Where Realms Collide

Michelle Lee

BLUE FORGE PRESS
Port Orchard, Washington

Where Realms Collide
Copyright 2022
by Michelle Lee

First eBook Edition May 2023
First Print Edition May 2023

ISBN 978-1-59092-872-1

All rights reserved, including the right to reproduce this book or portions thereof in any form whatsoever, except in the case of short excerpts for use in reviews of the book. For information about film, reprint or other subsidiary rights, contact: blueforgegroup@gmail.com

This is a work of fiction. Names, characters, locations, and all other story elements are the product of the authors' imaginations and are used fictitiously. Any resemblance to actual persons, living or dead, or other elements in real life, is purely coincidental.

Blue Forge Press is the print division of the volunteer-run, federal 501(c)3 nonprofit company, Blue Legacy, founded in 1989 and dedicated to bringing light to the shadows and voice to the silence. We strive to empower storytellers across all walks of life with our four divisions: Blue Forge Press, Blue Forge Films, Blue Forge Gaming, and Blue Forge Records. Find out more at: www.MyBlueLegacy.org

Blue Forge Press
7419 Ebbert Drive Southeast
Port Orchard, Washington 98367
blueforgepress@gmail.com
360-550-2071 ph.txt

For Stacy, who tolerated me through a year's worth
of deadlines and let me bounce off him every
random thought that sprang to life in my head
and then popped out of my mouth.
I couldn't have done this without his support.

Acknowledgments

I'd like to thank my parents for helping me nourish the dream of being a writer and for being a sounding board for some of the prompts.

I'd like to thank Jennifer, my publisher, who offered advice and tutelage that helped me hone my storytelling skills. It's people like her that help dreams come true.

I'd like to thank Jonielle for always being my guinea pig and beta reader with the things I write. She's my soul sister and I'd be lost without her.

To Shannon U, Arianna, Pam, Kapua, Nathan, Renee, and all the others, you have my deepest gratitude for allowing me to ask countless questions about the prompts and what you thought of when hearing them. Your ideas helped shape the stories I wrote and gave me direction when lost.

And finally, to Stacy, thank you for everything.

Table of Contents

Where Realms Collide

Michelle Lee

The Silence Screams

I peered out from the tent and the dense air swallowed my quiet gasp. It was snowing. Not the gentle drifting down snowflakes that make you wish you were sitting in front of a blazing fire drinking hot cocoa and reading a steamy romance book, either. It was the type of snow that came down so thick and heavy that it felt like a freezing curtain draped over the land.

Isolation closed in around me and the warm air of my breath died inches in front of my face. I couldn't even hear the icy river rushing over the rocks that flowed less than seven feet in front of me. The only sound was my heart thudding in my chest.

I'd wanted peace and quiet to heal, and it seemed the universe had answered my plea. I hadn't packed for heavy snowfall and it hadn't been in the forecast. I mentally went through my pack's belongings and knew I wouldn't be in danger; I always had thermal clothes with me no matter the weather. It might be a sketchy trek if I had to move locations, though. If by some chance people showed up.

I stuck my bare arm through the door of the tent and watched the pure white flakes fall on my brown skin. It was mesmerizing. I felt like the only living thing breathing on the entire face of the planet. I knew it was a ridiculous thought, yet I couldn't help feeling that way. I zipped the tent back up and retreated to my sleeping bag, sitting as still as the air around me.

The last conversation with my family played on repeat in my mind. It had only happened the night before, so it was all fresh:

"Shannon, you don't have to do this," Gerard pleaded. "We'll figure it out. The kids'll go crazy without you here."

I couldn't respond with my voice. I grabbed the paper I had been writing on and scrawled the message: My being here puts you all in danger. This virus is scary serious.

I had three masks on my face, one an N95; Gerard wore two and made each of the kids double-mask after thoroughly sanitizing themselves after he got the news. He had set the oldest on wiping the house down with disinfectant wipes.

My job as a certified medical assistant at a lab where we ran patient trials on new medications and vaccinations had exposed me to a new strain of a particularly virulent and nasty virus. I was the manager in charge of all the other CMAs and got called in to help with the patient, who turned out to be my friend that I had met for dinner a few nights before and shared a drink with, unfortunately. The exposure part wasn't the issue; the issue was that none of us knew the virus had mutated again until it was too late. We were used to exposure.

Things had been on a quieter scale with the virus, the strains getting weaker with each mutation, so restrictions had loosened for the general public. Jessica and I had been friends for years, and neither of us gave it a second thought to share a beverage, eat off each other's plates or steal a napkin when we'd shredded our own. Jessica hadn't had any symptoms of any illness other than looking a little tired, which I chalked up to her working extra long hours.

Every person in the facility was now at risk because I had gone to work as usual the next day. Four workers had turned up positive. What terrified me the most was the way the virus mutated and spread. My dinner had been three nights before Jessica showed up in the office, looking like she was moments away from death. We ran test after test, hooked her up to IVs, and got her on antiviral meds but nothing helped ease her symptoms. The test results were terrifying. After we realized it was a mutated version of the virus we'd been fighting for over a year, I left for home.

The virus still traveled through the air, but it seemed as if the vibrations of voices activated the spores and accelerated the process. In three days, Jessica had sprouted open blisters that wept on her body, a fever that wouldn't break, her eyes were glassy, and she appeared delusional. She couldn't stand on her own without assistance, her voice sounded like someone was strangling her, and her fingers, toes, and lips had a blue tinge to them.

I couldn't knowingly stay home with my kids and risk infecting them because they did something to annoy me, and I yelled at them. There was zero chance they would understand the risks associated with me being home. I didn't want them to see me like that, nor did I want them to go through it. I had to leave.

I shrugged it off—I'd made my decision—and pulled the thermometer out of my backpack. I wasn't symptomatic yet, but we all knew that the potential for me to be a carrier of this new strain was exceptionally high. I popped the thermometer into my mouth and waited.

That's why I came out to the middle of nowhere in the winter. I had to quarantine, and since this spread through air and voices seemed to activate and accelerate the incubation period, out here, there was no one to infect. I would have, of course, preferred a four-star—five-stars would be expecting too much—hotel and someone waiting on me but given the situation, that didn't seem probable.

I waited patiently for the thermometer to beep and checked my temperature. The screen read 99.6, slightly elevated. It concerned me, but not overly so that I freaked out. That was my first symptom other than general tiredness. Easily explained away by life. Though, since those were also symptoms of the virus, I couldn't risk it. Not with Gerard's compromised immune system.

We were still in that warning period where his body could quickly reject the liver transplant. I'd come close to losing him too many times and wouldn't be able to live with myself if I was the reason he died. I sighed again as I tucked the thermometer back in the small medical kit I'd brought.

I'd packed more food than anything else, and my campsite by the river took care of the water issue. I had a portable filtration system to eliminate bacteria in the river, though now I could also catch the snow and melt it.

I doubted that my solar battery charger would work with this much snow falling, so I needed to limit my Kindle reading and playing of phone games to preserve the batteries; there was no cell signal out here in the woods, either, and I didn't want to go through all my books in three days. That meant I needed to find something else to do to occupy myself during the day. I wasn't great at being idle.

I could insulate my tent with tree branches to help keep the snow off it. I pulled my outer clothes on and donned my waterproof coat. Thankfully my boots were waterproof, insulated, and lined. They wouldn't hold up if the snow got deep, but for now, they would keep my feet dry enough for me to gather the limbs to put up around the tent.

It was what the people in the reality survival shows did, so it made sense for me to do the same. I took a fortifying breath before unzipping the tent again and climbing out. I'd need to try and start a fire, too; I hadn't done that last night. I felt reasonably confident that I'd packed some matches. I'd been in a hurry; there was a slight chance I forgot. I turned back to the backpack and rooted through the pockets until I found the small box of wooden matches and stuffed them in my coat pocket.

I began to gather boughs to cover my shelter. The snow wouldn't last terribly long, but I'd be out here at least two weeks, which was the best case scenario if no other symptoms developed. The world was in crisis mode and there were people far sicker and in more dangerous situations than I found myself in. I was a healthy woman and rarely got sick, so I hoped this wouldn't be awful.

The general population hadn't been all that good with social distancing or mask-wearing, so I wasn't too hopeful they would all remain silent. Maybe quarantining and isolating myself out in the wilderness was a chicken shit move. However, it seemed logical when we found out the sound vibrations accelerated the virus. Being silent in an increasingly noisy world was impossible. At least in city life.

Isolation wasn't excellent for mental health, and I knew that. I'd made the extreme choice as a sacrifice to keep my family all safe, to keep everyone safe if I was a carrier. It may have been misguided, but it was my reaction. Sometimes, it felt selfish of me, and other times it felt selfless—I wavered between the feelings. My car was only about a mile away, and I had cell reception there, weak, but it would do. If I wasn't too sick, I could walk and text my family to let them know I was okay. My fear was I wouldn't be able to make the walk if things got dicey. Jessica had barely been able to stand.

Out here in the blanket of snow, cover of trees, and Mother Nature, silence reigned queen. How quickly would the virus die if everyone could be this quiet? That deep thought made me wonder how silent it would be if everyone perished because they couldn't keep their mouths shut. I blinked slowly.

Too much reflection time! I did my best to put a lid on my mind while I sought out limbs that had a lot of pine needles on them for insulation. The mundane task worked and three hours later, I had managed to prop the branches up teepee style over my tent and created a system to keep the snow from piling on the roof and caving it in. I even made an overhang over the front to give me a drier spot to get out.

I moved on to making a fire pit under the tree cover with high clearance. Starting a forest fire wasn't high on my list of things to do either. I was actively trying to avoid people, not bring in droves of firefighters for me to drool over.

I took my time, and a couple of hours later, I had a lovely fire going, managed to find some downed logs that I dragged over to create a place to sit in front of the fire, and felt toasty warm. I was proud of myself. Not bad for my second day camping by myself.

I used the fire to melt some snow for drinking water and poured it into my insulated bottle. Survival was a choice and I made it freely. It might not have been the ideal situation but I was making do to keep my family safe.

A silent world was scary to contemplate. This quiet was healing and damaging at the same time. I could only do it so much before fear overwhelmed me and I retreated to the tent to read. I swear my mind was my worst enemy. I imagined scenarios of mass death or that the few sounds I heard were someone stalking me to kill me; my brain went totally off-leash.

Little did I know that this would be my routine for the next month as more and more symptoms arose. The first week, it was a slight fever and tiredness. I made the walk to my car twice to send texts before I was too tired. It wasn't the same as hearing their voices, but it was human contact. Then a painful dry cough started, which I tried to make myself believe resulted from the cold snow. It was plausible; that was what I told myself.

However, when I brushed my thick black hair, clumps came out the second week. Hair loss wasn't present in any of the other strains. That had nothing to do with the snow and a lot more to do with a virus I felt sure was fully activated in my body. Since it was a new variant, I had no idea what to expect other than the symptoms I had seen in Jessica. There had been so little time for me to observe and learn. The thought sounded harsh in my mind since she was a good friend.

My fever grew the third week and my muscles

ached with a fierceness that sucked the energy from my body. I couldn't make the walk to my car to text. I would have fallen and died. There were hours of the day that I wanted it to be over. Whether it was me recovering or succumbing, I didn't care. I was miserable. I had blisters and random bruises with chills so violent I thought the ground was shaking under me. My lips were cracked and it hurt too much even to cry.

I missed my kids and the thought of Gerard being left alone without me would have made me cry despite the pain if I'd had the strength. I didn't, though, because I wanted to live. I preserved my energy and battled the deafening thoughts in my mind. Those tore me apart as much as the virus did.

I sincerely believed the fever made me delusional or the never-ending silence did. It could have been a combination of the two. My heartbeat, my raspy breath, my eyes blinking, all of it. I became so attuned to each minuscule sound my body made that it sounded like a rock concert to my sensitive ears.

The wood cracking in the fire could have been a war zone. A clump of snow falling out of a tree was a bomb going off. I was slowly losing my mind and I wasn't sure what to attribute to the virus, the silence, the longing for my family, or something more sinister like death that felt like it was hovering too near.

On one of the rare days that tricked me into thinking I was getting better, I made a trek out to my car, grabbed a notebook that one of my kids left there, sent a text to my family that I was sick but alive, and brought the notebook back to the tent with me. I didn't have the energy to wait too long for a reply, and after I got an, *I love you, get better,* I headed back. I began to draw the weird visions that would pop up in my mind, dark and foreboding. It became a graphic horror journal.

My dreams were twisted, cryptic, and black and white like an old, silent horror movie. I'd wake up with more bruises on my body, another symptom of the virus no one had seen in the other strains. I looked like I'd lost a boxing match.

The snow had melted, then fallen again, but the silence never abated. I'd thought I'd have heard animals at least, yet the thoughts in my head told me that they knew death was around me and kept their distance. I didn't know whether that was true or some figment of my disturbed brain.

On the third day of the fourth week, I woke up with enough energy to start a fire and sit outside instead of crawling back into the tent and passing out. The fresh air was comforting, and it was the first day with no fever, no morbid thoughts, and me feeling like myself. Just tired.

Hope crept into my thoughts that I was on the other side of this virus. I wasn't delusional enough to think I was over it but maybe well enough to say that the worst had passed. I desperately clung to the optimism. I needed it after the past few weeks.

My food supply was running low. Thankfully I hadn't eaten much while in the throws of the virus. I drank more tea than anything else and I'd never been as thankful for an insulated bottle as I was during the worst of it. Despite the lack of appetite, my body needed nourishment, and I needed to eat something to regain energy.

I set about beginning to prepare some food, and once finished, I ate slowly. It tasted like the best meal prepared by a famous chef. Okay, not really, but it was good, and I could actually taste it which was a plus. Tasteless food sucks.

The noise I made seemed overly loud to my ears and the random thought popped into my head that I didn't even remember what my voice sounded like anymore. It was depressing, yet the fear of what it did to this virus kept me from talking. Silence still reigned.

That meant when a voice speaking my name broke through, it scared me badly enough that I almost fell into the fire. With my heart punching my rib cage hard enough to hurt, I spun around, and my jaw dropped open. It was so loud to my sensitive ears that it sounded like a bullet went off next to my ear.

Gerard stood there and took in my appearance. With no mirror handy and too afraid to use my phone to check, I could only assume I looked awful. I knew how much hair I had lost and assumed that what he saw was close to a rotting corpse.

"Gerard?" I whispered, my voice sounding foreign to my ears. Was I hallucinating? Did the virus have a second lifespan?

My husband took a step closer to me and I reeled backward, worried for his health. "It's been over a month, baby. I doubt you are still contagious, and I don't have it. An article in the news said four weeks after contracting this, and you would be safe. It may be true, or they could be full of shit, but after a couple of weeks with no text, I decided it was worth the risk." Gerard told me with a soft smile that melted my heart. "Why are you whispering?"

I shook my head. "I'm not used to sound." I kept my voice as low as possible. "I don't know if it's safe for you to be out here or for us to be talking." With everything that I knew about this virus so far and its various strains, once you got it, the antibodies helped build your immunity to that particular strain. There was every chance I could get it again, but it wasn't likely I would get this same strain. I wasn't worried about myself.

"Don't worry about me," Gerard reassured me with a careless tone as if he could read my thoughts. He lowered his voice to match my volume, understanding that my ears were sensitive.

I looked him over with a practiced eye and saw that his skin pallor was paler than usual, and he'd lost weight, his cheeks sunken shadowed a bit. He was still devastatingly handsome. Tall and dark with those disarming eyes.

"I'm supposed to worry about you; it was in the vows, remember?" I replied jokingly. Those were words he'd said to me when I had told him not to worry about me. I enjoyed throwing them back at him.

Gerard grinned at me. "I'm guessing you got the virus or am I talking to a zombie?"

I nodded. "Both. I feel human today. No fever when I woke up either. It's an improvement."

"I don't care what you look like, baby. You are still gorgeous. Can I get a hug?" Gerard held his arms open.

I moved as fast as I physically could and let him wrap me up in an embrace. It felt so phenomenal I sagged against him and cried. Gerard kissed the top of my head and rested his cheek there.

"I've missed you, Shan. The kids and your sister are out of the danger zone but still in quarantine to be safe. I just decided that I don't give a shit anymore;

consequences be damned. If I get it, I get it, and it won't matter either way. I needed to see you."

I choked on a sob and clutched him tighter. I wasn't ready to examine the rest of his words yet. Nothing could have made me feel better than Gerard's touch, his voice, his smell. My husband's touch was healing and worlds better than a text. Doctors had underestimated the need for social contact with those you love as a balm for a hurting soul.

I was starting to believe that things became more evident in all that silence I endured. That what truly mattered in life became obvious when the lack of noise cleaned out the clutter in my mind. The everyday bullshit that bogged us down amounted to nothing other than a waste of time better spent in the arms of the ones you love.

"Is it safe to go back?" I whispered.

"No. You wouldn't believe the craziness out there right now, Shan. I can't even understand how no one has found you out here. It's not like your car is in hiding." Gerard pulled away and looked down at me. His face was tired and drawn, something I hadn't noticed when he stood across from me with a distance between us. "Let's give it a couple of days."

"You hate camping," I pointed out, frowning.

"No. I hate camping with the kids. It's a nightmare and total chaos. With you, it's a vacation." Gerard grinned at me again. "Plus, I figured you were about out of this nasty dehydrated food. I brought food from your sister."

"Whatever it is, I'm sure it will be delicious. Later. I just ate. Would it be terrible if we took a nap?" I suggested. Not even because I was worried about him—

which I was—more because I was still exhausted, and the emotional upheaval that went through me at seeing my husband wore me out. I wasn't out of the woods yet; the thought made me chuckle silently.

"Sounds perfect."

Gerard followed me back to the tent and we napped. The first solid sleep I'd had in a month. A straight five hours too. No nightmares, no delusions, only blissful sleep. I woke before he did and I watched him for a bit. I wasn't overly fond of how tired he appeared and I began to wonder if he wasn't well.

He awoke before I could examine him further. Gerard's eyes were intense on me. We were both silent and it was then I noticed the yellow tint behind the bloodshot veins. My heart started to race as the reality of what I was seeing sank in.

Gerard moved out of reach before I could feel his forehead or demand to see his abdomen. The signs of liver rejection were a fever, swollen abdomen, jaundiced eyes and skin, fatigue, itching, dark urine, headache, and irritability. I was now going to be watching for all of them and had mentally ticked off the present ones. In my heart, I already knew, but I wasn't going to admit it. Not yet.

"Tell me the state of the world outside," I requested softly, aiming for distraction.

"Do you really want to know?" Gerard pushed back.

That told me a lot already. "I do."

"People are going crazy. Remember how insane people went with toilet paper and hand sanitizer? It's that all over again, only with talking. If you're outside your home, they have it mandated that you can't talk; no going to stores either. National Guard delivers a set amount of groceries to every home based on the number of people living inside. You aren't allowed outside if you have symptoms and the house is marked. You have to remain inside for a minimum of four weeks. The Guard make rounds to watch the marked houses and you're fined if you're seen outdoors. It's martial law to the extreme. Those that need medical care are seen virtually and in silence with words on the screen, and then the medications are dropped off by Guard medical personnel that are in biohazard suits."

I absorbed that information in shock. "How did you get out?"

Gerard shrugged. "It's been four weeks. I also learned about their rotations. Not all of them are super smart. The ones that are were assigned to watch the houses that have the most infected people. The houses that have reached their four weeks? They have the peon guys checking on us."

I half-smiled at him. "So you snuck out and ran away. That sounds about right. How is Jessica?"

"She died," Gerard answered gently, his eyes sad. "Tell me, Shan. How are you bathing out here? I imagine that river is mighty cold and not something I'd be interested in skinny-dipping in with you." Gerard wagged his eyebrows and made a goofy face at me, changing the subject.

My heart broke at the news of Jessica, but I knew that Gerard was attempting to get me to smile so that I didn't cry. I laughed weakly at his expression but didn't feel it the way I knew he hoped I would. "I heat water and use a sponge for bathing, then I use the rest of the hot water to wash my hair, and I rinse it with the cold." I fingered what was left of my hair. "It keeps it from drying out, what's left anyway."

"I have my very own corpse bride. I'm good with that." Gerard reached out and moved the hat I'd put on so he could see my entire head. "It could be worse."

I nodded because he wasn't wrong, and that was usually my line to him. "I can give you a sponge bath," I offered generously.

"I'd rather give you one. I think you could use it more than me." Gerard's face shuttered closed for only a moment but it was enough for me to see it happen. There was something he wasn't telling me.

"Are you saying I stink?" I laughed softly. I didn't push for an answer, knowing he'd share when he was ready.

Gerard held his finger and thumb an inch apart and smirked at me. The banter was so similar to how our lives usually were that I forgot we were in a less than stellar situation amidst world strife.

"Okay, big shot, now that I've done the hard part and got the fire started, go ahead and heat the water and bathe my stinky ass," I taunted him.

"Challenge accepted, my corpse bride. Good thing I brought some good smelling soap, so you don't stink us out of tent and home." Gerard dug through his backpack and pulled out a bar of my expensive soap. "See, babe? I planned ahead."

Oh, how I loved this man. "You knew I would be smelly?"

"Duh. You've been living out here in the woods for over a month during winter and being sick. Doesn't take a genius-level brain to figure that out." He pulled out a loofah next and winked at me. "Get ready for bath time."

"Does it include a happy ending?" I couldn't help it; the question had to be asked.

"Only if you are a good girl," Gerard drawled as he crawled out of the tent. "Strip."

An hour and a couple of happy endings later, we went back to bed after dousing the fire. I'd seen the evidence I needed to see to know that Gerard was hiding something serious from me and that it wasn't good. I waited until we were both settled before I started with the questions.

"Are you going to spill whatever is on your mind?" I began cautiously. My head was on his shoulder, his arm around me.

"What makes you think there is anything on my mind?" Gerard fired back while he stroked my side.

"We've been married a lot of years now; I know." I tapped my finger against his chest. "I'm not above torturing it out of you."

"Shan, I just saw the ravages of this virus all over your body. I don't think you have the energy to torture me."

He had me there. "Fine. Then I'll pull out the big guns. Stop hiding things from your disease-ridden wife. We don't keep secrets from each other, so let's not start now. You knew the reasons I came out here. I don't know the reasons that you did."

Gerard whistled low. "Wow. Went straight for the heartstring and the guilt trip."

I remained silent. I knew Gerard was thinking about how he would say whatever he needed to say. Every instinct I had told me I already knew. I'd spent years with this man, enough to know how he reacted and the choices he would make. Gerard didn't waffle around. He made informed decisions and then planned out his moves methodically.

"My body is rejecting the liver, and there isn't anything they can do about it. Not in the middle of a pandemic. The specialists gave me some medications to prolong my life, but it wouldn't be a quality life. It would put unnecessary strain on you and the kids, which isn't worth it to me. I'm dying, Shan. Probably in the next couple of days," Gerard confessed, his tone melancholic.

I held my breath for as long as I could and let it out slowly. I had desperately hoped that the news wasn't going to be that, but I'd seen the signs. "Do the kids know?"

"They do. I told them a couple of weeks ago and then stopped taking the medications. I can't lie; it was rough. We hashed it out, the anger, the tears, all that fear, and we made a sort of peace with it." Gerard paused. "I told them I was going to find you and spend my last days with you. That is my wish."

Gerard fell silent as I absorbed his news. This silence was different from what I had lived with the past month. This quiet was heavy and filled with immense sorrow. I rolled my body into him, positioning myself to not cause pain to the sore abdomen I knew he had.

"I guess that means I should use the penis mold now so that way I always have a part of you with me," I joked feebly. The tension in my gut needed to be broken with some of my husband's laughter.

Gerard laughed heartily. "That's my girl." He hugged me tightly. "It's not something I ever wanted to tell you, and I'm sorry, baby."

I knew he was sorry. So many times, we'd had the

conversation about what would happen if the transplant didn't work. Those talks were some of the most painful we had ever had and blunt in the raw honesty we expressed. It sucked then, and it's worse now that it's a reality.

Living with the threat of death hanging over your head gives you a twisted sense of humor and it was something we both definitely possessed. I wasn't naïve enough to think that anything I said would change Gerard's mind. I respected his decision on how he wanted to live his life and how he wanted to die. Had the roles been reversed, he would have given me the same consideration.

"I'm sorry, too." I buried my face in his armpit and bit back the tears. "You could have used a bath too; these pits are rank."

"I love you, Shannon," Gerard laughed at my continued attempts to ease the tension.

"I love you, too." That was as mushy as either of us would get.

We spent the rest of our time together talking, joking, having fun, and being together. We slept a lot. He lasted a few more days before his body shut down; it happened quicker than I had hoped. The last day wasn't pleasant, but it was a sad reality that we had prepared ourselves for years ago. We said our goodbyes in the few lucid moments when he was awake.

When Gerard died, my world fell silent again. I screamed and railed inside, yet the silence felt like it was louder than I ever could be. I slowly made the trek back out to my car and called for an ambulance. I gave specific directions on where to find us and what the situation was, that they didn't need to hurry or put lights on. I warned them I had suffered the virus but was past the worst and on my way back to normal. Whatever that was.

I walked back and sat there with Gerard until the EMTs came to take him away. I kissed him one last time while another of the medics checked me over, asked questions, and declared me safe to go home while lecturing me on the dangers Gerard had taken to come out here. He also quickly informed me that I had to follow the martial law in place. I was in no state to argue.

After they left, I packed up my campsite and carved Gerard's and my name into the closest tree. I didn't think I'd ever feel the same way about silence. It swallowed the cries I made and left me with only salty tears that finally fell. It had taken everything.

Broken-hearted, I drove home. The sound of the engine, the tires on the pavement, the blinkers—all of it was a cacophonous rock concert to my ears as I adjusted to the different kind of silence I would face at home: Life without the sound of my husband's voice.

I found Gerard's will, his last wishes that his body be donated to science to help further my career, and letters that he'd written for each of us on the counter in the kitchen. Oh, how the silence screams louder here than anywhere else. Even in a silent world that shouts for relief from a deadly virus spread by sound.

Contract Void

Have you ever felt like you stepped directly into an odd-shaped inkblot that someone looked at and saw an image of their mother stabbing their father and emerged as darkness so dark that it swallowed all light? That's what I remember as my awakening, though I highly doubted that I came through a splatter of ink on a piece of paper to wherever this existence was this time.

It was my second awakening. It happened similarly to one of those dreams where you are falling relentlessly, limbs madly flailing as you would imagine an uncontrolled windmill might. The scenery on the way down blurs into a kaleidoscope of colors. Then, as you see the approaching ground reaching up to you, you jolt awake at the moment of impact with your heart racing and thumping in your chest. Only I don't have a torso.

I don't walk as a man walks; I don't appear as a human appears. I am neither of these, yet as alive as a walking, healthy human man in his prime. I have no previous knowledge of how my existence came to be. I only know that I blinked into reality as abruptly as the impact of the falling dream.

Back to the inkblot image: If I had to describe my appearance, the inkblot wouldn't be a far stretch. I was the darkest dark, a black vortex that swallowed all color and became a swirling mass of roiling energy that encompassed the vilest of emotions.

I've tried countless times to step into the light, to experience something other than the by-product of human hate, but it hurts like a bolt of the purest white lightning striking the deepest parts of me with poison so strong it kills instantly. I longed for it.

The pain made me realize I was alive. I detested the light and the colors of life, yet I wanted it more than anything I'd ever craved before. A very human emotion, if you think about it. Most people desired what they couldn't have and they spent their lives trying to attain, only to die a miserable failure for not getting what they worked so hard to achieve. None of them ever stopped to think that maybe what they were striving for would be the ruin and death of them.

I couldn't deny that I was any different (though, maybe a tad more devastating). In my wake, I left a path of destruction on my way towards experiencing the light. I didn't care who I took down. Why would I? It was my purpose of being.

Some have said that I was born from the bowels of Hell in some recessed cave no one remembered was there. I've been called the devil's pet and referred to as an embarrassment. Maybe I was a demon, I couldn't say for sure, though I strongly felt that I was not born in Hell; humans created me.

Admittedly, not all of them were terrible people, the two that I have experienced, anyway. Dormant for years between summoning, I observed life, behavior, patterns, and learned. I am a sentient being, and I adapt to my surroundings the way most viruses do in the fight to survive in a hostile environment. That's not to say I was a virus either.

I was the direct result of profound suffering by traumatized humans who could not see the gift of light in front of them; the same humans that were afraid to be happy because if they were, life would take it away from them. So, they stewed in their hate, in their trauma, and they lived for it. Which was ironic because they weren't truly living.

Those humans were so lost in their pain that they created me with all those emotions that tumbled through them, coalescing into impenetrable darkness because they wanted something that validated those feelings. That something was me.

Those feelings fed me, nourished my energy, and made me more powerful than demons that possessed stupid humans seeking power. I didn't need human energy to survive. I only needed their emotions which never stopped. I sustained the human, not the other way around.

My energy became free when my human perished until I felt that call to return. As I've mentioned, it's happened twice now. The trick was my energy needed to be in the vicinity of a person drowning in those toxic emotions that held them captive. As usual, the timing was everything.

I traveled to the places where I felt the darkness undulating like an endless night, yet the people I found there were happy in the shadows. Not a self-seething cesspool of oily black hate that made them want to act out, but instead a group satisfied with anger and the loathing they spread; it gave them joy.

I wasn't without limits, though. I'd recently found

out I could be banished or destroyed, as it were. I don't mean destroyed permanently, obviously, since here I am, but killed in the manner that my energy was spread across several planes and took longer for it to rejoin its other particles.

I can't say I particularly enjoyed being destroyed. However, I appreciated the learning experience it provided me. The pain was exquisite, though, perhaps more than I anticipated.

The woman behind the act, I despised her. The female was a human referred to as an empath. I felt this girl before I even saw her. The flashing beacon of her soul screamed as a danger to me and enticed me to go after her in any way that I could, using whoever was available to me.

Yet, this woman fascinated me because of the simple selflessness she deployed to sacrifice herself for the sake of others that welcomed me into their bodies. Even though she died fighting me several times, life would not leave a body so willing to share the light with those that might not deserve it.

The experience left me wary of encountering another empath, though, since through those encounters I have adapted, grown, and learned; and I believe she is an anomaly of her kind. Regardless, I am paying more attention to the souls around me and hovering near those that would give me an opening to plant myself inside them to grow their seeds of disdain.

This point is now where I found myself. There is a promising individual I have been watching and waiting patiently to reach out to me. They are on that edge of calling out something to understand that darkness dwelling in their hearts. They crave that something that will feed it and give their life meaning. That is when I step in and grant them the favor of my presence. I am a gift.

I prowled the streets, unseen but hardly unnoticed. People gave a wide berth around my essence and didn't even know why they were doing so. With the intelligence I've gathered, my presence felt like an unnatural void to them, something they could fall in and be lost forever. It's not far from the truth.

Those who aren't ready for me—the people who don't honestly want to hear their authentic voice—flirt with the danger I present yet run from it simultaneously. I seek the one that will embrace me like a long-lost lover. He's near; I can sense him. He only needs to open himself to my endless possibilities of ways to express that voice he's afraid to use.

It won't take long. The desperation my new host caged inside of himself clawed at me to release it, so its anguish had a voice to be screamed to the skies. That's what the initial contact felt like to me. A mass exodus of energy harnessed over the years, trapped and then released when the hinges snap from years of rusted neglect. Not quite sexual, though close enough that it's immensely satisfying, and it sings through me in a rush. All that pain, agony, and trauma leaves me exhilarated and powerful.

I was ready for that feeling to wash through me again, which left me a little impatient. That is why I prowled the streets, a predator searching for its prey, not to kill but to command.

It was a different world this time. Not literally, but other than how I left it the last time. I knew apocalyptic events had taken place. The population had dwindled drastically, making it harder for me to find the right person, yet easier to sense their location due to the amount of trauma experienced.

I'd come across a few empaths on this journey. However, none of them were similar to the one that could defeat me. Not even an affiliation with a demon prince had been able to keep me in place when faced with her.

I guessed that was the power of love at work. I couldn't say for sure because it was not an emotion I had ever experienced. I was intensely curious about it; though, like the light, it caused me a tremendous amount of agony.

My last host was far from perfect. His darkness was enticing, embracing, yet threaded with ribbons of colorful light, hope, and love. He was somewhat of an empath himself, which surprised me that he could manifest me.

I believe that those emotions made it easier for him to cage me when faced with impossible hope. It was an exciting battle with him, and those times I took over his being were glorious. Even when contained, I felt a spark of admiration for this man that continued to hurt me with those hopes and dreams. It made the victory sweeter, the pain more intense.

Maybe I was the villain in that story, and perhaps I am in all of them. Yet I refuse to see myself that way since I am what those that called me created me to be. I was pieces of their trauma, molded into the sentient perfection that I am now. I devour light and thrive in the darkness and pain.

Ah, the man that was almost ready to call me was closer now. I could feel the pulsing line of his energy that sought me out when others veered away. Raw need thrummed through my essence the closer I came. I would be this man's downfall and his graceful rise to the perfect instrument I would create.

A piercing arrow of agony shot through me as I rounded the corner of a building. It was a familiar pain. An empath was near and in the process of doing whatever those overly caring, sensitive people do. Not the same one that scattered me to the winds, thankfully, as that particular empath would be able to sense me before I ever got near her.

Still, the sensation gave me pause and halted my momentum, and a stab of yearning tore through me. It probably made me sadistic that I craved that pain that only light could bring. It was a paradox.

I stopped to watch the disdainful act the empath performed by simply existing. I couldn't help it; I liked train wrecks. It appeared as if this could be a colossal one, too, with disastrous consequences for me.

Two men sat on a darkened porch outside an apartment building on a rundown street that has seen better decades. One of them was the man who would welcome me into his soul soon, the other, the empath.

They were talking in hushed voices, the empath more passionately than my next host. A few random words floated in my direction on the dank air that drifted from the alley on the other side of me: Mentions of suicide, depression, rage. All emotions that were in my wheelhouse. Feelings I spoke of when I inhabited my previous host.

A tremor of excitement vibrated through my essence when I saw that the empath was not reaching his goal. My new host had stepped too far into the darkness inside of him to see the offered branch of light extended his way. It worked in my favor.

I dealt with the pain; it was worth my sacrifice to remain in place for the despairing spectacle. Soon, a new host would be mine. He would make the call, beg for something to take him, to make him feel, make him whole. He would cry out for something to understand him, and I would step in like the savior I was.

The call came earlier than expected. The dark void expanded from my new host, and I dove, absorbing it. I was a new darkness inside of this man. He was mine. I swallowed his soul, making him the devourer of light.

It was the sweetest ecstasy. I stretched my essence to expand to fill every available space in this new body. It was the taste of freedom, and I let it encompass me entirely until I fully settled. Then it was all about making the mental connection to communicate. The first acceptance of a host was images I needed to send telepathically, and the second, I simply spoke.

I couldn't be sure what this time would be, and I waited for that electrical charge that told me I'd successfully tapped into the man's thoughts. I wanted to see if I could visualize the thoughts my host projected before I spoke. That would grant me an idea of how to communicate with him and what thoughts would be have the most impact to gain my goal of spreading.

The connection was slow to take hold and my frustration mounted. The emotion made my host agitated, and he jerkily paced about, muttering incoherent words. If I'd had eyes, I would have rolled them.

Stop moving! I thought, irritation leaking out

of me.

"Wh-who said that?" My host halted in his tracks and began to look around.

I stretched a bit further and realized that I could see through his eyes. Interestingly, the connection had been made and I hadn't known it; my, how this one was susceptible to me. I rather liked the feeling of power it gave me.

You called for me. I'm inside you. The statement was a risk I was willing to take since I already inhabited every possible space in this man's body. He couldn't eject me. Not without a powerful empath to sear my connections to his soul. He'd lose pieces of himself if he went that route.

My host's body remained still as he processed the information that he was no longer alone inside his mind. Little did he know that I'd reached so much farther than that. My essence had fully embedded into his soul with roots that bloomed like magical trees in fertile soil.

"Are you a demon?" my host's whispered, ragged breath wheezed out the words.

No. You may call me Void. I'd thought the name up spur of the moment. It suited. The truth was: I didn't have a name. The empath had called me Darkness. Void had a better flare.

"Void?" my host echoed.

You don't need to speak aloud to communicate with me. I'm inside you, and speaking aloud while alone might lend to someone thinking you aren't mentally capable of taking care of yourself; we don't need any interference. This man was putty in my hands. It was too easy.

"There is no one here but me." The man's tone

was angry. Perhaps I'd been too condescending. His mind was weak, but there was steel in there somewhere.

What is your name? I tried with a conciliatory tone.

"Gregory. What do you mean I called you?"

You wanted something in this universe to understand the anguish that lives inside you. That is me. I understand it. I hear your authentic voice, your desire to inflict the same trauma on others so that you don't feel so alone in the world. So that someone else will know why you are the way you are. I felt my words resonate with Gregory.

"What are you?" Trepidation seeped into Gregory's voice.

I am the darkest of nights, an existence without light. I devour it and revel in the pain it causes. I am the energy that people like you create with the emotions that eat you up and leave you wallowing in self-pity. Does this cause you fear, Gregory? I cajoled a bit to see if I could rile him to act defiantly against me. I needed to know my limits with this host.

His anxiety increased with a shot of adrenaline through his veins. It wasn't only fear Gregory was responding to; he needed to feel what I offered him. His emotions told me that I would meet very little resistance to my suggestions, or even if I took over for him.

That knowledge shot through me with a tremor of exhilaration that bled into Gregory's emotions. For a split second, there was a moment of light that had me withering into a small ball of pain inside him before my essence demolished it.

Everyone who has wronged you will kneel before you, I promised with a hard-won arrogance.

I didn't expect the laugh. The sound burst from

Gregory's lips in a symphony of darkness that created the most beautiful sound of villainous laughter I've ever heard. For about two hairs widths of time, a trickle of fear shimmered through me with the thought that maybe I'd gotten in over my nonexistent head.

"Let's begin," Gregory announced.

I should have examined those memories I rifled through a bit better. Maybe then I would have been able to exercise some foresight.

Gregory didn't need a list of people who'd wronged him. He was so far lost in his sense of righteous anger that anyone he encountered was already on that list. People that Gregory didn't even know were on the receiving end of black anger that far surpassed the rage incited by a homicidal maniac.

Gregory cut a swath through the city that left it reeling in his wake. It was a brilliant and stunning display of what my essence could do. Little pieces of me were left inside his unknowing victims to multiply and dominate. I would be unstoppable in no time.

I allowed myself to be distracted and frolic in the emotions cascading through my willing host. It was the most unbelievable feeling in my existence. Neither of my previous hosts had experienced this or been willing to share such a wonderful experience with me. It was a heady feeling, and it made me sloppy.

Gregory spewed vitriolic words like he was singing a children's nursery rhyme during a happy family gathering. Except it was poisonous barbs that left people standing stricken by the verbal blows he doled out like candy to trick-or-treaters.

Too much of a good thing is still too much.

Unchecked darkness could render me powerless, and I didn't see any circumstances where that would be considered a positive. Even I admitted to a balance to everything that needed to be maintained.

Gregory was weak enough to call me, yet strong enough to stay within the lines of breaking the law. He used his tone, expression, and words to inflict maximum damage and douse the light. He never physically touched anyone or anything; he didn't even brush up against anyone.

I almost found myself giggling with giddiness like a little school girl playing recess games with her friends. However, my voice of reason still came through the cloud of glee surrounding me.

Gregory, slow down. He heeded my warning, albeit slowly and in the wrong context.

Gregory slowed his walking pace down, and now instead of spreading his dark behavior, he began to encourage others to contribute to his efforts. Never at my most imaginative would I have envisioned this. It was gasoline on a wildfire.

Thugs breaking into parked cars on an unlighted street were praised for how the windows shattered, making it look like art. Prostitutes got advice on milking more money from their marks with less work. Teenagers who hid in doorways and experimented with drugs received wisdom on maximizing their highs.

It was despicable, and it was glorious. It began to grow almost immediately. I exerted no effort and became essentially useless to my host as he handed out unseen pieces of me to remain behind and ensure my continued presence on this planet.

The problem this presented was that all this

success, the light growing dimmer and weaker, would leave me with nothing to learn, nothing to feed on and fight. Even I needed to have a purpose. The light required dark, and vice versa. The growth rate of this expansion would leave nothing, and I would wither away, fighting nothing but myself.

Gregory, we must let it rest. You've planted seeds that far outmatched my expectations, and now we need to leave them time to grow. I did my best to keep the alarm from my tone and remain calm in the face of his destruction. I still found it breathtaking, though I had a sense of self-preservation. The light may hurt me, but I knew I needed it to exist.

Just as I knew, I needed him to rest so that I had time to filter through his mind and try to figure out what had happened to him to create such an effective weapon of destruction. I might have been too quick to declare Gregory a weak-willed person. The passenger seat was not where I wanted to be in this host.

The 'be careful what you wish for' lesson flitted across my mind like a warning flag and reminded me that I was not infallible. As quickly as that thought left my mind, I realized I needed to protect the one thing I wanted to destroy. The empaths. The very beings that killed me, I now needed to save. How ironic an existence I lived.

"I don't need your permission, you know," Gregory muttered under his breath like a petulant child.

Indeed. It was all I said.

My last host had had a balance inside him that worked well with my plans. Gregory had none. He might have before I entered him, but it seemed as if my presence erased that, which told me he wasn't a balanced person before I came into the picture. Apparently, my selection process needed some refining.

Be that as it may, it was something I would work on in the foreseeable future. Yet the Gregory I now inhabited was different from the one who called me, and I couldn't pinpoint why. I felt torn between abject horror and utter fascination. The old cliché of an evil genius wasn't far off track in this case.

I watched from behind Gregory's eyes as he tied rats to strings in such a manner that they could chew themselves free. I didn't admit the genius behind it until I observed him hanging those rats from bridges over walkways.

People's terrified screams as rats fell out of the air on them gave me a little shiver of delight. Gregory's gleeful giggles were a bit over the top but deserved. I can't say that was something I would have thought of on my own.

It was for that reason that I didn't interfere. I wanted to see what Gregory would come up with next. Technically, he wasn't hurting anyone or doing anything that would draw the attention of the police, as scant as they were in this new world.

Empaths had done a remarkable job at finding people to recreate cities and join them so they weren't alone. It didn't seem as though they paid a lot of attention to their proclivities since this newly formed city teemed with the darker side of beings.

It could also possibly be that she put them all here in this place so that they didn't affect the others that thrived in the light. Either way, this entire city would be overrun with the essence of me in no time flat.

In less than twenty-four hours, there had been rats falling from above, snakes coming up through toilets, deadly spiders traveling through vents and dropping down into homes and businesses. Fear was contagious, and even stray animals hadn't stuck around.

There were five empaths in the city of varying strength. Their efforts were futile against the expanding void of darkness that made up my essence. Yet, they still tried to reach people, to help them see that light can't exist without the dark and that this will pass.

Maybe if they combined their efforts, the empaths would be more effective. Not against me but in helping individuals find their strength and combating the dark thoughts crowding their minds, or at least getting them to leave the city.

I supposed they might not know each other or that they were empaths. Those poor souls were too busy trying to figure out why they felt the way they did and if those emotions were theirs or the overwhelming number of people that had entered a helpless depression or rage and sprouted violent tendencies.

Gregory was more than I hoped for and too much at the same time. I stood by with my mental decision to save the empaths so that a balance remained. I had to choose my timing wisely, though. Eventually, Gregory tired and settled into an abandoned apartment to rest.

In this state, his mind was vulnerable, and I would be able to search through the stored memories and learn what I needed to, to halt the uncontrollable spread. Gregory would help me stop himself without his even knowing.

I bided my time until I felt him slip into that deep

sleep stage where he wouldn't be easily disturbed, and then I set forth. I tested doors and boxes and found that only the most inane and useless would open. They offered nothing of value except one image that sprang up several times: A wolf in a sheep's skin.

Somehow Gregory had managed to protect his mind without me knowing he was doing so. He'd thwarted me. Who the hell was Gregory, anyway? What had I stumbled upon, what was his goal, and had he known I was coming? Was the whole introduction nothing more than an act?

Perplexed, I retreated into myself and set up barriers around my thoughts. I couldn't be giving Gregory any advantages over me, at least not more than he naturally had, which was a mobile body. If I couldn't see his mind, then he couldn't see mine. It was an even playing ground that way.

I wasn't sure what was worse at this point: Being destroyed by the empath or being bested by my host that I took to be weak-willed. Shame washed through me as the old thought of 'third time's the charm' went through my mind. Obviously, I just proved that theory incorrect.

I began to plan and pooled my energy into a void within me that I would pull from later. I drew power from the scattered remains that Gregory had dispersed, thankful that there was a lot to draw from since I would need it.

I was going to have to attempt a takeover. It was dangerous at this juncture of our joining. I could end up frying Gregory's neuro system or burning myself out to the point of being useless. Our connection was untested at the energy capacity I would have to use to take control... though it was easy to admit I would take the risk.

I didn't have an emotional attachment to Gregory in the way I had formed one with my previous host. That man had been hard to deal with but his darkness was mesmerizing and it spoke to me. Gregory's despair called to me, too, but it was different. I would have reconsidered had I taken the time to explore it before diving into him.

In my defense, I would still be considered a being in my infancy since this is only my third host. The argument remained that I should have been more careful, and I couldn't ignore it. I probably shouldn't dwell on it the way that I seemed to be doing either. Introspection was a sharp, double-sided sword.

I sank into a rest phase, let my energy build, and stored it in my void for me to call on later. That was as close to sleeping as I would get. Yet even in this phase, I was still hyper-aware of my surroundings and poised to react should something threaten my host and, therefore, me.

Thankfully the hours passed quietly and when Gregory roused, there was precisely one weak moment where he was who I had thought he was. Then it was as if a switch had flipped and he became someone else. It was interesting to witness, though I had no idea how to process the information or what it meant in the bigger picture. I stored it away for future reference.

I remained quiet while Gregory went through his waking up routine. I recorded his patterns and mannerisms to help create the profile that I was building in my mind. All the information was helpful as it told me the story of Gregory.

The order and behavior he displayed spoke of a creature of habit, things he had been doing for years. If he were planning nefarious deeds he wanted to perform throughout the day, I wouldn't know it. His face in the mirror gave nothing away. It was so blank Gregory could be mistaken for a simpleton. I mean, I had made the same assumption. Only, I now knew it was a lie.

I remained a passive passenger in his body and kept from mentally stretching on the chance that he paid attention to my movements. It bothered me that I couldn't decipher if Gregory was working in opposition to me or had the same goals, his just being too extreme.

Good morning, Gregory; I tested the waters. *I trust that you slept well?*

"You know that I did," Gregory's tone was on the cooler side of emotions and carried a distance with it. That didn't bode well for me.

My perception can be different than yours, I conceded. I only got a grunt in response.

Gregory fell silent as he perused the cupboards, looking for shelf-stable food that he could pilfer and eat. He managed to rummage up a can of refried beans and a wrapped cupcake. The combination sounded putrid to me, though to be fair, I'd never tasted food. I didn't need it to survive.

"How did you come to be, Void?" Gregory asked conversationally while the beans heated in a microwave.

I was created by humans and destroyed by one. I don't believe I can die unless all the dark emotions disappear from people. I threw that in on the chance that he asked how to kill me. I couldn't be too sure.

"What do you mean?" Gregory scoured the drawers for a smaller spoon than the one he'd previously found.

I explained: *I am excess energy released from a human and coalesced into a sentient being who fed on that negativity. Much like the place where you mentally were when I found you, that is how I was created; I am a combination of the darkest emotions. They were so alive that life breathed into them, and my essence was born, something that could speak back in understanding.*

I was hesitant to go too far in explaining myself. I wasn't sure Gregory could expel me, at least not without the empath I encountered last time. The more he learned about me, the more he could use against me.

"You inhabit the willing body and then what?" Gregory wondered.

I hadn't explicitly gone over things with him when I joined his body. I only promised that those that wronged him would kneel. I paused before answering to choose my words carefully.

I work with you to help you achieve your goals. My response was purposely vague. *I am here so that you don't have to feel alone. I am what understands that agony inside you and gives you a companion. That is what you called for when I arrived.*

"Does that mean you are here to serve me?" Gregory's tone changed to one with a sharp edge and commanding presence.

No. I needed to derail that train of thought. *What we have is not a Faustian contract.*

A dark chuckle escaped Gregory's mouth as he shoveled in a spoonful of the refried beans. The spoon clanked against the bowl, his mouth smacked when he chewed, and his knee jiggled constantly. He said nothing else and noisily ate.

I began to think that I wasn't alone inside Gregory, though I couldn't prove it or sense another presence alongside mine. My keen intelligence and intuition told me repeatedly that this wasn't the same person I'd occupied when I was called to him. Whatever was going on, the extra part of Gregory that wasn't him was at a bare minimum as intelligent as me, perhaps more so.

The more discord Gregory sowed, the more of my essence he left behind to grow, plant roots, and multiply. My essence, my energy, was created to spread. I don't know if there is a science to it, but I liken it to something akin to an airborne virus.

It wasn't simply by Gregory being somewhere or even speaking. It had to be him giving voice to the darkness inside him or acting on it. For example, Gregory walking down the street and simply being surly wouldn't leave traces of me behind.

However, if he was actively engaged in giving action to the thoughts? If he was thinking about how to make someone who gave him a cold get something else, and he was actively searching his mind for a way to make it happen, my essence would leak out of him.

It wasn't a straight line, and sometimes I don't think my energy should have leaked out, but it did, and it made me reevaluate myself and my power. This thought process was what was currently happening. Gregory was actively engaged in his thoughts, trying to develop creative ways to achieve his revenge goals if his crazy muttering was any indication.

My last host was somewhat of a reclusive individual and avoided large crowds unless he was at work, so he didn't spread my energy around as much as Gregory did. I can't say I expected to feel as depleted as I did, and I desperately tried to regroup as quickly as possible so that I would be ready for a takeover when the moment arrived.

Each time that pieces of me were left behind, a little of my stored energy was drained. I needed to be in a restful state to refuel, much like humans did. A relaxed state of mind was not what I felt. I was on constant alert, waiting for something disastrous to happen. That in itself was a drain.

It might have been intentional on Gregory's part, though I don't think he was aware of how it affected me. He hadn't given me a single thought since he set out on foot, wandering through a busy yet still partially destroyed city.

"What are you doing here?" Gregory asked, jarring me out of my thoughts. He wasn't speaking to me.

"Oh, hey, G. I'm exploring. Sometimes when I feel overwhelmed or over-stimulated, I come out to these ruins and look for pieces of those that are gone and try to find a way to tell their story." The voice was a female, one I hadn't encountered yet. "What brings you out here? And by the way, you look more rested than usual. It's a good look for you."

Scorching pain tore through me that had me convulsing inside Gregory. My essence recoiled, split, then crashed back into itself in a tsunami of agony. This strange woman could only be an empath, and she'd just given Gregory a ray of hope that blossomed into that beautiful but deadly light that I craved and hated.

Gregory's reply got lost in the white noise of my mind while I tried to reassemble myself and calm the rapturous pain. I was mentally twisted. I wanted her to do it again. Then maybe once more after that. Would I adapt to the feeling? Grow numb to the stinging ache?

"Oh? I haven't seen anyone else but you."

The soft timbre of the woman's voice was what I imagined sandpaper would feel like on a bleeding wound. I wanted her to keep talking and become silenced simultaneously. My desires confused me. Or it could be that Gregory's emotions were feeding my bafflement. The woman created a weakness in Gregory that I might exploit if I needed to.

As if he sensed my latching onto that fact, a swarm of spiders that I didn't believe native to this area crept out of the rubble and over the old building's broken bricks. I said nothing nor attempted to stop Gregory. I observed.

Gregory experienced guilt when the woman shrieked, remorse when she tripped and fell over something behind her. He reveled in the glee that he had managed to make it happen and displayed apathy when he didn't help her.

"Gregory!" the woman yelled. "Be careful. Get out of here! These spiders are dangerous!"

The warning she offered up to the man that caused the chaos sent another wallop of torturous throbbing agony through my being. This person spared no ounce of worry about herself, only for Gregory.

Not one tiny atom of my being got stuck to the woman; she repelled my essence, and I wanted nothing more than to devour her soul and let it split me into a wild array of nothingness that would take four times as long for me to regroup.

Gregory absorbed the words and the warning, nodded and ran like a coward. With a blinding flash of understanding, I realized that at one point in my host's life, he had loved this woman. Perhaps he still did, only now he was lost in the pain of not having her.

I was an apathetic being. I had zero empathy for people's plights, emotions, tribulations, or anything at all. But it was that split moment of understanding that made me flex my nonexistent muscles and force Gregory to act and recall the spiders back into whatever hole they seeped out of into this world.

I didn't make him go back and help the alluring woman. That would have been too much. I don't fully understand my actions in stopping the horror, only that it felt right, which confounded me further. This single act by me was the first of this type. I fell into contemplative silence instead of observant silence.

"Do you know what Vantablack is?" Gregory's voice snapped my attention back to him. I took a chance and looked through his eyes and saw no one. Who was he talking to this time? "Void, I know you are there."

Vantablack. I can't say that I did know what that was. It had never come up in any of my previous experiences. Would it be detrimental to me if I admitted that I didn't know? I didn't suspect that it would harm me, and it would offer an opportunity for me to learn something new. I spoke no words but grunted acknowledgment.

"It was something created that is considered the

blackest of black. It's paint, scientifically made to absorb light from any angle. I'm not going to get into the details of the science behind it. I brought it up because you mentioned yesterday that this wasn't a Faustian contract. I know that to be true, but it feels like I need to name it anyway, and while I was sleeping, the name Vantablack popped into my mind. You devour light the same way it does. We have a Vantablack contract." Gregory sounded pleased with himself.

Upon awakening in this time and place, I noticed that humans felt a need to label everything. It wasn't a practice that made sense to me beyond a surface level of identifying who you are. I ignored it. I'd never even had a name until I called myself Void.

You may call it what you'd like. That was all I said. I wanted to appear agreeable but aloof. I needed Gregory to trust me but I didn't need him to like me; the two states weren't mutually exclusive.

"Thank you," Gregory replied with an amicable tone. "I like that we get along."

Gregory was a fool. I didn't care what he thought of me; he couldn't eject me. If that's what he had to tell himself to be okay with it, I didn't mind. I had more important things to think about than my host liking me.

I began to create an image of the woman we had encountered and visualized her hurt and in tears. I let it leak through my thoughts, making it visible to Gregory. I followed it up with another image of the female covered in blood and released it moments later.

Gregory's body jerked and he made a choking sound but quickly clamped it down. His reaction wasn't something he wanted me to witness; that much was clear. It told me everything I needed to know. The woman was a weakness I could use to control Gregory, just as I'd thought.

Now I only needed to find a way to put that information to good use to slow down the erosion of light so that balance remained in the universe. I wasn't entirely sure what my plan would be but I needed to keep in mind that something else other than me might reside inside Gregory. I needed a contingency for my first course of action, to get my act together and plot.

Meanwhile, Gregory was trailing my essence in a wave of depression behind him. I was thinking in circles and frustrating myself. I didn't have a lot of time to waste figuring things out before droves of people started committing suicide at a rate that would draw a lot of unwanted attention.

Every person we passed suddenly became despondent. It indeed was a sight to behold and if I weren't worried about Gregory spreading too much, I would be proud. Since I was blocked mentally, I could only guess that he was dwelling on something that made him feel despair.

In my first awakening, the concept of Heaven and Hell being physical places that a soul departs to once leaving the realm of the living was a joke. I've since learned that they are places but not in a sense like a town. They are more of a different plane of existence. Both were as real as where I currently reside. But there were rules to abide by for anyone to reach them.

Not the religious texts that people lived by, but more of a scientific nature. Light and dark existed in different realms, and when they mixed, you got the land of the living. Earth. A place of shadows that constantly shifted. My second awakening taught me that valuable lesson.

By nature, it was easy for me to communicate with other beings that dwelled in only the darkness. Communication with those that repelled those creatures was immensely more complicated. That was my stumbling block in coming up with a plan of action; how could I breach that barrier without using Gregory as the tool to do so and still keep him from finding out that I was working against him?

One could argue that it was entirely my fault that I was in my situation. Honestly, I was the cause of the imbalance the last two times I'd inhabited someone. It was true. Had I not settled into Gregory, he wouldn't be doing what he was doing. Chances are, he would have taken his own life in a tragic story that would get told on a local news channel.

One could say there was a pattern here, and you can't keep doing the same thing and expect different results. I was aware of that dichotomy. However, I wasn't insane. I couldn't say the same for Gregory; I only spoke for myself.

I'd ignored my host and his actions in all my musings. I tuned in as he threw a punch at who I assumed was a law enforcement officer. Gregory had taken this too far, too fast, and now there was very little time for me to find a way to correct the path he was on. My essence jolted with the white-hot electricity of what I believed was a defensive device that got shoved into Gregory's side.

My mind reorganized and I found my host semi-conscious in a locked cell. My thoughts spun frantically, trying to come up with a plan. It would be easier to get an empath in here to rescue Gregory than it would be to find a way to entice one to Gregory in the outside world. This prison could work to my advantage. Those were words I never expected to think.

Which empath? My mind felt torn between the male I had seen trying to help Gregory when I joined with him, or the female Gregory had stumbled upon earlier, who seemed to impact his mental state so profoundly.

My choice would be the woman because I could exploit his feelings for her. However, that could backfire as well. The man already invested himself in trying to help Gregory, though his effectiveness was nil. Despite that, there was also history between them. Hence the torn feeling.

I formed images of both people and discreetly pushed them into Gregory's frontal lobe while he wasn't fully aware of his surroundings yet. Several blurry impressions were already there that had leaked out from his weakened state of mind. I didn't have time to examine them thoroughly as Gregory became more aware.

Hastily, I added as many more images of the two empaths as possible before being forced to retreat, so he didn't find out what I was doing. Wresting control hadn't been easy in my previous awakenings, and I had every suspicion that the feat would be more difficult with Gregory.

With that thought active, I checked my grasp on his soul and felt satisfied that if anyone tried to expel me the way the empath had with my last host, Gregory's soul would get torn to shreds and he would die. I would perish as well; only, eventually, I would return. I felt no remorse for this.

I took a backseat when Gregory stirred from his electrocuted slumber and scattered thoughts. I hoped he wouldn't do anything to make that happen again; it wasn't an experience I wanted to repeat.

"Hey, asshole!" Gregory shouted while he gripped the iron bars of the cell. "Let me out! I get a phone call!"

The efforts were futile. Wherever the person was who locked us in this place wasn't within hearing distance. Yet he continued to shout and make noise, essentially acting as though the Gregory I had initially encountered was the only thing possessing this man now. No traces of the other, of which I kept getting glimpses and impressions.

"Void, help me!" Gregory implored helplessly. "I'll die trapped in here. I'm terrified of enclosed spaces."

Then why did you assault the man who put us in here? Gregory being claustrophobic might be helpful information to remember.

"I don't know." Gregory fell silent and began to pace with agitated body movements, his arms unable to remain still. "Something came over me and my mind went blank. I thought it was you."

Proof. Gregory's words were solid proof that I was not the only being inside Gregory, or at least that something else could join both of us without disrupting my hold on him. It spoke of something infinitely more powerful than I.

Sit and close your eyes. Forget about where you are and think of a time when you were happy. The suggestion flowed freely into Gregory's mind without resistance. He was receptive to the idea and sat on the cold metal bench.

The sliver of light that blinked into existence was

enough to hurt but not severe enough to incapacitate. I still consumed it until it was no longer shining, however dull. I waited until after Gregory had gone to whatever memory brought him that joy and it showed me that his happiness had been with the woman we'd encountered.

What is the phone call you expect? I wondered once the glimmer of happiness disappeared.

"Due process when someone gets arrested. The cops are supposed to allow you to make a phone call to tell someone where you are or whatever. Like, call your lawyer, parent, or spouse." Gregory shrugged. "I have no idea who I would call; it was the only thing I could think of doing."

Would you not call the person you thought of when you were happy? I fed fuel to the fire of the thought.

"Ramona is a part of my past. I ruined my relationship with her by dwelling on the bad that my life had turned into; I doubt she would be willing to help me get out of jail. Ramona is one of those naturally optimistic people; being around me was hurting her, so I told her to leave." Gregory shrugged again. "Probably the only selfless thing I've ever done."

I reflected on Gregory's statement. A constant factor of my existence has been evolution. I learn more each time, evolve, and become more than I was the previous time. In the beginning, I hated the light, and now I wanted it. I've never experienced anything other than dark and some part of my essence yearned to feel something different. It was knowledge, is how I looked at it.

I'd be better and more effective at deciphering emotions if I experienced them. I didn't know how to make that happen but something in Gregory's tone when he spoke of Ramona caused some part of my essence to shift. I didn't know what that meant, but I associated that tone of voice to my last host and the range of emotions that rolled through him constantly, especially when the empath was present.

Was it wrong for me to want that? I didn't think so. It was an emergence. Maybe this was the beginning of what should have been happening all along. I didn't know. Confusion was new to me too.

"It's a new world, man. Civilization almost got wiped out, and the old school police forces went with it. What you have now is something different. I don't have to give you a phone call. Why should I? You sucker-punched me in the face, and for what?"

Gregory paced a bit in the cell as the law enforcement officer held his ground and stared at us, or rather, Gregory, with his arms crossed over his chest. The man's posture was rigid and imposing, and his jaw ticked with restrained anger.

"You don't remember me, do you?" Gregory finally asked. He stopped moving and stared with a penetrating gaze back at the man.

"Have I brought you in before?" There was no change in the man's tone or stance.

"No," Gregory shook his head. "But you pulled me off the bridge and threw me to the ground. Told me not to waste the new city's resources cleaning my guts off the rocks below. You told me to grow a pair and be a man, that everyone suffers, and I was no different than anyone else."

"Obviously, you needed a wake up call. Still do if you wound up here," the stone-faced man declared.

"Whatever. I'm a dick. Sue me. If there's someone out there that can bail you out of here, then call them. If I haul you in again, you won't get out."

The officer handed a corded phone through the bars and waited while Gregory recited a phone number for him to dial. He stood there and listened. He didn't leave and give Gregory any privacy to make the call.

It enraged me, the arrogant attitude. I wanted to ignite Gregory's temper and make this man beg for forgiveness but that wouldn't serve my purpose of slowing Gregory down. The fact was that Gregory was still getting possessed by something other than me, and that entity had no bounds. I couldn't let it control Gregory and run unchecked. Gregory was my responsibility.

"Ramona, hi. It's Gregory. I know I'm probably the last person you wanted to hear from but I need some help. I've landed in jail. There's some money in my apartment. Would it be possible for you to grab it and bring it down here so I can bail out?"

"Do you still use the same hiding place?" Ramona asked gently.

"I do." Gregory sounded contrite. "Thank you." He slowly pushed his hand out through the bars and handed the headset back to the officer.

Are you angry with the words he said to you or that he saved your life? I bluntly asked after we were alone again.

"Both. Many people say suicide is a coward's way out, but to me, it takes courage to follow through on the feeling. It's brave to decide to put yourself through the pain of death. I don't know why people say someone died peacefully in their sleep. I've watched someone die and it wasn't peaceful. They suffered. Choosing to suffer isn't a cowardly act. I was completely aware that there was a chance I wouldn't be successful and would be bound to a life of constant pain. It's no different than what I am dealing with now. It's just a different type of pain."

Gregory's admission didn't move me, and I don't believe he expected it to. I experienced emotions like that. It's what created me. That helpless, there's no way out feeling. A need to end it all... but then not do it because they reveled in the despair. The difference was that Gregory had had the gumption to follow through and been stopped.

I could understand his anger over that because he was right. It took courage to get to that point and be poised on the edge of death and get denied the opportunity and then belittled and minimalized for it.

Not that the officer was wrong. Suicide wasn't the answer to end suffering. I wouldn't have been born into existence if that were the case. I wasn't the answer for ending the pain either; I simply gave my hosts a companion in agony to allow it to blossom into a thing of beauty.

It dawned on me that I might be a touch narcissistic in believing that I was intelligent and powerful and that my hosts should obey me. Part of my evolution and emergence, perhaps? Considering that some other entity saw the perfect vessel in Gregory the same as I did, it was possible. That other being wasn't present at the moment, or if they were, they were observing me and noting my weaknesses.

The assault was revenge then. It might go better if you plan out and observe your target in the future. The weapon the officer deployed was quite effective in stunning us both; I pointed out.

"Taser. It fires fifty thousand volts of electricity. I don't know what it did to you, but it made me flop like a dying fish on the ground, unable to use my limbs. I was carried here and dumped in the cell and jolted again with a lesser voltage to keep me incapacitated," Gregory explained in a monotone.

That was good information to store away and remember for the future. It seemed prudent to keep a list of weapons that could immobilize me; that way, I could avoid them.

"Gregory, are you alright?" Ramona's breathless voice roused Gregory. "Under your eyes looks bruised."

"I got tased." Gregory's voice was clipped and short. "Twice."

"That seems a tad excessive," Ramona gasped. "They're processing the payment and paperwork right now, so hopefully, we can get you out of here soon."

"I wish that you had told me no." Gregory rose from the bench. "Even more, I wished I had exercised more control and not called you."

"That's mean, Gregory," Ramona replied in a hurt tone. "You know that I still love you and want to help you however I can."

I didn't know whether Gregory knew; it was confident that Ramona didn't. The subtle change that came over Gregory could have easily gone unnoticed. However, his energy shifted in a way that told me Gregory and I were no longer alone in this body.

I genuinely don't know why that bothered me. Ramona wasn't my concern, and while Gregory might be,

I wasn't emotionally attached to him. I didn't get that way, but that was the only logical assumption I could make from how my energy reacted.

"You know it's not safe to be around me, right?" Gregory asked with a sneer.

It didn't match any of the reactions I had witnessed earlier with this woman; I didn't need more confirmation than this. This third being was the cause of the excessive spreading of my essence and the unrelenting cruelty.

Who are you? I asked, my curiosity unchecked.

"Ah, the smart question, who am I?" Gregory's tone changed. If Ramona's expression was any indication of Gregory's facial expression, it wasn't a good one.

"Gregory?" Ramona answered with a tremor. "What's wrong?"

"Sorry, honey. Gregory isn't present right now. Well, he is, but I kind of pushed him out of the way. But wait, there's more: It's not just me in here, there's someone else, and that's the real reason I'm here."

Alarmed, I remained silent. I didn't know what to think of this entity being here because of me. My mind raced with the possibilities of whose attention I could have drawn. It must have happened during one of my awakenings, but which one? Curiosity won out.

Why are you here for me? I did my best to keep my tone unreadable but didn't quite pull it off.

"We have a mutual acquaintance that seems finely tuned to your presence here," the entity controlling Gregory answered. "She was under the impression that I had a hand in it. Since I was accused, I wanted to check on the situation myself. I wanted to know what you were up to this time."

I was stunned. I didn't know who this entity was but I had a sinking feeling that I knew which female it was referring to: The empath that took me out of my host last time. The empath that kept me from spreading and continuously weakened me.

"What's happening?" Ramona interrupted. "I don't understand."

"Oh, my dear, it's quite simple. Gregory is being possessed by two powerful entities that stem from powerful darkness." Gregory's slightly amused tone rankled Ramona.

"Excuse me?" Ramona stiffened and her eyes sparkled with a fire I didn't expect.

Do not harm the woman, I commanded the other entity.

"I don't harm innocents. That's all you, bud. That is what brought me here. Though I must admit, those affected by our friend Gregory were not innocent. Something changed with you." Gregory began to pace again and his movements were jerky as if the man was working against the entity.

I am ever-evolving. My essence spreads quickly with you at the helm; it does not spread to people such as the woman outside this cell. I didn't know why I shared the information. Perhaps it was fear that the empath would return.

"Yes. I am now aware of your weaknesses. Nor did I mind sharing your essence with the humans that became stained with your impurity. I can safely return to my realm knowing that you have evolved as you say."

"You're a demon," Ramona stated. "I can feel the dark pull of you."

"I am not a demon," Gregory's voice vehemently

denied the accusation. "I command demons. I suggest not angering me."

My essence reeled in shock at the admission. I gathered everything that I could to me and took control. I met resistance with a violent force that drained my energy more rapidly than made me comfortable. Gregory shared the space with me, though I allowed him no room to take over.

"Ramona, take my hand, please." Gregory stuck his hand through the bars, his voice his usual tone that I was used to hearing.

Part of me wished that Ramona stopped and questioned the request given the information she'd just heard. Instead, her hand grasped Gregory's and squeezed.

Tell Ramona your truth. Tell her how you feel, why you ended it. Be honest. I still commanded Gregory as his thoughts and emotions were his. *I don't know how much longer I can keep this hold. You're spinning wildly out of control and spreading my essence at a rate that will throw the balance of the world off-axis. Yes, that was my goal my last awakening, though I have shifted and grown enough to understand that would be devastating for all concerned. Allow this woman to help you, Gregory.*

There was a brute force shove against my essence inside Gregory and I felt my grip loosening. I could only hope that Gregory would do as I told him to do, even though it meant the end for me.

"I love you, Ramona. I pushed you away because I didn't want to drag you down with me and some part of my fucked up brain decided that I enjoyed being miserable. Only the real misery didn't start until you left. I realized then what a mistake I'd made and convinced myself that this existence was what I deserved. I failed at us, at suicide, everything. I'm ugly inside and you are the definition of good and beautiful.

"I doubt I can make you happy or change who I have become. I'm not even sure that I want to. But I want to when I look at you. I don't warrant any glimmer of hope that simply being near you offers and you don't deserve the shit show that I am. The fact that you're here right now or even answered your phone amazes me." Gregory paused to take a breath.

That's when I lost my hold and the other entity took over with a bruising force. Ramona didn't release her grip when she realized that Gregory was no longer at the wheel. I doubted she could harm this being; I suspected I was the only one who stood to be hurt.

"Sweet revelation. Gregory was right that you deserve better. It would behoove you to leave him. I won't influence your decision, and I could because I am that charming. However, the other presence inside is bad news. Unfortunately, I can't remove him."

Well, now, that was interesting information. I didn't know if the other entity was notifying the empath of my presence or where to find me, and fear wasn't something I was used to feeling. It was almost as telling as the entity leaving as quickly as he'd arrived. Suddenly, only Gregory and I remained.

"All I ever wanted was you to ask me for help." A few tears escaped Ramona's eyes. "I don't expect perfection, Gregory. I never did. Depression is hard and everyone struggles."

Searing pain electrified my essence as light blossomed in Gregory's soul. So powerful was the ray of hope that I was unable to fight it. I was too drained, which may have been the point of the other entity battering me the way he had.

I was immobilized and in agony. But oh my, how beautiful it was to have that light shine. I felt humbled that something as simple as Ramona could shine a light on something so purely dark that it devoured all traces of brightness and diminished it to nothing.

Every cell of my essence was on fire as Gregory latched on to that hope like it was his lifeline. It was, though I felt a tad shocked that he grasped it as tightly as he did. There was a lesson in this pain that I needed to learn.

Dark couldn't exist without light, this I already knew, and each had its place and purpose. But choosing to die for it was an experience unlike any other. Ramona shone like the sun on the roots I had so carefully planted in Gregory and the way they shriveled and exploded into small pieces that fell helplessly to the ground was artful and more destructive than my last death.

I'm not advocating for this light, Gregory; it destroys me. Don't throw the opportunity it gives you away. You don't want me coming back. I wasn't selfless; I was selfish, though I handed out the warning freely.

I wanted him to ruin his chance at happiness because it meant I might have a willing host again. Yet, the light now devouring me in exquisite agony kept me thinking that this was supposed to happen all along. This experience was how I evolved into something better.

Perhaps it was the cruel streak of the other entity showing me something I could never attain or hope to have. Either way, it was a done deal. I would learn this lesson, file it away as valuable information, grow, regroup, and return. I would die knowing I chose this path. I became selfless, even if just for a moment. When I awoke, I would be unrivaled in my darkness and narcissistic once more.

I sent my last thought to Gregory right before my essence scattered in all directions and several realms: *Contract void. Goodbye.*

Conditioned Numb

The town could have been ancient ruins. Relics of a time gone past spoke of centuries of history and stories passed down through generations. Except it was a ghost town—a shell of a place that wasn't nearly as old as the beautiful ruins.

This devastation was remnants and ghosts of a bomb placed to destroy. Char burned cinder blocks, rubble, bricks that once cooked meals. Twisted and melted steel bed frames where children closed their eyes after hearing a bedtime story or where lovers attempted to create new life.

Why were we here? To serve as witnesses to the horrors of war? To kill any life that we found left? There were no choices for anyone on this team. We weren't here because we chose to be; we followed the orders.

Ten of us carry an extra forty or fifty pounds on our bodies in full battle gear. Our minds were on high alert, our bodies finely tuned for any sign of danger, or alternately, the opportunity to find someone alive that we could help. Or kill.

We carried everything we needed to survive and nothing that gave us a feeling of belonging. We weren't on a humanitarian mission; we were on strict orders to gather intelligence on what had happened in this town and several others just like it.

None of us knew what desires were anymore because all we'd seen was devastation and death. We felt like robots, the extended limbs of a puppet master who allowed no coincidence, nothing left to chance, only pulled the strings.

Hopes, dreams, wants all got beaten out of us in boot camp, and then they chipped away whatever remained until we simply did what we told. It didn't matter if the people giving the orders were wrong; we weren't there to question them or their authority. We were there to execute the plan and deliver.

How often could we see bodies of innocent lives lost to some power-hungry narcissist leader who craved domination and ultimate control over others and felt nothing? How many licks does it take to get to the center of that sucker? One? Two? Numb.

The hollowed-out pieces of a building that used to be a school was now the site of an incendiary device. Why would someone bomb a school? What could children have possibly done to warrant that? Why target the people that were teaching the future generations the knowledge needed to better the country?

Conditioned apathy and indifference oozed from our persons as we studied the bloodied shoes and remains of those in the school when the bomb exploded. We weren't supposed to cringe at the stench of decaying flesh. It wasn't allowed to feel anything at the sight of children's burned and bloody clothes that still had body parts in some.

No. We were specialists sent in to map out what happened, recreate the events, relay it to the chain of command so they could pretend to understand what made the aggressors do what they did. Emotions were useless in this place.

So many of us wondered what it would feel like to desire something, yearn for tears or a hug. We couldn't mourn because that would cloud our thoughts and sway our minds to think one way instead of seeing all options. Instead, we got scenes of massacres. The locations changed, but the bloody body parts didn't. This numbness was our reality.

A scant few words were spoken between us, and when we did talk, it was to relay information uncovered as we searched the grisly school. Two more towns existed in this place where some nameless group detonated IEDs. We didn't choose the school first because we suspected it would be worst due to children being present. We decided on this site merely because it was the first we came to; the helicopter had had a football field to drop us off. The rest we would travel to by vehicles.

It might sound like we were all heartless bastards, which could be true for some. Most of us were likable people, and some of us even had children of our own back in the states. It took great skill to compartmentalize our lives when we had conversations while deployed. Likewise, it required just as much when we were home pretending to be normal.

Our mourning came when we closed our eyes and visualized our children in place of the nameless faces we encountered; the sightless gaze of the person whose eyes matched those of our significant other haunted our dreams. The elderly couple who perished holding hands and sported matching bullet wounds could be our parents or grandparents.

We didn't cry while we were on location. We didn't even shed a tear while asleep. Our expressions remained rigid and passive, carefully blank. Our minds were so busy putting puzzle pieces together that we didn't have time to associate the scene with things that would make us feel. It only came when we were at our most vulnerable and had no control over the direction our brains took us when our eyes closed.

The EOD technicians, Explosive Ordinance Detectors, flashed upon the undetonated ordinance we almost stepped on that one mission a while back while they dreamt of their kids that like to go metal detecting and be treasure hunters. Our NBC, Nuclear Biological Chemical warfare specialist, would see visions of melting flesh from a chemical attack on his children's faces when they dressed as zombies for Halloween.

Numb was a safe place for us to exist. It was a necessity.

It took us seven hours to clear the school, plot out a sequence of events and possibilities of how we believed the detonation affected the area, the structure, and the people, and declare the site free of chemicals and radiation. There were no survivors.

According to satellite footage and reports to the authorities, the school wasn't the first detonation. It happened no more than two seconds after the first bomb went off. Two of the other locations were simultaneous; the other three explosions were one to two seconds apart. In under ten seconds, three cities had plunged into utter devastation.

We didn't believe that it happened the way it was supposed to. Our thoughts were that the explosions were supposed to be staggered to drive more people to a meeting area. It was a gut instinct that more than a few of us had. The rest hadn't formed an opinion yet, so we weren't saying anything until we had checked out the other detonation site in this town.

We were heading there next since we still had daylight hours left. Not that we wouldn't work after dark, we did. Sometimes it was nice to have natural light, and we were used to fourteen-hour days. There were instances we worked a straight twenty-four and slept on the way to the next assignment. That wasn't the case today; at least we didn't believe it would be.

We traveled by vehicle to the following site as we picked our way through the collateral damage inflicted by the explosives. We figured the device had been planted on or around the boiler room at the site we left. The heat from the blast ignited some of the cars parked around the school. It was a domino effect, which often happened when explosives detonated in populated areas.

The following location was similar to what would be considered a town hall. It held courtrooms, offices, law enforcement, town records, and civil offices. We were inclined to believe that this should have been the first target. The structure was smaller than the school, but not by a large margin. We expected that the investigation would take the same amount of time as the last site.

The collateral damage was more significant in the town hall. A fuel station was within the blast radius and had ignited. Perhaps our hopes that the second site would be quicker were misplaced. Our expressions hadn't changed as we looked at the bodies in the street, yet some of us, if not all, were grateful it wasn't entirely children.

Our team got to work immediately. A good portion of the town had evacuated in panic after the melee of the explosions. Some lingered and observed us while we worked. An unnatural hush filled the air, and our footsteps echoed. A few were vocal in their declarations in stilted English that we were to blame for what happened, breaking the silence, and a couple of teenagers sat not too far away and sobbed while they held a vigil for whomever they'd lost in the blast. The sobs were the only constant noise.

It was a fact that not one of our team hadn't noticed the two teens. It would be hard not to. Two of our team were married, with children. Another three were single parents. The rest were all unattached and with no family alive, much like the wailing teens. After working sites like this, it wasn't a big shock that we remained single. Why put someone through this? Our work wasn't a safe desk job, and military relationships with active-duty soldiers weren't a cakewalk.

We worked diligently, adding to the sound and sometimes drowning out the teens until it was time to find the shelter we were assigned. It was nothing more than an empty store, but it would keep us warm, out of direct sight, and it had a bathroom we could use and wash in. Not all places had that luxury.

The next day, we worked from sunrise to sunset before we could clear the location. Our activity drew a few more observers, and we studiously ignored them unless they got in our way. We found the remote detonators were simple, nothing extravagant, though it looked like whoever put the explosive together at this site was far sloppier than the person who assembled the bomb at the school. It was still effective, though the shrapnel helped paint a clearer picture.

We found hardly anything from the detonator at the school. Here we uncovered several pieces that told their own story. It began to appear that our initial impression was that the two devices should have detonated at different intervals was correct. Our EOD specialist believed that there were two separate teams, or individuals, that had created the two explosives, and the styles proved that true.

The town hall bomb had done its job, and the boiler room had taken care of the rest. The fallout had been several other explosions that made a more significant statement and created the panic we believed intended. In this situation, the aim was to drive people toward a shelter or meeting place, usually a school or stadium.

We didn't know the why behind it; that wasn't our job to figure out. Senseless death held no logic for most people. Terrorists weren't like most people. We relayed the information we gathered back to command and headed to the next town. There was an empty warehouse waiting for us to bunk down in there. It would be too late for us to begin by the time we arrived.

We examined the bodies, rubble, shrapnel, and even pieces of the cell phone detonator that we could find, mapping out the chain of events. The towns could have been interchangeable, and the location and patterns were the same as the previous town. Even though it was more of the same, we still took our time and left no torched stone unturned.

To our trained eyes, the MO was the same. We started with the town hall, which had a courthouse appearance, and we ended with the school. Both buildings had housed elementary and high school combined. Both towns had people watching us work and mourning at the locations. Similarly, they had high body counts. Not only that, the construction of the explosives was identical. Only this town took us three days.

Communication on site was short and to the point. There was hardly any talk in the warehouse, just broken and staccato conversations with family members at home for some, which was a majority of the words spoken, while the rest of us found our spots to sleep and kept to ourselves. That's how we handled our demons.

It was hard to say if our quiet demeanors were due to the scenes we'd witnessed or pure exhaustion. Probably both. We didn't dare wish for home; wanting something was a dangerous pastime. However, we didn't want to remain here either, though we never voiced that. We stayed in our conditioned numb state to get us through. It was a sad existence, but someone had to do the job.

Day three, we wrapped up the location and headed to the next town some fifty miles away mid-morning. The drive between the sites was almost equal distance from each other through the remote and somewhat desolate terrain.

In this instance, there was no such thing as coincidence. It hadn't escaped our notice that almost dead center of this triangle of towns was a secret laboratory-type facility, privately funded but government operated. Whoever created these devices seemed to be trying to drive people away from their villages, perhaps to the larger cities over an hour away.

It led to questions about what went on at that facility. Our clearances didn't allow us to investigate that unless we were ordered to from the chain of command. If that happened, we might find out the why behind these attacks, though not one of us expected that to take place. We weren't part of that need to know.

Yet it was a guarantee that each of us was pondering the laboratory and how it played into these scenarios that we were picking apart, body part by body part at a time. Even when our training forced us to focus on the latter, we were still human though we rarely felt that way. It was natural to wonder the why instead of always the how.

As we drove up to the last town we needed to investigate, we noticed a drone flying high overhead. It could be one of ours. It could also be the people who set these devices off and killed countless people. Again, there were no chance encounters on missions of this type.

The EOD specialist was confident that the charges were all placed by hand in the boiler rooms, so if that drone flying were an enemy, it likely would not drop explosives on us. More likely, it was to spy on our activity or watch over that laboratory and report vehicles within a certain distance from the facility.

Three of our team dedicated themselves to watching the drone's flight and monitored it for indications of hostility while we continued to the next town. The others watched the road around us, looking for hostile forces that wanted to thwart our investigation. It wouldn't be the first time it had happened on a mission, though it didn't happen every time.

We had trained in combat, and we weren't easy to take down. However, it wasn't our specialty, and each attack rattled our usually unshakable demeanors. Those instances required downtime where we stared at our mortality and came to grips with how different it could have gone had we not prevailed. That downtime didn't happen, and over time, the fears came out in unexpected ways, usually at home where we could let our guards down.

It was a luxury that not one of us could afford out here, and the worries and nerves got shoved into a dark recess of our minds while we concentrated on the mission at hand. Our focus remained razor-sharp on our surroundings, even after arriving at the last location.

This site was the farthest north, and the air was chilled more than the previous two locations and provided a peculiar quietness to the atmosphere. It created an eerie feeling as we unloaded our gear and prepared to get started on the investigation.

Fewer people lingered around the scene, and no one spoke, wailed, or shook their fists in anger at us. It felt like the people of this town had given up hope for safety and fled. We hadn't passed any vehicles on our way in, and they had likely left after the explosives detonated. Those that stayed behind paid no attention to us. They walked around with their heads down, their steps hurried, shoulders hunched.

This town was the smallest of the three, and our information told us that it had had the lowest population. While that may be true, the damage was the most extensive here. The initial blast had triggered several other explosions that left minimal structures standing.

The town hall here had been in the direct center of town. The losses were devastating. With our game faces on, our RTO called in our positions and communicated that we were beginning our investigation.

They say the devil is in the details, and we left no detail unexplored. Perhaps we were uncovering Satan as we worked. It took a particular type of individual to kill this many innocent civilians. Believing they were the devil wasn't that much of a stretch.

It took us three days to work our way through the town's rubble towards the school, which lay on the far edges of the location. Not many structures still stood between the town hall and the school, and our sleeping quarters were in the middle of the two sites. It took us another three days at the school.

The sleeping quarters didn't give us a feeling of security, and each night as we called in our progress, the tensions grew. We received information that another team had been deployed to the laboratory to investigate reported hostilities that had recently happened. We didn't dare feel hopeful that it wasn't us that was going.

We derived no pleasure from knowing our EOD had been correct in his assumptions that someone was trying to take over that laboratory and the surrounding areas. We didn't know what was getting produced there or happening inside the building. No one felt the need to tell us.

We received orders to wrap up as quickly as possible and that we were going to get sent home after. That was where our tensions stemmed from, the thought of home. We were due the break since we'd been deployed for over twelve months, and we were afraid to look forward to it.

How do we reconcile the two very different lives we lead? How could we go back to normal lives filled with petty grievances after seeing the worst humanity has to offer? How could we explain the awful things we'd seen and dealt with and how we couldn't react and keep going with only our deep and hidden anger fueling our need to finish?

Fear was a powerful motivator, and the fear we felt learning we got to go home was quite different than the fear we experienced when we entered combat. Combat could kill us. The psychological fear was for returning to normal and expecting the devastation we dealt with to wreak havoc on our bodies and minds.

It would have been understandable if we'd slowed our work down to delay the inevitable return to home, yet we didn't. We kept the fear under wraps and moved forward with the mission. That's what we'd trained to do, and we didn't veer off the path of our mission.

The closer we became to finishing, the more our anxiety grew. We wanted to want to go home, and one thing our positions in the military taught us was that wanting was dangerous. Beneath that want umbrella was hope and hope could kill. Coincidences put us in the cross hairs. The military provided us with everything we needed, and no logic dictated us to desire more than what we had.

Wishing for things is nothing more than greed, one of our drill sergeants told us in training. We came from a first-world country where people killed to have a TV to turn on. He declared himself the person that would beat our wants out of our system and provide us with what we needed and nothing more. All that good soldiers needed was to remain alive so that we could complete our missions and return.

That drill sergeant never taught us not to be afraid to return home. He never once explained that not having a family could be considered desirable or that if we did have families, coming home broken from seeing too many body parts could taint our home life. Some of it we understood without having to be told. We all knew what PTSD was and what the symptoms were, just as we all knew we were in denial about it.

What did it mean to want to have a night's sleep without dreams? What did it mean to desire a spouse, someone to hold you when things got bad? What did it mean to crave that feeling of needing someone to worry about you so that you looked forward to going home? Why was it wrong for us to want these things? Didn't we earn the right to want?

We'd had quiet conversations between our teams about this very subject. It was likely front and center in each of their minds as we concluded our investigation and submitted our final reports to our commanders.

We packed up our gear and began the long drive back to the first town to wait for our helicopter ride out. We received no praise for cracking the pattern of the failed explosions, the fact that there were two separate bomb makers, and that the explosives that didn't detonate on time were all made by the same person who was far less skilled than the person who made the bombs set at the schools. We received no thank-yous in identifying that the laboratory played a part in the devastation in all three locations.

Instead, we received the command to return to the

stadium, catch a ride on the helicopter to the nearest base, and hop on the next ride back to the states. For the briefest of seconds, flashes of something akin to hope brightened the faces of the parents on the team, only to disappear moments later. Home. This fear was what it meant to want.

Misconceptions

aimlessly wandered through the exotic jungle with my face tilted to the sky to see the petals that towered over my head like the skyscrapers that humans talked about when they reminisced. The sunlight filtering through the flowers cast light like I imagined a stained-glass window would when the rays hit. Not that I'd seen any of those things before.

I shouldn't even be here in this jungle. A deity privately owned it, and I'd heard that trespassers received severe punishments. The rumors were on the crazy side of the scale, but regardless, I was here, and I didn't care what happened to me.

I should probably stop calling the jungle a jungle if I'm being honest. It was a lush garden that belonged to a goddess. The space was meticulously maintained by sprites, humans, and the goddess's magic. Antheia was her name, and she was the goddess of plants. It was perhaps the most talked about, admired, colorful, and lusted after garden in existence.

Of course, the humans are how I learned about stained glass windows and skyscrapers. I'm a pixie— everything is a skyscraper to us—but humans spoke of buildings so tall they kissed the clouds in the sky. Some had windows that looked like rainbows with bursts of color and when the sunlight met them, they had the power to mesmerize with their beauty.

Today was my first day breaking the rules and going on an intentional adventure. The human realm would have to wait for my courage to recover. One day I would travel to that realm and experience it for myself.

I doubted that anyone would see me here. On a human, I would fit in their palm; on a goddess, I would fit on her fingertip. I was small. And underneath these flowers and plants, I was all but invisible. My wings had a gossamer shine if the sunlight caught them, but the vividly colored petals and leaves above me provided plenty of shade.

This jungle-like garden exuded happiness and glorious joy with various greens, pinks, yellows, oranges, and all the other colors. It was the happiest place I'd ever seen. This place was perfect for me to mend my dented heart, and that's what I intended to do on this little adventure of mine.

The sloped leaves of the lilies could be velvety slides like nonother I've ever experienced, not even when I was a child. The thick, slick texture of the leaves could work as a trampoline and launch me into the air without the aid of my wings. It could be an amusement park! My inner child was crazy with delight.

The adult part of me looked at some of the lush leaves and petals as the perfect place to nap and gaze at the clouds looking for shapes and daydreaming. The air was tinged with the scents of tropical flowers. It made my mind relax and forget about the arguments with my careless and selfish siblings.

The pollen-fattened bees buzzed around from blossom to bud, taking their fill and doing whatever it was that bees did. The humming of their wings was a pleasant sound when it wasn't too close to my head.

I sauntered over to a thorny vine that hung heavy with ripe fruit. I desperately wanted to sink my teeth into that fruit and let the juices dribble over my lips like sticky sweet syrup. I used the thorns as a ladder and climbed up past the aromatic berries that left my mouth watering hungrily.

This garden has to be what heaven is like, I thought to myself. *It's perfect.*

I grabbed one of the vines above my head, swung myself across to a tulip leaf, and slid down to the stem. I lay back, propped my feet against the stem and stared up at the petals of the white tulip that looked like someone had dipped it halfway in burgundy-colored wine.

I dozed for a bit, gently swaying like I was in a hammock, without a care in the world. Maybe I should apply for a job working in the garden here and answer only to the goddess. What a dream that would be! Unfortunately, I don't know enough about plants or flowers to entertain the thought for long.

I rolled over, jumped off the leaf and glided down, dodging thorns and bees. There was so much more of this place to explore and I wanted to get started. I'd wasted enough time in this paradise already. My trespassing had to wield more excitement than a nap on a leaf.

The domains of gods and goddesses were grander than those of humans or pixies. Maybe because their sheer size was so much more, everything else just accommodated their largeness so it didn't get outclassed.

I'd lived my entire life without ever running into a

god or goddess. Some of them were rather intimidating and plain rude. I'd obviously heard stories about them but had no solid evidence that the rumors were true.

I'd just crossed into the greenest grass when a gust of air ruffled the blades. It sounded like knives slicing through the air past my ears. The sound gave me goosebumps and a shiver went down my back and made my wings quiver.

I hurried through to the other side, anxious to get out of the thick velvety green prison, and stepped happily down into the dirt. I'd no sooner gotten underneath the bright yellow looming sunflowers than a shadow passed overhead.

I scooted over to a violet pompom-looking flower and paused when I saw moisture clinging to the delicate ends of the tendril-like bloom. The dewy appearance gave the flower a prism-like glow when the sunlight filtered through it. It was like a fantasy, and I was mesmerized.

I swiveled my head over to the illuminated dahlia, looking for a similar phenomenon, and saw no droplets. However, when I turned around, I spotted an orb. It was the only one, and it slid off the petal of a brilliant red flower as if it were shedding blood, the essence of life. Except it was translucent, prismatic, capturing the light and making rainbow reflections as it splashed down, leaving nothing but a mud puddle that I could jump in if I were so inclined. I stepped out from under the leaves I hid under and glanced up at the sky, expecting to see clouds and raindrops. There was only blue sky.

Puzzled, I spun in place again, and the corner of my eye caught more movement. Two more perfectly round rolling balls clung to the tips of lavender and pink-colored orchids before falling to the ground in rapid succession.

Where were they coming from? I wondered. There wasn't a cloud in the sky.

I leaped over the puddle to the next flower stem. It was slightly smaller than the others and allowed me to see up above it. Maybe I chanced upon a sprinkler somewhere? I needed to be careful of those things; they could drown a pixie. I let out a little sigh of relief when I didn't spot one and slumped against the stem.

That was when I heard an echo of my sigh, only much louder and more forlorn. I froze, terrified to move my head in case my movement caught the eye of whoever was out here with me. I became even more aware of my situation and my crime of being here.

A few other colorful orbs dropped, and I held my hand out, interrupting the droplet. It drenched me, but I'd confirmed my sneaking suspicion that these were tears; the liquid was salty. Someone was out here crying, nursing a wounded heart just like I was.

My curiosity overrode my sense of danger and I followed the trail of puddles until I could see a hunched figure sitting in the vividly green grass. Long tresses of hair fell in waves over her shoulders, face, and back. I saw golden strands mixed with a deep auburn and brown mixed with chestnut. I realized I gazed upon a goddess—a miserable one, to my amazement.

I couldn't see her face as it was buried in her arms, which rested on her bent knees. The grass, trees, flowers, and living plants turned toward her as if trying to ease her pain. Something in my gut told me with certainty that this was Goddess Antheia.

I felt drawn to the goddess and not purely out of

curiosity to see what she looked like either. I could feel the anguish radiating through her, and I yearned to help. I made my way closer to her, flying to get there faster.

Grateful that she didn't swat me out of the air like a pesky bug, I landed on the petal of a peach rose in full bloom. The rich scent soothed the ache in my heart, and the soft texture had me enthralled for a moment.

I snapped out of it, remembering why I'd risked exposing myself to a goddess's anger at my blatant crime. I still couldn't see her face, and I doubted she knew I was there. Or maybe she did know and assumed I was an insect. Either way, I had a few moments to study Goddess Antheia.

Her skin was the perfect golden color of one who spent time outdoors among her plants. Her body was long and lithe; though, for all I knew, she could be the smallest of the deities that lived here.

Her hands hung limply over her leg and her nails were a frosted pink, a shade that matched some of the blossoms. Her toes peeked out from her strappy flat sandals and those nails were a robin egg's blue with tiny white daisies on them.

Antheia wore a white sundress that looked gauzy and soft. Perhaps the same material that the elder gods and goddesses wore, but in a more modern fashion. A dainty silver chain hung around her slender ankle with a charm in the shape of the tree of life.

Before I could think about what I was doing, I leaped off the rose petal and landed on one of her pink fingernails close to her ear. For Antheia to hear me, I'd need to be close.

"Goddess Antheia," I called out. "How can I help ease your pain?" My voice trembled as I spoke to the legendary goddess. I was a tad afraid she'd smite me.

Antheia's head turned only a smidge. Just enough for the corner of what I thought was an emerald-colored eye to peep out. Long, dark, curled lashes framed the almond-shaped eyes, and I didn't miss the moisture that clung to the tips of the lashes.

"Who are you?" Antheia raggedly whispered. Her voice was husky and alluring.

"My name is Rosella," I squeaked. I resisted the urge to fly away. "I know I'm not supposed to be here," I began to ramble anxiously. "But my heart was hurting today, and this place feels like healing."

My statement made Antheia lift her head and straighten her body. Penetrating violet eyes landed on me, and my heart clenched in fear. They weren't emerald at all; that had been purely a reflection of the vegetation around her. I wasn't sure what would happen next.

Antheia was stunningly beautiful, as are most of the gods and goddesses, but in my opinion, there was something more about her. She was extra. Looking at her made me feel like I was looking at sunshine, as if her rays were something I could see as they fed life to the realm.

"Rosella." My name rolled off Antheia's tongue. "Today, we are sisters in pain. What caused your heartache today?"

Antheia curled her finger until it touched her palm, and she motioned me to stand in her hand. I stepped carefully and kept my balance as she stood. She walked us through the garden and held her hand open and out so I could see where she took us.

"You must be careful here," Antheia cautioned me. "This place is a haven, of that there is no doubt, but it is also deadly." Antheia fanned her free hand out to show me a section marked by a chain across the front of the entrance. "These plants are some of the most beautiful in the universe, and they are the most fatal. One touch for someone as tiny as yourself, and you would die. Yet for a god, I would need to crush the petals of the entire plant into a poultice and dissolve it into a drink for the same effect."

I was aware there were poisonous plants; I wasn't stupid. The other side of that was that I couldn't identify them either.

"Are those mixed in with the other flowers?" I asked as I thought about how many flowers I had touched since illegally entering the garden.

"In some areas, yes. The pollens they produce help grow some of the harmless varieties. I'm not angry that you are here, Rosella, only that you were here unaware of the dangers. I would hate to have your death on my conscious because of one of my beauties," Antheia explained. "I wish you would take that frightened look off your face. I am not going to punish you."

Antheia's speaking manner was so much more formal than my typical chatter that I wasn't sure how to respond. Before I could formulate an answer to her statement, she lowered us both to the ground and propped her back against an ancient-looking oak tree.

"Now that we settled, how about sharing our woes?" Antheia suggested. She held her open palm to a mauve flower petal reminiscent of a hammock for someone my size. "Make yourself comfortable. Have no worries; none of the rumors about me are true, Rosella."

I didn't know how to respond to that, considering I hadn't thought anything about those rumors since I laid eyes on Antheia and decided to try and help. I figured a nod of acknowledgment would be good enough of an answer. I settled down cross-legged on the swaying petal.

"Are you sure you want to hear of my petty issues?" I began.

"I do," Antheia answered with a sigh. "Though, please, don't think something that hurts you is petty. It hurts, and that is what matters. You undermine your worth and value as an emotional being by thinking your woes petty. That's a trap so many of us fall into, accepting that our hurt is childish and not worth the time it takes to understand why it happened and how we can correct it. Don't compare what hurts you to things others are dealing with in their lives."

I pursed my lips as Antheia's words sank into my mind and I processed them. The goddess had a valid point, and I can't say that I'd looked at it from that point of view before.

"Thank you for saying that. I didn't realize that I was minimalizing my emotions," I conceded. "You are wise, Goddess."

"Hardly," Antheia let out a harsh laugh. "Otherwise, I wouldn't be in the garden crying with you. Tell me what has made your day less sunny than it should be."

"I have three siblings," I sighed, giving in to the request. "I'm not the youngest or the oldest. I'm third in line, and my family owns a cleaning business. My parents have never pushed me to be a part of the business, though my other three siblings all bought into it and made that their livelihood."

Antheia nodded her understanding, her beautiful

face expressive with empathy. The fact that she listened to me made tears glisten in my eyes.

"My passion is more artistic. I help out when my siblings have more work than they can handle, and I feel no shame admitting it's not my forte. I do a passable job and haven't had any customer complaints. However, my siblings have lists longer than your arm of my shortcomings." I shrugged my shoulders and looked down at my hands. "I shouldn't let that bother me, but it does."

"Why shouldn't it bother you?" Antheia asked quietly.

"Siblings often disagree. That's what my mom says." I shrugged again. "Anyway, I know I'm not the greatest at making things spotless. My talents lie in designing fashions. I designed the uniforms they wear, sewed them myself, and gave them as a gift. I even embroidered the company name on each of the overcoats. That's what I want to do with my life."

"That's a thoughtful gift that came from your heart." Antheia smiled softly at me. "Did they not like them?"

"Oh, no. My family loved the uniforms and asked me to make an extra set for each and the rest of the employees. That made me feel good, though they expect me to pay for the materials and don't want to pay because they are family. But I'm even okay with that because I can use those designs for my portfolio," I explained.

"All right. So something else happened then. Was it today?" Antheia correctly guessed.

"It was. This morning, I made a pot of coffee for everyone as a good morning gesture. My oldest brother was the first one to the kitchen, and he gave me one of those frowning looks that means he's disappointed with something I've done or said. I brushed it off and went back to sketching an idea for a gown that came to me in a dream," I told the goddess.

I paused to blink back the tears that threatened to surface over the recent slight. I fell back into the same old thought patterns: I sounded so petty. My problems were insignificant compared to the issues that some dealt with daily.

"Stop whatever you are thinking, Rosella," Antheia interrupted my self-loathing. "Your face betrays your emotions, my little friend. Continue your story."

"Paulie, my oldest brother, sat down in front of me and said nothing. He only stared with that condescending look as he watched me sketch. My older sister was down next, grabbed a cup of coffee, then walked over and snatched the pencil from my hand and snapped it into three pieces. Corrina, that's her name, stole the paper I was using, crumbled it up, and stuffed it into her coffee cup," I blurted out.

"That's awful!" Antheia cried out.

"It is," I agreed tearfully. "My youngest brother came down after that and saw me upset and asked what was going on. I've always been closest to him, probably because of our ages, but it felt like he was siding against me. They all sat down around the table and told me that they would have an intervention so that I stopped wasting my life on silly drawings and joined them in the family business to honor our parents and the sacrifices they made for us."

Antheia made a humming sound and frowned. She didn't even have frown lines that marred her perfect face. She clicked her tongue against the back of her teeth in frustration. Instead of speaking, she waved her hand in a motion for me to continue.

"I didn't respond to the comment at first, but the more I sat there, the angrier I became. I didn't cry because I was hurt. That was probably why I *didn't* cry. You know when the hurt is so deep that you can't cry? That's what it was like; however, there were those angry tears that came even though I didn't want them to," I babbled. "I didn't want to give them a reaction at all. Them knowing they hurt me gave them power."

"You only give them power if you hand it to them," Antheia corrected me gently. "Showing a reaction doesn't do that. Though, little one, you had a good reason for feeling heartache today."

"I'm tired of feeling second-rate to my siblings because I follow my heart. It's what my parents taught me to do. They taught all of us to do that, yet I am the only one who did. Paulie wanted to be a veterinarian. Corrina wanted to be a teacher. Only Hunter wanted to join the business," I kept going.

"They're jealous," Antheia stated. "That's not your fault. Your siblings' jealousy is proof of their unhappiness and insecurities; it has nothing to do with you. It's a tough lesson to learn, and almost everyone goes through it. I'm not saying that to take away from what you're feeling. I'm telling you on the chance it was something that you didn't realize yet. I apologize for interrupting you; I only wanted to help you understand why they do things like that."

Antheia made a motion with her finger, and the petal I was perched on wrapped around me like a cocoon. At first, I thought it would be a Venus flytrap scenario, and the plant would consume me. Then I realized that I wasn't trapped.

"You are far too small for me to hug, so I had the flower do it for me," Antheia gave me a hesitant smile. "I hope that didn't scare you."

It had, though I didn't want to admit it. Antheia's gesture came from a caring place, and in a startling moment of clarity, I understood that she didn't often get to be in this position: To be totally herself with me who expected nothing of her.

"In a nutshell, that's my story. I had a pity party with myself and decided to do something illegal and trespass in your haven. I feel awful for intruding, but I'm also happy that I got to see the beauty you've created, and I'm lucky for chancing upon you and getting to meet you," I quickly finished.

"Thank you for the compliment," Antheia bowed her head gracefully. "Did you design the clothing you are wearing now?"

"I did," I smiled proudly. The dress was one of my favorites. I used bright colors that were in a large swooping floral pattern. "It takes a long time to make the fabric if I am designing from the start. I don't do that every time, but I had an idea and ran with it for this one."

"It's divine," Antheia agreed. "I quite like the design. Even more so now that I know you created the fabric as well. You are quite impressive, Rosella. Would you be willing to accept a commission to design and make a gown for me?"

I practically fell off the flower petal at her question. I thought she was joking at first, but her earnest expression assured me the request was genuine. I quickly tried to mentally calculate how long it would take me to make fabric for a goddess and got overwhelmed.

"How quickly do you need something?" I swallowed the fear that I would have to turn Antheia down.

"There would be no deadline. I just want it for myself because it would be an original and make me feel pretty. I understand where the question is coming from, and I can offer some workers to help you make the fabric. I understand that doing something on this scale would be daunting given our size differences," Antheia assured me.

"Okay," I breathed out a sigh of relief. "I'd love to design something for you."

Antheia smiled in response, but again that haunted look settled behind her eyes. Before I could blink, the goddess had bent herself in half, and those bowling ball-sized teardrops spilled from her eyes in a waterfall. Each tear rolled off the flower petals under her face, creating small rainbows as they caught the light before landing on the ground.

The visuals were still mesmerizing, though I was far more concerned with the goddess's mental state than with the spectacle of the orbs. I jumped up before one of the tears bounced me off the petal and I hovered in the air a moment.

"Goddess, please. Tell me why you are hurting. It's your turn now. Unburden your soul," I begged. "Allow me to return the favor."

Antheia swiped at the tears on her golden face, and a stream went streaking through the air, narrowly missing me. I swooped around and landed on a different flower, out of target range, and waited patiently while the goddess composed herself.

"Please, come settle on my shoulder." Antheia wound her wavy locks up out of the way. "That way, if I need to walk as I talk, I won't leave you behind and be talking to myself."

I silently did as she asked and slid my feet through one of the loops on the shoulder of her garment, so I remained anchored in place.

"My heartbreak is self-inflicted," Antheia began. "I am not smart enough to see through the lies fed to me by the one that my brain thinks is the right choice of a life partner. When you are immortal, life is a long time."

Antheia fell silent. From this vantage point, I couldn't see her eyes as her head was straight. I didn't need to see her face to hear the anguish in her voice, though. I could feel it resonating in the air, and I swallowed thickly.

"So many of the gods are fickle and selfish beings. I know because I am one. I've learned through my workers the art of empathy, kindness, and selflessness. I try hard to practice it instead of taking everything for granted because I am a goddess. Did you know that I am the goddess of human love as well as plants? Wouldn't you think from that alone that I would be wiser to the ways of men?" Antheia asked rhetorically.

"No," I answered, even though I suspected she wasn't looking for one.

"Why would you answer that way?" Antheia was clearly surprised by my response.

"Because it's a lot easier to see things looking from the outside than seeing them when your heart is invested and involved," I replied. I sounded like I knew what I was talking about, I hoped.

"I suppose you are right," Antheia responded slowly. "I also wrongly assumed that you are young based purely on your size. I'm unaccustomed to pixies; most of them shy away from deities."

"That's true," I nodded agreeably. "I think most have had bad experiences, intentional or unintentional. We tend to stick closer to the smaller species. I say smaller, though they are all still larger than pixies. Anyway, please go on."

"Right," Antheia sighed. "Where do I start?" She fell silent for a few moments, and I let it hang in the air. "I've been romantically involved with Rogagi, a demigod. We've been together for centuries, and maybe I should have expected that infidelity would happen, though I didn't."

I, too, have been a victim of a significant other stepping out on me. I didn't open my mouth when Antheia fell silent again but waited patiently for her to collect her thoughts and what she wanted to share.

"The first time it happened, I felt crushed beyond anything I could have imagined and questioned love's existence. I let requests go unanswered for a time, and Aphrodite herself came to visit me and raise my spirits. Aphrodite convinced me that love is real but that perhaps Rogagi wasn't the one for me or that he wasn't ready for love. That got me over the initial hump, and I decided I wouldn't take him back," Antheia confessed.

I hummed my agreement with that sentiment. However, Antheia must have done what she didn't want to do since she was out here and had been crying over a broken heart. I patted her shoulder consolingly and kept quiet.

"Rogagi came to me a week later, distraught over

his careless mistake, and told me that he was raised to believe that it was okay to have multiple partners because his father, a god of pleasure, had several. It was a convincing argument and one that I felt I needed to consider as I hadn't been raised the same way, so my values were different. I agreed to take him back but made it clear that I wouldn't tolerate it happening again." Antheia's voice had gone soft.

There was a train of logic to the argument that I would have been inclined to excuse, though, personally, I don't believe I would have. I knew for someone suffering those internal wounds of betrayal it would be even harder to see that as nothing more than an excuse to get away with the infidelity. It was easy for me to think that way when I wasn't in the situation.

"My trust in Rogagi came back relatively quickly, and I didn't give a second thought to a repeat offense. He'd explained himself and his actions in my mind, and now that I knew and had spoken to him, it was no longer a concern. That was my mistake, and I own that. Matters of the heart are never straightforward. Choosing to love someone is hard, and it hurts," Antheia explained.

The light hit another tear. This one was not perfectly round, though not any less prismatic in the sunlight. It left a trail down Antheia's cheek that sparkled, and the tear clung to her chin, forming a marble shape before it fell. It shattered on the blades of grass as they sliced through the water.

"My forgiveness cost me because Rogagi did it again. I was absolutely furious, and I unleashed a torrent of magic that had plants blooming and growing, and others withering and dying. I should have learned at that point. Only when he turned the tables on me and blamed *me* for his actions, made *me* the villain, did I accept it," Antheia whispered brokenly.

"Why?" I couldn't help but ask.

"The old adage that love is blind comes to mind, though it boils down to nothing more than an excuse. The truth is, my devotion to Rogagi made me think that maybe what he said was true. Perhaps that was due to his explanation of his method of betrayal. My fury turned to depression and self-loathing as I took his statements about my shortcomings to heart." Antheia fell silent. "It was a pattern I frequently saw in humans and those seeking me out. I counseled them to not be deceived, and here I was doing just that."

I leaned my body into her neck as a show of support. I knew Antheia wasn't finished talking, so I said nothing and simply sat with her as she revealed her wounds to me, a stranger. It was an honor unlike any other I'd received.

"Hold on, Rosella," Antheia warned as she stood. "I want to show you something as an example."

Antheia's strides were gigantic, and she traversed the garden that she'd created with an ease that spoke of intimacy with the place. She crossed into a chained-off section that housed some of the most gorgeous blooms. The fragrances were heavy in the air and clung to my skin like the morning dew.

"Everyone has misconceptions about gods and goddesses," Antheia began. "I am sure you did too, and no, I'm not taking you to task for it. I want to explain why I feel the way I do. I didn't choose to be born who I was. It's something that was out of my control. Certainly, I had privileges that many others didn't, but I did not take them for granted. Yes, I have powers that were gifted to me upon my birth, but again, it wasn't a choice. Yet there are still those who hate me for who and what I am."

Antheia couldn't see me, but I nodded right along with her. What she said was true; I've heard people scorn deities for their power and privileges.

"Even those who claim loyalty to us loathe that we can do things they can't. Growing up, we had parents, some of us, though they weren't truly parents like yours. They taught us to use our gifts, take control of our domains, and dish out punishments to those we thought deserved it. There was no abundance of love and support. We were issued demands and expected to obey, or the punishments would be severe, sometimes even death. We didn't get time-outs or restrictions. We had power stripped from us or received brutal beatings when we crossed lines," Antheia described.

The picture that Antheia painted for me was drastically different than what I'd envisioned being a goddess was like. I knew it was for this reason that she explained herself, and it made me look at her in a different light. I was shocked and silent.

"See this plant?" Antheia stroked a lush and velvety petal. "It smells divine. It makes you want to cut some of the blooms off and put them in a vase. Yet if you do that, the liquid that would seep from the stem would cause deadly toxins to enter your bloodstream through your skin. Death would come in minutes, and it would be excruciating as it attacked your nervous system. Do you understand my comparison?"

"Yes," I nodded. "Looks are deceiving."

"They are," Antheia agreed sadly. "This plant didn't choose to kill; it just grew as it was supposed to. Now here's the kicker: If you take that liquid, boil it, and add in some select herbs, it becomes a sleep tonic that can help those who struggle to find rest. Not what you would expect from a deadly plant, is it?"

"No," I shuddered. "Misconceptions, like you said earlier. Some would hate this plant purely because it could kill them, never knowing that it could also be a remedy for an ailment that could cause death. Putting that into context, everything we know about deities could be false."

"Or just shades of the truth," Antheia granted. "The rumors about me are not true. However, my rage where my magic went out of control was witnessed and then taken out of context. From there, the rumors were born. You and I, we aren't so different. We want to be seen for who we are, not what we are expected to be."

"Yes," I breathed out in a rush. "That would be nice for once."

"Today marks the fifth time that Rogagi has been unfaithful to me. Five times and it's only today that my heart has decided that it needs to let him go. It is finally in agreement with my brain. I can't begin to describe the agony I have gone through with this man. Those tears you saw or had to dodge were the release I needed to experience. It hurts, but there is also a sense of freedom that I can't explain," Antheia admitted.

"They didn't feel happy," I replied skeptically. "There was a heaviness to those tears as they fell off the petals."

"Yes," Antheia nodded. "Those toxic emotions were releasing. I'm sorry you had to experience that. I was just so tired of being the punching bag for his defensive behavior and weak excuses. I fled the house and came here, where I know that I'm safe and protected."

"That's what I felt when I snuck in here," I confessed.

"I made this garden," Antheia gestured around her. "Every plant in this garden was planted by my two hands and raised from seeds. My blood, sweat, and tears nurtured them to grow. I talked to them and told them my deepest secrets, and I sang them my joy. Here I receive love. In the house, I receive lies."

I gazed out over the expanse of the blooms, shrubs, and trees. Knowing Antheia herself planted each and every single one impressed me. It wasn't often that you heard of a goddess getting down and dirty with the earth to create something so wondrous.

"Did you know that my tears are magical?" Antheia asked me suddenly. "Aphrodite's are too. A little-known fact for you: Mine make things bloom. My blood from cuts and scrapes nourished the soil. Rogagi once tried to rip a plant out of the ground by its roots when I didn't fall for the lies he spewed. It caused me physical pain, and I instantly knew what was happening. Sadly,   I will admit to pleasure in hurting him to make him stop."

"Revenge," I whispered.

"Avenging my creation. These plants are my children." Antheia began to walk again. "Misconceptions are dangerous, Rosella."

The goddess ran her fingers over a large-leafed tree's dark brown, rough bark that emitted a spicy smell. I knew better than to follow her example and touch. She'd already told me that several were deadly to all but her.

"I am not trying to scare you, my new little friend," Antheia's tone softened. "I suppose I am still leaking out the toxins that have built up in my heart. Shall we make it rain?"

"What do you mean?" I glanced up at the sky.

"You have resentment stored inside, the same as I do. Am I wrong in that assumption?" Antheia shrewdly asked me.

"I do," I cautiously admitted.

"Let's set it free, raise it to the heavens and let the universe answer our plea for release," Antheia raised her arms and tilted her head to the sky. "A benefit to having Zeus as a parent."

I didn't understand what she was saying, but I mimicked her movements. From my perch on her shoulder, I threw my head back to the sky and stretched my arms as far as they would go, palms face up.

"Let your heart feel everything you need to get rid of," Antheia instructed me. "Let it flow through your veins. You'll may feel overwhelmed; if you need to cry, let yourself."

I'd worked so hard on suppressing my emotions so that I didn't feel that relentless disappointment pressing down hard on me, knowing I couldn't live up to my family's expectations. I knew that Antheia was correct: It wasn't my problem! But it didn't feel that way. I tried hard to let those feelings wash over me and not feel ashamed.

It took me a few moments to understand that was an emotion I needed to let go of too, and anger, disappointment, rejection, and sadness. They all bubbled up inside me, and I began to feel as though I was about to implode.

I was so in the moment of ridding myself of the toxicity I'd stored away that the sound of an electric, raw and anguished scream hadn't penetrated the fog my brain had dragged my heart into at that moment. Not until one of my own matched Antheia's.

The combined energy of our voices filled with our agony, anger, resentment, and self-loathing reached for the sky. I put everything in my body into that scream until my throat felt like it would bleed itself raw.

Antheia, I was sure, did the same. Tears spilled from our eyes until dark gray and purple roiled threateningly, answering our call. Electricity built, I could feel it penetrating my skin. As lightning flashed in a brilliant ribbon across the sky, my scream died away, and thunder vibrated through my bones.

Unlike any other that I've ever felt, a peace settled on my being. The sky was acting out those emotions we'd set free, and it was the most amazing sensation to see it in motion. The fury unleashed in violent displays of lightning, pounding rain, and whipping wind that stung my skin.

Electric blue, violet, silver, shades of gray and purple lashed out in a punishing force. I didn't know how long it went on, but suddenly, all fell quiet again. The clouds dissipated slowly, and sunbeams reached out for our skin, sharing their warmth.

The wind died down, and the air currents heated up and kissed our faces with gentle caresses that let us know we'd been heard. Blue sky peeked through and smiled upon our supplicant bodies, and both Antheia and I smiled.

I can't say what we did solved anything. Our problems still existed the same way they had this morning when we woke up. I can say that I wasn't a prisoner to those feelings anymore. I could look at my issues and see them with a clearer head, a heart unburdened. I felt lighter.

I stood and took flight from Antheia's shoulder and flew to a spot in front of her, where I could see her face. It was a world of difference and the goddess was as beautiful as her garden. The shadows were gone from her eyes. I could only guess that her heart was lighter as well just like mine.

"You are stunning, Goddess," I sighed happily. "Thank you for that invaluable lesson."

"I don't know about you, but I feel better," Antheia smiled graciously. "May I be so bold as to ask if you would be willing to return and visit me when you have time? I'd like to consider you a friend now, and I have so few of those."

"Of course," I blushed happily. "It would be an honor. I have to return anyway to get sizing for your gown."

"I know this," Antheia responded. Her face fell slightly. "I hoped that you would return without having to do work. We could spend time in the garden talking, or having a picnic. Did you see how lovely it is after a rain?"

I turned and hovered not far from Antheia's face and gazed upon the wondrous garden. Thousands of little rainbows filled the air from the sun's rays penetrating the various drops on the leaves and petals. Heavy drops rolled and fell, making the flora shake from the weight of the releasing water. Brilliant colors shone throughout. Paradise would be an understatement.

"The word 'lovely' doesn't do it justice, Goddess. Nor does a simple phrase like: 'You do good work.' I'll return whenever you'll have me. Not just because of this place, but for your presence and friendship. Now, tell me, have you decided what to do about Rogagi?"

A slow smile spread across Antheia's face, and I had chills race up and down my spine. Antheia had proven to be a gentle soul, but there was no mistaking the calculating look that entered her eyes. She was about to prove one rumor true: Gods and goddesses can dole out punishment quite well.

"I was thinking of letting my father handle him," Antheia responded with a cold smile. "After all, it wasn't his first offense."

I shuddered and felt immense relief that I wasn't on the wrong side of Antheia. She'd given me a lot to think about over the course of the day, and one thing that stuck in my mind was her telling me that we weren't so different.

"Our insecurities don't make us weak," I finally said. "It's how we deal with them that defines who we are. I don't condone Rogagi's actions, but perhaps instead of allowing your father to deal with him, ask your father for counsel?" I suggested as kindly as I could.

Antheia frowned, and a distant look crossed her features as she contemplated my suggestion. I threw it out there as a token of my trust, as she had been bluntly honest with me regarding my own situation.

"I suppose you are correct," Antheia admitted. "I need to handle this on my own and not involve others. Asking for Father's counsel is a wise idea. It allows him to help me without expecting him to handle my problems.

Thank you, Rosella."

"Friendships form when you least expect them to," I replied with a smile. "Today was what I needed, and I can't thank you enough for sharing your time, feelings, expertise, life, and the garden. I can't wait to get started on your gown. Not only that, you've inspired me to talk more frankly with my parents about the situation with my siblings. I don't expect it to solve anything, but it might help reaffirm that they aren't disappointed in my choices."

"Indeed," Antheia agreed. "Please, keep me informed. I have enjoyed this more than I thought I would. You are the silver lining of my day. I'm so happy that we've met, Rosella."

Antheia walked me out and handed me a vial tiny to her but nearly as large as my body. It was surprisingly light enough for me to carry, yet it also felt somehow heavy. I patiently waited while Antheia fashioned a sling for me to carry it over my back.

"This vial contains one of my tears that rolled off a specific flower. It contains powerful magic pertaining to emotions and seeing clearly. If I am unavailable and you need a friend, dab your finger in the vial, and the essence will assist you," Antheia explained. "Keep it safe, Rosella. This tear is part of me."

I knew I would treasure the tear for as long as it was in my possession, and I told her so. Our size differences made it impossible for her to hug me, but I gripped her finger as best I could and then we parted ways.

As I flew home, the sunlight reflected off the tear in the vial so it appeared as if I were flying with a rainbow. It was hard to dread the upcoming conversations I needed to have with such a view. Instead, the prismatic powers of that tear made me look forward to the changes headed my way.

Tears were powerful; it was a misconception among many that they were a bad thing. I knew differently now.

Uncovered

My eyes snapped open to inky darkness instead of a starry night sky with clouds under me. The air was dank, stale, cold, yet humid, and smelled of urine. My mind was hazy and mixed my last memory with scenes from the raid. I struggled to remember what had changed between my last memory and how I now found myself.

I'd been flying my plane toward Saint-Nazaire, France, region looking for ground troops needing assistance from our fleet in the waters. That was the last that I remembered. The British had successfully raided that city, though we still had control of the town and surrounding areas.

I wouldn't likely forget the repurposed warship crashed into the dry dock; it wasn't something seen often. They'd snuck troops and explosives in the old ship, and rammed it into the structure. I'd been there after the raid happened and helped evacuate the wounded from the ship's delayed explosion; it was seared into my mind. The chaos and broken and bloody bodies were unforgettable. The detonation had been devastating to troops and land alike. That single event cost the German forces a port to repair their war-damaged ships, three hundred and sixty soldiers, a Generaloberst, and faith in their abilities to fight back against the calculating allies.

After the raid, German efforts had received new ideas, structures, and orders to focus our efforts on protecting and reinforcing gun emplacements and bunkers on the Atlantic Wall. Our Fuhrer wanted assurance that another raid such as that, the one they called Operation Chariot, would not happen again. That order was why we had been on a flight over the area, patrolling and searching.

My copilot had seen a couple of flashes of light during our recon flight but no signals telling us we needed to send help. Not that we had a lot of people or equipment left to utilize a rescue attempt without heavy loss if we became infiltrated again. Also, thanks to that raid, there wasn't a functioning dry dock left to help the Wehrmacht with their war efforts.

Back to my current predicament, the last thing I remembered was some form of a shock wave after the flashes had been spotted. I had to have crashed, which would explain the throbbing skull pain. I don't remember the impact, what area I'd landed in, or why I lay in this state of darkness. My memories failed me.

I hadn't lost my sight because I could blink my eyes and feel them try to focus on pinpricks of light that my mind told me I saw. I supposed it could be a head injury causing me to see things that weren't there. Either way, I didn't believe I was blind.

However, I did believe I was alone. Perhaps captured by enemy troops and held captive in a pit somewhere. I did my best to keep my mind from running wild with possibilities and sending myself into a panic.

I slowly lifted my arm, which felt like a dead weight, to see if something was before me. I painfully brought my hand close to my face and splayed my hand out. When my pinky didn't touch something, I knew there existed at least eight inches between my nose and whatever was above me.

I exhaled a hot, smelly puff of air that bounced back to my face. I might have eight inches of space, but there wasn't much more than that. My lips felt cracked, and my throat was dry. At some point, I'd soiled myself. All of it told me I'd been in here for longer than a couple of hours.

I took a chance and softly cleared my throat, tasting blood. Immediately, there was a noise from somewhere above me.

"Hush, brother," a deep, gravelly male voice replied in English with a heavy French accent. "There is still danger present. I am keeping you safe."

There was no argument from me. I hated everything about this war. I never wanted to be part of it; I certainly never wanted to be identified as a Nazi, or desired to be the person pulling a trigger on another human being, regardless of their race or country of origin. Truth be told, if someone uncovered my secrets, I'd be a *target* of the Nazi party.

I didn't understand who the French man was hiding me from—it could have been resistance fighters, Nazis, or Allies. I was in my Luftwaffe uniform, my name (Wagner) in clear sight, flying my German airplane, over German-occupied France, with Allies doing air raids. Any or all could want me as their prize.

I drifted back off to sleep with nothing else to do other than wait for rescue or get killed. My dreams were a muddled mess of bombs, fighting, burning ships, flashes of light, and fading. I couldn't distinguish reality from horror movie nightmares, though it could be that the two were the same.

"Wake up, Wagner."

My shoulder shook, and my eyes cracked open. The sudden bright light hurt my eyes, and I closed them again, much to the man's unhappiness. He shook me again, a little harder this time and persistently until my eyes opened, to my annoyance. It made my head hurt worse.

"I'm awake," I muttered. I tried to use my arms as leverage to sit up, but pain lit like lightning through my limbs and back.

"Do not move. Allow me to help."

I was thankful that my parents made me learn English when I was in school. I hadn't been then, but now, it was our common communication thread in a foreign land since I hadn't bothered to learn French.

English, however, had had a draw to it. My parents told me that if I ever wanted to move to the United States to pursue my dreams, I would need to know the language. They called it the Land of Opportunity, and the war had taught me that the Americans harbored hate just as much as the Nazis did. It contradicted what they had described with all the land's opportunities, though it still called to me.

With a grunt, the man heaved me out of the hole he'd buried me in, which eerily felt like a coffin. His arms were under my armpits, and he used his legs for leverage, the proper way to lift. Electrical pain shot through my body, and for a brief moment, I thought that I would lose the contents of my stomach if I had anything in there.

My legs loosely dangled as my body cleared the pit, and I wondered if I had lost the use of them. That thought lasted only long enough for the pain to flair through the useless limbs and caused them to stiffen and cramp with agony.

I bit my lip to keep myself from crying out. I didn't want to draw the attention of whoever this man had hidden me from. I tasted blood but didn't unclamp my teeth until the man dragged me into what I assumed was his home and deposited me unceremoniously on the floor.

I struggled to sit upright and catalog my injuries. One of my legs had broken; I didn't need a doctor to tell me that. It lay at an uneven angle below my knee, blood staining my uniform. That would explain why I hadn't been able to use it.

My arms hurt similarly to my legs, though they hadn't snapped; I guessed they had some fashion of fractures. I could bind those to keep them from moving too much and hope for the best. The cuts, scrapes, bruises, and burns would have to heal independently; the breaks and fractures were the more significant concerns.

"Here," the man walked up to me and dropped to his knees with some thin pieces of wood. He was a tall, athletic man with sun-darkened skin and deep brown eyes. "I will help. What do you call yourself?"

"Drexel Wagner," I found my manners and introduced myself. "Thank you for the assistance. How shall I address you?"

"Jehan," he told me. Jehan set to work cutting my uniform leg open and didn't bother to hide the grimace that came over his face as he looked at it. "This will hurt."

Jehan gave me no time to prepare and jerked my bones back into place. This time, I couldn't hold back the scream, and my voice echoed off the walls. My head swam, and my torso swayed with the waves of pain. I began to dry heave and flopped back on the floor with a jarring thud to my already throbbing head.

Jehan quickly wrapped my leg using the wood and torn bedsheets to form a splint. He was efficient, if not gentle. All I could do was grind my teeth and hope I didn't pass out from the pain. It was my first injury of this type or severity, and for a few moments, I wished I was home getting taken care of by my mother. I found it sad that I wanted to revert to childhood, but life was simpler then.

"Would you like a sip of brandy? I might help with the pain," Jehan offered when he finished.

As before, Jehan didn't wait for me to respond. He turned and walked off with long strides, then returned and handed me a small tumbler with a few fingers' worth of alcohol.

I gulped it down gratefully and waited for the pain to subside. It took longer than I had hoped, but it did the trick. While I sat there, Jehan got me a warm washcloth and a clean towel, and I did my best to cleanse my injuries and the blood from my body. My head was tender and sensitive to my touch.

"I'm sorry," I apologized, looking at the washcloth. "I've ruined your washcloth."

"It is fine," Jehan shrugged. He took the soiled linens from me and tossed them in a bucket before settling himself into a rocking chair. "You talk in your sleep."

I jolted and sent a bolt of agony through my abused body. I didn't know how to respond. I hadn't exactly been asleep, and there were countless alarming things I could have aired to the stranger. None of them would have been to my benefit, though it seems the man had no interest in handing me over to anyone.

"Did you see another man when you found me?" I finally mustered the courage to ask after my copilot. I was ashamed it had taken me this long to do so.

Jehan nodded slowly; his intense brown eyes focused on me. I supposed I didn't need the words spoken to know that Roland's fate was not as fortunate as mine.

"I could not help him; he was already gone. Wehrmacht found the body, took it away." Jehan waved his hands through the air with a finality that I felt deep inside.

In grief, I hung my head to my chest; I felt heavy remorse at his loss. Roland and I shared many similarities. We both hated the war, the Nazi machinations of soldiers committing atrocities against fellow humans. We both had gotten conscripted and pulled from our schools against our will. The soldiers told us we would be killed as traitors if we didn't go with them.

"Who were you hiding me from out there?" I bravely asked.

"Everyone," Jehan answered after a pregnant pause. "You talk in your sleep," he reminded me. "Dangerous habit."

I swallowed my denial and tried to push the excuses out of my head. It was easy enough to surmise that whatever words I'd uttered weren't things I wanted out in the open. Jehan wasn't stupid, and treating him as if he were wouldn't do me any favors after the kindness he'd shown me.

"You speak German?" I asked in German after a

long and awkward silence stretched between us.

Jehan nodded in response. He was considerably older than me and perhaps a farmer or laborer of a type. His hair, which was longer than military issue, draped over his forehead with his nod.

I took my time and thought about what to say to the man. Not that his appearance would tell me anything other than he wasn't a man of wealth. I studied him a bit more and tried to figure out his motives for helping me.

Jehan's face bore lines as though he worked a great deal outdoors, and he kept a neutral expression in place. There was stubble present, but not enough to tell me if he wore a beard or it was a day's worth of growth he hadn't gotten around to shaving.

"I speak English now because there are fewer of them out there looking for you." Jehan gestured to my uniform. "There are more of your party comrades than Allies. Rifle fire took your engine out and another shot punctured your gas tank. The plane exploded from the back end and broke apart. It was a sight that everyone could see."

That explained what happened, and the flashes that Roland saw must have been the gunfire. I was tired when we took off on our flight, but I didn't realize I was tired enough not to know the plane had taken a hit. Then again, our aircraft was in dire need of repair, and we patched it up daily.

"I went to look for survivors," Jehan continued. "It isn't right to let people sit there injured, suffer and die, if you can help. I am no Nazi," he spat in disgust. "What they do in the name of their Fuhrer is reprehensible. I resolved not to feel hate for someone following orders, and if you were violent, I would notify your comrades of your location so they could come get you."

I absorbed Jehan's information without a word in return. I silently agreed that the Nazis were doing horrible things to people, and I didn't condone it. That is why I chose to become a pilot or, rather, I hadn't argued the assignment. I would not get sent to work in a camp or another post where atrocities were expected of the soldiers.

"I found you buried under your parts of the plane," Jehan told me. "It was easy to find, and it happened to be that I was closer than anyone else. I followed the smoke. I didn't expect survivors. Your partner was further away, and I do not believe he suffered if that helps you."

"It does, thank you," I feebly offered up and said a silent goodbye to Roland.

"You were talking, which is how I found you in the wreckage. I moved some of the parts and freed you, and I tried to arrange them in a manner that would look natural, though I might not have succeeded in that task since they were looking for you."

I bit my tongue to keep from speaking. I am more than positive that I revealed things I shouldn't have said aloud while in that semiconscious state. I believed that Jehan wasn't someone who would turn me in, though I wasn't entirely sure.

"The only way I could hide you was to bury you, the same way your plane had buried you," Jehan explained. "Under my garden is a trap door. I put it there for situations like the one I found you in. I planted plants on top of the door to hide that there was a hole. It makes it heavy, and the plants move, but it has remained a secret. When I use the hole, I pretend to be fixing the garden due to a critter that got to it."

That answered the other questions I had. However, they weren't the questions pressing heavily on my mind. Yet, knowing Jehan buried me alive almost distracted me from seeking out those answers. I was grateful for not being aware of the situations as they happened.

"How long ago was the crash?" I asked after a few minutes of silence. The sky outside had darkened rapidly, and I realized I didn't even know the time.

"Two days," Jehan admitted. "Would you like some cushions to lie on?"

I wanted that badly but did not want to fall asleep before finishing this conversation. I nodded before worrying that I would soil up Jehan's furniture with my odors and blood in a moment of weakness.

Jehan got up and walked into his kitchen, filled a large bowl with some water, and brought it back to me with some clean cloths and a bar of soap. He set the bowl down next to me and dunked the linens in the water. I saw steam rise and understood that he brought me the water so I could bathe myself.

"I will leave you for a few minutes so you may clean without me watching. Leave the clothes in a pile, and I will bring you fresh clothing." Jehan stood and left the room, only to return shortly with some clothes that he set next to me. "Do you need help removing it?" He gestured to my uniform.

"I'll manage. Thank you for your kindness, Jehan," I told him gratefully.

Once he left the room, I peeled my uniform away from my rank body as best as possible. It took me more than a few minutes to wiggle out of the pants and boots, and the efforts left me sweating profusely, nauseated and panting. The pain was almost unbearable, yet the desire not to inflict the odors on someone else was strong within me.

Once I got my breathing under control, I began to wash and spotted several more injuries, but none were alarming in nature. I pulled on the clean clothes and felt marginally better than I had when he deposited me on the floor. I thought to myself, *I could use more brandy to numb the pain.*

Jehan returned with a narrow mattress that he settled on the floor, covered with a blanket, and then moved to help me onto it. He handed me a pillow and placed a blanket over me.

"It still gets cold at night," Jehan told me. "It's the only extra one I have that will keep you warm."

"It's more than I expected, Jehan, and I am grateful for it," I murmured tiredly.

Jehan picked up my uniform and turned to me with a questioning look. "Are you attached to this?"

"No." I had no energy to laugh. I hated that uniform.

Jehan nodded once and then threw the offending clothing into the fireplace. He walked away, and I closed my eyes, only opening them again when I sensed him standing over me.

"Water," Jehan held a cup out to me. "You need to drink." He held out a second cup with amber-colored liquid in it. "For the pain. We'll talk more in the morning. The pan is there if you need to relieve yourself."

I gulped the brandy and gave Jehan back the cup, and then sipped at the water. I rolled to my back and let my eyes close. Not that I remembered enough to argue because I remembered nothing after the shockwave. I needed sleep and time to process Jehan's version of events.

My sleep was restless and consumed with pain. I couldn't toss and turn due to my variety of injuries so I'd lay still with just my eyes snapping open until I'd force them shut. The night chilled the air, yet I had to push the blanket off due to sweating.

It was both the best night and the worst. The pain was unlike anything I'd ever felt before, and the other side of that was that the Nazi party most likely considered me dead or captured. For all intents and purposes, I was a free man.

That was the thought that I drifted in and out of sleep thinking: I was free. Maybe I could escape to the United States and live free for the rest of my life. It was a thought. It kept me going and stopped me from giving up and surrendering myself to either side.

My eyes opened when I smelled food cooking, and my stomach rumbled. I propped myself up as best as possible and tried to peer into the kitchen. The vision of a young woman around my age caught me off guard, and I fell forward, jostling my broken leg.

I let out a grunt of pain and tried to push myself back onto the narrow mattress. I didn't know if I should be alarmed or not. Jehan never mentioned anything about another person living here. Panic crept in around the edges of my heart because there was no way I could escape if this were an enemy.

"Sit still." The woman ran up to me. "Did you hurt yourself?" Her English was better than Jehan's but still heavily accented French. Aside from the fact that it sounded much more alluring coming from her mouth than Jehan's.

The woman looked me over with assessing eyes, then made matters a little more uncomfortable by running soft fingers over my limbs. Thanks to the war, I was almost twenty-one years old and had not been with a woman before. That didn't mean my body wouldn't react to her touch, and it did. Not enough that she would notice, but I realized it and flushed hotly.

"It's okay. Jehan is my father. I'm Coralie. You are Drexel, yes?" Coralie quickly tried to reassure me. "I'm a nurse. He told me he could use my assistance and had an accident while working. It's our secret code; if intercepted, it won't raise suspicion."

My panic receded, though my racing heart didn't but that was for other reasons. I took the moment that getting moved back onto the mattress offered me to study the woman. She didn't look like Jehan, and I could only guess that she favored her mother's appearance. Fair skin, thin lips, an upturned nose, and strawberry blonde hair that was straight, tied back away with a few loose tendrils that floated about her face. She was beautiful.

"Are you escaping the Nazi's capture?" Coralie asked gently.

"I am one," I bluntly stated after clearing my throat.

Coralie paused and sat back on her heels, her face a careful mask of indifference as she processed the information. I could see it all play across her delicate features as she wondered if she were now in trouble for the things she'd revealed to me.

"He's more than that," Jehan's gruff voice came

from behind me. "You've nothing to fear from him, Coralie."

No, she certainly had nothing to fear, considering I was at their mercy. However, it felt like a vindication to have someone else feel caught off guard other than me. I wisely kept my mouth shut after Jehan's revelation and watched the small smile that teased the corner of Coralie's lips.

"Ah, a defector," Coralie surmised.

"Not that either, yet," Jehan chuckled. "Are you hungry, Drexel?"

"I am, yes." I nodded at Jehan as he walked into sight. "The smell of food woke me. I haven't smelled anything that wonderful in quite some time."

"Well," Coralie said as she rose to stand. "Let's get you to the table so you can fill your belly."

Jehan and Coralie took place on either side of me and put their heads under my arms. They lifted me effortlessly and carried me to the table, setting me gently on one of the hardwood chairs. Pain rolled through me like a tsunami wiping out everything in its path.

"I brought some medication to help you with the pain," Coralie told me with a kind voice.

"Put your head down until it passes," Jehan ordered.

I hung my head and closed my eyes. I could hear them moving about the kitchen, murmuring in French. I heard plates and cutlery getting jostled, water running, and cupboards opening and closing. I missed the sounds of ordinary life. I missed my family.

I opened my eyes when a glass clinked on the table before me and saw water and a couple of pills. I didn't question what they were. I silently took them, swallowed them down with a gulp of water, and voiced my thanks.

A large platter of scrambled eggs was plopped down on the table, along with smaller plates of bacon, sausage, and toast. Then came the mouth-watering aroma of freshly brewed coffee. The supply of decent coffee had dwindled since the rationing began the previous year.

Coralie let out a delighted peal of laughter when she spied the expression on my face. I flushed bright red and reminded myself to count my blessings. I could be dead, imprisoned, or back on the battlefield.

"Would you like a cup, Drexel?" Coralie offered with a smile.

"Yes." I nodded gratefully. "Very much so."

Coralie placed a steaming cup in front of me, and it was all I could do not to cry. I inhaled the rich aroma, savoring the smell as much as I anticipated the bitter brew on my tongue. I sipped slowly, not wanting the cup to end too quickly.

Jehan and Coralie made plates of food—hard to come by food at that—and ate their meal with quiet contemplation. Before too long, Coralie got impatient with the fact that I wasn't eating yet; I was still sipping the coffee. Rather than wait for me to do it myself, she made me a plate heaped with more food than I could possibly eat and shoved it across the table at me.

"Eat. You need to regain strength. It is not every day we have food like this. We are more fortunate than most; however, you still need the nourishment." The stern look I received from the young woman had me picking up my fork.

"After, it is time you talked while awake," Jehan

reminded me. "War is a never-ending cycle of history repeating itself. Whether human or animal, one race is always working on making another extinct for some perceived slight," Jehan muttered the words low in his throat so quietly I almost could not hear him.

"My father fought in the first war," Coralie frowned at her father. "Thankfully, they deemed him too old and broken to serve their purposes this time on the front line. Now, they make him build things for them until his fingers bleed."

I dropped my eyes to Jehan's hands and saw the truth of his daughter's statement. How I didn't notice it before now, I didn't know. I also took in the calluses and dirt under the nails that would never come out.

After that, we all fell into silence and ate our meals, ensuring that we consumed every last bit to hide the evidence of the bounty we'd shared. Coralie and Jehan washed the dishes in practiced moves and had the chore done in no time flat.

They came back to the table with the last coffee and split it between us before taking the kettle back to the sink and washing it out. All traces of the coffee disappeared except for what was in our cups.

Jehan waited until Coralie sat down and then looked at me expectantly. I nodded in response to let him know that I understood what he wanted, and I tried to gather my thoughts into a semblance of something recognizable to myself. My life was something never shared with anyone other than my parents; not even my siblings knew my truth.

"Please understand this is not easy for me to speak about," I began, my tone more defensive than necessary given the circumstances.

"We, too, have secrets that we shouldn't explore. We understand," Coralie replied sympathetically. She reached her hand out and placed it on top of mine.

I had figured as much. "I am twenty-one, as of later this year. My father was in the first war and wound up on the wrong side of some political types. I heard he had strong opinions that weren't popular. After the war ended, he met my mother, and things progressed to the creation of myself."

"Drexel," Coralie interrupted. "You don't need to tell us everything about yourself."

"I wouldn't tell you if it weren't relevant," I promised.

"Let him continue," Jehan stopped Coralie from arguing.

"We need to listen for the warning," Coralie reminded her father.

"I'm always listening, daughter." Jehan smiled softly at Coralie before nodding at me to continue.

"Okay, yes," I said and paused. I needed to get past my fear of speaking truths about my parentage. "My father was born in Germany; my mother moved to Germany from Poland."

I let the statement hang in the air for a moment, and I am sure that Jehan was not surprised by the revelation. On the other hand, Coralie didn't appear as if she'd expected that news.

"After my parents were married and I was growing in my mother's belly, my father ran afoul of the law." I paused again and gnawed on my lips. "My father was imprisoned, and my mother had nowhere to turn other than a childhood friend of my father. Their political views were similar, and his wife was also pregnant. Since the police were looking to blame her for aiding my father, she hid out with these friends."

"You speak as though you don't know them, your parents," Coralie commented. She'd sat back in the kitchen chair and crossed her arms over her chest. I didn't know if that was a casual posture for her or if she were cold.

"Let him continue," Jehan told Coralie gently.

"I was born in that house under the careful eye of a trusted and loyal midwife. Three days later, another boy was born to the woman of the house. The midwife reported and recorded that the woman had fraternal twins. I only knew my mother for the first three months of my life. I don't remember anything about her or even her name. I was one of the twins that the other woman bore as far as Germany knew."

"Wait. Your family in Germany isn't your family?" Coralie sat forward and stared at me, aghast.

"They are my family. They raised me, cared for me, loved me, and never treated me differently. They sat me down and told me the truth when I was thirteen, and they only told me. My brothers and sisters never learned these secrets. My father told me about my biological parents when he received news that they were both deceased." Scenes from that conversation played in my mind.

Coralie's eyes appeared to be watery, and her hand covered her mouth. She stared at me in horrified wonder, not speaking or moving. I didn't know how to interpret her behavior, and I shifted uncomfortably in the hard chair.

"There is more, yes?" Jehan looked at me expectantly, ignoring his daughter.

"Of course," I nodded in response. "By that time, I knew that being Jewish was something that could get me killed. Hitler's propaganda had begun, and my adoptive parents made me promise never to reveal what they'd told me. Yet, here I am doing just that." I shook myself and went on. "Being thirteen with a bit of a rebellious nature, I secretly studied Jewish traditions, faith, customs, and history to learn as much of it as possible to feel closer to my mother. I had to admit that something within that religion spoke to me."

"Because it's a part of who you are," Coralie whispered tearfully. "I couldn't imagine not knowing my father."

"But I did. The man who raised me is my father," I argued quietly. "I understand what you mean because there was a brief period where I had the same thoughts and then anger towards my biological father for leaving me. It took the war beginning for me to understand that it wasn't their wishes not to raise me; it was fear for my safety. I mourned their loss, and when my adoptive parents saw that, they incorporated stories of their childhoods with my biologic parents into our conversations. They showed pictures they had and brought them to life for me. I was their child as much as the children they'd created."

"A parent's love has nothing to do with the blood that created life in the child," Jehan commented. "Finish your story."

"My father is influential, and when they started conscripting men into the party, he pulled strings, and my brother and I began university instead of joining the party. They weren't taking students yet, not if they could prove that we were learning of the Nazi party and willing to take part once we completed. The recruiters were happy enough to leave us alone. That only lasted until the losses began to pile up. The party called my brother into service first." I remembered the day in perfect clarity.

"A man walked up to us in the library. Hans never noticed him at all, but I did. I watched as he went from person to person and handed them papers commanding them to report for service. There was a pattern to this; the man only went to the largest and most solidly built first... which Hans was. My heart began to pound, and I kicked at Hans under the table and tried to get him to pay attention to what was happening. For as smart as Hans was, he could be oblivious at times, and this was one of them. He didn't look up from his book until the papers were slapped down in front of him."

"What did he do? Was he for or against the war?" Coralie wondered.

"Our parents raised us to accept all people, and no one in my family supported the war. We did what was expected of us to keep under the radar, but there was no overt excitement to join the efforts. My father claimed to others that we were getting an education to join the party and be of use in the efforts behind the fighting. It worked for me but only until the Poland invasion began," I told them.

I fell silent for a few minutes, remembering that the letters from Hans had grown fewer and fewer at that point, even though he'd only been enlisted for about six months. Hans hadn't made it secret that he despised the killing. He was on the front lines in Poland, and our father feared that his letters weren't making it through due to the content.

"When I received my conscription, I was drafted into the Air Force. They lacked pilots, and since I had an education, they put me in the pilot program and rushed us through training. Way too quickly, in my opinion, but what I thought didn't matter. Before being conscripted, a pilot was my choice, so there were no arguments. The philosophy the men training us used was to 'Learn to fly, or crash and die,'" I recited the words I'd heard too many times. "I spent hours at night memorizing the books, the instrument panels, and the lessons of flight so that when they put us in the planes, it became a simple recall situation or putting words and pictures into action. Not to say that it wasn't scary because there were moments that I was sure I would die, but I took to the plane quickly."

"Were you part of the recon units?" Jehan paused me to ask.

"I was. We still had to fight our way out more than once, and it caused such moral dilemmas in me that I got sick. None of the commandment cared and they sent me out anyway; that was my first crash. We'd landed in enemy territory in Poland. Uninjured, thankfully, but we had to fight our way through troops that wanted nothing other than to kill us to try to make it back to German ground troops. I had to stare down the barrel of my gun and pull the trigger on a Polish man because Hitler believed they weren't good enough to live." My voice trembled.

"It was easier to be above the fighting than a part of it," Jehan guessed correctly. It was the entire reason that I wanted to be a pilot if I had to join the war.

"I couldn't reconcile killing people I rightfully belonged to; I was killing people who could have been my biological family. Yet, I could say nothing, or they would have killed me and called me a traitor to my kind and a stain on the party. I wanted to die. I wanted to help the Jews. I wanted to be captured and spill my secrets to someone so they knew I wasn't an enemy. I was an unwilling participant. If I told, then I would put my family at risk. We've all seen what happens to sympathizing Germans. I didn't feel human, yet I was a part of this war machine, and it clawed at the inside of me." I hung my head in shame and cried.

"Drexel, you are not what the party is trying to make you," Jehan declared. "In war, everything you are doing is something someone told you to do. You are carrying out orders, which soldiers are trained to do. You questioned them, maybe not verbally, but you aren't like the ones out there killing innocents for sport."

I shuddered. I was not one of those, though I had met the type. I had seen the monsters in action. Jehan's statement was true, but it did not excuse me for killing when I didn't want to. That mark on my soul was all mine.

"Do you want to fight on the side of the Allies?" Coralie finally found her voice and asked me.

"I don't want to fight at all," I responded immediately with a thickened voice. "It's senseless."

"That it is," Jehan agreed. "No matter how you look at it, that body is someone's child, regardless of race or religion."

I numbly nodded. I'd thought the very same thing each time I pulled a trigger. I'd wondered if a sister was waiting for a letter from her brother, a mother who had sleepless nights of worry over her child, a father that was proud of his son but only wanted him to come home. I squeezed the trigger so my family wouldn't have the same fears.

"There are so many more like me in the ranks," I whispered. "If I had to fight, I would fight with the Allies, but killing people that feel the same way I do doesn't make it any better or easier to cope."

"More Jewish soldiers are fighting for Germany?" Coralie asked, stunned. She'd taken my statement too literal.

"I meant that there are more soldiers that don't want to kill innocent people because one man feels they are dirty or subhuman or whatever adjective he uses to describe people not Aryan. Soldiers that think the way I do; I didn't necessarily mean Jewish soldiers," I corrected.

The sound of a bird of prey screech filled the air, and Jehan and Coralie jumped to their feet. The two of them had me under the armpits and out the front door before I could understand what was happening. Instincts had me keeping my mouth shut and not questioning them.

We were back in the garden, Coralie supported my weight while Jehan lifted the trap door then he helped Coralie get me back inside. I understood that I needed to remain silent, and I locked my jaw shut and did my best not to panic as the door closed on top of me. Buried alive again.

Sitting there in the dark while I listened to Coralie and Jehan chatter naturally in French with each other pretending to garden, I imagined. It took me a few minutes to understand that the bird's call was the warning they'd listened for when we talked.

It didn't escape my notice that these two angels of mercy most likely worked for the resistance. They were one of the pockets of French people who didn't want their country under Nazi rule or taken over by the Allies either, though I understood that they often aided and helped the Allies.

I figured I presented a conundrum for Jehan and Coralie. I didn't know much about the resistance efforts other than the party hated them because they were fighting on two fronts, and it was much harder to smoke out the resistance fighters. I had no intentions of making things harder for them and would cooperate with whatever they thought best. Needless to say, their secret was safe.

I lay there a few more minutes until I heard halting French with a German accent. No doubt the party was looking for me. I'd heard my name spoken several times and a physical description. I couldn't understand what Coralie and Jehan responded with, though their tones were sounds of denial. I felt reasonably confident they wouldn't give me up to the Germans.

I wasn't even sure why I was worried about it. The party didn't know my back story; they didn't know I was Jewish or Polish. My paperwork was solid. My parents made sure of that. Everything about my birth got filed and recorded correctly, and coincidentally, I looked enough like my mother that there was no questioning.

Drexel Wagner was the property of the Nazi party and Luftwaffe. They might question what happened and pick apart my story, though I don't think they would harm me. My belief was they just wanted their pilot back because they needed me. I could be wrong; one never knew with the Nazis.

Indignation boiled up inside me, and I struggled with containing it so that I didn't get Jehan and Coralie into trouble with the soldiers. My need to get away from the party intensified and helped me solidify my decision to abandon my duties and defect, despite being considered a war crime.

It was something my father had drilled into me time and time again when we talked about my conscription which he knew would come. My dad told me he would rather live his life knowing his son was a traitor to an awful party and alive somewhere than brainwashed and turned into something he knew I was not.

I felt a nervous flutter in my stomach when I thought about America. Would I be allowed to learn more about my heritage there? Could I go to school or find work? Would the American people accept me? I had too many questions and not enough answers.

I knew that anywhere in Europe would remain unsafe for me. I could try my hand at Africa, though I knew there was unrest there. Australia, perhaps?

A few hours alone in the dark hole and too much time to think left me jittery and anxious. When the lid opened, I tried to lift myself out and became dismayed when I couldn't. I needed to move from here so that Jehan could get on with his life.

"Allow us to help you," Jehan growled. "Injuries like these take time to heal."

"Time you don't have," I answered but stopped struggling. "I'm putting you in danger."

"Nonsense," Coralie argued. "Once you can move freely on your own, we will get you out of here."

Stunned, I stared at the beautiful woman. I swiveled my head to look at Jehan for clarification, but he only nodded and smiled cryptically. Could it be that simple? I had my doubts. Once back inside Jehan's home, I dared to ask.

"You will get me out to where?" I glanced at Coralie for an answer.

"America, if you agree. That would be the safest choice." Coralie moved toward me and checked the wound on my head, which I had yet to see. Then she moved to the rest of the injuries. "I'll go home tonight and come back with more medication and supplies in a few days. I'm worried about an infection in your leg."

Coralie lifted my pant leg to examine the limb to prove her point. My flesh was an angry red and a swollen yellow around the opened skin. Farther back, the color changed to deep purples, blacks, and blues that you see in severe bruises.

I knew Coralie wasn't wrong, and I let her complete her examination, treat or redress the wounds she thought needed attention, and offered no argument. I was grateful for the attention and care and didn't feel worthy.

That was how the next three weeks played out. Every three or four days, Coralie would come to check on Jehan and me. When she was gone, I helped Jehan however I could and spent time in the hole when the warning calls came. Jehan and I would share meals, speak of our lives, and sit in comfortable silence more often.

When Coralie was present, she would ask me questions about my life and, in return, allowed me to ask about hers. I felt a growing attraction to her that I had no right to foster while people around us fought and died in an ugly war.

By the fourth week, I could get around on a pair

of makeshift crutches and would accompany Coralie on short walks about the little village. My hair had grown considerably, and I let my facial hair grow at Coralie's suggestion. She told me that it made me look less like I was when Jehan found me.

Jehan said they had given up looking for me and I was presumed dead. It broke my heart to think that my parents had received notification of my death, and I hoped that they didn't believe the news. At the six week mark, we had established the pattern of the German patrols and knew when they would arrive for their checks.

Once eight weeks arrived, I began to walk using the injured leg. Short distances only at first, and then I would accompany Jehan when he had work to complete. The drastic change in my appearance ensured that the soldiers didn't look twice in my direction. They assumed I was an apprentice of Jehan and followed his orders.

War raged on around us, and bombers flew overhead daily. Germans and Allies alike dropped their bombs on innocent French cities in the name of Adolf Hitler or in the name of stopping him. Those that believed in his mission and those that wanted him dead. Places like France were casualties of war, a calculated loss that I knew the German forces didn't care about.

Twelve weeks into my recovery, Coralie and Jehan began their work of extricating me. The father/daughter duo worked in tandem with their resistance contacts to get me new papers. Coralie passed messages along the route that I would be coming through, and our goal was never to travel through a checkpoint. The papers were merely insurance while in France.

Switzerland was our target, and my traveling

wouldn't be solitary. Some Jewish refugees would join me in hopes of avoiding the Nazi war machine. Our route would mainly stick to forests, mountains, and villages not on maps and depend on the kindness of strangers in this network of resistance fighters.

As the departure approached, my attraction to Coralie grew. It wasn't arrogance that had me believing she felt the same; it was the expressions on her face when she thought I didn't see her looking at me. We left the truth of our feelings buried with the secrets we harbored.

"Drexel!" Coralie's excited voice floated on the air currents to me. "I did it. I got a message to your parents. They know you are alive!"

Love and fear crowded my heart, overwhelming me to the point of my knees buckling. The motion of me dropping garnered Jehan's attention and he made swift movements to assure himself something hadn't gone wrong.

"Remember his new name, Daughter," Jehan warned Coralie once she reached us. "Drexel has passed from this life."

"*Conrad*, sorry," Coralie flushed from her blunder. "I sent a message to them that said nothing more than 'May we meet in the land of opportunities.' Don't you think they will understand what that means without giving away anything?"

I considered her words, fear still battling for control in my heart. It might arouse suspicion, but nothing to tie to my existence, especially if she sent it from where she worked. My plane had gone down north of Aisne, and she worked east of Saint-Nazaire. I supposed that if someone were to look closely, they could draw a correlation, though I was positive that Coralie used a secret radio location to transmit the message.

"Thank you, Coralie. I can't express how much that means to me," I responded before her face could fall. "I will miss you and our talks."

Jehan cleared his throat. "Perhaps she could visit you once you settle."

Jehan had talked with me about this and his concern about getting discovered. He wanted Coralie to have a future, and he'd planted the seed in my mind that he could very well send her in my direction if things got worse.

"Nothing would please me more than to have you both as guests," I responded. I wanted to remind Jehan that there would always be a place for him wherever I landed. We knew firsthand how brutal and unforgiving war was, and I would be dead if he had not intervened. The debt I owed Jehan was more significant than he would ever admit.

"Get ready. We leave after dark." But Jehan gave me a curt nod to show he understood my message.

I bade my hole in the garden a fond farewell before I met my three traveling companions. I would never forget the sensations of being buried alive, nor how grateful I was that I was allowed to experience it.

Four Months Later

After a physically grueling journey filled with sleepless nights, terrifying encounters, and countless faces of the resistance movement in France, I stepped onto the boat that would carry me across the expanse of ocean to America. We'd traveled through underground tunnels, over mountain passes, hid in caves with barely enough to keep us alive, but we'd made it this far.

Sure, there was a chance I could still get captured, but I didn't believe it would happen in my heart. I felt as though God wanted me to survive this. Something better waited for me across that water, and if it meant I slept in an engine room hiding from patrols, I would gladly do it.

I would honor the sacrifices of all the people who had helped me stay alive. I would arrive at a place where I didn't need to hide who I was from anyone. I was a boy of twenty-one years old and had already lived a lifetime of horror... which was nothing compared to those captured for being Jewish.

My adventure began now, and I was ready.

Realizing the Lines

There was no recollection of how she arrived here, though it was a road she was overly familiar with due to years of driving its length. It began in nowhere and ended nowhere. She stood in the middle of the street wearing a befuddled expression, a pair of old jeans she'd turned into shorts, an aged Nirvana t-shirt, and her worn-out red Chuck's.

"Okay, Prudence, how did you manage this one?" she asked herself as she scratched her head. No one answered, of course, because no one in their right mind would be out in the middle of the desert during high summer in the heat of the day.

The sun's rays baked the pavement under the thin soles of her shoes. Shimmering waves of evaporating souls danced upwards, undulating as they disappeared into the heated air. Iridescent, wispy strands of silver that shouldn't exist as condensation on the once heavily traveled road.

"But it's a dry heat," Prudence said to the signpost. It wasn't a consolation to the handmade directional signs or her rapidly increasing body temperature.

Prudence stared at the signs that pointed in each cardinal direction. Since someone built the road around the signpost, it must have held significance to someone. Carved by hand many years before her grandparents were born, someone had a twisted sense of humor. Perhaps that is why they still existed here in no man's land.

"'North but not to Heaven 14.6,'" Prudence read aloud. "'South of Hell 7.34.' 'East to West 21.7.' 'West to Sunrise 2.81.'"

Many travelers theorized the meaning of the signs, though no one knew who made them or why they became labeled as they were. What made it even more puzzling was the road only traveled east to west. The northern and southern sides of the road were nothing more than the high desert ground. No indication whatsoever that a road ever existed that crossed this one.

To muddle it further, carved on the post was 18.5=1. Prudence wasn't great at math, but in what world did eighteen and a half equal one? She knew it must have referenced something but she hadn't been able to figure it out—not that she put a ton of thought into it. It was fun to pretend she knew what it meant and that the meaning was magical.

Prudence ran her fingers through her stringy, neon green hair and pondered her situation. People had accused her of being crazy before, and maybe it had finally happened. There was no sign of her car anywhere, yet here she stood, sweating the moisture out of her body.

"Well, this is one hell of a way to dry out," she snarked to the empty road. She didn't expect any response, though it would have been nice to hear a voice.

Prudence turned around in a circle looking for anything. Nothing stood out—no shrubs or greenery in sight. It was the same dry, brown, and red desolate landscape that it always was. However, Prudence knew that if she walked a mile to the south, there were a few cacti on the other side of the slope.

Come to think of it, the general landscape of the signpost area was strange. The road was generally flat from start to finish, but it sloped down in the area around the post—almost a bowl shape. The road on either side of the signs dipped down. Once you headed away from the oddity, you were climbing a slight hill in either direction.

Prudence had noticed it the first time she accidentally came to this place. She stood in the middle of the road and faced east; it appeared that the world ended due to the hill. Almost as if, if she walked up that hill, she would fall off like the flat-earthers believed would happen. When she turned west, it was the same.

One of Prudence's theories was once you died, this is where you ended up, and the signs were directions for something only a spirit would know. Having traveled this road many times, Prudence knew that wasn't the case, but the illusion remained. The shimmering air added to the ethereal appearance.

Prudence had imagined some wild scenarios happening each time she stood here. She even tried walking the numbers on the signs, using their values as feet or steps but nothing happened. It gave her endless thrills and she always stood for far longer than she intended.

"Pru, Pru, Pru," she mumbled. "Did you drink enough to get alcohol poisoning? Even if you did, it doesn't explain how you ended up here. Think."

Prudence sniffed and realized she smelled sour. How long had she been here, and when was the last time she showered? "Gross. You reek like you've been on a week-long bender."

Shrugging her shoulders, Prudence turned from the enigmatic post of signs and faced south. "South of Hell. Is this Hell? It feels like it, and here I am, having a full-blown conversation with myself while stranded in the desert. Seven point three four. What does that even mean?" Prudence grumbled.

She walked a few feet, looked back at the post, and then faced south again. She would eventually reach home if she traveled due south for forty-five miles. She shuffled south again, then a few more feet. As Prudence turned back to face the sign, she took a small step backward and tripped.

Her butt hit the ground somewhere else. As in, Prudence landed on grass. But where? There was no rich, green, velvety grass in that desert, and she knew there was no oasis around that signpost.

"What is south of Hell?" Prudence wondered aloud as she took in the almost jungle-like place. "And how did I manage to trip over it? Why do I feel like Alice made her rabbit hole into a tunnel, and I boarded the bus to crazy town and exited in the middle of that tunnel?"

Prudence stood up and tried to wipe the dusty desert dirt off her shorts that had none. She took a few cautious steps and heard the sound of running water. Common sense told Prudence that she was dehydrated. She'd been drinking; she smelled like an old whiskey barrel on which someone rubbed rotten onions. Plus, it was blazing hot, and a dip in water would feel wonderful.

She kept walking in a straight line, trampling the grass that looked like it belonged on a world-famous golf course. She did it on purpose, so she had a way back to where she landed.

"If I'm in an alien world, I don't want to get lost here," she told the jungle. "I'll need to go home because I have a job. Not a good one, but it gives me enough to pretend that I'm making ends meet; the utility company doesn't believe the lie."

Prudence followed the sound of running water until she came to a small creek after five minutes of walking. It wasn't deep enough for her to stand in, but she could strip and lay in the water to try to wash the stink off her body.

This place wasn't barren like the desert. It was the opposite. Life thrived here... though she hadn't seen any other than plant life—more accurately: Grass life. That emboldened Prudence to continue with her plan to clean herself, and she began to strip off clothes, starting with her shoes.

"So south of Hell is this paradise?" Prudence asked the babbling creek as the rest of her clothes landed in a pile. "I would have pictured somewhere that looked like where I came from, not this fertile land."

She wandered to the bank and dipped her toes in, expecting the water to be frigid. Instead, it was surprisingly mild and pleasant. Prudence released a peal of delighted laughter and stepped fully into the creek.

"Do you take everything so literally?" a monotonic voice reverberated through the air.

Prudence started, slipped on a rock, and fell into the water. The landing wasn't as soft as she had hoped, and she did her best to keep her nakedness under the water.

"Where are you?" Prudence squeaked out. One arm snaked across her chest, and the other went down to hide her crotch. "It's rude to sneak up on a naked bathing woman," she chastised the unseen speaker.

"Your moss looks unhealthy," the voice spoke.

"My moss?" Prudence was confused. An uncouth man could have been talking about her unmanicured lady parts.

"The green is the wrong color."

"I call that my hair." Prudence almost snorted creek water through her nose.

"Oh. A human." This time the voice sounded affronted.

Prudence felt along the bottom of the creek with one of her feet. She found a deeper spot and moved toward that. She didn't know how to respond to the 'human' comment and saw no sign of any other entity.

Prudence painfully knew that being underwater didn't hide her nakedness from anyone. While she didn't live up to her name, she wasn't an exhibitionist. She began to rub her skin vigorously, trying to freshen up as best as she could without soap.

Wait. Didn't she have sex last night? Vague images of moans and sweaty bodies flittered through her mind. With no thought of eyes watching her, Prudence squatted in the water, spreading her legs wide, and touched herself. Yes, there was a tenderness to her flesh, so she'd had sex recently. Though that still didn't explain how she ended up at the signpost. Or here.

Prudence quickly dunked her head under the water's surface and scrubbed at her hair, hoping some of the oiliness would wash out. Once finished, she gingerly made her way to the bank while keeping the front of her submerged under the water.

"Close your eyes," Prudence called out. "I need to get out of the water and get dressed. I don't remember getting paid for a peep show."

"I have no eyes. I have no money."

"Yeah, okay," Prudence rolled her eyes. "Yet somehow, you knew my hair was green."

There was no response and Prudence was tired of crouching like some small, scared animal hiding from prey. She was no victim, so why did she act this way? She boldly stood and marched over to her pile of clothes.

Prudence wrinkled her nose in disgust. She should really rinse the clothes too. The air was warm enough that she should dry out quickly. With a shrug of her shoulders, she gathered up the odorous clothing and returned to the creek.

Feeling like one of those old-time prairie women, she submerged her clothes, rubbed them over the rocks, beat them a little, and then un-balled them and let the refreshing water run through them before putting them back on soaking wet. It might only be psychological but she felt better.

Prudence returned to the creek and gazed over the crystal-clear waters with the brightly colored rocks that lined the bed. She imagined this is what an unspoiled rainforest would look like if such a thing existed. This land wouldn't be an awful place to live if she never found her way out.

Prudence took a few steps upstream and found a place she could drink from without falling over. Bending, she scooped water into her cupped hands and sipped it.

She drank her fill, grabbed a large handful of the colored stones, and then sat back on a large rock, letting the heat warm her and dry her clothes.

"Are you done?" The voice was back and using clipped tones.

"Maybe. Why do you care?" Prudence lay back and covered her eyes with her arms. "I'm not hurting anything."

"That is your perception. Your human mind is limited. Selfish."

Prudence laughed. She knew she wasn't overly intelligent. She'd heard it enough throughout her school life. 'Imaginative' was the most common phrase used. Her grades were mediocre despite putting all her efforts into learning. This voice calling her limited didn't offend her in the slightest. Selfish, however, piqued her temper.

Prudence shifted and lay on her stomach, burying her face in her arms. Her hair wasn't thick and dried quickly in the warm breeze, though she supposed it probably did appear to be sickly moss. Finger brushing wouldn't help the situation.

"Why are you harassing me?" Prudence asked in a muffled voice.

"I'm observing an intruder. You came here uninvited, trampled all over, soiled the water, stole from me, and seem unaware that you are the harasser."

Prudence slowed her breathing and pondered the words. Her actions weren't meant to cause harm and seemed innocent enough. With the words spoken, though, she could see how someone could take her arrival and subsequent action in that way.

"You're the land? Give me a sign that I'm not crazy," Prudence finally asked in a skeptical tone. Maybe she was high, thinking that the land spoke to her. Was she that desperate for interaction in such a lonely place as the signpost that she talked to the land and felt that it responded?

Prudence pushed herself up and looked around. Nothing happened and the voice didn't speak. "Figures. I've lost my mind. I'm proving people right."

She slid off the rock and looked for the trampled grass to lead her back the way she came. She wandered for more than five minutes and saw nothing to show her how to get to the signpost. There was no trampled grass to lead Greenielocks to the Yellow Brick Road home and clicking the heels of her red Chuck's three times didn't work. Plus, she was mixing her literary illusions.

"Now what?" Prudence asked rhetorically. "I'm not a survivalist. I'll die out here as much as I would in the desert."

"Help me and I will help you."

"How?" Prudence cocked an eyebrow up.

"I'm dying. I need life to live."

"Don't mock me. I know I'm not the smartest but come one! If you have no life, you're already dead." Prudence crossed her arms under her chest and pursed her lips. "From what I can see, water exists. I used it. The grass is green. That's a living thing."

"Humans and their limited minds."

Prudence threw her hands in the air and turned full circle. "I'm waiting."

"Did you fail to notice there are no animals, no insects, no flowers? The waters hold no fish. The selfish humans that have landed here have bled me dry. You asked what is south of Hell? An area devoid of life. I cannot grow."

Well, Prudence hadn't noticed those things. She stood in a grass desert with a creek and pretty rocks. She took it in now and didn't even see any trees. How was she supposed to change that trapped here and having no idea how to return even if she did find her way out?

"This is your quest. You must find the answers and promise to help." The voice answered her thoughts with an exasperated tone.

"That's it. I'm still drunk. Fine. I promise to help you have life," Prudence called out.

A bright light made her blink her eyes rapidly and Prudence faced the signpost again. Baffled, she looked at the signs and saw she stood under the sign that pointed north. Was that a literal sign that she should head in that direction next? She had asked for a sign that she wasn't crazy. In hindsight, if this was the answer to that, it probably wasn't declaring her sane.

Prudence pivoted in place and faced the direction the sign pointed. "Fourteen point six. Clear as a mud puddle in a pig pit. Am I truly going to find life to bring to that place?"

A hot, dusty breeze blew in response to her question, and something inside her trembled. She guessed that was her answer. Indeed, she was going to seek out life to bring to the green paradise south of Hell.

"Looks like I'm going north but not to Heaven," Prudence mumbled. "Why not? There isn't much hope of anyone driving by and rescuing me from here."

She twisted her body to look south, trying to find how she ended up in that other place. All she saw was a rock, probably the one she'd tripped on. That wasn't much help. She saw nothing that indicated a portal or doorway existed in that direction, but she didn't know what that would look like either.

Prudence had never given a lot of thought about magic or other worlds. At least not in the context of it being something real, more along the lines of wishing for magical powers like the people in superhero movies. Everyone did that, though, right?

Prudence faced north again. She backed up until her back touched the post, started again, and walked perfectly straight. She began to walk what she thought fourteen feet might measure, and nothing happened.

"What's the trick?" Prudence asked aloud, the relentless heat making her irritable. At least her clothes were dry.

The sky appeared white with the sun so bright and hot. Prudence stood still in the same place and tried to puzzle it out with the heat practically melting the soles of her Chuck's to the ground. She needed to move so she didn't stick to the pavement.

Prudence backed up to the pole, stuck one foot in front of the other, and cart-wheeled. Too late, Prudence realized that her arms were not strong enough to support her in that endeavor and she cracked her head on the ground when her elbows gave out. Prudence rubbed the top of her head with a grimace. "So long, youth."

She pushed back to her feet and went back to the signpost. "When in doubt, dance." With that, she began dancing the only dance she could perform: The Macarena. Prudence hummed the tune as she moved away from the pole because she didn't know the words.

When she spun around, she found herself in a similar yet foreign landscape. Red sand surrounded her: Giant dunes, some rippled from the wind; intense heat beneath a sky that wasn't blue but rather an odd purplish color.

"Am I on Mars?" Prudence asked the desolate landscape, expecting an answer this time.

There was no response and she began to climb one of the dunes in front of her. Another thought of the flat earthers crossed her mind because this dune could very well end with a drop. It was a sobering thought and she slowed her steps and burned off any traces of alcohol that might remain in her system.

"Why is the sky purple?" Prudence looked up to distract herself.

She looked behind, seeing the falling sand from her climbing the dune filling in the traces of her footprints. All the hills looked the same, only varying heights. *It would be easy to get lost here,* she thought.

At the top, Prudence looked around and saw nothing other than a sea of red. At least in her desert, there were some green things and tumbleweed. If anywhere needed life, it was this place. She didn't think even camels could survive here.

She slowly turned her body and let out an ear-piercing shriek as she saw an entire dune move and the most enormous head she'd ever seen raise from the sands. Prudence jolted backward, slipped, and somersaulted heels over head down the dune.

The hot, red sand was in every crevice and coated her skin. Prudence flopped to her back and stared at the purple sky, trying to make sense of what she'd witnessed. Dragons were real. Violet skies were a thing. A dragon had been sleeping under the sand dune until she'd woken it up.

Is it hungry? Prudence wondered to herself. *Am I*

about to be a dragon's lunch? Should I try and talk to it? How do I know if it's a male or female? Are they friendly creatures? What will it do if I offend it? Will I get roasted by dragon's fire? Do they even talk? Am I on Earth still? Am I drunk? Does this mean magic is real?

Hundreds of questions flew through Prudence's mind and none had any accompanying answers. If this situation were anything like the last place, she would most likely have to interact with the dragon in some capacity because the sand dunes weren't talking.

Pointed ears rose above the dune that Prudence fell down and then the head appeared, followed by slit-pupil eyes looking right at her. Her veins vibrated with fear, and her knees knocked hard enough to leave bruises.

"I wouldn't make a good lunch for you," Prudence stated with a warbly voice. "Do you know how to dance the Macarena?"

"What?" The dragon's eyes blinked. "You are correct about lunch. Your bones would get stuck in my teeth and I'd be picking them out for hours. How did you get here and why?"

"I was hoping you'd be able to answer that. I woke up standing in front of a signpost, fell into another place where green grass was everywhere, then landed back at the post and danced my way into wherever this is. Are we on Mars?" Prudence babbled.

"What is the Macarena?" the dragon asked curiously.

Prudence couldn't believe she'd asked the dragon if it could dance. Now she had to explain the dance and its relevance somehow, not that it was relevant. It was just the only dance she was able to dance accurately.

Instead of answering, Prudence began to hum the tune and performed the Macarena for the dragon. She was positive that she looked like an idiot. However, in her defense, how many people could say they'd danced the Macarena with a dragon?

Deep laughter filled the air and Prudence slowed down, dropped her arms to her sides and stared at the magical beast. She didn't feel embarrassed, only unsure of how to proceed.

"Can you fly?" Prudence wondered.

"Can you?" the dragon quipped back.

"Do you see wings?" Prudence shot back. "You *are* a dragon, aren't you? Admittedly, my knowledge of such creatures is limited as adults taught children dragons don't exist. So if my question offends you, I apologize."

"Ah, a human," the dragon huffed out a puff of steam, still not showing much else than a portion of its head. "Why is the top of you green?"

"I'm an artist," Prudence propped her hands on her hips. "It's a form of self-expression and green is my favorite color."

"Does it taste different than brown?" the dragon asked.

Prudence wasn't sure what to say in answer. "It's totally gross," she settled on a response after a pregnant pause. "Green tastes rotten."

"You could say that of all humans." The dragon let out another huff, followed by a long groan that made Prudence tremble. "Now tell me: What does an artist do?"

"We do all sorts of things. Some people draw or sing. There are others called actors. I'm different than those. I do something called tattoos. I use a sharp-pointed instrument that draws ink into it and inserts it underneath the skin, creating art."

"Does this art hold a purpose?" the dragon wondered. "Here, when I see designs on skin, it usually means that person has magic."

"Magic," Prudence breathed out in awe. "What does it do?"

"Whatever the user intends. What does your skin art do?"

"It looks pretty." Prudence cocked her eyebrow. "I'm very good at it."

"Enough about that. Teach me about dance." The dragon was demanding and semi-rude.

"That's art too. I'm not very good at it. The only dance I can successfully do is the Macarena, and it's old and out of style," Prudence admitted. "You move your body to music however you feel compelled."

"Did you bring music with you?"

Prudence patted her pockets, having forgotten that she had a phone. The battery was probably dead or close to it. She pulled it out of her front pocket and saw about ten percent of life left. She brought up some downloaded music and hit play.

"Here you go," Prudence said and turned the volume up as loud as she could.

She swayed her body to the song's beat and gestured for the dragon to do the same. Prudence kept dancing, swallowing a scream as a massive body rose from behind the dune. She gyrated her hips, shimmied, spun around, and did whatever moves she could think to do to keep from freaking out.

The dragon was the size of an airplane. It was

magnificent yet terrifying. Beautiful, enormous, and could be deadly. Prudence felt every inch of her mortality when her eyes landed on the beast. The closest thing she could compare it to was seeing the ocean for the first time.

She hadn't realized she'd stopped moving until the dragon also ceased movement and stared at her. The urge to retreat was strong. What was the etiquette one should follow in this situation?

"Are you able to send me back?" Prudence abruptly asked.

"Do you not like my company?" The dragon's tone had an edge that made goose bumps rise on her arms.

"Oh, I do! That wasn't what I meant. I only wondered how I get back since there's nothing here but sand."

"There is a city some distance away. I prefer quieter and a space I can comfortably fit inside, though I often get lonely. To answer your rude question, yes, I can send you back. I won't unless you promise me something. A favor if you will."

"And what would that favor be?" Prudence sighed. She still hadn't completed the first promise she'd agreed to fulfill.

"Bring me something so I'm not lonely. I miss conversation." The dragon lowered itself back behind the giant dune. "If you promise me that, I will send you back where you came from if that is your wish."

What the hell? Prudence thought to herself. *Am I in some twisted fairy tale?*

"Okay, I promise," Prudence agreed, wondering how she would accomplish that without sentencing someone to give up their life to live in a sea of red sand.

"Am I going to need to travel all the directions of the signpost?"

"I can't answer that. The magic will deposit you where you need to be," the dragon replied. "Perhaps it knew I needed entertainment and delivered you. Maybe I'm supposed to keep you."

"Why now?" Prudence snapped, lashing out. "Why does the universe wait until I'm almost forty years old to decide to show me that magic is real? There were times in my life that knowing magic existed would have helped me get through them. Even if I didn't possess it, that belief would have given me confidence that the world isn't as awful as it seems. And for sure you don't want to keep me. My entertainment factor is limited and my list of things to do is growing."

"Is this what an angry human looks like? Or is this some other emotion?" The dragon's tone had a note of humor under it.

Prudence wasn't sure herself. "Frustration, I think." Prudence thought about it more before continuing. "You speak, you are aware, so I assume you know what frustration is. I'm not quite angry but it's a small part. I'm confused and unsure what my next move should be."

"Well, you need to fulfill your promise." The dragon snorted with attitude. "I am not unintelligent. Just unaccustomed to humans."

"I will keep my promise. Can you send me back?" Prudence asked in a gentler tone.

"I shall. Remember that the magic will place you where you need to be. It is not my doing."

That was the last thing Prudence heard before she stood

under the sign that faced east… only she faced west. Her confusion mounted and her frustration grew.

"Clear as mud. Should I go east or west? Has time passed or is it still the same time I found myself standing here before I landed in the strange places? If I wanted to go home, would I even be able to leave, and how would I get there?"

Prudence wasn't about to ask for more signs. She'd had enough of the ones she was under already. If each direction asked for something for her to leave, that would be four promises and she would have to figure out how to make good on all of them.

She could bring seeds to plant things back to the first place, the southern lands. Maybe try to capture some insects. If she introduced that stage of life, it would draw others. That was her supposition, anyway.

The red sand land didn't offer any life for her to take and there was nothing in the first place that she could have brought to the dragon to ward off loneliness. The last two directions had to have the answers that the first two needed… which then would mean those first two had whatever the previous two would need. Right?

Prudence stuffed her hands in her pockets and paced. Her fingers played with the gem-colored rocks she'd plucked from the stream in the southern lands. She pulled them out and wondered how she'd lost two of them. She'd had five and now there were three. She slid them back into her pocket because wondering about those rocks wouldn't get her to where she needed to go next.

"Okay, twenty-one point seven. East has the biggest number, why is that? I hate math, Universe, you know that, right? Logically, I know that my falling or dancing isn't what got me to those places. I know I had to have stepped in a precise location, which triggered the entrance, portal, or wormhole. I don't know what to call it. I'm just standing out here in skin-melting heat talking to myself and a signpost after seeing a dragon."

There was always the chance that she was over-thinking and making it all far more complex than needed. On the flip side of that, she could be oversimplifying everything and totally off track from what the answers were.

"Okay. Let's assume twenty-one feet and to account for the point seven, it would almost be twenty-two. Now how would I measure that with something?"

She looked around the barren landscape with little hope of finding anything. With her shoulders slumped, she leaned against the post and heaved a heavy sigh. That's when it hit her. Prudence looked down at her feet, which were a size eight. She could measure feet with her feet. Two footsteps would equal a foot and a half.

There had to be a trick to this. Placing one foot directly in front of the other, she precisely counted twenty-one steps, then one extra that she would take an inch away from the end. Nothing happened so she went back to the post, lost in thought.

She looked up at the numbers engraved into the post. Maybe that first number equals the distance in one step. She'd tried that before but perhaps she'd used the wrong measurement? She'd never attempted feet before. Maybe it was eighteen feet that measured one unit. For all she knew, it could be centimeters.

Prudence set out again, using feet as a measurement as best as she could without a measuring tape. This method took her quite a distance from the post and she held a straight line as much as possible. She kept a close watch behind her and stopped when she thought she'd reached the correct distance.

Nothing felt different here. Maybe there was nothing to feel. Prudence figured the air density would be different if a portal existed, although that was only a guess. She walked a few more feet and found herself in a bustling city.

It appeared like any other city and yet like nothing she'd ever seen before. Hundreds of beings hustled down the streets, their heads down as if they were enraptured by their cell phones like people were back home. She didn't think phone were what they were looking at, though. But what made it even more strange was there was no conversation and they weren't human. No human she knew had two heads and antennae and looked like a Cyclops but yellow.

There were no cars, trucks or motorcycles, though some bicycles existed. Even the vehicles on the street made no noise and appeared to be something similar to electric Vespas. What astonished her the most was the colorful skin tones that belied belief. It was like Skittles come to life and an utter contrast to the bleak gray of the place.

The rainbow hues of the people walking around were the only color. There were no plants, fluffy white clouds, blue sky, or neon lights. She'd stepped into a black and white film and was in the gray area; even the scooters and everyone's clothes were a shade of gray, along with the sky itself.

It was very different from the first two locations

and the air was cooler here. Prudence took a couple of steps before wondering if she was in danger. She couldn't name one creature she saw walking around. She couldn't help but wonder if they were real and not robots; they were so quiet.

Doors to buildings opened and closed with quiet hisses and people walked in straight lines four deep as they rushed to where they were going. She stood out like the intruder she was. Yet no one looked at her standing on a concrete block that might have been a bench of sorts.

Prudence looked up and saw lines that led nowhere and just floated there in the sky. There was something eerily reminiscent about how the heat shimmered off the pavement by the signpost reflected in these lines; she couldn't take her eyes off them. They had to have a purpose. Some other lines near them could almost pass for steps—though where they led remained a question.

She hopped down from the block and stepped into the procession leading closer to the suspended lines in the air; they drew her like a moth to a flame. She figured that was where she was supposed to head if they called to her so strongly.

This place was the most unique city she'd ever had the privilege to visit. She expected a park of some sort to be where the lines were, only it was more concrete. A rather cold feeling emanated from this location—probably from the lack of color but she didn't stop or feel endangered.

She wondered what she would encounter here, what presence would ask her to make another promise? She dared to wander off the path and stood under the floating lines that now appeared like a narrow path. It was an optical illusion that delighted her senses. Each angle she viewed it from changed what it seemed to be.

Prudence hopped onto another block, stood on her toes and extended her arm as far as she could until her fingers brushed the suspended line. It felt like rock. Wavy rock that almost seemed alive. Could it be a trick of the eye?

She pulled her hand back and moved away from the edge she stood on. She dropped down and fell back on her butt. She flung her legs over the side of the block without even looking. When her feet smacked into something solid that wasn't the ground, she let out a small shriek of fear and her knees pistoned up under her chin.

Fear crept along her spine as she realized she was in another world, distracting her from the lines. She had no idea what her feet had touched. Not that she could explain anything she'd experienced since she'd found herself standing in front of the signpost!

She folded her legs down and leaned forward to look over the edge. She jerked back almost as quickly and swallowed a scream. Every terrifying movie about snakes she'd ever seen flew through her mind as her gaze landed on a snake bigger than she imagined an anaconda. The body coiled around the corner of the block out of sight.

Silvery and charcoal-colored scales (is that what you called snakeskin or was that just fish?) in a widening chevron pattern moved up along the body away from the tail. It was beautiful yet it also made her pucker up in parts of her body. Yet curiosity drove her to inch along the block to see where the head lay.

Prudence wasn't dumb but she also let curiosity rule where logic and common sense should take over—for example, looking for the head of a gigantic snake that could eat her whole. Life was supposed to be an adventure! However, she never regretted taking the chance to seek answers because that's how she learned.

She reached the end of the block opposite where she approached it the first time and cautiously peered over the side. Utterly unprepared to see a human upper half of a body, she let out a surprised yelp and plopped back on her ass in wonderment. She'd read about werewolves and bears that could turn human but the thought of a snake that could do that had never crossed her mind.

"Didn't mean to startle you," a sleepy voice floated up to her. "Were you trying to climb the stairs?"

"Stairs?" Prudence echoed stupidly. "Those floating things are stairs? How are they held in the air like that? What's supporting them?"

"First time here, obviously," came the dry response. "It's rare someone wanders off the path of inane-ness over there."

"Uh, yeah. I don't know where I am, or what you are, much less what I'm supposed to do here before going wherever I land next. I feel like I'm talking in riddles. I'm not even sure what's scarier: The ginormous dragon in the other place or you."

"Pah-shaw," the snaked hissed. "I'm not frightening. Those mindless drones are a different story. Just look at them rushing from place to place in the name of serving others and never having a dream of their own to work toward. What separates them from each other than their skin color? Eh, whatever. I've been looking for a way out of this hell for years. I wish I knew how you got here so I could reverse the path and get out. And I can't answer the rest of your questions, which, if I may say, you have a lot."

"Where do the stairs go?" Prudence wasn't in the least offended.

"I can't say I know or I care. I've been stuck in this hybrid form since I've been here. It's not warm enough for me to shift fully into my snake or back to human. That's only one reason I want out of here. I'm not a fan of the concrete jungle. My advice, take the stairs. Then come back and tell me where they go. It would satisfy one curiosity that I've been unable to answer."

"You're half-human, use your arms and drag yourself up them," Prudence retorted hotly. "I'm not the person to talk to if you want to have a pity party. Laying there doesn't look like you are doing much to help yourself out of the situation you landed in. You hardly strike me as helpless."

"You're lucky I don't strike you, period. My energy reserves are low and those pink things don't taste like strawberries. I have no idea what you would taste like, though."

"Probably like rotten whiskey, not something you'd want to try," Prudence answered quickly. She scooted back from the edge, hopefully out of the strike zone. "I'm a little nervous to try my weight on those itty-bitty steps."

"Fine. At least I'll have company if you're stuck here with me."

Prudence frowned and rose to her feet with her knees cracking. She wasn't going to be stuck here. Nope. She walked back to the floating stairs that still looked like nothing more than lines in the sky and wondered how she would get up them. Her upper body strength wasn't all that impressive. Truthfully, her athletic abilities were zilch.

"Don't be over there having a 'pity party,' as you stated. Just go for it! Commit," the snake taunted her.

Prudence bit her tongue because snapping back wouldn't be the prudent thing to do in this situation. Instead, she stretched and grabbed hold of the bottom stair, leaving her toes barely brushing the top of the block. She could do this. She wasn't aware she'd said it aloud until the snake spoke.

"Of course, you can do this. I admire your tenacity, foolish as it may seem."

Prudence lifted her legs and swung them back and forth to gain momentum and then, like an acrobat, she hooked her heels on the next step. She jockeyed around until she felt confident enough to let go with her hands and hung upside down.

It was her first look at the snake in its entirety and she was glad she hadn't mouthed off as she typically would. She spied the nicely toned male torso and thought he could have at least helped her climb the stairs. He came off as lazy and probably wouldn't have helped even if she had asked. Whatever.

"Do the purple ones taste like grape?" Prudence blurted out randomly, so the wanton side of her didn't take over and comment on his physique.

The snakeman laughed heartily and shook his tousled head at her but said nothing. He merely watched her struggle to get upright on the narrow, shallow, floating steps.

Prudence hadn't done a sit-up since gym class in

high school twenty years ago. How she managed it now, she wasn't sure. It was probably nothing more than pride and not wanting to look weak or like prey.

She sat on the tiny stair and tried to figure out how to get from this position to the next step without falling to her death. It was melodramatic, but she couldn't help feeling that way. The next step wasn't that far, realistically, so she reached out and used it as a brace with her arms to rise to her feet. It sounded easier in her head when she coached herself but she managed.

Standing wasn't any less daunting when there were no supports, and one misstep would cause a devastating fall. With a deep breath, Prudence took the step and kept going with the forward momentum. Before she knew it, she could no longer see the snake or anything below her and came to one of the steep, narrow pathways she thought was a line.

She was way too far to think about going back, so forward it was. Her legs were tiring and it felt like forever until she reached the top. She stood there in a gray cloud, on a slab of gray stone, looking around at a lot of nothing.

It shouldn't surprise her but it did. Cautious of falling off where she stood, she only moved a few feet in either direction to see if she could spot anything or anyone.

"Hello? Is anyone here? I climbed your steps and I'm here looking for answers and a way to get back home. Anyone? I get the sense that I'm on a schedule, yet I don't know what it is. But I feel a pressing need to hurry," Prudence called out into the gray.

"You were right to think of them as lines," a low-pitched voice rumbled.

Prudence immediately picked up on the male vibes instead of the androgynous tones she'd gotten so far. She felt sure she spoke to someone of great age and that they should be respected and revered.

"Well, that's what they looked like: Lines floating in the sky that go nowhere. Lines like these should intersect somewhere to create something and have meaning. It feels disjointed right now." Prudence felt like she was babbling about art, but once she opened her mouth to speak, those words chose to come out. Her artistic soul was hardly wrong about these things.

"You are perceptive and intuitive," the unseen entity replied. "Tell me: Do these lines mean anything in your life?"

Prudence was startled at the bold question. As she thought about how to answer, she realized she hadn't drawn any correlation between these locations and her life. Was this the actual test? Were these promises things she needed to fix in her world? Or was this a case of her over-thinking things again?

"I haven't thought it about," she answered. "Is that the trick to all this? Find how it relates to my life and vow to fix it?"

"What do broken lines amount to?" the voice asked.

"That depends. It could be art or a puzzle. Some lines shouldn't ever cross or intersect; they only run parallel to each other. And if that were the case, then they aren't broken; they are a larger part of a whole. A line could also be symbolic, like a boundary, and those lines are there as a safeguard." Prudence's mind began to wildly spin as connections became evident in her mind's dark corners.

"I see I have given you something to consider. I will elaborate further to aid you. Centuries ago, there was a large dispute among a ruling family. So deep ran the anger and the hate, the world cracked open and the color bled away, leaving everything desolate. Magic can't fix everything, nor should it be allowed to have that power. But choice—ah, the power of choice—leaves a rippling effect across several lives and worlds." The entity's voice drifted off, his nostalgic tone hovering in the air.

Prudence looked deeper than the surface of the words and tied them to her existence. Right or wrong, choices formed lives, and several she had made throughout hers left broken lines.

"My choice was to give color back to the worlds that broke off and separated. I bled it from my body, soul, and very being so that others could still find happiness, even if they hadn't reconciled their choices and repaired those lines. The world you see now, devoid of color, is what's left due to my decision. I don't regret it, except those who remain here are deprived of the beauty that thrived."

Prudence blinked slowly at the similarity to her life. Except for the color part. Her world was colorful but lonely without family. What didn't make sense was how each location tied in with her or her situation. That part she still needed to ponder on.

"What is it you need me to do?" Prudence asked the expanse of gray. She had a sinking feeling she already knew the answer.

"Fix the lines," the voice confirmed her suspicion. "By doing that, the color will fill this world again. Something other than this bleakness will exist and perhaps I'll have hope that the lines inside me will begin to repair."

Prudence cleared her throat. "How do you see that happening? I don't understand how to fix the lines. I don't even understand how I arrived at each of these locations or how I get sent back."

"You carry the keys with you, child. Those keys allow entry and exit."

Prudence wanted to scream. What the hell was this thing talking about? What keys? She didn't even have car keys on her. All she had was the damn rocks she'd picked up in the first location, which she kept losing. You'd think they'd stand out in the places she'd been to with their monochromatic schemes.

"What happens now? Do you send me back or do I need to climb down and go back to the ground and that smartass snake?" Prudence resisted the urge to put her hands on her hips like when she did when customers got sassy with her.

"The naga can be of assistance to you if you allow him. He has his uses. Though, I will not lie: He borders on the lazy side."

"Thanks, Captain Obvious," Prudence couldn't help but snark. "I caught on to that pretty quickly. He didn't even move when I stepped on him by accident."

A deep chuckle floated past her ears. "For me to send the naga with you, he must be with you. I'm afraid that means you will have to climb down."

Prudence grumbled under her breath and sighed. "I don't think the down trip will be easier." She was correct; down was a hundred times more terrifying. She made her way to where she had entered and searched for the path to the sound of more laughter.

She put her mind to work to distract herself, trying to figure out how each location and promise tied into her life, no matter how obscurely. If she made a connection, she vowed to search for a real-life solution to the issue and hoped that would lead her to an answer to fulfill the promises.

When she thought of life, what came to her mind was a failed pregnancy and awful miscarriage. The whole reason she'd packed up her life in the middle of the night and moved to a middle-of-nowhere desert. But that wasn't really life; that was the loss of life. A life that should have been but never was.

How did that relate to South of Hell? That place, too, was experiencing the loss of life. It was much easier to bring seeds, some insects and fish to begin repopulating that place than to figure out how to add life to her life. It wasn't like she could just go out and get pregnant; honestly, the thought of that scared her deep down to her soul. There had to be more to that one than having a baby, an impossible task for her.

The loneliness promise was much more straightforward by comparison. Prudence needed to find a compatible companion for the dragon that could exist in the sand. She knew in her life that she needed to find better friends and work on maintaining the relationships instead of letting them wither away to nothing. The people she called friends now were only her friends because of what she could do for them. It was one-sided.

Those were workable issues, though they didn't lead her to brilliant conclusions on how to fix floating lines to reconnect broken pieces of this world. That problem was intimidating to lay at her feet and expect resolution.

Prudence looked at the block and wondered how long she'd been in deep thought. It felt like it had taken her no time at all to get back down. She briefly thought about jumping but wasn't sure her knees would take the abuse.

"Hey, naga," Prudence called out. "I could use your help down."

"Why do you insist on interrupting my naps?" the snake man answered. "What do you want now?"

"An entity told me that I could take you with me if I could get back down to you but the only way the magic would work is if you were with me. I thought that maybe with that kind of incentive, you'd be less lazy and more willing to help. But if you want to stay here forever, that's fine too. I'll make the trek back up and get sent back." Prudence cocked her hip to the side as much as possible without throwing her balance off and falling.

"If you're joking, I'll eat you." Tousled dirty blond hair became visible as he peered over the block at her. "For reference, the yellow creatures are rather sour but don't taste like lemons. How is it you think I can help you?"

"I could use a hand down from here," Prudence gestured around her. "I'll hurt myself if I jump. I'm too old for that shit."

The snake slithered closer, the muscular torso an enticement of future dreams. Of course, that thought led to what a forked tongue would feel like on her body. None of those musings were helpful to the situation at hand but Prudence wasn't one to pass on a good time either.

"You do look a little seasoned," the snake drolled. He rose as much as he could and held his arms out.

"Come on, then. We don't have all day."

Prudence rolled her eyes, took a leap of faith and fell forward. Steely strong arms wrapped around her, squeezing more than was necessary, and set her on the ground.

They were in front of the signpost, under the west sign, declaring: 'Sunrise.'

Prudence looked at the naga and saw a man. A very handsome and well-endowed naked man lay flat on his back, soaking up the heat with a rapturous expression on his face. There was no shame felt on Prudence's part for looking her fair share.

"How long has it been since you felt this way?" the naga asked, practically writhing on the ground.

"Less than twenty-four hours," Prudence absently responded as she admired the way his body moved.

"I was speaking to myself. Dare I ask what you're referring to?" The man suddenly sat up and rested his dark, sinuous gaze on her. "And thank you for getting me out of there."

"I was talking about sex. You're welcome, though whoever was at the top told me that you might be of help to me, that you have uses." Prudence bit her tongue before she could suggest carnal pleasure. "Also, you might not thank me. It's dangerous here. Humans are careless and seem to disregard other creatures that occupy this planet."

"Ah, yes. Freedom is never free. So, if you do not want sex, what am I supposed to do for you?"

"I never said I didn't want it. I am saying that I feel my time to solve the issues presented to me seems to be running out. I want to fulfill the promises I've made before that happens. We are under the west sign now, and it seems that we need to head that direction and get the last wish spoken," Prudence explained.

"Fill me in, then." The naga crossed his arms and smirked when Prudence's eyes roamed over him.

She quickly brought him up to speed on what she had seen and experienced up to that point. She gestured at the signpost behind her and then fell silent while the naga seemed to absorb her explanations. His gaze flickered over the signs, back to her, then to the landscape around them.

He stood and approached Prudence, taking liberties to run his hands down her sides and slide them into her front pockets. He withdrew the gem-colored stones and held them out to her. Only two remained: A beautiful ice blue stone that reminded Prudence of the pristine glaciers in Antarctica that reached for the sea floors and a brilliant emerald green one that made her think of lush rainforests. Each was as equally stunning as the other.

"Humans," the naga scoffed. "So complex at times and yet simplistic beyond all reason. If you spoke the truth, I believe these are the keys that the entity you spoke to told you about. If one of these stones is required to enter or exit that domain that would be why they keep disappearing."

Prudence slapped her palm against her forehead. "Excuse me for not picking up on that when I didn't even know magic, dragons, nagas, or alternate universes existed due to a random signpost in the middle of a shithole desert. Yeah, it makes sense after you explained it. However, it doesn't explain how I got into the first location. I didn't have one of those stones then."

The naga walked to the signpost and traced the numbers etched onto it. "This tells you how to reach the entrance. These numbers are a form of measurement. Eighteen point five equals one. The numbers on the signs multiplied by eighteen point five give you a precise location. Take a step for me."

Prudence blinked her eyes a few times and then took a step. She'd figured out that the numbers meant a measurement but she hadn't multiplied the numbers. At least, she didn't think she had. She couldn't remember now. Plus, she was distracted by a naked snake man bent over in front of her.

"Let's assume that one step you make is eighteen point five inches. The sign for the west says two point eight one. That would mean you would take two full steps and then almost another. It would require some precision and, for these entrances, it would make sense that precise measurement gets you in. I'd say you got lucky for each one and hit the line of demarcation right on the nose," the snake man explained.

He made it sound so simple that she felt stupid by comparison. It wasn't a complex code or a riddle; it was math. A universal language that someone left the answer for right on the pole. Prudence slapped her palm against her head again and shook it.

"The simplest answer is usually the right answer," Prudence grumbled. She quickly did the math in her head. "Almost five feet. How tall are you?"

"Over six feet. Probably close to six and a half feet," the snake man answered. He dropped to the ground and lay down, using himself as a ruler. "So we'll take some off the top and then a little more. We should be able to find the entrance much easier."

Prudence moved and marked the top of where his head lay and stepped to the side so he could get up. If this worked, she would find a way to kick herself. Plus, she'd have to admit the gray entity was correct: The naga had proved helpful.

Together they measured what they thought a foot and a half might be and then took off another eight inches. The naga had made a lewd suggestion on how they could measure the eight inches. Prudence almost agreed but they had more important things to worry about than boosting egos.

"We should at least be close, within a couple of inches," Prudence muttered as she toed around their measurements.

"Together, human," the snake man insisted, holding his hand out to her.

Prudence didn't argue. She took his hand as they moved carefully around the area they'd marked on the road. Prudence had no basis for understanding how magical entrances worked. But each of the previous times was quicker than a blink of an eye.

Cold arctic air swept across Prudence's bare legs as she stared in astonishment at the top of a mountainous snow-capped valley with a golden sky. The sight was breathtaking and condensation billowed from her mouth as she exhaled.

"I definitely don't want to stay here long," the naga muttered. "My nether regions that you keep staring at are receding into my body. Snakes like heat; this is hell for me. Remind me again why I came with you?"

Prudence didn't have a good answer and asked herself the same thing, though she also didn't let go of his hand. She turned to look behind her and saw the giant gaping mouth of a cave. The ground they stood on was icy with a drop-off in front of them.

"It's probably warmer in there," Prudence pointed with her free hand. "Let's go that way and get away from this cliff."

The naga strode in front of her, dragging her behind him as he barreled into the cave. He didn't even think about checking to see if something scary occupied the space that wouldn't appreciate the intrusion. He stopped suddenly and Prudence plowed into his back.

"It's too dark to see anything," the naga whispered back. "All I can pick up on is our heat signals bouncing off the walls. This cave isn't normal rock."

The cave seemed to radiate blackness. They hadn't gone far from the entrance, and the light diminished to the point that Prudence couldn't see her hand in front of her face. The wind wasn't blowing against them but the air was still below freezing. Prudence was immensely grateful she wasn't naked like the naga.

"Hello?" Prudence boldly called into the black abyss in front of them. "Is anyone here? It's cold and dark and we don't want to fall into a crevasse or anything else."

Her voice echoed off the black walls giving the cave an eerie feeling. As she stepped closer to the naga, he moved forward another few feet deeper into the darkness. She wasn't sure which unnerved her more, walking in the pitch-black, not knowing if they would plunge to their death or running into a creature that would want them for a snack.

"It's obsidian," the naga whispered. "The cave is

made of obsidian. Fascinating."

"How do you know?" Prudence raised her eyebrows, not that he could see the expression on her face.

"Obsidian is used to help ward off negativity. It takes away stress and protects from attacks of the psychic variety. That's why neither of us are freaking out. The obsidian is calming us and absorbing our anxiety."

Prudence said nothing because she had nothing intelligent to contribute to that statement. She took his word for it and sucked some cold air in to call out again.

"Wait. I can see a heat signature. A large one. Let's walk slowly toward it and feel our way."

"You better know what you are talking about, snake man. I do not want to die at the bottom of some crack in the mountain." Prudence followed because it was better than being left alone in an obsidian chamber, unsure which way was out.

"You were told I would be useful. How about you trust me so you can do whatever you need to do here and get us the hell back to somewhere warm," the naga snapped.

It felt like it took hours of inching their way through the dark, using the cave wall for guidance. They stumbled over obstacles they assumed were rocks along the way but eventually the naga stopped and held Prudence in place.

"Whatever it is, it's right in front of us and one of the biggest signatures I've ever seen," he whispered. "I can hear breathing too, so it's probably asleep."

There was a brief moment where Prudence considered saying nothing because she didn't know what was ahead of them but time mattered in this situation.

She assumed so, anyway, because her instincts told her that.

"Hey!" Prudence yelled abruptly. "Wake up!"

The naga hissed at her in annoyance and then fell silent when a bone-rattling roar shook the cave walls. It was immediately apparent that they were the prey in this cave, not the predators. Regardless, Prudence suspected this creature was who they needed to see.

"Sorry to disturb you but we need your help. Or maybe you need my help, and in turn, you'll end up helping us. Whichever the case may be, we are here and freezing. So, let's talk," Prudence rambled.

"Oh dear, you gave me a fright!" a decidedly female voice sprang out from the dark. "How did you wind up here? There have been no visitors in centuries."

"Would you mind turning a light on?" the naga asked cautiously.

"That roar was us frightening you?" Prudence asked incredulously, ignoring the naga. She wondered what the response would have been if they had angered the female. Then again, she might not want to know the answer to that.

"Indeed, I was scared." There was the sound of something making a scratching noise, then the darkness disappeared with a flash and became replaced with a warm yellow glow.

The female voice belonged to an exquisite beast. The obsidian walls reflected the light and revealed a Caribbean blue dragon. She was the color of tropical seas or, more accurately, the hue of the glaciers outside the cave.

"Another dragon?" Prudence breathed out in excitement. "You're beautiful."

The naga looked unsure if he should run or move closer to the fire. The heat won out and he inched closer with his eyes fixated on the mammoth creature.

"You've met another?" The dragon cocked her head to the side inquisitively.

"I did. Only he—I think it was a he—was in a land of red sand and purple skies and it was oppressively hot there," Prudence told her.

"Take me there," the naga mumbled.

"Ah, so you've met my brother. How is the selfish bastard?"

"Lonely," Prudence responded. "That was your brother?"

"Sadly, yes. Is that the only other dragon you met? You didn't meet my father or grandfather?"

Prudence could almost hear the light bulb sparking to life in her brain. "The four directions. The four pieces of the world that broke apart! The four family members... the four sets of broken lines. I didn't see anyone in two of the locations, so I'm guessing that would be your father and grandfather. I only spoke to them. I never saw any indication that there were dragons there. Incredible."

"My brother is the fire dragon. I'm the ice dragon. My father is the water dragon because how else do you tame a fire or melt ice? Now, my grandpa is the ruler of our kind, and as such, he is considered an elemental dragon. He has the power to use all elements and control them. It's spectacular to watch and downright terrifying to be on the receiving end. How is it you saw neither of them?"

Prudence blinked and processed. "Where were they?" she wondered aloud. "What does that mean? Fire, ice, water, elemental?"

"Well, instead of breathing fire, my father breathes water when he attacks or punishes unruly children who set fire to things. My brother breathes out fire. Me, I exhale ice. Now, my grandpa can control all of them. He can choose what to dole out and you never know what it will be. He can also be invisible. My dad can be invisible, too, as long as the water is around him. It's illusional magic."

"I never knew that was even possible. Simply amazing. Do you by any chance know how I travel between your locations?" Prudence asked while the dragon was in a sharing mood.

"Hmm," the dragon tapped a claw on the ground. "I'm guessing you saw my dad first. Was there water there?"

"There was," Prudence confirmed. "The purest, clearest stream I've ever seen. At the bottom were all these brightly colored rocks that looked like gemstones. The naga believes these are the keys but I am unsure how they work or how to get more."

"Well, if you made it out of that world without him taking them from you, that's a plus. You can only get them there if he's in a sharing mood. He's an impossible dragon. His stubbornness is why we're all separated. Not that I mind the solitude."

"May I ask what happened?" the naga finally spoke.

"Several years ago," began the dragon with a heavy sigh. "I was sure I'd found my mate. Unfortunately, he was my brother's rival and that caused tension between us. I wasn't overly close to my brother but I was close to my father and grandfather. My brother threw dramatic tantrums and created a divide between my father and me that grew deeper the longer it continued. My grandfather tried to intervene, which caused a rift between him and my father."

The naga listened intently to the story and Prudence tried to gather as much information as possible to figure out how to repair the broken lines. She figured that the key stones played a part. But maybe there would be a clue in the story the dragon told. There might also be a connection to her life that she needed to draw on to help solve the problem.

"One afternoon, when my potential mate and I were working on the bond we shared, my brother interrupted and caused an altercation that turned into a brawl. My brother drew first blood, which my mate had to answer to maintain his position; it's a whole caste thing. Anyway, it drew the attention of my father and grandfather. My grandfather, the Dragon King, intervened and demanded a cease. My brother refused to listen and kept right on going as was his typical style."

The ice dragon paused and seemed to gather her resolve as if continuing caused her pain. Prudence figured it probably did because the familial ties caused her anguish. That's the way it happened in her family, too.

"My brother lashed out when my mate had ceased as ordered and struck a fatal blow. There was nothing anyone could do to save him and, in doing so, he injured my grandfather and me. My father retaliated by defending my brother when I struck out. His siding with my brother broke my heart. Watching the dragon I thought would be my mate die felt like my heart disconnected from my body, permanently. The first crack appeared when my irrational father saw my grandfather consoling me. The reactions from all of us deepened them until we all separated."

Prudence empathized. Her experiences with loss were similar. Only the earth didn't crack and separate. She ran to the desert to hide away from everyone. The action had the same consequence on her family. They'd fractured.

"I'm sorry that you had to deal with something like that," Prudence finally offered.

"That's why I'm in this obsidian cave. I sometimes think that the cave expands because the obsidian breaks from all the negativity it absorbs from me. Though I can't lie, I feel safe in here, in the dark. Yet my heart tells me to be honest and admit I am lonely and miss them all. The loss of my potential mate has me believing that I will never find a love like that again and no matter what I do, I can't fill the hole that remains." The blue dragon was free with her woes and showing her pain.

"But you can," the naga spoke up. "'Potential mate' is different than a real mate. Not even death can sever that bond. If nothing else, that should bring you comfort and hope that someone is still waiting for you. You have to leave here to find them; maybe that's too daunting for you. I get not wanting to experience loss again but I've learned that no matter where you are, it finds you."

Surprisingly wise words from the snake man, and Prudence couldn't help but feel mildly impressed at the display of empathy. She hated that he'd nailed it on the head for the dragon and for herself. She couldn't dwell on it; she had to solve the issues and to do that, she had to push the dragon for answers.

"The rest of the dragons all extracted promises from me before sending me on. What is it that you need from me to send me back so I can get started on fulfilling the impossible tasks?" Prudence felt like a heel.

"Show me I'm not alone in my grief. Tell me what made that look come across your face when I told you what happened to me."

The naga turned and cocked an eyebrow at Prudence. His hands dangled freely at his sides, yet she saw how he balled them into fists and she suspected that he had a tale of his own to tell. However, that wasn't what the dragon had requested.

"Will it truly help you?" Prudence hedged. She'd never shared her story before now. No one in that remote desert town even knew her past.

"I believe that it will," the naga answered for the dragon. "I also think it might help you solve what you need to solve."

Prudence cursed under her breath at the nosy snake man and wished she'd left him behind to sunbathe at the signpost. She didn't understand why this was so difficult for her, considering she'd just asked a strange dragon to do the same to help her on this quest. It was rather selfish of her not to give the same when it was her request.

"I used to live near my family in a mid-sized town far from the desert. I had a good life; I worked as an artist and would often take commissions to do portraits for families or their pets. And I did landscapes to balance that out when it became tedious painting people. I had talent and I loved what I did. Then I met someone that I thought would be my forever."

Prudence paused, unsure how to go on. The small

details wouldn't matter much to the story's overall theme, and she didn't feel like she needed to share those intimate details that she raked herself over the coals for practically daily.

"We dated and grew together for about two years when I became pregnant. I was over the moon happy. My family has old-fashioned values and were less pleased that I wasn't married and settled but they supported my decisions. The thought of a grandchild excited them. The love of my life didn't share the enthusiasm. After he found out, he told me he'd never wanted children."

Prudence breathed as the familiar pain ran over her nerve endings, reminding her of everything she had lost. It was water under the bridge now, the pain shouldn't stun the way it still did and it made her feel ashamed. She swallowed it down and continued: "We became distant as the pregnancy progressed. By the sixth month, I realized that he wouldn't be around much longer. It hurt terribly... but not quite as much as learning he was already married and had three children he'd abandoned. I should have known. The signs were there but I chose to ignore them. Come to think of it now, I think my family suspected but they kept their mouths shut. I don't think they expected a haggard-looking mother of three to show up in town and confront me at a baby shower. I know I didn't foresee that happening but that's how I found out."

Prudence sighed heavily. The face of the woman haunted her, along with the disappointed stares of three beautiful children. The accusations the woman had been enough to bring Prudence to her knees. She'd cried for what the woman had been through, ignoring her own feelings.

"Needless to say, the relationship was over at that point. It might as well have been a death that caused the end and I swear it felt like a part of me died. Then it happened: A part of me did die. I had a miscarriage that night when he showed up at my place and accused me of digging into his past and trying to ruin his life. His words were cruel and felt like physical punches. I believe the stress of the situation and the way I handled it caused my baby to die. I would have had a little boy."

The naga shook his head and clucked his forked tongue. Prudence couldn't decipher his expression if it were disgust or blame; it didn't matter anyway. It was over and there wasn't anything she could do about it now.

"I left after the hospital released me. It was the middle of the night. I was a coward and couldn't be there anymore. I packed up the things that meant the most to me, took my clothes, and left. I didn't tell anyone. I canceled my phone, changed my name, and never picked up a paintbrush or pencil again. I kept driving until I could sell my vehicle for something else, then I landed where I live now. That's where I've been, stuck in a cycle of self-loathing, making foolish decisions, sleeping with whoever strikes my fancy and avoiding my family."

Prudence backed up a few steps to put distance between them. The dragon's eyes were sorrowful and five-gallon tear drops fell from her eyes. It felt like tearing open her heart again and she couldn't take it for much longer.

"You can't keep running," the naga scolded. "Where are you going to go? Out into the snow? To the signpost, if she sends you back? You have to face it, human. What happened was tragic but it doesn't mean your life is over. You should know precisely what needs completion to finish your tasks. Not theirs: Yours."

"Would you like me to freeze him?" the ice dragon offered.

Prudence let out a bark of laughter but shook her head. "He's right. He's an asshole but he isn't wrong."

"Perhaps, you both may be right," the dragon considered. "You've given me some big things to consider and process. The second part of my wish is when you come back, you tell me how you have mended some of the broken lines in your life."

In less span than the blink of an eye, they were looking at the signpost from some distance away. The naga sank to the ground and relished in the heat as he had before. He paid not a lick of attention to Prudence as she marched back up the signpost and went right to the South of Hell sign.

She made the mental calculations in her head and began to measure the distance to the entrance. If she were going to complete these tasks, she needed more of those stones. A lot more. She also wanted to give the water dragon a piece of her mind for not giving her more information from the start.

Right as Prudence began to step into where she believed the entrance to be (considering the rock she tripped over was a good indication), a hand wrapped around her bicep.

"Not alone," the naga informed her. "If my fate is tied to yours, I want to ensure this is done correctly."

"Well, this is a barren paradise," the naga hissed as they

landed on the grassy plain.

"I know who you are!" Prudence called out, ignoring the snake man. "Show yourself!"

"This is the life you bring me?" the water dragon answered after a few moments. "Hardly acceptable."

"The naga isn't the answer I present. I'm here to gather more stones to manage with all the problems I have to fix. He simply brought himself along with me, though I can leave him here as collateral if you'd like," Prudence suggested with a smirk.

"What?" the naga hissed again. "I'm not a bargaining chip."

"You're whatever I say you are. I didn't have to bring you with me, nor do I have to bring you back," Prudence snapped, tired of his haughty attitude.

"Is my family faring well?" the water dragon asked.

A shimmering wall of water appeared in the distance as the iridescent green dragon made himself visible. The water dragon was as breathtakingly stunning as the others. Prudence only allowed herself to gawk for a second before schooling her expression into one of indifference.

"They are not. They all suffer to some degree. Are you willing to admit your mistakes and make reparations?" Prudence crossed her arms defiantly, despite the fear that coiled in her belly seeing the angry eyes of the water dragon land squarely on her. "I have to own up to my shit. You need to own up to yours."

"Take the rocks you need," the water dragon growled menacingly. "I'll do what I deem necessary."

Prudence shrugged in response and made her way back to the stream. She took off her shirt and loaded it as full as she could with stones, making a knapsack out of the clothing. She slung it over her shoulder and walked back toward the gaping naga.

"Send me back so I can fix things," Prudence requested with a no-nonsense tone.

The naga barely had time to reach out and grab her arm.

"Maybe you should be less rude to creatures that can kill you in less than a second," the naga complained.

"Don't lecture me. Tell me how I get home," Prudence demanded.

"Easy enough," the naga shrugged. He pointed to a bleeding wound on her leg that she swore hadn't been there until just now. "Wake up. I'll wait here."

Prudence opened her eyes and realized she lay on the grass of the guy she'd been drinking with the night before. Her shirt was off and tied up knapsack style next to her on the lawn. She breathed a sigh of relief that it all hadn't been a dream and then sucked in a lungful of air because that meant it had happened and she had a lot of work to do!

She sat up and saw her quasi-friend staring at her open-mouthed. "What, Derrik?"

"I blinked and you suddenly had your shirt off and it's next to you all tied up. It's been, like, a half a second. How did you do that?" Derrik spluttered.

"No time to explain." Prudence stood and picked up the very heavy shirt of stones. "Is my car here?"

"Are you still drunk? You are standing in front of your car." Derrik frowned at her.

"Oh. Yeah." Prudence shrugged it off. "I've got

things to do. Catch you later, Derrik."

"Hey, next time you fall over and slice your leg open, don't use peyote like its aloe vera. And don't forget your phone," Derrik tossed her phone to her. "Hope your vision quest was worth it."

Prudence gaped at him for a moment before turning back to her car and getting in. She shoved her hand under the front seat and found her keys where she usually stashed them. Peyote? Vision quest? That couldn't be right. The signpost was real and how else would she have gotten a bag of gemstones if she'd hallucinated the entire thing on a peyote high?

Before pulling the car out of the driveway, she untied a corner of her shirt to reveal a pile of gray stones. How could that be? It didn't make sense. Prudence had met four dragons and a naga and had made promises to each of them. She'd learned magic was real. But why was there a bag of dull gray stones if it was?!

Prudence headed back to her place. She was tired and her mind spun out of control. A shower, food, and perhaps some meditation was in order before she opened this can of worms. That was her plan of action.

Yet when she got home, the first thing she did was grab a notepad and pencil. She sat down at the kitchen table and began to sketch. She drew the obsidian cave, then the ice dragon that lived there. She moved on to the concrete jungle with its Skittles-colored people. She flipped the page and penciled the broken lines that she climbed up to the platform where she spoke to the dragon king. She even sketched out the naga in his hybrid form and, of course, the naked physique. The last two pages held the fire dragon and the water dragon.

Each picture was a perfect likeness. Prudence had

had some vivid dreams before but she knew they were dreams. These places, these creatures, they were real. Every bit as authentic as her family was to her. Prudence stared down at the notepad filled with fantastical pictures and smiled. It was the first time she had sketched anything in over thirteen years and it felt magnificent.

So then why was she crying? Exhaustion pulled at her bones. She dragged herself to the shower and stripped, plunging into the icy water before it could heat up. It helped and the hot water eased some of the stress from her body.

Prudence got out, toweled herself dry and lay naked on her bed. She did some of the meditations she used to do when she practiced yoga regularly. They were good for getting her mind centered where she needed it to be when dealing with stressful situations. And calling her parents 'stressful' was an understatement.

When she was ready, she reached for her phone, made sure the charging cord was plugged in and dialed the number she'd never forgotten in all these years because it was home. She listened to it ring twice before her nerves failed her and she almost hung up.

But she didn't. Prudence prided herself on her courage; it had taken her this long to realize that she had it in spades. By the fifth ring, she was about to assume her parents weren't home when the phone stopped ringing.

"Hallo! You better not be coming to arrest me for Social Security fraud. Or telling me my 1956 Ford pickup truck warranty has now expired or I will hunt you down and handcuff you to a pole, roll you in cow livers and stake you up as dragon bait," Prudence's father hollered into the phone. "Speak now or pay the consequences!"

"Hiya, Pop," Prudence spoke softly. "I'm calling to pay my consequences."

"Julianne Buttercup! Is that you, darlin'?"

"It's really me, Pop. How are you and Mom?" Prudence answered, feeling like a child again.

"We're old, Julianne. We miss you. For so many years, we thought you might be dead. Which, if you're a ghost, then I guess you are dead. But you sound real. Are you real?"

"I'm not a ghost, Dad," Prudence chuckled. "But I do go by Prudence now. Tell me: How are you and Mom?"

"She's right here, honey. Hold on. I'll give the phone to her."

Prudence smiled at the way some things never changed. Her father's swings between forgetfulness and total lucidity were one of them. At least it was due to a head injury he'd sustained when she was a teenager, not dementia.

"I'm surprised to hear from you," her mother's voice floated across the line.

"I've had some mental clarity recently and realized I needed to apologize for my behavior." Prudence didn't waste time with small talk or formalities. Her mother hated it. "I'm sorry, Mom."

"You were always a spontaneous person. We just figured you'd let us know that you were somewhere safe. That was the hard part, Julianne."

"Prudence, call her Prudence now," her dad's voice came from the background.

"I use Prudence as my name now," she reiterated her dad's statement. "Mostly because you always used to tell me: Would that be prudent of you to do? It seemed fitting. White noise filled my mind, so much anger and grief I couldn't really think straight and that was the only name that came to mind. Plus, it's my middle name."

"Are you still doing your art, dear?" her mom asked. It was a slight dig that she wouldn't use her name but Prudence had expected that to happen.

"Not how I did it before. I'm in the desert, by the way; I'm doing tattoos. I just picked up a pencil for the first time in years tonight and it felt fantastic." Prudence knew her dad was listening by the echo of the speaker phone.

"It's good to hear your voice, honey," her dad said. "Are you married? Do you have children?"

"No, I'm not married," Prudence answered with a crack in her voice. "I can't have children, Dad. That was the final straw that made me leave. I felt like staying there would break me and I'd do something stupid. So, I ran away. I told myself never to look back and leave that life behind me."

"Are you coming home?" her mother asked with a tremble in her voice.

"Would I be welcome?" Prudence whispered with tears in her eyes.

"You're our daughter. You're always welcome," her mom replied. "I wish you would have told us, Jul— Prudence. I would have understood your pain."

"I'm learning these things now. I'm taking that step to mend the hurt I caused. I was selfish and that wasn't my intent. I truly mean that and I hope you can forgive me. I want to start a new chapter of my life and want you both to play a part. Maybe I can start by coming for a visit after I finish up some things here?"

"Are you covered in tattoos?" her dad wondered.

"No, Dad. I give them to other people, not myself. However, I was considering getting one. A dragon," she told them. "Are you guys busy in the next week or two?"

"Will you be flying in?"

"Yes, Mom, I'll fly." Prudence winced a little at the harsh tone her mother used. "If you'd rather me not come, I can stay here and rebuild with you over the phone."

"Let me know what day and time your flight is and I'll pick you up from the airport. I need to get your father ready for bed now. We'll talk with you soon, dear."

Prudence was startled at the abrupt end of the conversation but it didn't anger her. That's how her mother had been for as long as she could remember. Hope blossomed in her heart that she could repair the damage she'd left behind her in her mad dash to flee. She was more than aware that the rift was her fault but maybe that broken line in her life could be made whole.

The following day Prudence woke with a start, the dream she'd been in the middle of fresh in her mind. She jumped out of bed and rushed to find the notepad she was drawing in last night. It was nothing more than a vision but it felt like a solution.

Before the image could fade from her mind, she began to sketch. The more she drew, the sharper her memory became. Details emerged that she added as she went along, immersed in what she was doing.

It took her over an hour but Prudence sat back in her chair and breathed a satisfied sigh. She knew what she had to do. She dressed, grabbed the notepad, her phone, keys, and purse, and headed out. She needed to pick up a few supplies before she drove back out to the signpost.

Distracted driving was illegal but Prudence couldn't stop her brain from solving the puzzle of the broken lines. She didn't remember driving to the art store, hardware store, pet store, or gas station. She wasn't aware of anything until she arrived at the signpost and saw the still-naked naga basking in the sun.

She grabbed the rocks she'd transferred into a reusable grocery sack and the supplies she bought. With her arms loaded, she got out of her car and set everything down at the base of the post. She returned to the car under the watchful gaze of the naga and moved it off to the side of the road about a hundred meters away.

With a bottle of water in hand, she set back toward the pole and the naga. She reached into the bag of stones and grabbed green, red, clear, and blue ones. They went into her pocket and she pulled a measuring tape out of the bag from the hardware store.

Prudence pulled the end out and kept pulling, pushing the tape along the ground until she reached the precise measurement of the first location. She locked the tape, grabbed a piece of chalk from the art bag and went to mark the spot that she believed the entrance to be. She did this for each location, keeping the line straight and true to match the direction of the sign.

"Clever girl," the naga drawled. "What will you do next?"

"Buckle up, buttercup, we're about to get wild," Prudence told him. "Let's go."

With a sigh, the naga pushed to his feet and followed Prudence to the west. Wisely, he didn't ask why that direction first. He simply grabbed hold of her arm and followed her to the mountain.

The icy air stung their skin but they walked into the black with no fear this time. As an added measure, Prudence had her charged cell phone in her pocket and pulled it out to use the flashlight app so they didn't stumble.

They made their way back to where the blue dragon lived and managed not to stop and stare in amazement at how enormous the cave was. There wasn't time for that and, if she were allowed back, Prudence fully intended to explore the wonders of the cavern.

"We're back!" Prudence called out. "Hello?"

"No need to shout. I'm awake," the dragon answered as they rounded the corner. "Have you mended some of your life?"

"Oh, yes, and I've only started. I picked up a pencil and drew for the first time since I fled." Prudence pulled the folded drawing of the ice dragon out of her pocket and displayed it. "I also called my parents. I apologized, briefly explained, and asked if I would be welcome if I visited them. My instincts told me they might receive my story better in person, where they can see my sincerity and emotions. It was a huge step, and the jabs that my mother threw hurt, but I took it."

"You *have* taken great strides," the dragon responded hesitantly. "What if my steps are not welcomed?"

"Then they aren't. If they don't accept you, they have to live with that. But at least you will have tried, which is easier to live with than the guilt of never reaching out. I'm not saying it won't hurt, but remember:

You already lost them. There isn't anything left to lose." Prudence shrugged, hoping that the words sunk in.

She folded the drawing and slid it back into her pocket. She waited in silence, watching the dragon's face as she struggled with overwhelming emotions. The dragon's eyes were expressive beyond belief.

"So be it. If you can reconnect the lines, I will do my part to mend what's broken," the dragon finally acquiesced. "Would you agree to return and visit with me?"

"I'd love to!" Prudence quivered in excitement.

"Very well," the dragon huffed unhappily. "I will swallow my fear and give you my word that I will attempt reconciliation."

There was no warning, just the signpost. Prudence smiled happily and dragged the stunned naga to the southern sign after she picked up the bag from the pet store. There was a reason she chose this order to make her marks before beginning the final plan.

The humid air took the chill off her skin as she glanced around the grassy plain. She didn't call out this time as she had with the ice dragon. The water dragon was a mite touchier and she'd angered him the last time she was here.

Instead, she headed for the water, releasing the naga as she walked. He could follow her of his own free will or he could stand there and wait to see what happened; it didn't matter to her. She felt reasonably certain this wasn't the world he wanted to be stranded in, so he'd follow in case she got sent back before he could join her.

Prudence walked right up to the water's edge and opened the bag. She pulled out a few varieties of freshwater fish that would flourish in this environment. She sat on the bank, plopped the plastic bags into the stream to let the water in the bag acclimate to the temperature of the stream.

She'd figured out the time it would take for this to happen and planned accordingly. She knew the water dragon was near because the naga (who had reluctantly followed her) became skittish. She ignored both of them and pulled out a bag of crickets and some other insects that the store specialized in—spiders, bees, worms, all things creepy and crawly—and released them.

It was with a happy heart that she watched the creatures take off and do whatever they did to ensure the life-cycle of nature. After another couple of minutes, Prudence untied the bags of fish and let them go as well.

It wasn't a massive addition to life but the storekeeper had promised her that there were enough of each to reproduce and continue the circle of life. She stood up and pulled the variety of seed packets from the bag she dropped in before driving to the signpost.

Prudence walked out to the middle of the field, opened a wildflower variety, and spun around in a circle, flinging the seeds in all directions. She moved to another area and did the same with a different type.

"You'll need to do your part with the seeds. They'll need water," Prudence stated, sensing a large presence near her. The naga had reappeared and held on to her. "You should also know that I spoke with your daughter again and she said if I can mend the lines, she will do her part to try and patch things up between you. Don't make the mistake I did and think you can just exist out here with some bugs, fish, and flowers. Meet her halfway. Don't miss out on the rest of her life because if she meets the mate she longs for and has children? You'll want to know them."

"You fulfilled your promise," was all the water dragon replied. But his tone told Prudence her words had made an impact. There was hope for the crotchety old dragon.

Prudence rolled her eyes when she saw the signpost again, only farther away. She chuckled as she trudged back to the post and looked between the western and eastern signs. Before moving on to those, she grabbed more chalk and began to draw on the pavement.

An intricate design began to emerge between the southern and western signs and western to northern. There was no question magic was involved as the pavement started to change colors—and not just from the chalk. Prudence was so involved in what she was doing that she didn't even realize that not once did she pull the drawing out to look at as a reference.

The naga simply watched in silence and admired the skill displayed by the strange green-haired woman who'd rescued him. It took her approximately an hour to finish the drawing and then she moved to the northern sign.

This area was the sign that had the most significant distance from the other two and now she understood more as to why that was. The fire dragon was the instigator and had been placed the farthest from his sister. It also explained the loneliness he felt. This direction is where she would part ways with the naga.

"Come along. This direction will be your new

home." Prudence held her hand out to the naga and they began walking to the entrance.

The sea of red sand dunes was the same as they were when she'd been here last time. Though now that she knew the history of this fire dragon, there was a tad more trepidation than there had been the first time she'd arrived here. It was because of that that she clutched the naga's hand tightly.

"This is the land of the fire dragon," Prudence relayed quietly. "He wished for something so that he wouldn't be lonely. Since you are a fan of the heat, I figured this place might appeal to you and also appease his wish. I won't make you stay if you don't want to."

The naga looked like he was experiencing a state of nirvana. There wasn't any other way that Prudence could think to describe the rapturous look that settled on the snake man's face.

"Is he going to kill me the way he killed the blue lady's man—err—dragon?"

"I haven't killed in years." The dune in front of them began to move again. "But probably that's because there isn't anyone here to kill. Now that you are here, that might change. Who are you?"

"You wanted something to combat loneliness and I brought you a creature that can survive in this place. He's a bit snarky at times and rather lazy but he has uses other than looking good naked. He helped me get to the other locations and back. I've met the rest of your family and I've got to say: You stand a good chance of remaining lonely if you don't own up to your actions and work on appeasing those you wronged. I've had to do the same thing, and boy, let me tell you: It's not for the faint of heart," Prudence fanned herself.

"Please let me stay," the naga pleaded. "This sand feels divine. And as a bonus, I'm not human." The naga swiftly became the complete snake form Prudence hadn't gotten to witness yet. It creeped her out, as all snakes did, yet he was oddly beautiful.

"Interesting. I can hear the snake speaking in my mind. He may stay. You, on the other hand, are becoming a nuisance with your lectures. I can't apologize when I can't get to where any of my family are."

"Funny you should mention that. I'm working on repairing those lines. I'll have them completed within the next couple of hours. So, man-up and make things right. This dude here sleeps a lot. He might not be the companion you hoped for. I also know that your father and grandfather miss you. I believe your sister might but it will be harder to crack that one." Prudence shrugged again because the ball was in the courts of the dragons.

"I'm assuming you want to go back now?" The fire dragon huffed and a sheet of sand rained down on her.

"Please. If you would ever like me to visit again, send the lazy one back to find me and I'll return, maybe even teach you a new dance," Prudence offered and gave the extra stone to the naga.

Prudence dropped to the ground between the southern and eastern sign and got to work immediately. She continued the drawing, filling the space between those directions with more of the elaborate picture that seemed to be etched permanently in her mind. It took three times as long to complete this section but she did it and was extremely thankful that she brought water with her. Before heading to the eastern entrance, Prudence moved to complete the drawing between the western and the northern.

She didn't feel like she needed to speak to the king about wanting to see his granddaughter; she already knew that he did. The remaining part of the sketch would be between the northern and eastern signs. The rest of the drawing was almost complete. It was gigantic, enigmatic, magical, and beautiful. After speaking with the king, she would complete the last section and then add the final touches that she believed would activate the four worlds to reform.

Prudence stood and looked at the three-quarters of the way done drawing. The scope of the art was astounding. Some of her finest work ever and it gave her a sense of satisfaction. She trudged over to the entrance to the east and stepped back into the concrete jungle.

Prudence made her way through the Skittles-colored people and found the block she'd stood on to get to the line. As she'd expected, her artwork filled in some of the gaps. It was much easier to get up onto the stone steps that brought her to where the dragon king hid.

Her excitement propelled her to move faster than she had previously and it wasn't because she was almost done with her tasks. She moved faster because she wanted to get home and book herself a flight to see her parents!

"Hello? King? Are you up here?" Prudence called as she paused at the top. "Your granddaughter told me a little more about you and that she misses you."

The air shimmered in front of her. It was similar to

the hot pavement by the signpost, giving an illusion of dancing steam at a rave. Prudence waited somewhat patiently until a dragon head appeared. But it wasn't that that shocked her: Color was returning to the king's scales!

"It looks like it's working!" Prudence crowed. "Your color is returning."

"Yes, but it's not complete. I am sorry but I can't say you have fulfilled your promise and that saddens me." Sorrow lined the king's eyes.

"Of course it's not complete. I wanted to talk to you before I finished. I needed to see if it was working or not. I've delivered on the other three promises. Only yours remains. I have spoken to each of your family and planted the seeds they need to forgive and move on. Your son and granddaughter are ready. I can't speak for your grandson but I believe in my heart that he will attempt to mend bridges."

"That gives an old dragon hope. Thank you, kind human. Now please return and finish mending these lines so that I may see my family again before I die."

"Wait. Before you die? Are you sick?" Prudence halted her steps and looked back at the king.

"Heartsick, yes. I have been waiting centuries to see them and I am rather impatient now that the possibility is at my doorstep. Here's a little secret for you: As the mender, you'll have access to all these lands for the rest of your life. It doesn't matter what any of them say because only I know that you have the power to undo what you have remade. You have my eternal gratitude. Now, please finish."

Prudence gave a tremulous smile and began her descent then paused. "Wait. I don't have to go this way.

You can just send me back."

The king winked at her and nodded.

Prudence finished the drawing right before the sun set in the desert's inferno. She ran to the bags of rocks and began placing them all in specific orders relating to the sign. Each direction would have a set of stones that each touched the other colors, woven into the design. She hoped that this particular pattern would draw the worlds together like stitches. As she placed the last stones and stepped out of the asymmetrical oval shape, she thought it looked like an egg. An odd-shaped egg; perhaps a dragon egg.

The air twisted into the egg pattern, those intricate designs rising right off the road and with a shriek, Prudence realized she'd drawn a map connecting each world. She'd just figured that it looked like roots and that's what she thought she'd created: A root system for each dragon to remember where they came from. Yet she failed to realize that she'd given them a map that told them the same thing.

Whatever it was, it worked because the map snapped together with a crack in the air and then disappeared. The gem-colored stones and the marking were just gone. But when Prudence walked toward the post, she felt the air change this time. She'd fulfilled her promise. The rest was up to them.

Prudence sat in front of her computer and clicked 'Purchase,' buying the airline tickets she'd been staring at for too long. She packed up her suitcase, let her boss know she'd be gone due to a family emergency, and locked her house.

It was time for her to fix her own crossed lines because, during the dragon process, she'd realized that her lines hadn't broken, they'd just gotten crossed. After these years of thinking her parents hated her, she wanted to hug them more than anything else.

She grabbed her bag, got it loaded into the car, and looked fondly at the house that had kept her safe these past years; she waved goodbye and apologized because she didn't know when she would return. But she would return. She had some new friends of the dragon variety that she wanted to check on after a while; she just wanted them to have time to heal before she barged back in, of course.

For the first time since her miscarriage, Prudence felt good. Not just okay or looking for another man to entertain her, but well and truly good. She looked forward to what would happen with her parents.

She knew there would be anger and tears, but the hugs and smiles would make up for it. There would be derogatory comments about her hair and clothes, and she eagerly anticipated that. It meant they still loved her enough to pick and pry.

Once seated on the airplane, Prudence rested her head on the back of the seat, staring out the window. It could be her imagination but it looked like a dragon swooped through the sky doing acrobats and smiling.

Maybe the end of the world *was* just over that small hill and that's where the dragons lived. She'd only needed to fall off to find them and to find her own family as well.

The Culling

The smoke still clung to the air like a blanket of fog, only it had the stench of sulfur to it and made your eyes burn. One hundred years after the Corona virus mutated to the most virulent strain of anything ever seen before and wiped out three-quarters of the world's population, there was still a small pocket of people that celebrated the Fourth of July.

The new government refused to acknowledge the holiday after the world settled after losing everyone. The population was now less than the previous population of New York City. Most people had migrated west feeling like there was danger in numbers; a populated city was breeding ground for a virus.

It seemed that most people believed that because their family members survived the decimation of the virus, they had antibodies that would keep them immune from future mutations. The Corona virus hadn't disappeared the same way scientists hadn't eradicated smallpox. Diminished it, yes.

Regardless, the new governing body of the United States were all employees, or in the pocket of the owner, of the one primary business that remained after the superpower's collapse. They declared some random day the new Independence Day, the day the world became free from the Corona virus. That was the line they tried to sell people.

Eighty percent of the population of the United States lived in Seattle. There were secluded pockets of people spread out over the rest of the country that wished to remain separate. Seventy percent of Seattle worked for Boxy. The tech mogul and entrepreneur Jeremiah Thomas Bronson Sr. was a brilliant and savvy businessman and moved quickly to take up power. Now his son Jeremiah Thomas Bronson Jr., also a high-ranking government member, had put himself in a position of power after his father's death.

In fact, Sr. had so much influence that he had hand-picked the rest of the governing body. They all bowed to what he wanted, followed where he led and praised him continuously. None of that would be an issue if Jr. weren't a complete narcissist and an utter tool.

He told people to call him Jerry in an attempt to be personable yet he advocated for an artificial intelligence society. He'd already replaced a large portion of his employees with AI robots stating that they were there for the employees' benefit so that when sickness happened, there would be no delay in business.

Most believed he used the AI so they wouldn't argue with or try to overthrow him. AI workers were only beginning to become popular when the last surge of Corona virus struck. That was Jerry's platform to kick off the fundraisers he launched for those that still had money to throw away.

The only people with money now were the people in the government and the few independent restaurants left open. Even those places had barely any to spare after paying their workers fair wages.

Not to mention that good old Jerry was pressuring those places to sell out to him, promising that he would make them rich so they could live their lives in comfort and style. It was an appealing offer to those who struggled but their independence and different viewpoints kept them from signing the dotted line.

Boxy hadn't even been on the map until the business Jerry modeled Boxy after went under when Corona virus wiped out the Board that ran it. It was a billion-dollar empire just waiting for the greedy hand to take it over.

Boxy offered a variety of goods, groceries, entertainment services, and even medical and delivery if you signed up for an account and paid a yearly premium. It sounded like a sweet deal until you realized they owned you, body and soul.

Jerry bought up all the businesses that would allow a person not to use Boxy services, effectively trapping people in his web. It was a dismal situation since there weren't a lot of options for people to choose something else.

The virus had wiped out so many trained professionals in various fields like agriculture, medicine, education, and pretty much everything. The virus spared no one except those left alive, obviously.

They did their best to restart their lives and build a community that covered all the basic needs. The virus didn't affect the books written about those fields, so training guides existed, and they utilized them for training the next generations. The doers became the teachers in their downtime. That's how they rebuilt under the watchful gaze of Sr..

With Jr. at the helm, things became more

aggressive and the Declaration of Independence signed in 1776 became null and void. That single act had spurred on a small group of resistance fighters, only without the violence. They called themselves Anti-Sheep and among their ranks were some of the most intelligent people in the country.

Unbeknownst to Jerry, one of them sat on the Governing Board. That's what Jerry named it, the Governing Board. He was under the impression that running the country like a business would work. Jerry wasn't wrong in some instances but for most issues that the Board brought up, that method wouldn't work. He'd started an uprising among the people.

The Anti-Sheep had moved to the city's outskirts and lived off-grid as much as possible. Their footprints were small and largely unnoticed by those who should be paying attention. Members that remained within city limits kept careful notes on routines and happenings. Participants working for Boxy became the ears and eyes on the company, working on sabotage from the inside.

It was insane for people to believe that Jerry held the answers for a happy and well-adjusted advanced country. Especially considering he went and razed the empty buildings to the ground to have his army of AI robots build more outbuildings for his company.

Families that had lived in their family homes for years got forced out and into Boxy housing facilities where they still had to pay rent and work more than forty hours a week for wages considered below fair, simply because there was nowhere else for them to work. It didn't matter to Jerry whose name was on the deed. Not to mention the listening devices planted into each building that he had AI listening to for keywords that would signify something dangerous toward him.

To make matters worse, the employees had to sink their hard-earned money back into Boxy to obtain the basic supplies they needed to keep living. They didn't even get an employee discount. It was a corrupt system run by dishonest people.

Plans were in the process of overthrowing but many pieces had to fall in place before the plans could reach realization. It also seemed like someone not part of the Anti-Sheep had caught on to the movement.

City boundaries were tightening their security and the number of AI unmanned drones increased. They flew over the city outskirts looking for people trying to sneak in, so they said; it was more likely they were watching for people to sneak out.

Seattle was the closest thing to a police state as it could get. A curfew wasn't in effect but it might as well have been. Guns were outlawed, except for the higher-ups in law enforcement, which was the military.

Crime still existed, it still happened daily, but when caught, those received severe punishments, some with a death sentence. Only not everyone received punishment. If any Governing Board member did something deemed illegal, it was for the betterment of society and forgiven with a stern warning that no one else should attempt the act.

It was fortunate that Iris Saxe was in the position to be on the Governing Board and the founding member of Anti-Sheep. She was also the person inside Boxy. Iris managed the Procurement Department for the company. She rose through the ranks quickly, repeatedly proving that she could efficiently solve problems and source whatever the customer sought.

Jerry favored Iris and did nothing to hide it. He frequently asked Iris' advice and counsel on issues with the company, though he often did what he wanted, disregarding the wisdom offered. He was the most intelligent person, or so he thought.

Iris learned early on to let no emotion show around the man, to stand firm in the face of adversity, and she had no problem stepping on the yes-men that supported Jerry's asinine initiatives. It wasn't something she was proud of but she understood the necessity of the behavior to get her where she needed to be to help stop the insanity. That was her goal from the start.

Iris' family was one of the displaced people forced to live in the company housing facilities. It wasn't necessary at the time, and she and her husband had lived there until her twins were eighteen and then Iris and her husband moved out, leaving the house to them. Iris herself hadn't lived there, but her children had. Iris kicked herself constantly for not getting the deed to her grandmother's house changed.

Then a heart attack happened and her husband died. She'd been too grief-stricken then to think of the deed, and only after Sr. passed on had she understood what was happening all over the city. Jerry was planning on achieving the title of the largest landowner and exerting more control over the people.

It sickened Iris, and that was why she set plans in motion over three years ago for a slow rollout on ousting him from office and taking down the Governing Board with him. So far, the little changes hadn't drawn notice from anyone. It was easier to trick a human than it was to trick an AI programmed to look for mistakes or anomalies.

AI vastly outnumbered the human workers but there was a human in the IT department, Emmer Young, also a displaced individual. Emmer was a phenomenal coder and could find bugs before they could get reported as issues by the app users. He worked with a rogue coder hacker (IciT was the rogue's tag) that Iris had placed outside the city borders.

IciT's real name was Burnett Downs. That was the only name Iris ever knew him by, though rumors existed that he'd changed it to that from Thomas Green. IciT, pronounced I-See-It, had been in the military when Sr. was alive. His job was to destroy, hence the name change.

Even though years had passed since the devastating strain of Corona virus, Sr. ordered destroyed all buildings that had seen and treated patients with the virus. Enter Burnett. He'd heard 'burn it down' so often that it seemed fitting. A fellow soldier would point and Burnett would respond, 'I see it.' That's where his online tag stemmed from and was the only way several people knew him.

When it came to skill, Emmer and IciT were the top tech people in the country. Emmer kept most of his talent hidden from the company's eyes, and IciT hid nothing. He had a notorious reputation and became hunted by the government for his many crimes. That's how Iris found him.

Iris juggled so many pieces that it was awe-inspiring to witness and hard to figure out how she did it on top of her job with the company and inside the Governing Board. She wasn't the only one pulling the strings. She'd designated other people within Anti-Sheep to take part.

Jed was the manufacturing genius and came up with the mirrored surface on top of the vehicles they used to transport goods to other areas in the country. It consisted of a material that hid the gas engine's heat signature and absorbed the infrared rays that the unmanned drones shot down looking for people.

It was a crime even to own a gasoline engine. Thankfully, Seattle had several areas underground to hide those vehicles and the stockpile of gasoline they used. Jerry had shut down trade routes with other countries except those with leaders willing to bend over and kiss his entitled hind quarters.

Jed maintained the vehicles and their camouflage so that Anti-Sheep could transport goods and pick up things needed within the city to supply their underground chain in preparation for taking over.

Iris had made contacts across the country under the guise of supply chain and sourcing trips sanctioned by Boxy. For the past three years, she had put together a network of farmers, craftsmen, tailors, mechanics, and cooks. It wasn't hard to find dissenters among the scattered population.

It was a matter of using IciT to fudge the trackers on the vehicles making deliveries to help them. She had them loaded with supplies Iris' contacts needed and swapped for whatever they had that Iris could store to help the underground supply chain. The less the remaining restaurants had to rely on Boxy, the closer to fruition her plan became.

Iris wasn't doing any of this because she wanted a place in a position of power. She spearheaded this project to put the people back in control. The United States had never been a dictatorship, which is what it is now. Removing the current Governing Board and handing over the reins to the general population to nominate people and have an election process was what Iris intended to do. Reinstate the Declaration of Independence.

Emmer relayed planted bugs in the app to IciT so that money got diverted to a pool that IciT moved to an offshore account that Anti-Sheep had set up to filter money back to the people that Jerry and Boxy trapped. Over the past three years, they'd accumulated just over three million dollars.

By any standards, that was a lot of money. Yet Jerry hadn't noticed a penny missing in all his arrogance. More surprisingly, neither had the AI that was in charge of bookkeeping. Taking random pennies from orders placed daily added up quickly. That proved how effective Emmer and IciT were at their jobs.

IciT made it look like a bug within the app, and Emmer planted it in a well-concealed place within the coding that he could easily detect should it trigger anyone's alarms and make it look like he was a genius for finding it.

Without guns, it was harder to overthrow a government, and while Iris could find and source those should it come to that, she would rather undermine him from the inside and topple the empire. There needed to be more businesses opened and run by the people. Let the country have options on where they shopped and who they bought from. All those years ago, that was the reason people moved here, to live out their dreams.

It was Iris' dream to reinstate that. She hated watching people live like prisoners, walking around like robots with lifeless eyes. She longed to hear children playing in parks and on the streets. It made her livid that there were restrictions on how many children people were allowed to have. How was the world supposed to grow without having children?

The history books, old printed newspapers, and even social media from the past were clear that the United States wasn't a peaceful place. Corruption, crime, pollution, greed, political divides, social distress, racial issues, and dissent among the people were rampant. But the other side was that people could open businesses, celebrate holidays, and choose where to buy groceries or clothes. There were storefronts and restaurants galore.

The only good thing with the United States now was that pollution was as low as ever. With fewer people, no fossil fuel vehicles, and solar-powered electricity, the earth had begun to heal itself. Wildlife rebounded from the overpopulation issues of the past and roamed freely in the unoccupied land.

Bald eagles battled the drones that circled the Space Needle, which Jerry had taken over and used as his residence. The skyscrapers that helped define the Seattle skyline had morphed into employee housing, in which Iris now stood in the penthouse, her allotted space, and stared at the once-popular tourist attraction.

Four months ago, Emmer and IciT started the next phase of their plans by purposely messing with the orders that shipped overseas. The number of calls that came into the call center daily was staggering. Thanks to Emmer, the AI computers were overwhelmed, and Jerry had to hire humans to answer calls.

This phase was working beautifully. The company's profits were tanking. Jerry looked like a horrible businessman, and the refunds issued were for fewer dollar amounts than should be. That was again thanks to Emmer and IciT.

Wrong product was getting shipped, orders misplaced, delivered to the incorrect addresses, arriving damaged, or simply not shipped at all. Jerry was becoming frantic and agitated.

He'd ordered audits on the warehouse staff, which was primarily human, another way for him to demoralize the people that 'served' him. Word had gotten back to Iris and she'd asked Emmer to plant a bug in the software that kicked orders out to make it look like Jerry's program was the problem.

Thanks to the listening devices, Iris couldn't pick up her phone and call anyone about the Anti-Sheep plans. She had to use code words that wouldn't trigger the audio bugs to focus on her. Regardless of the sentence she used them in, the words 'meet for dinner' meant she needed to meet with the key players in the resistance.

Iris picked up her phone and texted: Sorry, I won't be able to meet for dinner tonight. I'm too tired and not up for company. Can I offer you a raincheck?

Iris did nothing other than stand at the window and stared out at the other buildings while she waited for the return text. She was worried about pushing things too fast and having an unstable governing body in the aftermath of the tumble. On the other hand, waiting longer would cost people their lives.

The suicide rates were rapidly rising at an alarming rate. No person other than Iris had brought that fact up in the planning session. Jerry called it population control and survival of the fittest. He stated that if a person is suicidal, it's better to do it rather than draining the healthy people of resources. Because if you were suicidal, you weren't mentally fit to be a productive member of society.

Iris felt horrified at the apathetic response to the issue, considering Jerry and his rules were why people dropped into that bleak mental state. It was yet another reason to bring that man down.

Iris' gaze settled upon the Space Needle with derision. Not for the first time, she wondered if there was a way to topple the landmark without hurting anyone else. She'd had dreams where the monument sunk to the bottom of the Puget Sound and sharks feasted on Jerry's remains. The vision was dark but uplifting in Iris' mind.

Iris' phone buzzed in her hand and she glanced down to see the message: Sure. Maybe I should make you some chicken soup. I've heard that it helps heal the soul.

Iris smiled, reading the keyword chicken. That was the okay that a meeting would happen. They used chicken to say yes. It was fun getting creative with the sentences sometimes.

Iris hit send on the text, which told Emmer and IciT that she would be in their designated meeting spot in an hour: If I'm hungry, I'll go to one of the restaurants in an hour, grab some chicken soup, and put it to the test. Thank you.

If anyone intercepted the texts, which wasn't likely, and they looked at the security cameras, they would see Iris leaving about the time she said she would. If she were under suspicion for anything, they would see her walking into a restaurant as she said she would.

Iris used the busiest restaurant in the area that

she knew none of the Governing Board would go to as they saw it as dirty and beneath them. There was an underground tunnel that would take her to the outskirts of Seattle via an electric scooter. She'd return to the restaurant in under an hour and head home with a soup container.

For three years, Iris never heard an inkling of doubt about her activities. There was no reason to believe the location had gotten compromised, and the workers there were a part of her group and routinely confirmed that no one showed up questioning anything.

Iris wasn't overly worried about it though she didn't let herself get comfortable in thinking she was in the clear either. She knew better than most how quickly Jerry turned on people. She took several precautions when the Anti-Sheep met, and she knew after her response that the text tree was in motion, alerting people to move to their designated places to watch. Each member contacted would watch for tails on Iris or unusual activity like more drones or AI on patrol, even military showing up.

Lady Luck must be on the side of the Anti-Sheep since nothing had happened as of yet. Iris crossed her fingers, even though she wasn't superstitious, and hoped nothing would happen to reveal their movement. It would mean death for all of them. Probably a public one for herself.

Iris went about preparing to leave. She put a blanket on the couch to make it appear she'd been lying there. She put the book she'd read face down as if she marked the page to hold her spot. She left some wadded-up tissues in the garbage can after she blew her nose and left a half-drank cup of tea with the tea bag still in it on the side table.

Iris wasn't sick, though. She did have allergies, and her staging would explain either. For that matter, so would the tiredness. She placed an opened box of cold medicine on the bathroom counter and an empty package to make it appear she had taken one.

When Iris returned home, she'd take it back out and put it in the box with the unopened medication. However, if it looked like someone had been in there, she'd leave it be in case they counted how many remained in the pack. It seemed paranoid to feel that way, yet it wasn't due to the extremes she'd seen Jerry take.

Once Iris staged her place, she pulled a scarf from her dresser, draped it over her head, and then tied it in place. She put a raincoat on even though it wasn't raining and changed her shoes to tennis shoes. It was the same one she wore every time she had done this. Thankfully these meetings happened infrequently in this manner.

Iris headed out after another few moments of taking the time to put her ID in her pants pocket alongside her cell phone. She didn't bring cash or credit cards. She would put the soup on her account. She kept her head pointed down inside the elevator and slumped against the wall. Her gait was slow, and she slouched her shoulders forward to look tired.

She shuffled her way to the restaurant rendezvous with the electric scooter. Only when she was inside, made eye contact with the cook, and received a nod in response did Iris slide into a closet and open the hidden door to the tunnel. She climbed down the ladder, reached her hand out at the bottom, and felt the scooter handle right where it should be.

Iris maneuvered herself until she straddled the scooter and unplugged it from the wall. She hit the button and turned it on, the headlight illuminating the dark tunnel in front of her. She took off, throttling the little machine to the max. It wouldn't take long to get there, only about ten minutes.

The meeting would be quick; they always were. It was by design. Anti-Sheep hadn't gotten this far because they were stupid. The United States was at stake, and the consensus was that people wanted the country to have the freedoms it once had. They wanted to be able to explore the historical landmarks of their ancestors that lived during the initial outbreak of the Corona virus.

Iris shook her head and came to the designated cutoff that would lead her to the ladder to get to the surface of the meeting place. There was a space for Iris to plug the scooter in, and she did before climbing to the top. She knocked on the door in the pattern that would let whoever was up there know it was her.

A few seconds later, the door opened, and IciT's face smiled down at her. IciT wore his usual jeans and t-shirt with a vintage denim jacket. He dropped a hand for Iris to grab hold of, and he helped her out, even though it wasn't necessary.

"Nice to see you, boss. The group is ready," IciT told Iris and led her to the secure room he had set up in the old abandoned shop front he'd converted to his base.

Iris walked in and saw the monitors lit with the faces of the critical players placed across the country and one dark one on the end. The last screen lit with Emmer's face half in shadow. A zap of excitement shot through her veins, knowing they were reaching the final stages of their well-thought-out plan to bring Jerry down.

Emmer's joining caught her off guard, but she knew he wouldn't participate if it compromised his position in Boxy or the Anti-Sheep. He threw out a silent wave to those who were already online.

"Horace," Iris began, wasting no time. "How are the crops all coming?"

"Beautifully. I'd say we are at pre-pandemic levels for growth and storehouses." Horace was the mastermind behind the agricultural parts of their plan. "I received the list of supplies that the restaurant the Governing Board uses. I have some product that is on the verge of going bad. By the time it reaches the restaurant and gets used, some grains should be at the end of their lifespan and cause hallucinations. Make sure that no one else goes in that place. We don't want the general pop suffering."

"Understood." Iris nodded her head in confirmation. "Jed, are you ready to implement?"

Jed's mission was to mechanically alter the delivery vehicles through his network of mechanics by little issues that would either cause the delivery van to stall or break down mid-delivery or not even be able to leave the parking lot. Once the repair request came through, the mechanics would quickly replace the part, and the vehicle would continue its route. The process would repeat a minimum of three times a week.

"Ready to roll," Jed confirmed. "In the last phase, I need the coders and a two-week lead time. There are a lot of logistics to pull off for that one."

The last phase was crashing one of Jerry's planes into his warehouse, where Boxy stored the overstock. There were no humans around that area, so there would be no loss of life to lay on Iris' shoulders. That was important to her. This situation wasn't to be a violent uprising, only one where Jerry had a mental break in front of his peers so that he would get ousted from his position.

It sounded awful to hear but if he could be proved unstable, they wouldn't have a choice with pressure from the leaders of other countries saying that Jerry needed to resign. Along with that thought process, the stigma of mental instability would keep Jerry from a governing position in the future.

"Thanks, Jed. We'll do this phase for at least two months before we step into the next one. That will give us a little time to tighten those steps before implementation. If we are right, the loss of the plane, the warehouse, and the product will cause Jerry to snap publicly. Is that the consensus, Dr. Adin?"

"Correct, Iris. With the behavior patterns displayed up to this point and his narcissistic mannerisms, we have no reason to doubt this," Dr. Adin confirmed. "I'm surprised it hasn't happened yet as he seems to believe he is infallible. The current events and mishaps happening have already had an impact on his behavior when speaking. He is quick to point the fingers at others."

Dr. Adin was a psychiatrist who specialized in mental illnesses and people thought him to be the leading expert in behavioral patterns in the world. Countless agencies contacted him for help, and he liked to think of himself as a profiler. He had yet to be proven wrong in his statements.

"I've noticed the same. Before I head back, are there any other issues that have come up since our last meeting?" Iris looked across the screens at the people that worked with her.

"More drone activity over the Midwest," Horace mentioned.

"Same on the East Coast. Though I think there is some other group at play besides us," Alonzo, the east coast head, answered. "I've seen a few drones get shot out of the air. It's not good for us as it means someone will come here to investigate, and that puts us on high alert and slows our movements."

"I can hack in and reroute some of them to fly in the opposite directions and have erratic flight paths," IciT offered. "All I need ahead of time is where you plan to be so I can focus on those."

"Will do," Alonzo nodded. "I'll get my team to send me mapped out plans so we can accommodate for that. Thanks."

Iris nodded after no one else spoke up. "Very well. Stay alert. We are close, my friends."

Iris stepped out of the restaurant with a large container of chicken soup in a bag hanging off her wrist. She walked with purpose but kept her gaze to the ground, inviting no one into a conversation.

Iris' surprise was genuine when a vehicle pulled up next to her and Jerry motioned for her to get in. Iris' heartbeat quickened though no one would ever notice due to her cool demeanor. She calmly slid into the passenger seat and cradled the soup in her lap.

"Did you need something, Jerry?" Iris asked evenly. In the confines of the vehicle, her heart raced.

"You look a little under the weather. Are you feeling okay, Iris?" Jerry's tone dripped with concern. "I can't lose my best employee."

Iris' stomach cramped sharply with the unwitting confession that Jerry was indeed spying on conversations. At least the conversations of the people in his inner circle he deemed trustworthy. That told Iris that he suspected something was amok among his ranks.

"Overtired is all. I don't feel unwell. I went and got some chicken soup. Comfort food for me." Iris tapped her finger on the bag.

"You should have gone to a better restaurant, Iris. This one doesn't get excellent reviews," Jerry scoffed, accepting her explanation.

"Perhaps but this place makes their chicken soup like my grandma used to make it. It keeps me coming back for that bit of comfort. Was there something else you needed?" Iris kept her tone even.

"If the soup is that good, maybe I should try some. A little comfort food wouldn't hurt me." Jerry's voice held a hint of something Iris couldn't put her finger on.

"You can join me for a cup if you'd like. There is enough here for two," Iris offered. She didn't bother to hide her emotional exhaustion at dealing with Jerry. All he would hear was the tired tone. He wouldn't see that he was the reason for it.

"I guess you got extra so you could have dinner tomorrow too?" There was that tone again.

"I did. If I am going to make a trip out here, I might as well get more than one meal out of it. If there is nothing else and you aren't going to join me, I'm going to get going so I can eat and go to bed early tonight." Iris put her hand on the door handle, waiting for Jerry's answer.

"Go ahead," Jerry sighed. "I don't want to keep

you up."

Iris nodded and climbed out of the car, waved goodbye and kept walking toward home. The episode made her wary but she was glad that Jerry had confirmed that he was suspicious and indeed listening and tracking her phone usage. Thankfully, IciT had spoofed a friend's phone number so that it would like she texted one of her old friends, also a member of Anti-Sheep.

The following week at work, Iris made a point to send an email to Emmer through the work email stating that one of her vendor websites had changed and was forcing tracking cookies and felt suspicious. She told him she didn't want to lose the company's money and wondered if he could check her computer to ensure it wasn't compromised.

The email also requested that Emmer scrub all phone location software, which was something he already did weekly. It was heavily coded but would tell Emmer that tracking was happening, Jerry was suspicious, and to be on high alert. She also knew that Emmer would let the rest of the group know via the back channels he used to communicate with IciT.

Jerry's spying wouldn't change the plans that were already in motion. If anything, it reinforced why they needed to continue, only using extra precautions. Iris would refrain from using her phone unless absolutely necessary and would instead communicate through Emmer using work as the guise.

They'd planned for this situation and had vendor websites set up already. That way, if Jerry went looking, he'd see what Iris claimed. On top of that, the vendors were false fronts for Anti-Sheep, where Boxy bought items already stored for their underground black market. It was a genius idea from IciT who legitimized everything and covered their tracks.

Emmer replied within minutes that he would work on Iris' request as soon as he finished troubleshooting mechanical errors within the delivery fleet.

Iris smiled at the honest email. There were no codes within that one. It told her that Jerry was in the room with Emmer, demanding answers on why so many mechanical breakdowns were happening across the country. Iris read into the email a bit, but it was in what wasn't said that told her Jerry was near Emmer.

Iris sat back in her office chair and allowed herself a slight smirk. It lasted only a few seconds before she schooled her face back into business mode and continued with her day. Throughout the rest of the week, Iris heard several stories about the delivery vehicle issues and Jerry's temper regarding them.

The outside world caught wind of Boxy's recent struggles and the seed blossomed suddenly. Jerry was in the unfavorable spotlight, and the watcher became the watched. It was a snowball effect. It didn't settle with him and he vented to the Governing Board more than once on the matters.

Iris knew the plan would be effective, as did the rest of the Anti-Sheep. No one could have predicted the level to which it rose. Jerry made himself a household name worldwide for his temper tantrums and finger-pointing. It worked beautifully for the Anti-Sheep.

After two months and hundreds of thousands of dollars in replacement parts, labor, lost products, and refunds, Jerry called a meeting. Iris tamped down her joy when she informed Jerry that two significant suppliers of products from overseas were pulling their business from Boxy. Jerry's notoriety was harming their business and it wasn't worth the risk in the new world. Jerry's decline was well underway.

On the Governing Board meeting day, Iris sent Emmer another email requesting assistance for her lagging computer. She cited long load times and freezing screens and wondered if a virus had gotten in somehow.

The hidden meaning of the email was to hold off on skimming money and notify the group that the next phase was almost upon them. Emmer, of course, knew about the meeting from inside Boxy. He knew of Jerry's unraveling from Iris.

The meeting would give Emmer time to set up and double-check the coding for the plane crash and confirm the details with IciT. Things had gotten intense for Emmer when Jerry kept pressuring him to figure out what was wrong with the vehicles. Once Emmer proved nothing in the programming, Jerry had to admit defeat, accept that parts wore out, and eat the cost of the replacements. Which, they weren't really replacements. They were the original parts that had gotten removed before the vehicle set off for its deliveries.

There was no reason to believe that Jerry wouldn't immediately come to Emmer's office after the plane crash either. IciT would control that event, and Emmer would be covering his tracks. It would be far more complex and the most significant challenge Emmer had ever faced. He was terrified and excited simultaneously. One misstep could ruin the entire plan. The pressure was insane, and Emmer hoped he held up on his end.

Iris sat in her chair and listened to the nonsense Jerry spewed about Boxy and the entire country. He even began to trash the leaders of other countries and not one person interrupted him, even the president. They only sat there and nodded their heads like lap dogs.

"Jerry, I think you need to sit and calm down," Iris interrupted. "You are going to give yourself a heart attack. That won't solve any of the issues."

Jerry's bloodshot and red-lined manic eyes landed on hers. Iris knew that he was about to blow up on her. Suddenly, he collapsed in his chair and dropped his head to the table. His breathing was erratic and his hands fisted on the table sat next to his ears.

Iris wasn't sure what would happen; Jerry's body language was all over the place. She tried to think of something bland to say to keep him from exploding at her when he jolted upright with a wild look.

"I'm the smartest and richest person in the world. These problems should be happening to someone else," Jerry snapped.

Iris barely resisted the urge to laugh. For a fact, she knew he wasn't the wealthiest person, especially now, and as for the smartest, not a chance. The most brilliant minds in the United States were in Anti-Sheep. All people that Jerry looked down on and sneered at for various reasons.

None of the other Governing Board members spoke and not one of them met Jerry's eye as he scanned their faces. It was the first glimpse Iris had seen that the Governing Board wasn't as solid and in Jerry's court as it seemed.

"Maybe we wait to have this meeting and let

things calm. It doesn't appear you've gotten much sleep, Jerry. We all want these issues solved, and we all are tired from running around trying to put out the figurative fires. What if we went home and got some rest and reconvene in a couple of days?" Iris suggested, keeping her tone as gentle as possible.

"I second that," the president, Herschel McKenzie, or Mac as his friends called him, voted.

"Yes," two others chimed in.

"Mac, as president, is this vote called?" Iris asked.

"Accepted. Let's meet in three days. I ask that each of us bring a suggestion to the table on how to circumvent these issues and find a solution that will work to bring Boxy back into a positive light." Mac gave a thankful look to Iris for taking the meeting over.

Jerry said nothing, but the vengeful glare on his face spoke volumes. He silently fumed as each person stood up and filed out of the room without another word. She only stood after the last person other than Iris left, pushing each of the chairs under the table. She put a hand on Jerry's shoulder and squeezed.

"I know this isn't the way you wanted this to go. I do feel it was the best solution since no one had anything constructive to say. Giving the others a few days to think of something instead of only reacting could be useful to everyone. We all want what's best." Iris squeezed again.

She only marginally glanced at Jerry to see him zoned out, not listening to her. Iris wasn't going to waste her breath talking. She padded out of the room and silently cheered at the turn of events. The empire was crumbling.

Boxy's runway used to be owned by the airplane magnate that originated in Seattle. He'd razed all the hangars to the ground and put in an enormous 'L' shaped warehouse spanning the runway length. It included a refrigerated and frozen section for the grocery side of Boxy. Across the runway from the warehouse were the Boxy hangars housing the cargo planes.

Inside the warehouse was an automated system similar to what airports used to move baggage and packages about the airport. Only this was for the orders to get loaded on one of the Boxy airplanes. They shipped out to different parts of the country or the world.

Deliveries to this warehouse happened multiple times a day, and a few humans oversaw the processes to ensure machines were running as they were supposed to operate. The trucks delivered the orders, AI put them on the conveyors and scanned the locations and delivery dates and they got routed to the different sections of the warehouse where they waited for transport.

When the time arrived for the packages to get loaded on the airplane, the AI moved them onto another conveyor belt and loaded them into the cargo plane's belly. The process was typically smooth and required very little intervention on the human worker's part unless something was off with the programs.

When that happened, the few human workers couldn't solve it, given the size of the warehouse and the number of orders moving through there on any given day. It required several phone calls to the IT department of Boxy, which depended on whether Emmer was at work or not if it happened after hours.

With the issues Emmer and IciT implemented into

the delivery systems, those problems had more than quadrupled for those employees in the warehouse. They were being run to the bone, called on the carpet for the issues they had no control over, and treated as less than human.

Not all the people that worked in that warehouse were members of Anti-Sheep but at least one member of the group existed on each shift. Given the nature of the last phase, those employees got included in the meticulous planning to pull everything off without a hitch.

Three weeks had passed since the rescheduled meeting of the Governing Board and Jerry's unraveling had progressed even further. Iris wanted no loss of life, so she insisted on multiple meetings with the key players involved on the ground level. It was risky but worth it.

The board had suggested plans for dealing with the issues that plagued Boxy but Jerry wanted nothing to do with them since they all involved hiring more human workers to oversee more of the operations process. He didn't see that as a solution when he believed AI was the answer to all his issues.

Jerry was an intelligent man; Iris knew this much. But for someone as smart as he was, he couldn't see that AI manipulation could happen and work against him. Jerry failed to see the obvious, and that would be his downfall. It worked out well, his ignorance.

Iris had gone out of her way to ensure that she attended none of the meetings and only communicated through coded text messages and emails when she needed to know something. She focused her energy on doing her job and making a half-hearted show of support for Jerry's well-being. She had a hunch that someone still monitored her movements.

The other Governing Board members had disappeared into the shadows after the rescheduled meeting, where Jerry derisively shot down their solutions. Then after the meltdown on public TV when Jerry spoke in a derogative manner about other countries and their responses to everyday business issues like vehicles breaking down, the board members fell silent to all Jerry's requests.

Iris knew the last phase had begun, though she didn't know when it would execute. IciT said that it kept her in plausible deniability. A plan that started almost four years ago now would reach completion sometime soon. All their hard work, strategizing, growing, planning, and putting things into motion would either work brilliantly or fail terribly.

If it worked, and Iris truly believed it would, the people would rise up and demand a new election and begin plans on taking Boxy apart and separating it into different companies. Iris didn't think that would work, but Jerry going down would allow other companies to open and offer the same goods without ordering through Boxy. They'd be able to walk into a store and choose.

Medical offices could get established without having Jerry able to snoop through medical records to see if people had too many children. The world would once again change, and hopefully this time, for the better.

Iris checked her watch and leaned back in her desk chair. She needed to go home. She'd been in the office far too long already, trying to source the items that Jerry insisted they needed to stock. Items that realistically no one would order. She'd stayed late, hoping to reach an overseas office when they opened, though her efforts weren't successful.

With a long back stretch, Iris moved and began closing her office. She turned to shut off the lamp on the small table by the window when motion drew her eyes to the left. The Boxy building wasn't far from the Boxy airport and her eyes ran the length of the runway before turning upward.

It took a couple of seconds before it registered in Iris' mind that the last phase was happening right now. The motion that caught her eye was the plane coming down. The wings were at an angle, and she had only a moment to dash out of her office and frantically stab at the elevator button.

Iris heard the impact before the elevator arrived and she turned to look out the bank of windows that faced the runway. It felt like watching a slow motion movie. It was awful to see yet caused a thrill to run through her body.

The wing struck first, sending the giant cargo plane into a spin defying logic, immediately crushing the landing gear into useless junk. Sparks flew everywhere as the aircraft spun like a top, the wing wiping out the warehouse like a knife through melted butter. It was mind boggling the amount of destruction that happened in less than five seconds.

A raging inferno now gripped the clothing part of the warehouse. The tail obliterated a giant section, and various small fires erupted as the sparks ignited the flammable cardboard boxes that orders shipped in. It didn't take long for those to become larger and spread.

The horrifying sound of ripping metal tearing

through fiberglass and concrete filled the air as the cataclysmic plane crash enacted out its death scene in front of her eyes. The devastation of the last few seconds was nothing compared to the finale.

The plane's fuselage slammed into the refrigerated part of the warehouse in a fury of sparks and flames. In less than a second, a fireball lit the Seattle sky crimson and shattered the windows of all the buildings around the field with a massive concussive blast. Crystalline pieces flew through the air like millions of little deadly diamonds.

Iris never heard the elevator arrive or open behind her. She never even had a chance to scream. She felt the windows' shards tear into her face and body as she was flung backward into the elevator like a rag doll. Then nothing else.

The elevator plummeted as the cable snapped, throwing Iris' battered and bloody body around the compartment until it crashed into the ground with explosive force. Iris never felt a thing because she had died when one of the glass shards pierced her eyeball and embedded into her brain.

IciT and Emmer tried for hours to reach Iris when Emmer received word that the Boxy headquarters had taken heavy damage after the plane exploded. Emmer raced to the office, knowing that Iris had still been at work when he left. She'd told him she would be right behind him when he walked past her. He could only conclude that Iris was still in that building, no longer breathing. Otherwise, she would have answered their texts. She never not answered.

When he arrived and saw the extensive damage,

his knees hit the ground. The warehouse had gotten demolished. Buildings on the outside of the warehouse had taken damage they hadn't thought of happening. The runway was blackened and fires still blazed up and down the street. Had Emmer known that Iris would still be in the building, he would have warned them to hold off on the last phase until she was clear.

Emmer diverted his attention to the angry screams coming from the entrance of the ruined office building. Jerry was there and created a spectacle that put all his other antics to shame. He needn't have worried about spreading the word, media was already present and recording the furious rants.

There was nothing more Emmer could do, and he rose and walked away with tears stinging his eyes. He looked to the sky and vowed to see Iris' vision come to pass. She'd started Anti-Sheep to replace the dictatorship the United States had become because her daughter had gotten caught up in the ridiculous rules set in place by Jerry.

Emmer bit his lip, realizing someone would have to notify Iris' family, and it should be someone who cared for her. He changed his direction to head to the restaurant and underground tunnel to deliver the tragic news. They had work to finish and Iris' family to care for now.

Over the course of the next month, in which the last phase had proven to be an utter success, the Anti-Sheep watched the society that Jerry carefully crafted crumble to nothing. The Governing Board destabilized drastically and half the members ended up resigning.

The fight wasn't over and Anti-Sheep had a lot to

do to get the country set up in a way that would honor Iris' vision and stay true to what the people wanted. Boxy went out of business as Anti-Sheep planned, and Jerry had a mental breakdown in front of a group of world leaders, resulting in him getting arrested and incarcerated. He'd accused each of them of conspiring against him in the act of corporate espionage and attempting a hostile takeover.

Perhaps the most surprising development was that Iris' daughter had become the spokeswoman for political change. She used her mother's death as a platform and set the world on fire with her passionate speeches about reform and the power of love. People flocked to her with ideas and potential prospects for future office holders.

No one, or no entity, should have absolute power. One decision by a strong woman who acted out of love set the wheels in motion to put the power back in the hands of the people that worked to support the country.

Anti-Sheep stayed together to ensure that the change happened and that people like Jerry didn't end up in control.

The Mushrooms

A thick, velvety, heavy cloak of fog clung to the trees like a second skin. It almost felt safe despite the danger the woods presented. The shadows were deep and dark and the sporadic, faint breeze gave it an eerie feeling. Yet the sunlight filtering through trees made the forest feel magical and removed from the real world.

I sat there perched on a mossy limb that extended toward the sky. My feet were propped before me and basked in the fading light. I wasn't worried about falling. I'd been sitting like this for years. It was my favorite place in the forest.

Tucked back from the entrance far enough to keep me hidden from sight but close enough that I wouldn't get lost if I had to run home or call for help. The perch was on an old maple tree with low branches large enough to support an entire family, and they were perfect for climbing. None of the other limbs had moss, and I suspected someone put it there to cushion the spot for sitting long periods.

Nothing beat the afternoon light as the sun lowered itself into the sky when it filtered through all the green leaves. And when dew drops clung to pine needles and nestled on the leaves, they looked like jewels when the light struck them. Glistening prisms that made my imagination run wild with possibilities.

From the bottom, you could see a ring of mushrooms with blood-red caps right next to the trunk. My mom called it a fairy ring. I didn't know if that meant anything, but I believed in the possibility of magic. My mom told me when I was younger than I am now that I should never discount what I couldn't see or didn't understand.

A hint of a breeze wafted through the leaves, causing them to rustle and dance. The light danced around like a kaleidoscope. On the air drifted a female voice. It flittered through the leaves with a haunting memory that I couldn't grab hold of; it flittered away just out of reach.

"Enzo," the whispering voice trailed off, drawing my name out for at least ten seconds. Like it had to travel a long way to reach my ears, as if from a great distance away. In the recesses of my mind, I knew the voice. However, no amount of searching my memories could I produce a face to match it, though my instincts told me that voice belonged to someone I loved.

It wasn't the first time I'd heard my name called out. It had been happening more frequently lately and I wondered why. To make it even more frustrating, it only happened when I was on my tree, in this very spot.

I shouldn't say that because I did hear that voice in some of my dreams. Each time, I reached for the mysterious girl, and she slipped from my fingers like a mirage. I knew her. I know I did. When I felt like I was getting close to remembering, I'd get a bad headache that made me sick.

My dad told me I imagined things and my mom

said nothing. That was after the first few times it happened. I stopped talking about it after that, and my dad pretended nothing happened. Though he wasn't happy that I spent as much time in the forest as I did, and he'd never tell me why.

I figured it was all connected. I was only fourteen, so I had time to put the pieces together and the patience to wait for the puzzle to reveal itself further. These hauntings, which was the only word I could think to describe them, had started two years earlier.

"Who's calling?" I dropped my legs to either side of the limb, straddled it, and sat forward.

The light was waning but there was enough for me to clearly see that I was alone in the woods. As heavy as the mist was, I wouldn't even be able to see an apparition. That word sounded better than ghost. It made me feel older and wiser.

Oh well. It was time for me to head back to the house anyway before my dad got mad. If he weren't home yet, he would be soon. Then I'd get the speech on spending too much time in the woods instead of doing something productive like learning a new language or doing math problems to make myself smarter.

"Enzo," the voice called again as I swung my legs down to the limb below the one I was on.

It was so faint, like the echo of an echo, and drawn out, and I thought I imagined it. I paused and waited to see if she would call out again, but there was only veiled silence. Sighing, I began my descent again, carefully, limb by limb, until I planted my feet on the ground next to the mysterious mushrooms.

"I have to go home now," I told the forest. "I'll be back. I promise. But if you want to talk to me, you must help me remember. Maybe show yourself," I suggested with a shrug.

I turned and walked back toward the house, my steps slow and even. I trudged through the woods and before I reached the perimeter, I felt a tug on the leg of my pants and an icy grip on my ankle before it slid away to nothing.

I turned to face the direction of the tree and grinned. I didn't expect to see anything and it was possible I imagined it since communication with the other side was something I wished to experience. I should have been scared, yet I was only fascinated by the prospect that a spirit touched me.

"Thank you for letting me know you are here. Maybe next time I'll be able to see you." I threw a wave to the woods and continued my walk home.

It wasn't far. The forest, at least that part, was on our property. I had to go up a grassy hill and then the house was in view. It was one of those old Victorian-type mansions that people associated with haunted houses. Perhaps that was why the subject matter interested me so much.

"Vincenzo!" my mom called out to me. "Get in here! Your father arrived home."

I put a hop into my step and sped up. If my mom called me, that meant he was in a mood. That was the pattern. I never heard him take it out on my mom but he sure lit into me. Sometimes I wish he'd hit me instead of the verbal swordplay. I hadn't gotten any better at dealing with those wounds over the past few years. Bruises healed much easier.

I broke into a jog and ran to the back of the

house. My mother shooed me inside and pointed to the cupboards for me to start setting the table. I knew the routine. I kissed her cheek and got to work.

My dad was one of those very Type A personalities. He had a precise schedule, and if it wasn't strictly adhered to, he lashed out. Sometimes he passive-aggressively took it out on my mom, using his monotone voice with barbed comments like she must not have had as much time to prepare dinner; the seasoning didn't taste right.

It typically rolled off her back and she went on with the evening as if nothing had happened. A few times, some of the blows landed and it threw her into a funk that lasted for days. I never quite figured out which comments were the ones that triggered that behavior, but it made me more careful with my actions when I knew he was already upset by something that happened during his day.

My dad was a criminal lawyer and good at what he did. That was why he bought this place that was secluded and hard to find. He didn't want the people he defended to locate him. That was his story anyway. The house was in my mom's name.

My mom was born in Italy and came to the United States to attend school. She, too, had studied law; that's how they'd met. My mom never finished her degree, though, because she married my dad and he wanted her to stay home and take care of the children. Yet there was only me.

When my dad brought up things around that fact, I knew those words cut my mom like a knife, and she either lashed out or slunk away like an injured dog. I hated seeing my mother like that. It was terrible to witness, and I was thankful those strikes didn't come often.

Once I finished setting the table, I wandered into the kitchen to see if there was anything left that my mom needed help with to complete dinner. I noticed she had a pot roast set on the counter with some carrots and potatoes around it, a basket of bread, and a bowl of salad.

My mom was filling a water pitcher with ice water and had the decanter of wine with glasses on a platter. I patiently waited for her to finish and carried that to the dining room. I sat it on the table out of the way of the food. I grabbed the plates, moved them to the table, arranged them the way my mom taught me, and went back for the rest.

My dad walked down then and glanced at the table, a slight frown on his face. It eased when my mother walked in with the bread basket and placed it on the table. My dad held the chair out for my mom, pushed it in as she sat, and then took his place. I didn't seat myself until after he was sitting.

Manners mattered to my dad. I wouldn't intentionally push his buttons, knowing he must have had a bad day at work. I kept my mouth shut and watched while he carved the meat and served himself, then my mother. He handed me the serving utensil for me to dish myself a plate.

We ate silently for ten minutes; the only sounds were chewing and swallowing. My dad poured himself and my mom glasses of wine, and they clinked glasses with polite nods. After he took a sip, and only then did the conversation start at his bidding.

"Stella, tell me about your day," he requested.

"There isn't much to tell. After Vincenzo's doctor's appointment, I changed the bed sheets, had a piano lesson with Vincenzo, and made dinner. Same thing." My mom shrugged and practically chugged down the rest of her wine.

"How was the appointment?" My dad looked between my mom and me.

"Same thing," I echoed my mom's words. "Nothing has changed."

I saw my dad's face pinch and steeled myself for some disparaging remark but nothing came. I had spotty memories of my childhood, all of those which I remembered included happy and more relaxed parents. My dad told me I'd sustained a head injury a couple of years ago. I remembered none of it, yet they had to have me checked frequently. For what, I wasn't sure.

"He is correct, Nicholas. The doctor repeated his words that sometimes the memories stay gone." She gave my dad a pointed look.

There was a battle taking place on his face between relief and disappointment. They never spoke to me about what happened other than saying I received a head injury. There are no scars on my face or head that I'd been able to find, so it made me wonder if it was really that serious. I wouldn't find out any time soon.

I wandered through the trees the next day. I stuck close to my tree but explored a little, looking for signs that maybe someone else had been here recently. I only saw evidence of game: The usual raccoons, squirrels, bunnies, deer, and the occasional coyote.

"I'm back like I promised I would be. Where are you?" I kept my voice low. "Do you need help with something? Is that why you keep calling me?"

I talked to her as if I knew she was a ghost and that was only a guess on my part. For all I knew, one of the bullies from my school could be out there taunting me. They were undoubtedly cruel enough to sink to that level. And honestly, I didn't know *what* was calling my name. Maybe it was a byproduct of whatever head injury I'd sustained.

I circled back toward my tree and spotted the mushrooms that seemed to always be in season. I never picked them or touched them on the chance they were dangerous. They were intriguing, though, with their vivid red color that never faded year-round.

I gave them a wide berth as I approached my tree and climbed up to my mossy spot. Today was clear with no mist. The sun wasn't setting, but the light filtered through the leaves from above. The weather was warm and humid. No cool sun rays to admire, yet I'd had the foresight to bring my sketchbook.

I pulled it out and fanned through the images of someone that kept appearing in my dreams. I didn't know who the girl was, though she was just a girl, perhaps my age, maybe a few years older. When it was hard for me to fall asleep at night, I would try to imagine who she was and why I dreamed about her. My favorite was that she was someone I was supposed to meet.

I found a blank page and began to sketch the forest from this viewpoint. I had several similar to this in the book, but I wanted to see if I could get the mist right; that was something I hadn't perfected yet.

I lost myself to the drawing to the point that everything faded away except the paper in front of me. I never noticed the fingers of fog that reached for me, wrapping their cool touch around my arm and helping guide my pencil. I'd never heard of psychography before, and I wasn't aware it was happening to me at this moment.

My mom used to dabble in art when she was a kid, or so she told me. When she saw my sketchbook for the first time, she said that she had talent and used to draw when she was young. She'd said she was happy that she passed that talent on to me. It was one of the few memories I'd retained.

Drawing relaxed me; it was only while I was out here on this tree that I would allow myself to entertain the thought of making a career out of it. My dad envisioned me having what he thought of as a prestigious career in law or medicine. My mom told me to follow my heart; she just wanted me to be happy doing whatever I chose.

I didn't know what I wanted to do with my future and I chose to live in the moment during the summer. I didn't care for the piano lessons, learning a new language, sailing, or perfecting my chess game. I didn't mind golf, but I preferred swimming.

I kept sketching, pleased with what I saw emerging on my paper. The sun filtering through the mist appeared in the shades of gray pencil lead. I smiled as my pencil flew over the page.

I stared intently and suddenly jolted as I realized a face had appeared through the mist. My eyes rose from the paper and I saw the same misty face in front of me; I didn't scream because I was scared. I yelped because it startled me. My sketch pad dropped to the ground and I lost my balance.

My heart froze in my chest as the branch below

me loomed in my vision. My stomach plowed into it, causing me to lose my breath. The ground rose up to catch me with a thud, and my elbow cracked down onto a rock with blinding pain.

"Enzo!" The haunting willowy voice reached me. It didn't stretch out this time, but it felt faint and like someone breathed on my cheeks.

The face in my drawing and the one that appeared in the mist in front of me. Why did I know that face? Who was she? Did I see the face in front of me only because I was drawing it that way?

I picked myself up off the ground and dusted off the leaves and other debris that stuck to me. My sketchbook landed far from me and I walked over to pick it up. It landed open to a drawing of the girl from my dreams, reaching out as if she wanted me to take her hand.

"Who are you?" I asked the sketch without picking the book up. "Is this you?" I pointed to the picture. "Are you trying to tell me something?"

I stood back up and bit back a groan at the stiffness of my body after smacking into the ground. I'd have bruises tomorrow, that was for sure. I stretched a bit to try and alleviate some of the pain. As my back cracked, the page of the book turned.

It was one of my more unsettling drawings featuring those mushrooms with a hand coming up from the ground below them clenched into a fist in the center of the mushroom ring. It felt like a spark zapped the back of my brain and my vision went hazy for a second.

"I don't understand. I need more than that." Yet the book remained still, opened to that page as if being held there by an invisible hand, which perhaps that was the case.

There were a lot of conclusions I could draw from that picture but they all would be nothing more than a guess. I rubbed the back of my head and focused on why my mind went fuzzy. Had I hit my head when I fell? I didn't feel any lumps back there.

"What is happening?" I muttered. I bent over to pick up my book and met resistance for a second and a half before it gave, and I rose with it.

I wanted to stay out there and explore what could happen, but my head began to ache fiercely and my body rivaled that pain. I needed to go home and take something, grab an ice pack, and lay down for a bit.

"I've gotta go. I'm feeling that fall."

I turned and stumbled, my equilibrium failing me. I never hit the ground, though. If I did, I don't remember it, and maybe there is something to be concerned about with my memory if that is true.

My eyes opened to see the sun dropping in the sky. Moss was under my head, and a dream's remnants clung to my mind. To anyone that might have chanced upon me, it would have looked like I made myself a cozy place to take an afternoon nap.

I snatched up my sketchbook and pencil in front of my face and pushed myself to a cross-legged position. I flipped to a blank page and let my pencil guide my hand connected to the loose threads that remained of my dream.

"Remember when," the girl's voice whispered in the air.

"I'm trying," I mumbled half-heartedly. "Give me a break."

My hand flew over the paper as the vision came to me. I was a kid on a fiberglass horse mounted on a carousel riding in a circle. I could practically hear the music. My head was looking up and I was laughing, holding one hand out to the girl from the other drawings. She reached for me in the same way with a broad smile.

That carousel was no longer working. It sat derelict in an old amusement park, a ghost itself. I had no memories of my time spent there, which wasn't surprising. If this picture was correct, I had been there at least once, and from all appearances, I knew the girl that filled my sketchbook.

I kept drawing the little details of the animals on the merry-go-round, presenting as they appeared in my dream—not new, but clean and well-loved. The girl's sundress was next, and the patterns on the fabric, a large floral design, came out. I didn't use a colored pencil, but the material was vibrant and cheery in my mind's eye.

Brown hair, a couple of shades lighter than my own, streamed out to the side, caught in the wind. The smile that graced her face reminded me of someone, though I couldn't place who. Her age could have been ten or somewhere in that area. I was probably about four or close to it.

"Is this you?" I looked up from the finished drawing. Of course, there was no answer. Nothing stirred at all. It was the same empty forest I entered every day.

I sighed heavily and turned to go home. The words 'remember when' echoed in my mind, still buzzing. Her voice had been so sad and pleading. It's possible I superimposed my own spin on it, but that's what it felt like when I heard it.

"I know I just took a nap, but I need another one,

and it's almost dinner time, so I need to go home." Not even the hint of a leaf rustling. Nothing tried to stop me either. "I'll try to be back tomorrow."

I sauntered through the forest heading home, my body aching. The sketchbook dangled still open to the carousel drawing, my finger hooked through a rung of the spiral binding, and my pencil tucked behind my ear.

It took me twice as long to reach the house as it typically did, and when I walked in through the mudroom into the kitchen, my mom shouted in surprise. Her hands flew to her mouth and she dropped the cup of water she'd been drinking.

Water splashed across my shoes and the bottom of my pants. It took me a moment to understand my mom's reaction to my appearance. I should have considered it when I was on my way home but it never crossed my mind.

"Enzo! What happened?" my mom whispered, running to me. Her hands yanked on my arms and twisted them around so I could see the bruising and dirt on their back. For sure I'd landed on rocks and roots.

"I fell, Mom. I'm fine." I set my sketchbook down on the kitchen table and allowed her to finish examining me. Once she was satisfied that I wasn't in grave danger or had anything broken, she frowned at me, saying nothing.

My mom walked back into the kitchen and cleaned up the spilled water. That was when I noticed that she wore fancy going-out clothes. Hopefully, it was something only my dad and she needed to attend, not me.

"You look nice, Mom," I tried. My response was a hefty sigh that told me she was agitated.

"Don't you remember? The charity event is tonight that your father insists we attend." She finished mopping up the water and carried the wet towels to the mud room, where she tossed them into the dirty linens bin.

"I don't remember, sorry. Is this something I am supposed to attend with you guys?" If it were, I would catch grief for not remembering and probably have to go to the doctor again for memory loss.

"Not this time. It's a cocktail party and not something for children," my mom told me, frowning again. "Did you hit your head?"

"No," I sighed. "I just fell. It happens to everyone at some point in their life." I knew my tone was exasperated and I didn't care.

"I'm your mom, Enzo. It's my job to worry about you." She angled her body toward the door as we heard my father's footsteps on the stairs.

I cringed because I knew there would be some sort of reaction from him. I should have escaped to clean up before he came down but there wasn't enough time. I dropped my eyes to the floor and saw the mess of twigs, weeds, and dirt that came off my clothes while my mom looked at me. He wouldn't be happy about that either.

"Vincenzo!" My father's shout made me jump. "What is the meaning of this?" His tone was pure rage.

I looked up to see his face red, his eyes wide and wild, and he pointed to the drawing on my sketchbook on the table. He never liked my hobby, but this was an over-the-top reaction. I hadn't expected the anger to be because of that.

"It's a drawing I drew while I was outside," I snapped back. I was tired of constantly defending myself.

"You know, pencil, paper, and talent make that happen."

"Stella! What do you have to say about this?" My dad yelled, the veins on his forehead popping out.

My mom paled and moved to look at the drawing, then took two steps backward, one hand over her heart and the other over her mouth. I didn't understand their reactions and bravely stepped closer to look at what they saw, even though I knew nothing was wrong with the picture.

"It's a merry-go-round," I muttered. "What's the big deal? I know that kid is me, so I've been on it at least once if this is something from my memory. I don't understand why you are acting this way."

My dad picked up the book and threw it across the room, the pages madly fluttering until it landed with a *thunk* on the floor. I resisted the urge to roll my eyes and went over to pick it up and close it, lest he saw any of the other drawings.

"You have better things to do with your time than this nonsense! You have a future to prepare for and skills to build." My dad was fuming, his hands shaking with the hot anger running through him.

"Nicholas, enough," my mom put her hand on his arm. I saw the tears pooled in her eyes and I wanted to scream at him, but it would be futile. "Enzo, go clean up. I ordered pizza delivery for your dinner along with some salad. We should be home before midnight. Please remember to set the alarm after we leave."

I nodded at my mom and left. I hated doing it, but I knew she would handle my dad in whatever way worked. I also knew it wouldn't happen if I remained in the room. I didn't know what it was about me that incited that behavior in my father. But it reinforced my decision to leave the house as soon as possible.

I entered my bedroom, stripped off my dirty clothes, and dropped them in the hamper in my bathroom before turning on the hot water in my shower. I let the steam well up a few minutes before I got in.

I stood under the rain shower head of my shower and let the hot water run over my sore back and arms. I remained in the same position for a minimum of ten minutes before washing myself clean. The shower had erased most of the aches in my body but it hadn't done much for the mood my dad's rant left me in.

I was bullied at home and in school because I acted older than most kids. The school counselor once asked if someone abused me at home, and I had to think hard about my response.

When it happened at home, in the moment, it felt like verbally abusive behavior. Yet when I was in school, sitting across from the counselor, it felt more like a strict parent and nothing more than an abrupt personality on my dad's part. He'd never physically abused me, and I did my best to explain that to him when confronted with the question.

If the counselor asked the same thing right now, I'd probably say yes, my dad abused me at home. Lately, the tirades had gotten worse. Not only at me but my mom, too. I was tired of it.

It felt like I was fourteen going on sixty, and that was exhausting. When would it ease, if ever? What caused it? Had I done something when I was younger that I don't remember that is why he acted this way? Did he not like me? I had more questions than I had answers.

I turned to wash my hair and jolted into the wall behind me. On the glass door were the words 'remember me.' My next move was to cover my junk because that meant some spirit was in the bathroom with me, which wasn't okay.

"A little privacy please," I grumbled. I didn't know which way to turn or if it even mattered at this point. "I don't know who you are or what you want but being in here with me while I shower seems a little on the perverted side of things. Please leave."

I didn't know how long to wait before I finished showering and got out, and I was now self-conscious. My face was burning with embarrassment. If nothing, this was proof that there was a ghost at play since I knew I didn't write that on the shower door. It was both exhilarating and creepy.

Somewhat thankful for the steam, I wrapped a towel around me as quickly as possible and rushed to my bedroom to pull clothes on and cover myself. Sweats were the easiest thing and I yanked them on, wincing at the movement of the sore muscles.

Once clothed, I towel-dried my hair, stuffed my feet into slippers, grabbed my sketchbook and some colored pencils, and went back downstairs with my face still burning red. I knew pizza deliveries took at least an hour since we were out of the way, but the store accommodated us since my mom tipped them well. I could have made myself something to eat, but I didn't argue with the pizza order. It was my mom's way of showing she felt guilty for leaving me alone to fend for myself.

I ensured the security camera was on and went to the living room, where I flipped the television on, kicked up my feet, and relaxed into the overstuffed sofa. It was my favorite piece of furniture in this house other than my bed.

I stretched out and brought my feet over to rest on the arm. The fabric was a suede that felt soft against my skin, and the stuffing was perfect. It was enough to cushion and support you but soft enough to sink into and let my body go slack. If clouds were solid, this is what I imagined sitting on one would feel like while floating around in the sky.

I plopped the book in front of me and opened my tin of colored pencils. As if the event at the carousel were yesterday, I began to color the image. The more the vision emerged, the more something tugged at my mind.

I used a vivid sea blue color on one of the horses when the sofa cushion in front of me dipped down. I paused; the pencil froze mid-air as I stared at the indentation. Then I felt my hair moving, similar to when my mom tousled my curls.

My instinct was to scream in a high-pitched voice and bolt to the other side of the room. I didn't need more confirmation that ghosts were real. The events earlier had me solidly convinced. I wanted to move, but I became immobilized with fear. I don't know why this scared me more than the incident in the tree, but it did.

"W-was that you in the bathroom?" I stammered nervously. I don't know where my bravado went but it wasn't present now. "You sh-should stay out of the b-bathroom."

I swore I could see the faintest shadow of a girl my age sitting on the couch. The moment I moved to reach out, the television went to a white screen of static. The sudden noise made me jolt and spill my pencils. It made me think of the ghost movie with the creepy old man and the kid that reached out and touched the screen and got sucked in.

My gaze was fastened on the television while I waited for some voice to speak when the channel suddenly flipped and a news story about the anniversary of an unsolved murder played out. Electric pain zapped inside my head and I briefly wondered if lightning had hit me, but I knew better.

I'd started to identify that pain as something that got triggered when a memory was fighting to free itself from the confines of my mind. It hurt too much to focus and in the distant buzzing of my ears, I recognized the sound of the security camera dinging, letting me know that someone had entered the property.

My heart was racing; the air was bone-chilling cold. I didn't remember the pizza. I didn't even know where to look, at the screen and the news story I was guessing was significant, or at the shadow of the person haunting me.

Only when the doorbell rang five times in succession did the hold on me break, and I fell off the couch, scrambled to my feet, and bolted out the door to the front of the house. I flung the door open like a madman and startled the pizza delivery guy.

"Whoa. It's just pizza, man. You okay?" the delivery guy asked me.

"Yeah, of course." I grabbed the box and bag he held out. "Thanks, I appreciate it." I rudely slammed the door closed and made my way to the kitchen.

I unceremoniously dropped the pizza box on the counter and opened the bag, pulling out the salad container. I dumped the dressing on it, put the lid back on, and shook the container to mix the dressing.

I shoveled the salad in my face as promised, then

dove into the pizza with my mind racing. I needed to find my laptop and research that news clip that played on the possessed television. The thought of viewing it left me feeling anxious and on the verge of a panic attack. That concerned me because I wasn't prone to those types of things.

I ate three pieces before my stomach was too full to continue. I grabbed a soda out of the fridge, downed it, and raced to my bedroom to grab my computer. I didn't know why I was in such a hurry. Maybe my body was reacting to the adrenaline of the events that brought me to this point.

I rushed into my bedroom, pushing the door harder than I intended. It banged into the wall and bounced back to hit me in the arm because I never made it farther than the doorway. My feet grew roots and planted me to the floor.

Three mushrooms from under the tree were on top of my bed. The color was absolutely vivid against the gray of my comforter and looked like spilled blood except in the form of a mushroom.

I knew I hadn't brought those back with me. I never touched the mushrooms. Ever. Something about them felt foreboding, repellent. My mind reached warp speed as I tried to figure out a way to get them off my bed without my skin coming into contact with them. I wasn't even comfortable having them on my bed, touching my blanket.

Why were they even here? Who put them there and when? What did they mean? I had so many questions about everything and no answers to anything. That was the thought that made my feet move. I crossed the room without looking over at the bed, snatched my computer off my desk and left.

There was the possibility that watching the news story would leave me with nothing more than more questions, but there was always the chance that it would provide answers to some of the mysteries collecting in my head. I kept feeling like I was missing something obvious.

I didn't return to the television room. Instead, I went to the kitchen and sat at the table. After turning the computer on, I started an internet search for the anniversary of the missing teen girl in my city. Several stories came up with a variety of teenage females that disappeared in a short span of time. However, I had yet to stumble across the one that popped up on the television.

I clicked furiously through story after story, reading horrible details on murders, speculation, the other side of the forest in my backyard, and unsolved cases. Was the girl I drew one of these girls? It would make sense that she kept trying to reach out. Maybe she wanted her story told or for someone to remember her.

A chill rolled down my spine from the top of my head and settled in my lower back. The sensation of icy fingers reached around my sides and inched its way over my arms to my fingertips. I could practically see my breath puffing out; the air was so frigid. I'd seen enough ghost shows to know that people said this signified that a spirit was around you.

It also struck me that this spirit must have intense energy to do what she is doing. Moving mushrooms, manipulating the television, touching my hair, making her voice heard. I'm positive I missed something because so much happened on this day alone.

Where Realms Collide

My eyes widened as my computer screen scrolled by itself until a link I'd missed sat in front of my eyes. I waited for the ghost to move my hand but nothing happened. I moved so cautiously that it took forever for my mouse to hover over that link.

My mouth dried, my heart raced, and my eyes wouldn't blink until I clicked it. Then they began to blink rapidly as the clip loaded. I watched that little circle spin round and round as the news story spooled. Little steams of air puffed out in front of my open mouth, hanging there in anticipation of whatever was going to appear on the screen.

The reel loaded and the first thing that appeared was my parents. The screen froze on their ravaged faces. My dad's eyes looked wild and dangerous; behind them was our home. Everything looked the same as it did now, giving me no real timeframe for when this was other than the headline saying two-year anniversary.

I didn't know if it was two years before today or if this was an old clip and the two-year anniversary had passed years and years ago. I tried looking for a date on the frozen screen but had no luck with it still locked. Something told me it had been longer than two years but I can't say what.

Suddenly, the news clip began to play loudly, the picture now of the reporter standing outside our gate in the dark. *It must be the original story,* I thought to myself.

"Tragedy has struck again as another fourteen-year-old girl has gone missing. Jadaea Heatherton was last seen in the woods behind her house with her younger brother. Her sibling has returned home, but Jadaea has not. This disappearance marks the fourteenth female teenager missing from this area this year. Sadly, police

recovered two bodies and the rest remain unfound. Please call the sheriff's office immediately if you see this young lady."

A picture of the girl flashed on the screen and my heart stopped. It was her. The girl in my sketchbook that I kept drawing. The face that I had seen in the mist.

It sounds so familiar. Jadaea, I thought in my head. I looked back at the screen as the clip changed to reporters sitting in the news studio behind a desk.

"No new information has come to light since this tragedy happened. There are still twelve missing girls out there with families waiting for any information about what happened to their loved ones."

The screen changed and I saw my parents again, grief-stricken faces looking shell-shocked. My dad spoke to the camera.

"Please bring my baby home. Whoever you are, she belongs with her family."

I jolted again. Hot fiery pain zapped through my head and it felt like the ground was falling out from underneath me. The air grew even colder, yet my body had broken out in a sweat. My stomach heaved and I shot to my feet, knocking my chair over behind me.

"Jadaea," I whispered out loud. "Is that your name? Are you my family?"

I looked back at the screen, no longer hearing the words. It felt like an angry bear was trying to claw its way out of my brain. The pain was excruciating and my knees shook like crazy.

"We must put this dark matter to rest once and for all. Justice needs serving to these families. Please, we beg you, if you have seen anything, heard anything, or know anything, call the tip line. I will personally offer a reward."

My dad's voice cut through the pain.

A buzzing sound in my ears kept getting louder until my dad's voice on the computer became distant. His incorrect use of dark matter struck me, though I supposed he meant it differently than the scientific term. Blackness was closing in on my vision, shrinking it until it was nothing more than a pinprick of light. Then nothing.

I came to with the words, "It's not a fairy ring." on my lips. I opened my eyes to see a mushroom in front of my face. That broke me out of whatever trance I had fallen into or passed out from is more likely. I pushed to my feet and backed away from the mushroom. I promptly stumbled over my chair that had tipped over.

Something was happening to me. My mind felt watery and hazy but I remembered things. I remembered the carousel. My mom was outside the fence, clapping her hands for us while we giggled. The girl must be Jadaea. Was she my sister?

"Is that it? Jadaea, are you my sister?" I whispered in horror. "What the hell happened that I would forget who you are?"

A memory of a birthday party surfaced where my dad was happy and smiling. He tossed me in the air and seemed actually to like me. He wasn't the same man he was now. He was relaxed and his eyes crinkled with laughter. They weren't hard, distant, and cold like they were now.

A family trip to Disneyland popped into my head. The memories of my childhood were hitting hard and fast now. It was staggering and they felt heavy as all those gaps in my mind began to fill. It wouldn't be so bad if it didn't hurt so much.

My stomach rolled, pushing me into action. I ran for the bathroom, dropped to my knees and relieved my stomach of any food that I hadn't digested yet. It was rapid and violent and when I finished, I rolled to the side and lay on the cool floor for a few minutes while my mind raced and tried to sort through the years of memories assaulting me.

It was too much for my body to handle and as I rose from the floor, I pulled myself over to the sink and ran some water in my hands, splashing it on my face and rinsing my mouth. I glanced at the mirror and my pale face stared back at me.

My milk chocolate brown, curly hair looked limp and lifeless, my eyes sunken in like I turned into a skeleton, and my face gaunt and startlingly like the color of the stems of those mushrooms that kept appearing. A sickly gray color that made me think of dissected brains. It wasn't my best look.

To make matters worse, I was still hungry but terrified to eat now. I slowly walked back to the kitchen, righted my chair, and closed my computer without looking at the screen again. Sooner or later, the memory of what happened would surface. I didn't want to force it due to my pounding headache.

I grabbed another soda from the fridge and sipped it as I sat back down. I didn't need the spirit to confirm anything for me. Jadaea was my sister, and she went missing. The memories of the birthday parties told me we had the same birthday five years apart. That meant that when she disappeared, I was nine years old.

I was now her age and that news story was three years old today. Today is the day she went missing. Or that something had happened. The news story said that I was in the backyard with her. I didn't fully understand why I didn't remember it happening.

I grabbed my sketchbook and flipped through the images I'd drawn. I could now place each image in a returned memory, except the unsettling ones. I tapped on one with the hands coming up from below the mushrooms.

"These odd drawings.... You were trying to tell me something, weren't you?" I spoke aloud as though the ghost of Jadaea could hear me and answer.

I closed the book and stared at the wall for a bit. A part of my mind was trying to reconcile the father I saw in my memories to the one I had now. They were polar opposites. In my memories, my dad seemed to like being around me. In fact, he'd been laughing and playing with me in several of them and holding me. I wasn't sure he even liked being in the same room with me now.

Was that all because of the disappearance of my sister? Did us having the same birthdays drive the point home that she wasn't here and I was? Did he wish it was me instead? Was that why he was so concerned with my memory? Did he think I had answers to everything locked up inside my head? Should I confront them about all of this?

Speculation ran rampant in my head and my insecurities began to take over. I wasn't some traumatized kid, or at least until now I didn't think I was, but I did have moments of self-doubt or loathing. It wasn't because of the other kids at school either. It was more that I felt different from other people and in my eyes, it made me stand out, which was uncomfortable as I didn't like being in the spotlight.

Feeling restless and frustrated, I paced the

kitchen. After a few minutes, I decided to look on social media to see if my sister had a presence there. I knew my parents didn't want me to have an account yet, but it might have been different for Jadaea. It was a starting point and that was good enough for me.

I opened my computer again and, in the search bar, typed in Jadaea Heatherton. I wasn't quite prepared for the barrage of images that popped up. One of the photos was the same as the one shown in the news story. The rest were of her with various friends. I didn't see a social media account for Jadaea but her friends had them.

I had stumbled on a treasure trove. I spent a few hours looking at the photos and posts that went with them to learn as much about my sister as possible. She spent a lot of time outside in the woods in his tree. Our tree, I suppose, since she's probably the one who put moss on that branch.

With everything I read, Jadaea was a happy and adventurous girl. Her friends liked her well, always had positive things to say, and she never stopped smiling. Her hair was a few shades lighter than mine, but the way the sun caught it made it look gold woven throughout the strands. Our eyes were identical, though, and so were the curls in our hair.

I stared at each picture for several minutes, memorizing her face. On some level, it felt creepy but I was only looking for the resemblance to feel closer to a sister I can't remember. I felt like I owed her.

When I finally closed the computer, my knowledge of Jadaea included her favorite color, red, that she loved dogs, volunteered to help clean parks in the summer, and had a very generous heart. A couple of her friends mentioned her trusting nature and willingness to help strangers.

"Did you run away, or did something more sinister happen to you, Jadaea?" I wondered aloud. I think the only thing anyone ever assumed was that someone abducted her, or worse.

Seconds after my question, the air became thick and palpable like a building electrical storm about to unleash violence on the earth. Then a distant scream reached my ears, barely louder than the whispers of my name in the woods, though it made my blood curdle as if it had been at window shaking volume.

"I'm sorry," I apologized once I got my voice back. "I didn't mean to imply you did anything to cause your disappearance. I'm just thinking out loud." I kept my voice as sincere as possible as I genuinely meant what I said.

The air went from thick to icy back to normal. I could only assume that meant Jadaea had left. Watching ghost shows on television didn't quite prepare you for the real thing happening to you where you lived. Unsettled and unnerved, I got up and paced again.

Seeing the news story jarred my memories, but I'd been in the woods countless times since her disappearance and nothing had come back to me. I needed to remember what happened to me in those woods that night. I didn't know how to make that happen.

I glanced at the microwave and saw that it was barely eight o'clock. I had time to go back out there and see if anything sparked. I'd never been there at night as far as I knew. It wasn't dark yet, but it would be soon. I figured I'd need a flashlight and something to protect myself with should I run into trouble.

I ran back to my bedroom and grabbed a pocket knife someone had given me. Back to the kitchen, I went to grab a flashlight from the pantry where we kept emergency supplies for a power outage. Armed with both, I headed out the back door.

I thought more than a few times that it might not be such a great idea to be out here at night in the dark. This place *was* where my sister went missing and others, according to the articles I'd read. Perhaps someone evil dwelled in that forest like in fairy tales.

The mushrooms were a fairy ring, my mom had said. I couldn't outright dismiss that idea since they appeared in the house by themselves. However, I attributed it to Jadaea trying to tell me something I needed to remember instead of being moved by mischievous fairies. That made the most sense to me.

Today was the anniversary of the disappearance five years ago. Was there something magic in the number five? I shrugged to myself as I trudged through the grass to the forest. I can't say that I knew anything about numerology or magic. I was still only throwing ideas out to see if anything stuck.

As I approached the forest, an eerie chill settled over me. Possibly a reaction due to an overactive imagination though I couldn't discount paranormal reasons either. Not after everything that happened today.

I stepped into the forest and felt like I was on another planet. The air was still and utterly silent, with no insect noise or animals, only the sound of my breathing. It was unnatural and the hair on the back of my neck rose, making me want to flee.

I kept inching my way forward to my tree with my eyes wide open. Subtle differences started to catch my attention and I stopped. Bushes my height were suddenly shorter, trees not as tall or big around.

It took a moment for the scene to process in my mind and settle. I thought about it carefully and admitted that the entire thing dumbfounded me. It wasn't possible, yet I was standing here witnessing it, and I wasn't asleep.

"Have I gone back in time?" I whispered. "Is this confirmation that magic is real?"

I pinched myself to make sure I wasn't sleeping. Nothing changed. I was still standing in the woods at twilight, holding my flashlight and pocket knife. I didn't even think of bringing my cell phone. Not the brightest move on my part. No one knew I was here.

A few more steps in and I almost lost my nerve. I received the first glimpse of my tree, and I was on it. Only it was a much younger me. The moss on the limb was still bright green and spongy looking and there Jadaea was, sitting with me.

I didn't know how this was possible. I didn't understand enough about ghost abilities to say that it was something that could happen. Maybe it was magic. Or perhaps Jadaea's spirit was strong enough to show me my memories.

Jadaea and the younger me sat there on that limb and played with some pinecones she made into a little animal family. She spoke to me in a soft voice that was barely discernible. Yet she displayed nothing but patience and love on her face, even when I questioned what she did and why.

We sat contented until the light began to fade and Jadaea had to coax me into agreeing to return to the house. She hung from the limb, gracefully dropped down to the next and hit the ground with the ease of a gymnast.

My exit was a bit more clumsy but when I was one limb away, Jadaea held her hand up to me in a silent order to stop. Her head swiveled around to look behind her, then she slowly turned her body, her hand falling back to her side.

Don't move. I could see her mouth the words to me.

Neither version of me saw or heard what made her stop me or caught her attention. Both versions searched too. I was hyper-aware of everything as I stood there and observed my past self and sister. I knew another reason existed that I was witnessing this other than restoring my memory. I committed everything I viewed to memory, determined to remember every little detail as if I were taking a photograph of everything with my mind.

Everything slowed as if I were watching a movie screen in slow motion. Jadaea's hair fanned out behind her as she whirled to face the dark figure approaching. She stood in front of the terrified nine-year-old me, protecting me. I stared hard, waiting for the figure's face to appear from the mist shrouding it.

It seemed exaggeratingly slow that a black boot, combat style, came into view. The second boot quickly followed with black cargo pants tucked into the top. A slim man appeared wearing a black shirt tucked tightly into his cargo pants and a black hat on his head with a brim that covered his face.

I scrutinized every line, mark, shape, and color of that face as I watched him approach my sister. I listened as he taunted, saying awful things about my dad and what he would do to my mom and sister. It was hard to hear the threats as a fourteen-year-old; I can't imagine how my nine-year-old brain had reacted.

The man lunged for my sister, who leaped off to the side and caught a limb. She swung her legs up but her hair hung down, and he grabbed a handful of it, yanking her back. I yelled stop, scared, which distracted the man from my sister for a moment. He spotted me in the tree and menacingly stepped closer.

"Run!" Jadaea screamed. "Get out of here!"

I didn't get a chance. The man forcefully shoved me out of the tree with one hand and a firm grip on my ankle with the other hand, and I watched as my little nine-year-old self fell to the ground face first, my forehead smacking a rock. Blood blossomed and pooled under me as my sister screamed frantically.

The man ignored me after that, either assuming I was dead or unconscious. He went after my sister with vigor and she put up a fight. It was a terrible scene; he punched and beat her senseless, but still, she tried to fight him to get to me.

I sobbed and the horrific sight of her broken body that he dropped next to me. He kicked her limp form, kicked mine, then reached down and broke her neck. There wasn't anything I could do to save her or stop it. I screamed like a banshee... the fourteen-year-old me.

The nine-year-old me woke up, saw Jadaea and tried to wake her. I knew I didn't understand death then. What nine year old does? I watched as I dug a hole at the base of the tree and understood then that I was making a grave. Maybe I did know that she was dead. But as I watched, I never finished digging the hole. The man was coming back.

Instead, that younger version of me took her shoes and buried them in the exact spot where the mushroom ring now existed. Then he ran for home with tears streaming down his bloody face.

The vision blinked out and I stood in the dark woods in front of the fairy ring. I'd seen what I needed to see so I turned to go back home, picking my way carefully over the roots and stones. I felt tempted to dig for the shoes, but I didn't.

I don't know how long I'd been at it, but the moment I got home, I began to draw everything I witnessed. I drew each detail that ingrained itself into my memory. I cried as the pencil flew over the paper giving life to the vision gifted to me by my sister.

I was still at it when my parents got home. My mother's gasps and father's shouts didn't stop me as they looked at the fanned-out images across the kitchen table. When my father came to the sketch of the man's face, an outraged scream tore from his soul and he swept everything off the table.

He grabbed the pencil from my hand and snapped it in half, yelling at me as if I were crazy. How could I relay that Jadaea gave me the visions? How could I make them believe what I'd been through? That Jadaea visited me and spoke to me? The answer was I couldn't.

All I could do was tell them that my memory had come back. Drawing the visions was the only way I could show them what happened and give them the answers they sought to my sister's disappearance.

I think it broke my mom and set something free inside my father. Seeing all those images released the caged monster that hid deep in his heart after losing his daughter. His face twisted with rage, his lips pressed thin. He photographed the face of the man in a dangerous calm, then stormed out of the house.

We don't know what happened after that, and unless he tells us, I don't think we ever will. Sometime in the middle of the night, we received a courtesy call from one of the cops my dad kept in contact with over my sister's case. He let us know that my dad had gotten arrested on murder charges. In the following sentence, he told us that the man who killed my sister was dead; not a hard leap to make for the motive. He'd been the brother of a client that my father hadn't been able to get off death row due to the overwhelming evidence against him. It didn't explain all the other victims, but it told us why my sister was one of them.

When the sun came up, I went back out to the tree and waited for some sign that Jadaea was at rest or still hung around here. My mom wanted me out of the house while police interviewed her about my dad and showed them the pictures I drew.

I knew there would come the point where they would have to talk to me and I'd have to say what I witnessed and make it believable considering the head injury I'd sustained from the man. It wasn't like I could tell them a ghost showed me. However, I could give the truth that she was protecting me.

I sat on my limb and looked down at the mushroom ring. "They grew from our blood, didn't they, Jadaea?" I quietly asked. "That's where they get their color from, isn't it?"

"Enzo," Jadaea's voice floated through the leaves like a lost echo. This time she didn't say it with sadness. I considered it progress.

A year after my dad's arrest, cops again showed up at the house to tell my mom that police had retrieved bones from one of the murderer's properties during their continuing investigation. Bones of several victims were all in a pile and it would take time for them to differentiate the victims and get the loved ones' remains back to their families. They suspected my sister's remains were in that pile.

I wanted to bury Jadaea with her shoes under our tree. I knew my mom wouldn't go for it, so I didn't bring it up. I held her hand while she cried, then accompanied her to visit my father in prison to share the news.

Someday, I hoped he could learn to love me again if he ever got out. I felt he blamed me for Jadaea's death because I showed him how it happened through those pictures. I knew his harsh treatment of me was due to my sister's disappearance and his love for her. I didn't begrudge him.

Maybe the finding of her bones would help ease the burden from his shoulders. I didn't know. It's taken me a year to adjust to the loss that happened six years ago. I gained and lost a sister in a single day, and that was something that left a lasting impact. Having her bones returned felt like closure.

Jadaea still talked to me in those odd ways. I didn't know if that meant she still wasn't at peace and ready to rest or not. I knew now that she died protecting me, and it was a hard pill to swallow but also made me grateful that my sister loved me that much. Maybe today, she'd finally talk to my dad again; I wondered if that was the missing piece. I wanted them both to find peace after the tragedy. Jadaea deserved to rest and my mom needed to move forward with her life.

Unfinished business kept her and my dad rooted in grief. As we checked into the prison as visitors and my mom pulled her purse open to hand over her ID, I saw one of those blood mushrooms lying on top of her wallet. A stain of red against the dark black interior. Was it prophetic?

Rumors

Present Day

arlow, we're ready for you," a nurse called my name and watched as I awkwardly tried to get to my feet.

"Coming," I muttered lamely. I tried to get the crutches balanced under me correctly, but my center mass was off and I was a world-class klutz to the nth degree. Would it surprise anyone if I fell on my face? Probably not. Only I wouldn't land face first. I'd land belly first because I was six months pregnant with the universe's biggest baby growing inside me. I'm allowed to exaggerate.

Pregnant, on crutches, single, clumsy—one would think someone would help. Alas, it was not to be; they all wanted to see the circus act of a ballooned-up woman pretending to be an elephant walking a tightrope. Who was I to disappoint my audience?

I took one wobbly step with the crutch, my right knee buckled and my left shoulder decided to join the party. That was when the handsome man sitting quietly in the corner, keeping to himself, decided to look up and witness the spectacle I made.

"Perhaps we should get the wheelchair for you,"

the nurse, Mandie, piped up.

"Perhaps you should have thought of that before you opened the door and called her." The man helped me up, stabilizing me against his body, and shot a withering look at the not-so-bright nurse. "It's obvious to anyone that she's struggling with mobility."

At this juncture of my life, it would be a safe assumption to make that the situation I found myself in was embarrassing. Safe but wrong. I was the single source of entertainment for those that knew me. My life was a comedy of errors that played out in the most inopportune times with multiple sets of eyes watching.

"Thank you," I softly told the man holding me. I did everything possible to avoid looking him in the eye so he wouldn't see my reddening face. Mandie needed to hurry up with that wheelchair because, at any moment, I was going to pee myself.

Not to mention there was chemistry between this man and myself. It could be wishful thinking since I was single and my hormones were out in the stratosphere of wanting every sexual experience I could think of being involved in. My skin warmed and tingled where he touched me and he smelled amazing.

If he moved his hand one inch up, he'd be holding my engorged breast. I could think of worse places to be while I waited. I even contemplated shifting so his hand would go where I wanted it to and his fingers would found a stiff nipple. I was depraved.

Mandie came out pushing the wheelchair at her usual slow pace. She brought it around behind me, and I swore I didn't do it on purpose, but in my shift to plant my derriere in the seat, his hands ended up on both of my breasts with erect nipples pressing into his palms through the flimsy tanktop stretched over my belly.

As if that weren't enough to turn me cherry tomato red, I farted on the way down. Pregnancy wasn't for the faint-hearted. I couldn't even blame it on the seat making noise since I hadn't made contact yet.

"Oh!" Mandie exclaimed. "Experiencing some gas, are we?"

Okay, so it could get worse. The sporadic heartburn from hell caused by nothing other than growing a baby reared its head. There was nothing I could say to ease the embarrassment I was experiencing. I opened my mouth to apologize and belched.

The man hid a grin, bent over, and patted my leg as I finally sat. "I hope your day gets better." He dropped a card in my lap, offered to wheel me back to the room, and carried my crutches with him.

I mumbled another thank you as he left and looked at the card. "Sage Wilder," I said out loud. "Adventure Planner?" I read the words under his name.

I didn't know what an adventure planner did but my best guess was that it was what it stated exactly. Did Sage think I needed an adventure? *I* was an adventure all on my own.

I sat there and let Mandie take all my vital signs. She left without another word, and I patiently waited for the doctor to come in and check on my knee.

Maybe I should explain how I got to this point.

Three Months Earlier

I rushed around getting the office cleaned up, so when I logged in to do my online meeting with upper management and our client, they didn't see a messy room. I often felt like the youngest person in the company I worked for, yet I knew I wasn't. Maybe it seemed that way because I was the youngest in my position, which made me feel like the spotlight was constantly on me, which was stressful.

The company was prestigious, founded by a man wanting to make a life for his family, and ended up hiring most of his relatives and becoming the most successful design firm in the state. What made them stand out was that they included a marketing plan with their designs to help draw customers in and make the client's businesses prosper. It was a unique twist that I enjoyed.

Apparently, I had a flair for marketing, though my schooling and training were in design. That was why management had promoted me several times since hiring me five years ago. Senior management listened to me, asked my advice, and put me on as many projects as humanly possible.

I had a casual relationship with one of the other designers, which for our company, was strictly forbidden. They did not believe in mixing business with pleasure and they actively worked to keep the workplace drama free. I understood it but didn't follow the rules.

Work was the only place I had time to meet someone. They had me working on so many projects and I put in overtime daily; work was my social life. I did make it a point to keep things on the casual level and so far, it worked. Xander was my third of these relationships and the one that had lasted the longest.

Some days I felt like we could take it to a more serious level though I hadn't managed to figure out how to do that and not lose our jobs. Xander wasn't as invested in his job as I was. I loved my job, yet I was intelligent enough to know it wasn't my passion. I didn't know what was. I continued to throw myself into my career and would spend time later working on what made my blood sing.

Given my position and the trust of upper management, I worked most of the time remotely and went into the office for meetings. However, this time, the client was out of state and requested an online meeting with the company and the team I'd put together to go over the design scheme I'd worked up. It was imperative that I only showed my office and that it was clean and presentable.

It was a huge project. I was a risk taker by nature, albeit calculated risks, though the client was a family friend of the owners of the company I worked for and this needed to go off without a hitch. The client owned a timeshare building that had seen better days yet was an ideal location for people who needed a break from life. It had a historical city, perfect for tourists, complete with a coastline and an Olympic-sized pool on the property with plenty of activities for the adrenaline junkies.

These clients didn't need to see an exercise ball that had been the scene of many nights of sexual workouts. Not that they'd know what I used it for, but I didn't need to turn beet red thinking they did and then have to explain myself. I stuffed the ball into the closet, kicked some fun toys I'd used while on the ball and slammed the door. Those toys wouldn't need an explanation. Xander was game to try any whim that struck me when I felt creative and pent up with energy.

Satisfied that the space was clean, I got the presentations loaded up and ready to present. I checked the line of sight for my camera and decided I didn't really care if the bathroom showed; it was clean too. Down the hall was the rest of the house; while it wasn't a potential client meeting clean, it wasn't dirty.

I checked my watch and ran to the bedroom to change into the dress I had laid out, smoothed my hair and decided it was time. I heard Xander making noise from the living room, where he'd set up for the meeting in a corner where no one would know he was in my house. He didn't usually stay the night. I'd needed a tension reliever last night and he came over at the last minute. We'd fallen asleep on the office floor, hence the need to clean up.

I've been more tired than usual lately and had days that I simply didn't feel well and yesterday was one of them. By the time evening had arrived, I was in the mood for some extracurricular activity of the adult sort and I'd forgotten to take my monthly pregnancy test.

I did them out of habit because I was an active woman and didn't have time for pregnancy. Plus, I made sure all my partners wore condoms and I was on the pill. No doubt, during this call, I'd be able to run and pee on the stick while the big wigs talked. I wasn't in the spotlight for the whole meeting and wanted to do it while Xander wouldn't notice.

I settled into my desk chair and logged into the meeting. I was the first and since I created the room, I had control of it. I loaded my presentations, set the camera to look straight at me, so it didn't pick up too much of the background, muted my microphone, and patiently waited for the rest to join.

One of the admins was the first, his name was Chris and I didn't know him too well. Mikala quickly followed him, who was another admin. Her, I knew. She didn't have a stellar relationship track record or show up to work on time. I didn't know how she still had a job.

I unmuted my microphone and greeted them both by name and gave a friendly smile and wave. Xander logged in next and I was happy to see that all you could spot behind him was a white wall. That could be anywhere. I smiled and waved, receiving a cool, detached response in return.

I shrugged it off and focused on the managers popping up on my screen in rapid succession. The clients came on, and then lastly, one of the workers for the client, though his camera wasn't working.

"Welcome, everyone," I chirped. "I'm excited to be presenting to you today. Any questions or concerns before we get started?"

At the slow shaking of the heads, I launched into the campaign. There were about forty people logged in on the online meeting and it flowed smoothly. I ceded the microphone for my teammates to explain their ideas. I was elated.

I had four people that needed to speak before I retook the floor, so it was a perfect time for me to go pee since Xander was one of the people talking next and he wouldn't be paying attention to me. I clicked mute on my microphone and snuck away across the hall to the bathroom.

I nudged the door closed and grabbed the test out of the drawer. I was so used to doing these that I went on autopilot. I finished and opened the door to hear where the meeting was while I waited for the negative sign to pop up. The wall blocked me from sight unless I stepped into the doorway, so I wasn't worried.

I turned in front of the mirror and looked at my

side profile. My chest looked larger and I wondered if I had gained weight. I wasn't overweight but I also didn't want to buy new clothes. My dress fit tighter than last time and I vowed to eat better.

I paused my self-examination when I heard Xander talking and let out a little sigh. There was still one more person before I had to speak again. I pulled my dress up, tucked it under my bar, and looked at my chest and how my bra fit. It was an old one; I could probably do with a new bra.

I heard a cough and then the talking continued. I glanced down at the counter where I'd set the test and did a double take. I rubbed my eyes and took a step backward. I tripped over the bathroom rug, fell right into the wall and bounced against the door, my dress still up above my waist.

"What the hell?" I screeched and pulled myself up, the meeting forgotten. "Pregnant! That's not possible! I'm on the fucking pill and he uses condoms!"

I snatched the test off the counter and shook it like that would change the results. I treated it like an Etch-A-Sketch, hoping that line on the plus sign would just fall away to nothing and life would go back to normal.

"This is wrong! I need to take another test! I can't be pregnant!" I chucked the offending piece of plastic bearing terrible news into the trash can.

"Pregnant?" Xander's shocked question jarred me out of my stupor.

At that moment, I realized the meeting was still happening and I was standing in the hallway with my dress bunched up under my breasts and trying to pull my underwear off so I could pee on the stick again. I was in the direct line of sight on my camera.

"Uh, Harlow, your microphone isn't muted," Chris's voice came from my office.

It's like my feet had a mind of their own as they propelled me into my office, still showing a nearly naked lower half while I bent over and hit mute to eighty eyes staring directly at me with mouths hanging open. I assumed eighty since the black screen of the mystery man didn't show his face—but come on, he *had* to be looking.

Red hot flames of embarrassment licked at my face, and I saw myself turn an awful shade of crimson in my reflection on the computer screen. It practically matched my bra and underwear and the red plus sign on the pregnancy test that Xander now held in his hand behind me.

That was the action that brought me crashing back into myself. My hand unclenched and my dress fell back into place as my head swiveled between the computer screen and an indignant Xander. I was an island in the middle of a giant chasm with a white water river madly flowing around me.

"Are you trying to trap me or something?" Xander snapped, waving the test. "Why even take it now while I'm here?"

"Hi," Chris spoke again, the one voice among the stunned faces of the rest brave enough to speak out. "I think your wireless mouse might have a dead battery because your microphone is still on. Oh, and by the way, Xander, I don't want to go out with you anymore. Don't ask me again."

My utter humiliation didn't convert any shocked faces to my side or recruit sympathy among my coworkers. I suppose that I saw more than a few with the same flames of embarrassment flickering across their faces, or it could be anger. Mikala looked like lava.

"Pregnant?" Mikala spat, the second voice to break the silence. "I've spent the last six months doling out blow jobs like I was handing out Halloween candy just for you to knock up some other bitch? That's not how this works, Xander. Oh, and invest in a Sex for Dummies book, you lame fuck."

My jaw dropped once more and I spun to face Xander, who looked like he had swallowed a bucket of rusty nails. It took everything I had in me not to kick him in his inseminating nuts.

"You've ruined my life with your little game," Xander screamed and threw the test at me. "And balance balls aren't for sex with handcuffs. You and your fetishes are weird." He stomped out of the office and seconds later, I heard the front door slam shut.

I slowly turned back to the screen, dreading the expressions I knew would be there. To my surprise, Mikala and Chris were both gone. Unfortunately, all the rest were still there except Xander. I plopped down in my chair.

"I'm so sorry for everything," I began with an apology. I knew there would be fallout. There was no way there wouldn't be after that show.

"My office tomorrow morning," the owner stated and logged off. It was my publicly declared death sentence. Everyone followed suit and I was thankful for the silence and no one looking at me. I needed a nap and to call my doctor.

When I arrived at the office, I had all my arguments cued

up in my head. I was going to plead my case and beg forgiveness in the same breath. Yet when I walked into the office, the sudden silence caused all words to flee my mind. Then the round of whispering and everyone suddenly typing instant messages to each other filled my ears.

The rumors were rampant, I was sure. How could they not be after that? I had hoped that someone would take pity on me and try to quash them, but there was no hope of that when not one person would meet my eyes. Yet they all looked at the dead woman walking. I could feel their stares boring a hole through me with the fire of whatever concocted rumors they spread.

I kept my head held high and walked to the owner's office. I couldn't help but notice that Mikala's desk was empty. It gave me a slight sense of satisfaction. I stopped outside the vacant admin desk for the owner and waited.

Chris walked out a few minutes later, looking pale and nervous. He gave me a tremulous smile as he sat down. "A balance ball?" he snickered. "Please give me details on how to perform that way."

A wildfire blossomed across my face. I had no idea how to respond, considering I didn't know Chris well enough to discuss this topic. Thankfully I was saved by the clearing throat of the owner.

"Harlow, please come in." Mr. Smithers held the door open for me.

I scooted past him and stood in place until he closed the door and sat behind his desk. Only then did I take a seat in front of him and primly cross my legs and fold my hands over my knee. I kept my face blank while he stared at me in disappointment. It made me feel like a child getting scolded by a disapproving grandparent who'd caught me with my hand in the candy dish before dinner.

Mr. Smithers drummed his fingers on the desk and sighed. He hadn't blinked yet, and I wondered if the man was human. His eyes must be burning something fierce. What was I even thinking? I needed to be on my best behavior and focus on why he shouldn't fire me. Especially considering I was now pregnant.

"This behavior is not something I expected of you," Mr. Smithers finally said.

"Sir, it's not typical for me either. I stepped away to use the restroom, knowing that I had time before I had to speak again. The, uh, test is one of the things I do monthly as a precaution. I know you don't need to know that; I am only trying to explain," I rambled in a staccato tone.

"What you do on your personal time is your business," Mr. Smithers sat up straight. "Mikala and Xander no longer work here, and Chris is on probation. I would probably let this go if it weren't for our audience during that meeting. Due to the circumstances, I don't think I can be lenient. Rules are in place for this exact reason. For what it's worth, I'm sorry. Xander's behavior was abhorrent. No one should treat others that way. Given the situation, I have advised our benefits department to extend your healthcare for three months. After that, you will have the COBRA option to continue coverage. Truly, I am sorry to see you go. You were an asset to this company. Unfortunately, if I make an exception for you, it sets the tone that others will have the opportunity to follow the same path without consequences."

"I understand," I nodded. "I'm grateful for the concessions you made."

"Thank you for understanding." Mr. Smithers slid some papers across his desk to me. "I'll need you to sign the termination paper. I am giving you full pay for the rest of the month and the benefits as I stated. You'll get cashed out for any unused vacation time, which you have accumulated a large amount. On a personal note, I have written a letter of recommendation. You are phenomenal at what you do, Harlow. Something like a relationship shouldn't keep you from gaining new employment, nor do I want that. You will be able to use us as a reference. I wish you well with everything."

I knew that was my cue to leave, so I stood and shook his hand. I turned to leave and then faced Mr. Smithers again. "Thank you, sir."

"I know we didn't give you much of a personal life with as many projects as we placed on you," Mr. Smithers sighed. "I apologize for that, and I hope you can trust me when I say I understand why you chose to look within. I don't fault you, Harlow." Stunned by the admission, I could only nod and leave as quietly as possible before I overstayed my welcome.

Luckily, I could walk straight out the front doors since I didn't really have an office. There was a space I used when I had to be in the office though nothing personal was in there.

With my eyes pointed straight ahead, I ignored the furious whispers of the people I passed until I was safely outside the building and huffed out a sigh of regret. I could only blame myself. The company was far more generous than it needed to be on my termination, and I knew the rules and broke them anyway.

Well, Xander was to blame as well. I didn't get pregnant on my own; it took two. I think that most of my regret came from my choice of Xander. When you choose someone because of the way they look, it often ends in disappointment. Now I was left to make some difficult decisions that would be life-changing, no matter which way I looked. Not only for me, either. I sighed and headed to the bus stop.

I was thankful that I could get into my doctor today, even if only to confirm the results of the devastating test witnessed by all my colleagues. *The test heard around the world!* I thought to myself.

I sat at the bus stop and waited with a few other people for the next bus. I figured that was the safer route for me, knowing that my emotions were all over the place and driving like that was dangerous.

I positioned myself at the end of the bench just to keep some space around me because sometimes the bus stop had some crazy people. Ever vigilant, I watched around me and jolted when my phone rang. I looked down at the phone in my hand and saw Xander's name. I didn't want to answer but I did against my better judgment.

"What, Xander?" I answered, my tone expressing my irritation.

"You ruined my life and my career!" Xander shouted loud enough for me to hold the phone away from my head and still hear him. "Don't expect me to be a part of this! I don't even know if it's mine!"

"Listen closely, asshole," I snarled. "*I'm* not the one who was cheating. I don't want a damn thing from you other than your silence. Don't flatter yourself that you meant anything to me other than sexual release, and even then, I had to help you."

"*Lies.* Do that child a favor and get an abortion. You don't know the first thing about raising a kid," Xander snapped.

"Excuse me?" Fury boiled through my veins. "You don't know anything about me, nor do you get a say in what I do with my body or the child you planted there. Check the expiration date on your condoms or learn how to put them on correctly. Don't call me again."

I wished that I could slam the phone down. Aggressively pressing the red hang-up button wasn't the same thing. There was no satisfaction in that. I slouched back against the bench and fought the impulse to throw my phone into traffic. The nerve of that man-child to suggest I get an abortion!

A semi-truck going way too fast drove by at that moment, causing a gust of wind to blow my skirt up over my head. That set off a round of honking by passing cars while I windmilled my arms, trying to push it back down. That was the hundredth clue in the past twenty-four hours that the universe was trying to tell me Xander was a mistake.

"Sounds like you are having a bad day, dear." A lady patted my arm after I got my skirt back in place and my purse on my lap to hold it down.

"Understatement," I muttered. I'd experienced enough embarrassment already. *Where's the damn bus?*

Five hours later, I unlocked my front door and dropped my stuff on the floor. The doctor confirmed it. I was pregnant, three-plus months pregnant. If I traced it back, it would have happened one of the first times I was with Xander. Probably the first one where I hadn't bothered to check if he wore a condom or not. It was a heat-of-the-moment thing that lasted all of three minutes and twelve seconds.

I knew it was a situation I needed to address sooner rather than later but I also needed to process it. I walked into my home office and sat down to update my resume instead. I was worried that no one would hire me, knowing I was pregnant and would need to take time off to have a baby. I didn't want to lie to a prospective employer. That wouldn't build up any good karma points.

I had other band aids I needed to rip off, like telling my parents. How would that go? The answer to that would be: Not well. Especially when they learned of the events that led to me finding out—and they *would* learn. I'd already seen the clip on YouTube. It wouldn't take long before one of my cousins or other relatives saw it and shared it; they were helpful like that. It would be best if my parents heard it from me first.

"You are a strong, intelligent, independent woman," I told myself. "You can do this. It's just a phone call. Your parents love you." I sighed heavily. They might love me but they were opinionated.

I picked up the phone and scrolled until my parent's number popped up. I hit the call button and counted out loud the rings as I listened to them. Maybe the planets, stars, aliens, satellites, and guardian angels were all in alignment and I wouldn't have to have this conversation tonight.

"Hello, Harlow," my mother's voice broke the illusion. "You finally remembered we were alive?"

"It hasn't been that long, Mother," I drawled, rolling my eyes. "You do remember that the phone works both ways, right? You can dial as well as answer it." She was so dramatic. I'd talked to them last week.

"Be that as it may, why do you sound so desolate? I assume that's why you're taking the time to call us now. Tell me what calamity has befallen you." My mom's tone wasn't rude but the words rankled. She made it sound like I only called when things were bad.

"The next family dinner will have a plus one," I blurted out around my irritation.

"You are dating someone?" My mom sounded surprised. She didn't know about Xander because he didn't mean anything to me.

"No. Me plus one. I'm pregnant." I tore that band aid off and ripped every hair out while doing it. I might be bald now.

"Excuse me? I think we have a bad connection. It sounded like you said you were pregnant. I don't understand how that could be if you aren't dating anyone." Not much got by that woman, did it?

"You have three kids, Mom. I'm sure you know the mechanics of how it happens. Before you get on your high horse, soapbox, or whatever you want to call it, I used protection. Sometimes it can happen anyway, per the doctor's conversation with me this morning. Contraceptives fail. I'm not the first person it's happened to," I replied defensively.

"Where is the father of this little miracle?" My dad shouted in the background. "I'm going to give him a piece of my mind."

"Unnecessary, Dad. He's gotten several pieces of mine. It wasn't a serious relationship and I'm as stunned as both of you are, I promise. Maybe more so. Regardless, you are going to be grandparents.

Remember all those irritating conversations where you told me you wanted them and would never have them because your kids don't want them? Guess again. It's happening in approximately six months. Congratulations," I grumbled.

"At least you have a good job so you can support our miracle baby," my mom stated, ignoring my comments.

"Stop calling it a miracle baby," I snapped. "And I no longer have a job."

Dead silence greeted me. I pulled the phone away from my head and looked at the screen. I hadn't lost the connection to them. Silence isn't golden. It's a prelude to a verbal bashing about stupidity. I couldn't wait for the fun to begin.

"You can't move back in," my dad shouted. "We've converted your old room into my hobby room!"

"I don't need to move in with you," I sighed. "I have my savings to get me by until I can find something else." I was surprised that they hadn't asked me why yet. I wasn't going to offer up an explanation either unless one of them pushed me for answers.

"So what will our grandchild be?" My mom's tone when she asked was tight with frustration.

"I don't know yet. I've only had the pregnancy confirmed by a doctor this morning." I nervously fidgeted with a pen that sat on my desk.

"The father won't be a part of the child's life?" This time my mom's tone was accusatory.

"Most likely not. He told me to get an abortion," I growled, still angry over that conversation.

"I thought you were pro-choice," my dad shouted. I hated speaker phone.

"I am pro-choice, Dad. That means I believe people can choose for themselves, not that I want to get an abortion." I sighed in defeat. The conversation hadn't gone as badly as I thought it would.

"I can't say I'm happy with the circumstances, but I must admit that I am happy about a baby. As long as I don't have to raise it," my mom clarified. "God only knows your brother probably has a handful of them scattered around the country. I don't know where you kids get your cavalier ways, but it isn't us."

"Sky doesn't have kids, Mom." I knew my brother didn't have kids scattered around the country, for a fact. "He had a vasectomy to ensure that didn't happen." Well, crap. I wasn't supposed to let that out. Skyler wouldn't be thrilled with me, though it might throw them off me disappointing them.

"Oh, Lord." My mom huffed in indignation. "Why do you kids hate me? That was a bit extreme of him."

"No one hates you, Mom." I rolled my eyes. "I'm gonna hang up now and work on my resume."

"My knocked-up daughter needs a job," my dad crowed. "Get 'em, honey!"

I hung up to the sound of my mom berating my dad.

One Month Later

I had my feet propped up in stirrups and a phallic-shaped wand was stuck in places where I didn't want a device held by a strange man. It wasn't the most comfortable of things to experience. I'd expected the doo-dad that rolled over my belly. I wasn't fit to be a mother.

"Do you want to know the sex?" the doctor asked

me as he apparently tried to examine my throat through my vagina. He turned the screen toward me as he twisted the wand to the side.

"Yes, please," I muttered. "There needs to be some payoff for this torture."

"Look right here." He chuckled and pointed to the screen. "You are having a boy."

I knew this was supposed to be an emotional moment for me, at least by the standards of movies, but all I felt was anxiety. What did I know about raising a boy? Not like I knew anything about raising a girl except from my own life experience as a female.

"Are you okay, Harlow?" The doctor's kind eyes landed on my face. "Do you not want a child?"

"I never saw myself having children," I answered honestly. "I don't know the first thing about babies, much less boys. It's giving me mini panic attacks."

"Ah, okay, I see. Are you considering a late termination?" The doctor's careful question made me pause.

"No. I didn't consider that option once. I resigned myself to the fact I was going to be a mother. Can we have this conversation with the wand outside my body?" My muscles were all tensed up and the conversation didn't make the uncomfortable quotient any less.

"My apologies." He took the wand out, patted my leg, and then helped me get my feet out of the stirrups. "Are you going this alone?"

I nodded and rearranged my gown to cover myself. I scooted back on the exam bed and almost adjusted myself right off of it to the floor. I flushed hotly and refrained from movement. I decided then and there that I never wanted to have sex with someone endowed enough to be in the porn industry. That fantasy had shattered. Unfortunately, size mattered.

"Okay, Harlow. A few things I want to say. Being resigned to something isn't great. I'm happy that you will keep this child as they are a blessing though we might not always see it that way at first. Secondly, it's natural to be scared as a first-time parent. Don't beat yourself up over that. The simple fact that you are worried about being a bad parent means you care enough to try. Remember that."

A month of ruminating on everything the doctor told me had me semi-excited about the child that had now grown enough to make me wear a different size of clothes. I'd admitted to my friends that I didn't mind the stretchy pants; they were comfortable.

Lady Luck had blessed me with her presence because the prior week I'd received a phone call from the owner of the timeshare property that witnessed my fall from grace. He had wanted me to be the project manager for their remodel. He wanted my plan and me to oversee it coming to fruition. The salary offered was generous and I'd be an idiot to refuse.

I even went so far as to call Mr. Smithers and let him know that his friend had offered me the opportunity and color me surprised when he told me how happy he was that it worked out that way. This project was to last about a year, and while this opportunity might be temporary, it was something I couldn't pass up. It allowed me to work from home and make site visits to coordinate when necessary. I was excited because they saw me at my worst, knew I was pregnant, and wanted me anyway.

I called my parents and let them know the good news and my mom wanted to celebrate by taking me shopping for baby things.

There hadn't been one word from Xander since that phone call at the bus stop. That saddened me since he didn't want to be a part of the baby's life he'd helped create. Another part of me was happy because if he cared that little, I didn't want to inflict that kind of damage on an innocent child. We were both better off without him in our lives.

I didn't take the bus to meet my mom. I drove. I figured I'd treat her to lunch while we were out and try to get back into her good graces. I think I needed to do that for my brother, too. I'd gotten an angry phone call from him after my verbal vomit that outted him. Thankfully he'd forgiven me quickly after he found out about my situation.

I'd cleaned out the spare room, donated the mattress, and put the rest of the furniture in the garage for when the baby got older. I left the dresser in the room, though, and was trying to decide if I wanted to paint the room or not. I sighed and parked my car at the baby boutique my mom had wanted to look at, apparently for years.

I walked around the front of the store and looked for a sign of my mother. I hadn't seen her car in the parking lot but that didn't mean she wasn't there. Sure enough, she came from inside the store and dragged me in after her.

"Look at these clothes," my mother screeched. She held up a little set of overalls and a blue striped shirt. I didn't see what was so special about them other than they were tiny, which made them cute.

"It's cute. I think the itty bitty shoes are way more adorable. Oh, they even have cowboy boots. I'm getting a pair of those," I grabbed a random size and examined them.

"Honey, get staggered sizes, so you have clothes as he grows. The most important things right now will be a car seat, bed, and stroller. Have you thought about a theme you want to do? Like animals or colors or space?" she rattled off.

"I haven't even thought of a name," I responded sullenly.

"That's okay, Harlow." My mom patted me consolingly. "Sometimes, you must see their little faces before a name comes to you. Think neutral colors for his bed and stuff. That way, it will be easy to change the colors as he grows into his personality. A beige or gray color would be good, don't you think?"

"No beige," I thought quickly. "Gray."

My mom grabbed a cart and threw some clothes she'd picked out and the boots I clutched in my hands into it. I allowed her to pull me through the store to where the cribs and bedding were and my eyes bugged out.

"These are expensive! Why don't we go to one of the cheap chain stores and get this stuff there?" I frantically whispered.

"Because quality matters." My mom's tone and eye roll had my own eyes rolling into the back of my head.

"He'll be a baby. He doesn't need Tempurpedic." I absentmindedly rubbed my belly and followed my mother.

She had her eyes on a beautiful walnut wood crib

that made me want to sleep in it. It was elegant and rustic, and now I needed it. I ran my fingers gently over the smooth wood, admiring the swirls of the grain.

"We want this one," my mom told the clerk in her no-nonsense tone. "Do you do delivery?"

I let her haggle with the clerk on that and wandered down the aisle with sheets and blankets and saw a navy blue blanket that I fell in love with because it was so soft. I put that in the cart along with a cashmere gray set of sheets.

"Oh, those are nice. Good choice," my mom granted me her approval. She tossed in some onesies and directed me to the car seats where the clerk waited for us.

I listened to her talk about each one and she lost me somewhere talking about how they hooked to the car. I started to have an anxiety attack because I didn't understand what she was talking about with hooks. All I could think about was what would happen if I got in a car accident and couldn't figure out how to unhook my baby from a burning car? I got dizzy and windmilled my arms around to keep my balance. When my ears started to ring, my bladder did some strange cramp thing and I went down like an elephant hit with a tranquilizer dart.

My butt hit the floor and I peed myself on impact to my dismay. Was I wearing black pants? Nope, I sure wasn't. I wore a lovely pastel pink color that showed the spreading wet spot. My mother and the clerk stared at me in horror while I floundered around like a beached whale in a puddle of pee trying to escape.

"Oh, dear," the clerk broke out of her daze. "Hold on." She ran off.

My mom helped me stand up and the clerk

returned with a pair of black leggings and some wipes. She directed me to a bathroom in the back and I fled. Wetting myself was another new experience; I wasn't a fan of this either.

I peeled myself out of the offending pants and mopped myself with the wipes until I was sure I didn't smell like urine anymore. How humiliating but at least this wasn't on camera. Unless the security cameras in the store recorded that little accident. Hopefully, whoever monitored those had a heart and wouldn't post it online.

I shoved my legs into the new pants and ripped the tags off simultaneously. I cleaned up any mess I made and disposed of the wipes. After washing my hands, I splashed some water on my face and headed back out. I looked in the mirror and saw my face was pale with twin pink spots on my cheeks like some cartoon.

I wrapped my balled-up wet leggings in paper towels, and with a flush, I asked for a bag to stow them in. I felt terrible that the clerk had to mop up my puddle and I wanted to do nothing other than run from the store and never return.

"Please don't be embarrassed," the clerk tried to comfort me. "It happens more than you think. We've even had ladies who went into labor while they shopped. All of a sudden I'll hear an, 'Oh my, my water broke!' while I'm checking someone else out."

I made a mental note not to be anywhere other than the safety of my own house when it got close to my delivery time. I could only imagine me on a site location for work and something like that happening—utter mortification.

"Honey, what happened?" My mom rushed back over from where she had filled the cart with more items.

"Anxiety attack," I answered sheepishly. "I kept thinking what would happen if I couldn't get the car seat unlocked and out of the car in case of an emergency."

Understanding dawned on the clerk's face while my mother stared at me aghast.

I paced around my living room, arguing on the phone with a vendor about a delayed shipment of furniture to the job site. I was also texting my mother to tell her that I was watching for the delivery truck of furniture my mom had bought at the boutique where I could never show my face in again.

I was almost six months pregnant now and I looked terrible. I couldn't see my feet unless I bent over, which wasn't fun anymore. Backaches were getting to be a daily occurrence, along with heartburn. I didn't even want to get started on the memory issues popping up. And where the hell did my ankles go?!

I had three people see the video of me online showcasing the brilliant reveal of my pregnancy. I want to say I was past caring about it but that would be a lie. Rumors still spread about me, even through my family. However, even wildfires got contained and put out eventually. Maybe one day I'd laugh about it but not anytime soon.

"No, that's unacceptable," I told the aggravating person on the other end of the phone. "Doug promised those tables today; it's in the contract."

I turned and marched back into my office to pull the contract out. Before landing in hot water, I needed to make sure I knew what I was talking about and hadn't imagined it. I was almost certain that it was in the contract the vendor signed. I'd allowed the proper lead time and added another couple weeks to ensure this wouldn't happen. I knew I had.

I dug through my files until I found the one I was looking for at the back. I scoured through it until I found the section about the delivery date and stabbed the paper in delight. I was right! I went to battle with the vendor and ended up with a deeper discount due to the late delivery. That money would get funneled back to the employees as a bonus upon completion of the project.

Once I hung up with the vendor, I emphatically kicked my feet back and fell out of my chair into a heap on the floor. No audience this time and it made me laugh. I picked myself up, righted the chair and called the owner of the timeshare to let him know of the delay and discount.

The sound of a large truck jolted me out of my victory haze and I dashed out to the living room in time to see the delivery truck driving away. *How did I miss the arrival? That truck was loud.* I grabbed my phone to call the boutique and opened the front door. When I walked to the driveway, I saw the boxes.

"How am I supposed to get all this in the house?" I asked the empty street in desolation.

Wait! What was I even thinking? I could get this in the house. I wasn't a helpless, weakling! I was a fierce lioness that dominated obstacles put in my path. Furniture wasn't going to get the best of me! No way.

I walked around the furniture, found the smallest box first, and dragged it into the house, shredding the bottom of the box on the aggregate driveway. It was heavy despite its size. Yet the powerhouse I was got it into the baby's room and left it there.

On to the next box; I repeated the process until

the largest one remained. I think the package weighed more than I did. *Put your back into it,* I told myself. I did just that; I leaned into the box with my back and used my legs to push. I gained about five feet before I had to stop for a breather. I even had neighbors drive by and wave without stopping to ask if I needed help. Whatever, I didn't need anyone.

I started to push again, this time facing forward and I made it much farther. That is until the box hit the one step up to the front door. My arms buckled, my face smashed into the rigid packaging, and my knee hyper-extended with a white lightning-hot pain-filled pop that had me on the ground in less than a millisecond.

I yanked my phone out of my pocket and called my brother with tears stinging my eyes. "Sky! I need help!" I sobbed when he answered. *Okay, I needed someone.*

"What now?" Skyler's irritated tone came through the line. "I already forgave you. No need for the waterworks."

"I fell and hurt myself and don't think I can get up!" The pain was intense and my leg wouldn't move. My brain was fuzzy, so I quoted cheesy old commercials with old people lying on the floor.

"Are you at home?" Skyler changed his tone instantly.

"On the walkway outside my house. I think I peed myself again," I wailed helplessly.

"I'll be there in less than ten minutes." I heard Skyler curse under his breath before he hung up. He was true to his word.

"Sky!" I cried and held my arms out to him. I looped them around his neck as he gingerly lifted me off the ground with a loud grunt.

"Damn, Har, are you growing a sumo wrestler in there? And seriously, I thought you were kidding about the pee thing. Didn't you used to have ankles?" Skyler grumbled, carrying me around the box and into the house. "When did it start snowing cardboard?"

He managed to hit almost all my nerves and I didn't know whether to scream or laugh. I knew he did it to take my mind off the pain, but wow, all in one breath? That was a new record for him. I used one hand and flicked him in the back of his head when he set me down in the bathroom.

"Clean yourself before I take you to some walk-in clinic to make sure you didn't injure my nephew with your hair-brained idea of trying to move that box into the house by yourself." Skyler kindly returned the flick to my head.

I sat on the edge of the tub and turned the water on. There was no way I was about to ask my brother to help me strip. I'd deal with the pain. I peeled the wet pants off with memories of the baby boutique flying through my head.

My knee was huge. It wasn't good. I washed off as quickly as possible, wrapped my towel around me and hollered for Skyler. He frowned when he saw my knee and helped me to my room, where I directed him to a pair of sweatpants I knew still fit me.

Getting me into the car was a different ordeal and he demanded that I not pee on his interior. I wanted to say something witty back but the truth was it was possible even though my bladder was empty. I'd stretched out across the backseat so I didn't have to bend my knee, and Skyler had packed ice around it.

"Did you tell Mom?" I asked, wincing.

"Uh, no," Skyler hedged. "I was at her house when you called." His quiet snicker told me that the payback owed had arrived. "Sorry."

He wasn't sorry but I didn't care. I'd get a lecture for sure, and my mom might show up and hover over me if something was seriously wrong. Life could be worse. I could have parents that didn't care about me.

"Thanks for bringing that crib inside," I muttered gloomily. "I totally had it."

"I could tell." Skyler guffawed. "You just called me to gloat about it, I know."

I choked on laughter, momentarily forgetting the pain. Skyler knew how to take care of me. There was no question about who I would call to help me, even if he was mad. Thankfully the clinic was close to home and I was an established patient.

Skyler ran inside to get me a wheelchair and came back out with a stupid grin that could only mean he saw someone he wanted to date. He used that term loosely since he didn't 'date' people for more than a month.

He grabbed me under my armpits, hauled me out of the backseat with another grunt, and plopped me in the chair. Suddenly the chair tipped back and he popped me into a wheelie. I squealed in surprise and clamped my legs together, so I didn't wet myself.

I checked in and waited. The medical assistant took me straight to x-ray when they called me, took several images of my knee, put me in a room, and left me to rot. Okay, that wasn't the case but it felt like it considering I had to pee again. In desperation, I pulled the emergency cord and one of the medical assistants rushed in frantically.

The doctor finally came to check on me only to tell me that there were no breaks or fractures that they could see and he referred me to a specialist. He had the medical assistant wrap my knee and told her to bring me some crutches. I received orders to stay off the knee for a couple of weeks or until after I saw the specialist and heard what they had to say.

The visit wasn't exactly helpful. They did nothing to check on the baby either; I sighed and accepted the referral letter to an orthopedic surgeon. I stuffed it in my pocket, struggled with the crutches while a medical assistant watched and finally hobbled out the door to my waiting brother.

Present Day

"Hello, Harlow. I'm Dr. Courtney. I have your knee's MRI results, and it looks like a small partial tear. I think we can avoid surgery if you continue to stay off of it. How is the pain?" Dr. Courtney put some images up on a lightbox and pointed to the injury.

"Some days are worse than others. I can stand without the crutches but when I try to move, it feels like it's going to give out and the pain gets stronger," I told him. "It might be that I'm a wimp."

Dr. Courtney laughed and shook his head. He had me raise my pants leg so he could examine my knee and put it through some range of motion testing. The baby chose that moment to do some acrobatic moves in my belly, making me jump and accidentally kick Dr. Courtney in the chin.

"Oh, I'm so sorry. This entire pregnancy has been one embarrassing thing after another. I didn't mean to kick you. The baby moving around startled me," I babbled uselessly.

"You didn't hurt me, Harlow. Please stop apologizing." Dr. Courtney pulled my pant leg down and stood. "I'm going to print out some gentle exercises for you to do to keep the knee in motion but I am going to suggest that you continue to use the crutches for another three weeks. Use them with the foot on the floor, though. Don't put all your weight onto your arms and keep your foot off the floor; go through the motions but don't fully weight bear. Does that make sense?"

I nodded my assent and patiently sat while I waited for the nurse to return with the handouts and whatever else he decided I needed to do. I could live with crutches. It was a far better result than having surgery.

To my surprise, Dr. Courtney walked back in and reviewed the handouts with me, showed me how to do the exercises, and ensured I understood how to do them on my own and why they were important. It was nice that he took the time to work with me instead of handing it off to a nurse. Then he told me to allow one of the staff to wheel me out to the car so that no more mishaps happened. I think that last part was so I didn't become a liability while on the property.

I transferred myself from my chair to the car with little help and no calamity. I even got the crutches in the front seat next to me without breaking my windshield—all things for the win column. I headed home to pack an overnight bag because I needed to make a trip up north to the job site.

I had to meet with several contractors to close out some phases of the project and to talk with project managers about the stages that were about to begin.

The drive was about two and a half hours but the change of scenery was necessary.

I wasn't used to being cooped up and confined to home, with mobility being an issue the way it was right now. I've sustained injuries many times before, but none had immobilized me the way this had. Sure, I had crutches and could move around though it wasn't easy with my big belly in the way.

Once home, I maneuvered myself into the house without trauma and I had to admit, having my foot on the ground made a big difference not only to my sore armpits but to my balance overall. I had more confidence in myself that I wasn't making things worse by doing what I was doing.

Happy, I moved to my bedroom and picked a bag from my arsenal that was easy to toss over my shoulder and carry while using the crutches. I only needed a few things since it was only an overnight trip. I was going to drive up tonight after traffic died down and stay the night so I could be there in the morning and not have to get up super early to fight the traffic.

It was intelligent thinking on my part; that I could think this clearly during the pregnancy made me happy. Too often, I forgot the most straightforward and logical of things, like where I put my cup of herbal tea since I wasn't allowed to have too much coffee.

I brought my bag out to the car and went back inside to pack myself a few snacks to eat on the way. I was positive that I would have to stop multiple times because peeing every three minutes was my new hobby, and this baby seemed to want me to eat and drink just as often.

Both chores took me a couple of hours to

complete due to slow movement and taking the time to move the bags to the car, so I didn't do my standard try-to-carry-everything-at-once gig and injure myself further. The forward-thinking was something I was pretty proud of myself for completing.

I called Skyler to let him know I wouldn't be home for a couple of days since he had taken it upon himself to stop in at least once a day to check on me, not to mention he helped me set up the baby's room and assemble the furniture.

Finally, I left home and headed north to my hotel for the night. I'd packed enough clothes for three nights, or the chance that I did something to dirty up the clothes I wore. I couldn't be too careful, as life had taught me these past few months. The more accurate statement was that I *could* be more cautious, or I wouldn't be in this situation.

Thankfully the drive was uneventful except for the four stops along the way: Two coffee stores and two fast food chains that were still open because the rest stops that I drove through looked scary and I didn't want to stop there. The employees were friendly enough to let me use the bathrooms despite the late hour and the only part of the establishments open were the drive-thrus.

After checking in to the hotel, I was hungry but too tired to drive anymore, so I ate the snacks I packed, left crumbs all over the bedspread, and passed out. I slept so hard that I didn't hear my alarm going off.

I jolted awake with my hair flattened on one side and sticking up on the other with cracker crumbs embedded for extra texture. I was super cute and late. I needed a shower quickly. I rapidly sent texts to the people I was supposed to meet, letting them know I was running fifteen minutes late.

I rolled off the bed and hopped to the bathroom on one leg. There wasn't time for me to grab the crutches and make sure I didn't fall. I flung my rumpled clothes to the ground, cranked the shower, and went in. I let out a shriek at the cold water but kept going.

I'd never been late to a meeting, not once. This morning was terrible. I got out of the shower and blindly reached for a towel, only to realize I hadn't washed the conditioner out of my hair and had to get back in. Sadly, the towel came with me and I let out a stream of curses the person in the next room probably heard.

The day didn't start out well. Why did the hotel only put one towel in the bathroom and six washcloths? Whatever. I sat my wet butt down on the toilet seat and dried myself with each of the six washcloths and left them in a heap on the floor.

I used the wall as a guide to hop back out to the room, plopped down on the bed, twisting my body to yank the crutches closer to me, and landed on a pile of crumbs that shouldn't be in the crevices they ended up in.

Leveraging myself to stand again, I used my dirty sock to wipe the crumbs away as best as possible and flipped the bedspread over so I sat on a clean sheet. I dressed as quickly as possible and was immensely happy that I had worn boots on this trip so I could cover the cankles I had developed.

I pulled a brush through my wet hair and tied it in a ponytail. I scooted across the bed, used the mirror on the closet door to apply light makeup, and called it good. If I did anything else, it would only make me later and I needed to bring my bags so I could check out.

It took me longer than I would have liked but I finally made it out of the hotel room and to the lobby, where I dropped off my keycard and left a few choice words about the lack of towels before I departed.

I tossed my bag in the car, stuffed the crutches in and knocked my mirror out of place. I didn't care. Once in, I plugged the site's address into my GPS and drove faster than necessary to get there. Being late was a pet peeve of mine; I was more than thirty minutes past due now. It was not the impression I wanted to leave of myself.

The traffic wasn't awful and I made decent time. I parked the car, threw open the car door, yanked both crutches out over my head and hauled myself out of the vehicle. A few people looked over at me in curiosity as I hobbled to the main lobby where I was supposed to meet with the vendors.

Workers were everywhere and the building was an active construction zone. I didn't bat an eye when handed a hard hat; I simply put it on my head and kept going. I heard general conversation happening around me but I didn't listen to the words as I made my way toward my meeting spot. I ignored the eyes upon me because if I were honest with myself, I'd probably look at the weird pregnant lady on crutches in a construction zone too.

It wasn't until I was inside that all conversation stopped. Several eyes riveted on me in fascination. It dawned on me that they were talking about the video of my pregnancy reveal. *Why were people still talking about that?* I felt transported back to junior high and getting my pants yanked down in front of the entire school.

I fought back the impulse to snap at these men

and despite the red flames of embarrassment licking at my face again, I smiled and leaned forward on the crutches.

"Hell of a meeting, wasn't it?" I asked, putting myself out there. "Not my finest moment, to be sure. Can we move past that and get down to business?"

I heard the door open behind me and figured the people I was supposed to meet with next had arrived. It was as if I'd flipped the tables on who was embarrassed now. More than one face turned a shade similar to mine and they stuttered out their apologies. I'd acknowledge them when I finished with these guys.

I went through each of the vendors, signed off on the completed portions and dismissed them when I was satisfied with the work done. Wisely, only a few of them commented on my popularity and only one commented on my lingerie taste.

"What I wear is none of your business," I snapped at that last man. "The concern here is the project and I don't believe you have completed it to code. I'll have the inspector I hired speak to you after he checks everything over again. My inspector, not yours."

The man opened his mouth to argue with me and became silenced by a voice coming from behind me.

"That'll be enough. You heard the lady." The deep masculine voice sounded a bit familiar.

I turned and almost fell over when I saw the handsome man from the doctor's office that felt me up and gave me dreams of the delicious sort. My tongue glued itself to the roof of my mouth and my pulse rate jumped to racecar speeds.

"Sage Wilder." He held his hand to me with a crooked smile. "We met briefly before. I believe you have a crumb in your hair." He plucked it out and dropped it on the floor after I shook his hand.

"There's probably a whole meal's worth in my crotch," I blurted out without thinking.

The sound of several fake coughs to cover laughter reached my ears and I winced. My head swam and if it weren't for Sage again, I would have fallen in front of people that have seen the other video. I didn't need more rumors spreading about me.

"We've got to stop meeting like this," I grumbled. I righted myself instead of sinking into the yummy man.

Thankfully I completed the meetings and the inspections, wrote the job orders, placed orders for needed equipment, and visited the areas of the site I needed to see before we began the next phase—all of it which I did without further embarrassing myself.

Two weeks later, I sat in the baby's room and looked at what Skyler and myself had accomplished in getting it ready. It was a peaceful place, and I hoped the little guy would feel comfortable. The rocking chair was my favorite, where I currently sat and rocked myself back and forth.

The motion soothed the movements in my belly and I finally felt ready to be a mother. Maybe it was the series of humiliating events I'd survived and getting humbled into a pile of goo in front of people. I'd even watched the video that still existed on the internet without wanting to crawl under a rock.

Even more helpful were the comments from women who had similar wake-up calls to motherhood and the encouragement they directed at the poor lady in the video. Not that I was happy others had experienced bad things but it did make me feel less alone on that island of public humiliation.

My quiet reverie became broken by the sound of my ringing phone on the dresser across the room. I rolled my eyes but pushed to my feet. I could bear weight on my knee now and took a few steps to reach the phone. I didn't immediately recognize the number but figured it was work-related. I was wrong and right at the same time.

"Hello?" I answered, leaning my hip against the dresser. "Harlow speaking."

"Good afternoon, Harlow," Sage's voice greeted me. "Sage Wilder here."

"Hi Sage," I said more breathlessly than I intended. My hormones liked this man. "What can I do for you?"

"First, I hope you will accept my apology for calling on pretenses other than work. Since you never took me up on calling me after I gave you my card, I'm making the first move. Second, would you like to have dinner with me? I'm hoping you haven't eaten yet. Third, I wanted to let you know that my interest in you has nothing to do with work," Sage concluded with a smile in his voice.

"Have you seen the video?" I couldn't help but ask.

"Yes," Sage answered with a delicate cough. "I was on the call."

My world tilted again as I went through the memory of each of the images on that fateful screen. Sage had to have been the one with no face, the black screen. I couldn't go out with this man. Wait, yes, I could. He'd seen me at my worst and was still interested.

"Wouldn't that be a conflict of interest?" I asked. I had learned that lesson well. I wasn't keen to repeat it.

"I don't work for either of those companies. I am merely a hired contractor, much like yourself," Sage explained. "Otherwise, I wouldn't have made this call. I wouldn't intentionally put you through something like that again."

"In that case, yes, I'd love to have dinner with you. On the condition that we speak nothing about the project we're involved in," I amended. My hormones jumped for joy.

We set a date and time and before he hung up, he asked one more question that set my face afire along with my libido.

"Are you willing to explain the exercise ball?" he asked with laughter lining his voice. "My business is adventures, after all." I knew he was joking about the ball.

It had been one of the questions that several people on that call had been whispering about before it ended, not to mention in the office when I went in the next day to get fired. Funny how a rumor can come full circle and burn everything in its path like wildfire. When there was nothing left to fuel it, it died out.

"This might be the pregnancy talking, but if you play your cards right, I might even show you," I teased. We ended the call with laughter from both sides.

Sometimes life needed the fire to burn all the bad stuff out so it could begin again fresh and new.

Intentional Ruin

I stood on the outside looking in and it wasn't a metaphor. I'd been excommunicated. Banned. Burned. My morals were questionable and I couldn't argue with the decision. I don't know who I had become or if I liked that person.

Inside the warm living room sat the rest of the morality police. The phrase I coined—The Firestarters—was stuck on the end of my tongue like a scorpion hanging on for its life, eager to release its poison.

I found it funny, or perhaps more ironic, now that they'd kicked me out. It was easy for me to look at these people who thought of themselves as righteous and of high morals and ethics and see them for what they were: Judgmental and corrupt.

They sat before the fireplace and gathered around the small coffee table. They drank their warm cider, planning which immoral person they would burn next, which person struck a nerve with them enough that they should be brought down to understand the error of their ways. They'd plan an all-out assault designed to bring the victim to their knees and get them shunned by others; they would make them a social outcast, a pariah.

To think I'd been one of them once, a leader of sorts. I want to believe that my motives for helping create the group were altruistic but I don't honestly think they were. I believe I only wanted to get rid of a neighbor committing crimes. In my mind, it dirtied up the neighborhood and brought down our resale value. Thinking about it now makes me cringe.

Ultimately, it appeared the group accomplished what it set out to do. They burned me and I have learned from the experience. I saw what I became and am doing my best to better myself. I don't want to be one of them though I wish I still had a group of friends to spend time with instead of being out here in the cold watching.

I walked past the hanging 'For Sale' sign, the site of my demise and humbling. There was no atonement for me, only bitter disappointment.

Five Months Earlier

I saw the trucks and professional movers unloading box after box and remembered my experience unpacking and shuddered. I wished I had paid someone to do it for me. My back wished for the same thing.

I watched for a few minutes, not even pretending to do anything other than stare. Finally, I was rewarded with a non-uniformed female who walked out the front door. From my distance, she looked close to my age, dark-skinned, with jet-black hair, and petite. A couple of moments later, a man who looked much older than she did, came out. He had a paunchy belly, dark-skinned as well, but lighter than the woman, and the same color hair.

She might have been his daughter, though something told me they were husband and wife. I must have stared too hard because both turned and looked at me. I waved hello, shouted a welcome, and began my walk home.

I was surprised to see diversity moving into this neighborhood. Not that it was a bad thing. This neighborhood was notorious for being white; some color would do it good. It didn't hurt that the woman was attractive, either.

I went home, finished my chores, and relaxed until it was time for me to meet up with a group from the neighborhood for a night at the casino. There was a comedy show happening that we were all interested in seeing. A few guys wanted to play some card games and try their luck. Cards weren't for me but I was looking forward to the show.

I heard a horn honk outside and peeked out the front window to see one of the neighbors in my driveway. We'd decided to carpool to save on parking and gas and I hurried out the door, locking it behind me.

"Hey, Cole," Steve, the driver, called out to me with a wave. "Climb in."

"Are you ready to laugh your asses off?" I asked the rest of the passengers as I got into the backseat.

"Always," Mark answered. "Life is way too serious sometimes. And who knows, maybe one of us will hit a big win and come home rich."

"The house always wins, Mark," I reminded him with a shake of my head.

I never understood the draw to gambling that way. I worked hard to earn my money, and yeah, I liked to have fun, but throwing my money away on gambling didn't seem fun. I viewed getting drunk the same way. There were better things I could spend money on rather than something that would make me pee all night long. I drank a drink or two occasionally; I wasn't a prude but it wasn't something I needed to do.

When we pulled into the parking lot, the group in the car reached a new level of excitement and couldn't wait until we parked. I'd never seen these people this amped up before. It was amusing.

Steve found the car with the rest of the group, parked next to them with a honk, and shared waves. We were equal in the male-to-female ratio.

I was single, and Mark, Steve, and Renee were married. Those were the people in the car with me. John, Marnie, and Kiersten all had someone they were dating, and Polly was married to her job as a financial advisor. Those were the occupants of the second car. We all had similar tastes, thoughts, political views, and morals.

John thumped me on the back as I got out and chattered about his girlfriend as we headed toward the casino's entrance. I only half listened because I caught a glimpse of what I thought was the new neighbor but lost him in the crowd.

I refocused on John in time to hear him tell the others he didn't want to gamble and he would see if we could get seated for the show yet. Polly agreed, which didn't surprise me at all, and I followed those two because I had no desire to lose my money.

We wandered through the casino and found a place to get a light dinner since we couldn't get in line for another hour. It amazed me as we people-watched how many people threw money out like it magically reappeared in their pockets. I shrugged it off because it wasn't my money they were wasting and just watched the play of emotions on their faces. That's when I saw him again.

"Hey, Polly, did you meet the new neighbors?" I asked while watching the man.

"Yeah. I popped over and said hello and welcome to the neighborhood. Why?" Polly returned.

"Is that him?" I subtly pointed in the direction of the man. I hadn't taken my eyes off him because something struck me as wrong though I couldn't put my finger on it.

"Jeez, Cole. I only met them once, even though I live next door to them. It looks like him. Again, why?" Polly stared at the man with me. "Is something wrong?"

"I'm not sure. I thought I saw that guy with his arm around a woman, but the man in the cape blocked her. I'm pretty sure it wasn't his wife, though," I admitted, feeling guilty.

"Jerk," Polly grumbled. "I'm going to keep watching him now."

"Watch who?" John joined in the conversation when he returned from his trip to the bathroom.

Polly explained and all three of us sat there, our eyes glued to the man who was doling out money into the machine. His body blocked our view of the woman on the other side of him, but there was no mistaking the way he kept touching her.

"Wow," Polly finally said on an exhale. "His wife is beautiful too. Why do people have to go and act like that? Seeing it unfold like that doesn't make me want to find a relationship to throw myself into."

"Not all people are like that," John argued. "I don't flirt or cheat. Neither does Cole, Mark, or Steve. I don't see the point of it. If you are that unhappy, leave the relationship."

"Wouldn't it be cool if there was a group that monitored people for morality?" Polly mused. "They could out them or burn them when they do things like that to make them learn the lesson that they shouldn't do those things. Think of how many people could get saved from traumatizing heartbreak."

"I don't think it would necessarily save anyone from heartbreak," I replied. "Outing them or burning them, as you say, will still cause the other party to suffer. It might save them from a lifetime of being miserable."

"I suppose you are right. Still, the thought of a secret society of morality police is enticing," Polly claimed. "We could start one and test it out with people in our neighborhood."

"Sounds intriguing," John replied slowly. "Let's discuss it with the others and see what they think."

I mulled the thought over in my head and shrugged when they both looked at me. It was intriguing. I wasn't sure how great of an idea it would be to start with our neighbors and alienate people or create a hostile community where we lived. The flip side of it was that the concept held merit.

"Hey, guys!" Steve called out. "Ready to get in line?"

That was when Polly brought up her idea to the rest of the group. We all stood up and followed the rest to the growing line to get into the comedy show. It looked like everyone was interested and became more so when Polly and John pointed out the new neighbor and the woman who wasn't his dark-haired wife. She was blonde. That made it easy to decipher.

Everyone was silent as the event staff checked our tickets. We walked through metal detectors and joined another line to get inside the theater and find our seats. People were standing too close to us to continue the conversation without getting overheard. Once we entered the theater, we lucked out that no one was in our immediate vicinity, so we could finish talking.

"What are we going to call ourselves?" Renee asked the group, her voice a quiet hush. There weren't too many people in the room yet, so we could still hear each other.

"Firestarters," I answered immediately.

"Interesting," Mark drawled. "Why that?"

"Earlier, Polly said something about burning others. It stuck in my head." I shrugged, waiting for a better name. "No other ideas?"

"Eh, I like it," John added, looking around at the others. "I even have a person in mind we can start with. They don't live in our neighborhood, but I work with the guy."

"What's morally objectionable about him?" Marnie wondered.

"He's cheating on his wife and spending money on his girlfriend instead of taking care of his kids." John practically spat the words out and punched his hand for emphasis.

"You know this for a fact?" Kiersten sat forward and listened intently.

"He brags about it." John shook his head. "I hate it because those kids deserve more from their father than that."

No one argued that point and as more people began to take their seats around us, we dropped the conversation and settled into more effortless conversations while we waited for the show to start. My mind spun the entire time as I tried to figure out a way to find out more information on the new neighbors.

The Firestarters were well underway with their first burn victim. We organized watch parties where two of us would go, scope out the location, and try to spot the unlucky immoral man we wanted to take down. John supplied each of us with locations, photos, and names.

Meanwhile, when I was home, I spent a lot more time taking walks around the neighborhood that would take me past the new neighbor's house to try and spot them and open up a conversation. It wasn't as easy as it sounded.

It took me about two weeks before I saw the woman again and she must have been coming home from the grocery store. She held a paper bag in each arm and used her foot to kick the car door closed behind her.

"Hi, there!" I called out, perhaps a touch on the loud side.

Startled, the woman turned around and one of the paper bags fell from her arms. I felt terrible for scaring her and rushed across the street to help. The eggs were a total loss but the milk container hadn't broken open. I righted it and began to pick up the eggshells as best as possible.

"I'm so sorry," I began. "I didn't mean to startle you. I just wanted to introduce myself. My name is Cole and I live the next street over." I pointed to the cul-d-sac diagonally across from where we are. "Welcome to the neighborhood."

"Oh, well, thank you," the woman replied, picking up the spilled groceries. "My name is Saira. My husband is Nadeem. It is nice to meet you. Please, let me finish picking up; you don't need to clean up my mess."

"It happened because I was an idiot and scared you," I argued. Something about the woman made me want to help her. She kept her eyes downcast but her voice was firm and didn't waver. However, there were faded bruises on her forearms; I didn't want to make assumptions but I couldn't help it.

"Thank you," Saira told me when we finished and she stood back up. "I've got it from here. I must go get dinner started."

"All right. Nice meeting you, Saira," I responded and waved goodbye. She didn't see me because she'd already turned her back and walked up the sidewalk. It was dismissive, yet her tone had come across as nervous at the end of the conversation.

I didn't quite understand why I jumped to conclusions about this woman and her situation. And that each of those was negative. I was mild-mannered, typically non-judgmental, felt certain my moral compass pointed in the right direction, and kindness mattered to me. It made no sense that I wanted these bad things to be true because that wasn't who I was—being concerned about a fellow human was, though this felt like more than that.

I shrugged it off and went back home, sauntering. In two nights I was scheduled to be back at the casino for my watch of the current target. I didn't want to do it because I had no other reason to be at the casino. I didn't gamble, and I didn't drink. There wasn't a show going on that night, either.

Polly was my partner for that; we would be doing nothing other than wandering around the casino, not participating, staring at people, and taking notes. I felt like that would make us stand out more. Polly was set on it, however.

I spent the rest of the evening trying to relax by reading yet I found my mind wandering to the new neighbors. I imagined awful scenarios where the husband was hurting Saira. I finally put the book down and turned on the TV to distract myself with some sitcom.

During work the following day, I made a few mistakes that wouldn't ordinarily happen and people noticed. Some managers came down and asked me if everything was okay because I had entered the wrong dates. Simple mistakes that I hadn't made once in my entire career.

All I could think about was getting home and going on a walk to see if I could spot Saira or her husband again. I wasn't an unlikable person and had hoped that I would be able to be friendly and have the door opened for me. I wanted to have a simple conversation with her where I learned about her life.

What was wrong about befriending a neighbor? Absolutely nothing, I told myself. I was merely concerned for the health and welfare of a neighbor. And I finished my day at work with that thought invading my mind every time it wandered to Saira.

I arrived home, changed my clothes, and headed out for a walk. It was still earlier than most people got off work, so I held out hope that I would spot her again, and my luck held. The garage door was open and she was flattening some moving boxes.

"Hi, Saira," I called out less loudly than last time. She was facing me this time and gave a nod of recognition.

"Hello." She continued the work of breaking down boxes and stacking them.

"Do you need any help?" I offered, hopefully.

"No. There are only a couple of boxes left, thank you." Saira kept her eyes focused on the boxes, very careful not to look my way. "My husband will be home soon," she dismissively replied when I remained standing there.

A man she didn't know continued to show up at her house and invade her space; it hit me then that I probably came off as dangerous. I felt like an ass for not realizing it sooner and before I knew it, I was apologizing.

"What are you sorry for?" Saira asked in confusion, her eyes briefly lifting to look at me.

"Intruding. I just realized I was a stranger and probably made you uncomfortable by interrupting and bothering you. It was not my intent, honestly. I was only trying to be friendly and genuinely wanted to know if I could help you. I know how much of a difficulty it is moving," I rambled, trying to seem harmless.

That earned a laugh from Saira. She kept chuckling as she straightened the flat boxes and moved them to the recycling bin. She finally turned to look at me.

"You don't frighten me, Cole. Please don't worry about that. I am not accustomed to help; much less from strangers. I am used to doing things myself, that is all," Saira explained.

The woman had a feminine voice with a higher pitch, making her sound like a child to me. Her admission that she did everything alone riled me up a bit.

"Well, your husband should be helping you. A marriage is a partnership," I spouted off before I could stop myself.

"Maybe so," Saira shrugged. "I have an arranged marriage. That is the tradition my parents wanted to carry over when they moved us here."

Stunned, all I could do was stare at her. I watched as her expression shuttered with her confession, her mouth closed, and her lips pressed into a thin line. Behind her brown skin tone, I spotted a pink tint that appeared.

"If you'll excuse me, I need to get back to cleaning up." Saira gave me another polite nod and walked away before I could say anything.

I am sure my face gave away my horror at having heard that someone participated in the tradition of arranged marriages. It was narrow-minded on my part since I didn't know the customs of many cultures and barely knew the American culture anymore, if there ever was one.

My shoulders drooped and I walked back home feeling ashamed of the thoughts in my head. The flip side was that I felt reasonably sure I had developed a crush on another man's wife. Not only that, I was going to burn him, as Polly said. Plus, I believed it was the right thing to do.

Three days of the same routine until I spotted Saira again. It was the day after watching her husband drop copious amounts of money at the casino, with two women hanging on his arms. I can't say I've ever wanted to punch anyone until that moment. I was furious on Saira's behalf.

Today she was on her knees on the lawn, bent over a flower bed. Her shoulders shook as if she were bearing the world's weight on them. I almost didn't want to disturb her as she seemed very intent on what she was doing. Then I heard the sniffle. Maybe it was allergies but I didn't think so.

I stepped onto the lawn, my footfalls muffled by the grass. I gently cleared my throat when I got close and saw Saira flinch. In perhaps my wisest moment, I kept my mouth shut and didn't say anything. It took a few minutes before Saira looked up.

"Cole," Saira responded without looking back at me. "Should I be worried you *are* stalking me or is walking in the evening your habit?"

Evening walks weren't my habit until I saw them move in but I couldn't very well tell her that. That would make me a stalker; and while one could argue that it was what I was doing, I didn't want to think that.

"I like a soothing walk after work to ease the day's stressors away," I told her. "How are you?"

I could see how she was, the question was useless and we both knew it. Her eyes were bloodshot and swollen. Her skin had a paler hue to it than usual. Her limbs shook and her hands were unsteady.

"I've been better," Saira finally said after a few moments of awkward silence. "I wondered if you would be by today. I hoped that you had some knowledge about plants."

"Plants?" I echoed stupidly, trying not to look at the fresh bruises on her arms. "Well, let's see. I know they grow in sunlight, need water, and should be planted in dirt."

Saira's laugh made my whole day. She was a vision of beauty. Her face lit up and none of the stress I'd grown used to seeing was present at that moment. The delight lasted only a few seconds before her face sobered again.

I felt shame washing over me again for wanting something I couldn't have. Saira was married. I could admit that I tried to rationalize it by saying it wasn't a marriage she wanted, though that was presumptuous on my part. That was nothing more than the feeling I got from the mysterious woman.

"I apologize. I wasn't laughing at you. I take it from your response that you aren't a plant person, then?" Saira arched her back in a stretch.

"I only wanted you to laugh. I know a little from helping my parents and grandparents in their gardens growing up. What do you want to know?" I fell to the lush grass and sat next to her.

"How to be happy," Saira mumbled under her breath. "I want them to thrive," her voice strengthened and she went on as if she hadn't said that aloud. "Is the soil right? Is the placement right? Do I need to fertilize them? How often do I water? When will they bloom?"

"Well..." I cleared my throat. "Plants are a lot like people. Feed them, quench their thirst, treat them right, prune them, and they will be happy. Obviously, more goes into people, but you fill their basic needs. Each plant will be different on how much it needs water or fertilizing or where you plant it. The front here gets full afternoon sun, and the back gets the morning sun."

I twisted and looked at the flat of plants she had sat between us and sorted through them, creating two separate groups. I moved and placed the plants that would do well in the afternoon heat in front of us. I left the bulbs and starts of the more delicate plants in the flat to plant in the backyard.

"These are hardy," I explained. "These plants can take the heat and flourish in it. The rest should go in the back where they get full sun, but not the heat later in the day."

"Okay, great." Saira smiled. "Thank you for that."

"As for fertilizing..." I pulled one of the plastic info tabs from a plant. "These will tell you if they need it or not and how often."

"This will be the first garden I've ever planted," Saira confessed as she leaned forward and began to dig a hole. "My mom said it was relaxing but I don't feel relaxed. I feel anxious."

"The good thing is that the plants you picked lean toward fall planting. Have you considered growing your own herbs and some vegetables?" I asked. "Many people around here have fabulous herb gardens."

"That's a good idea." Saira sat back on her heels and picked up a plant. She pulled the tab out, read it, pried the plant out of the container and plopped it in the hole.

I reached forward, pulled it out, squished up the bottom, and then dropped it back in the hole. Saira looked confused and began to scoop the dirt back in to cover the roots.

"That breaks up the root ball, so it grows better," I tried to explain. I couldn't remember a better explanation of that to save my soul but she took it in stride.

Saira began the next hole, mimicked my breaking up the root ball, and planted it with a smile. She seemed pleased with herself and I didn't interrupt her. Eventually, she began to talk about her life. I learned about her parents moving here from the Middle East, how hard it was for her to adjust at first, and how she finally excelled.

I dug holes while she talked, got the plants ready,

and then planted them. We had a good system going and I didn't want her to stop talking, so I didn't interrupt her once to ask the thousands of questions that steamrolled through my head.

Saira hinted at the problems with her marriage but never came outright and confirmed any of my suspicions. I wanted to know everything about her. Her husband, that pulled into the driveway thirty minutes later, didn't change that. I knew wanting her was wrong.

"What do we have going on out here?" Nadeem barked as he got out of his car. His face was angry and his tone was biting.

Saira's demeanor immediately changed and she was strung tighter than a bow string. Her expression went bland and her tone almost childlike when she responded to him that we were planting a garden and I helped her figure out which plants should go in the backyard. She could have said I was here delivering a winning billion-dollar jackpot and his attitude wouldn't have changed.

"I was walking by on my daily walk and offered to help," I snarled, standing. I needed to rein it in. My behavior wasn't making anything better and fighting the urge to spill out Nadeem's nasty secrets was far too tempting. "I'll be heading off. Don't forget to water them, Saira, after you finish planting."

I stalked off unhappily and headed home to check in with where we were with the plan to out John's co-worker. The sooner we finished that we could move on to Saira's husband.

The Firestarters met at John's house, our first official meeting. We agreed to make it a democracy and vote on all matters, and first up, they voted Polly and me as leaders. They said it was because Polly and I had discussed the idea while the rest gambled. I didn't really care except that if I was a leader, I could push up the date of burning Nadeem.

"Everyone set on tomorrow night?" John asked. "I wish I could be there but I still have to work with him. I've never met anyone more deserving of what's about to happen to him."

I frowned for two nanoseconds because his joy at causing misery to another human sounded wrong but I couldn't fault him because I was plotting the same thing. If I were lucky, I'd also end up with a fantastic woman. I let my frown fade and refocused.

Renee, Marnie, and Kiersten were on duty for the first takedown. Marnie was an IT genius and they would take all their footage and make it viral. It was going to be splashy, technological, and very public. It probably wasn't how I would have had it play out but this was John's target, not mine.

"I think Cole is ready to begin collecting information on his target," Steve reminded the group after everyone settled. "How do you want it to go?"

"Less involved than this current one," I began. "I think if we collect evidence and just leave it for Nadeem's wife to find, it will do the trick. We don't have much evidence that Nadeem is doing wrong at work. So far, everything I have seen revolves around his wife: Cheating, gambling, and possible abuse."

"Wait, Saira's abused?" Polly interrupted. "Shouldn't we call the authorities?"

"I suspect she is," I informed them. "I don't have solid proof other than how she acts when Nadeem is around and the bruises I've seen on her arms. In the few conversations I've had with her, she hints about a bad marriage but has never come outright and said anything. I know it was an arranged marriage and she isn't happy."

Without going into specifics, I summarized my gardening conversation with the group and held out my arm to simulate the pattern of the bruises. Polly looked furious and Steve looked ill. It was my opinion that both emotions were valid. As a group, they all voted to begin unraveling Nadeem.

Polly spearheaded a tailing plan to see if our new target went anywhere other than work and to the casino. They'd collect evidence and proof and send it to Steve to gather and combine. I didn't have a straightforward way to present it yet but I had a couple of weeks to plot it out.

I'd stopped trailing Nadeem because my face was recognizable to him after our encounter in the driveway three weeks ago. However, in those weeks, the team gathered a large amount of evidence. Not only was Nadeem going to casinos but he also went to an establishment that we uncovered was a gentleman's club doing business under the guise of an exclusive nightclub.

Also, one of the women who had seen Nadeem confessed that he was excessively aggressive with her. She refused to admit that he was violent, only worded it that way to help protect herself. Besides, none of our group presented themselves as law enforcement, so she didn't need to talk to us but did anyway.

I'd kept up my walks while the rest of the group collected their evidence and had grown closer to Saira. She hadn't admitted anything else about her marriage. She talked about missed opportunities with school and I learned she had two master's degrees. I was adequately impressed and told her so.

My crush developed even further when Saira told me that she appreciated having someone to talk to. I required nothing from her, so it was time when she could be who she wanted and have no expectations placed upon her. It fed my ego immensely.

Polly had gotten Saira's phone number as a 'just in case something happened' sort of thing where they exchanged numbers as a neighborly thing. I was impressed with that foresight and wished I had thought of it myself.

There was another meeting of the Firestarters tonight to discuss how to burn Nadeem. I still hadn't come up with the best course of action nor could I foresee how it would play out. I think that was my hesitation in finalizing what should happen.

"How about a text message? Or at least a multi-media blast? We could spoof the phone number it comes from and send the pictures. Then hit her voice mail with the recordings we made and send links of the videos to the secure site Marnie set up," Polly suggested.

"It's a good idea," Marnie added. "She can't refute the videos or the voice recordings. You can fake pictures but not those—at least not by us, it would require a professional. Give me twenty-four hours to get the site loaded with the videos."

"It's also a hands-off approach that keeps us out of the firing zone or invading her space," Steve replied, seeing my skeptical face.

I was worried that she would get depressed and I couldn't go over there and offer my shoulder to cry on since I wasn't supposed to know what was happening. Maybe when it was all said and done, I could extend an offer for her to join our group. I shrugged to myself and saw that the others took the movement as a sign of my acceptance of the plan.

Polly's eyes studied me closely and a frown marred her face but she didn't say anything. I wasn't sure what I did to warrant that expression and didn't let it bother me. We moved on to the next target after Nameed.

"I have someone," Renee finally spoke up. "He appears to be stalking a woman he has no attachment to. I've been watching him and am worried about her safety."

"Oh," my curiosity was piqued. "Do you think the guy is dangerous?"

"Possibly. I've been watching this man and I think we have enough evidence for burning him," Renee supplied. "We can knock out two at the same time. Or within a day of each other."

"Sounds good. If we don't need to do any surveillance, then great," I replied. "Take charge and pull whoever you need to. Wow! This group is rolling right along. Anyone else?"

"Maybe," John answered me with a drawn-out voice. "I want to see how these two go first in case we need to revise our routines or anything like that."

"Not a bad idea," I agreed. It seemed a reasonable answer.

"I motion to close the meeting," Polly called out. "We've got two assignments to carry out and we will reconvene after they have finished to share information and discuss where we go from there. Everyone?"

We all agreed and I happily walked home, taking a detour by Saira's house. I didn't expect her to be out, so I wasn't disappointed when I didn't see her. That's not entirely true, I was, but it was easier to brush off since I wasn't typically out wandering around at this time. I went home and imagined that I would be the one Saira would run to for consolation.

I argued with myself over taking a walk the day the burn was supposed to happen. I knew it was probably something I shouldn't do but wanted to. I set out at the usual time and walked around the neighborhood to have the returning route pass Saira's house.

She wasn't outside. I bit back a groan of disappointment. In fact, all the blinds were closed and the house looked shut and vacant. Yet Saira's car was in the driveway. Perhaps she was sick. I crossed the street to knock on her door and check on her and remembered that I shouldn't do that even if it were the neighborly thing to do.

I kept walking and looked down at the ground as I passed her house. I crossed the street, rounded the corner, and headed home. I felt happier than necessary, yet I couldn't shake the feeling that Saira would run to me for consolation.

I had a restless night and my nerves felt electrified, keeping me from sleep. I read a book, listened to music, paced, checked emails, and finally, took an allergy pill to see if that would work. It did, though it wasn't quality sleep.

I woke the next morning to someone pounding on my front door. The *thump thump thump* was insistent and my first thought was that it was Saira needing help. It took me falling over trying to get pants on before it registered that the knock was too heavy for it to be her.

Then I wondered if it was her husband wanting to tear me apart for burning him but I didn't think he knew where I lived.

I eventually got my pants on, raced to the front door, and flung it open. The last person I expected to see standing there was a police officer with a complaint of stalking. With startling clarity, I understood that the target after Nameed was me.

Present Day

I stood on the outside looking in and it wasn't a metaphor. I'd been excommunicated. Banned. Burned. My morals were questionable and I couldn't argue with the decision. I don't know who I had become or if I liked that person.

Inside the warm living room sat the rest of the morality police. The phrase I coined—The Firestarters—was stuck on the end of my tongue like a scorpion hanging on for its life, eager to release its poison.

I found it funny, or perhaps more ironic, now that they'd kicked me out. It was easy for me to look at these people who thought of themselves as righteous and of high morals and ethics and see them for what they were: Judgmental and corrupt.

They sat before the fireplace and gathered around the small coffee table. They drank their warm cider, planning which immoral person they would burn next, which person struck a nerve with them enough that they should be brought down to understand the error of their ways. They'd plan an all-out assault designed to bring the victim to their knees and get them shunned by others; they would make them a social outcast, a pariah.

To think, I'd been one of them once, a leader of sorts. I want to think my motives for helping create this group were altruistic but I don't honestly think they were. I believed that I only wanted to get rid of a neighbor who was a convicted felon, not that I'd known at the time. In my mind, it dirtied up the neighborhood and brought down our resale value. Thinking about it now makes me cringe. The reality was that I wanted his wife.

Ultimately, it appeared the group accomplished what it set out to do. They burned me and I have learned from the experience. I saw what I became and am doing my best to better myself. I don't want to be one of them though I wish I still had a group of friends to spend time with instead of being out here in the cold watching.

I walked past the hanging 'For Sale' sign, the site of my demise and humbling. There was no atonement for me, only bitter disappointment. Disappointment in myself mostly, though I was disappointed in them as well. I'd tried talking to a couple of them and explaining that what we did was wrong and they didn't want to listen. They believed in their path.

I may have been right in that Saira was a victim of domestic violence but I was wrong in choosing to prove it the way I did. I had only been doing it because I figured I'd have a shot with her if I got rid of Nadeem. Yes, I'd been worried once I saw the bruises but that wasn't why I continued.

I was thankful the Firestarters burned me because the situation helped me right my wrongs. The protection order I got served that day is in a frame on my desk at home to remind me not to judge and to act out of kindness.

I never received a chance to explain to Saira. Marnie had followed through on her plan of sending all the information to her; only I hadn't known that the information included me and my watching Nadeem and Saira's house. I was in pictures and videos. They'd been thorough and included a warning to Saira that they believed I was stalking her. I saw now that they were right.

After that happened, while I was on a walk not past Saira's house, I encountered an elderly couple that told me Nadeem was a convict. Saira had confronted him in the driveway and several neighbors had witnessed the fallout. The police were there, ironically filling out the protection order paperwork to serve me, when the truth about Nadeem's past came out. He'd gotten too physical with an 'escort,' and she'd pressed charges against him. That was why they'd moved to the house in my neighborhood, except Saira didn't know that either. Saira ended up kicking Nadeem out.

I can't claim to know the intricacies of an arranged marriage or the customs of their culture. I'd heard Saira hadn't divorced Nadeem though she hadn't let him back in the house either. I didn't understand that but it wasn't for me to question. I let the people unload the gossip without stopping them but my heart hurt for Saira.

Of course, the older couple had no idea that I was the one stalking her, which is another thing I'm grateful for but the event certainly proved to me how damaging gossip was. I'd helped ruin Saira's life and I had to live with that for the rest of mine. It was the heaviest burden I'd experienced and there was no one to blame but myself.

I'd learned the lesson. I now understood how holy wars happened, believing that one group thought their actions were correct and forced their view on others. It didn't matter who you were; there would always be someone who needed to be exposed, even if that person was you.

Full Circle

*I*f you held hope for the future, you'd be wrong and correct. Confusing, right? Despite the mistakes of humankind, good things remained after the world destroyed itself. Yet it all came down to choices; you can make the wrong choice with the best intentions. It can all work out without harm to others, or it can tumble down, crack and cause rifts that aren't repairable.

What if those choices showed you the error of the directions chosen? Would you correct the course or continue on the path and hope that the greater good saw the same thing you saw and banded together to make a change? Let me summarize such a story for you. That way, you can take the good and bad decisions and be the judge yourself.

Did humans learn from their mistakes or is history repeating itself? Is capitalism in any form the right way to live or does it breed animosity and division? Did the history of humans come full circle?

"They send me off tomorrow," the ten-year-old girl named Kapua told her three friends. She stared down at her fidgeting hands, the nervous tremor apparent to everyone. "The Habitat. Did you guys get your summons?"

"My mom said there was one for me—the Fishbowl. She said I had three days to say my goodbyes," the blonde ten-year-old named Sunny replied. "Why the Habitat for you, Kapua? You are native to this land. I thought you would go to the Island."

"We are all native to the land, Sunny. None of us were born underwater or in space," the brown-haired little boy retorted smartly. His name was Han. "They are taking me to the Island."

"I didn't get anything," the brown-skinned girl named Zaralai answered. "I applied for the scholarship program to each faction."

"Why do you want to go, Zaralai?" Kapua asked. "I'd rather stay here with all my friends."

"I want to feel useful," Zaralai answered softly. "My family has no wealth and all of you are getting drafted. I'm smart; I could help."

Over three hundred years ago, a nuclear war broke out between the world's superpowers. Not all countries fired the warheads that destroyed the planet, though that was little consolation to those that didn't perish in the immediate aftermath.

Survivors flocked across the world to what used to be known as Australia, and there the new world formed. That continent was one of the few that hadn't been decimated. It was hit but far less than the rest of the planet. That didn't mean the air was healthy for any exposure longer than ten minutes or so, but most felt there was safety in numbers. People longed for that sense of community.

A group known as SSS formed twenty years after the radiation levels began to drop and people could surface. Space, Sea, and Surface are what they called themselves. People just shortened it to SSS. Experts in their respective fields headed up the three factions; people that at one time were considered extremists.

These leaders were some of the people that had foreseen the threat of nuclear war. They acted on their predictions to ensure their survival. They built bunkers underground, and one billionaire built a life-sustaining structure out in space that dwarfed the ancient International Space Station that would hold several hundred people. Another created an underwater station to house their family and friends.

Their foresight saved humanity, and when they all surfaced twenty years later, they met for the first time in the new world. Hundreds of others survived the years in scattered underground bunkers and those people were the ones that were now the wealthy class.

They'd stored food, clothing, supplies, seeds, and everything needed to thrive underground and sustain life. Those people knew that plants and animals topside would not be edible, so they created an ecosystem that would revive it. By no means was it primitive living.

It took hard work and willingness to keep it all running smoothly and those recruited to help had no worries. Sometimes through the security feeds, survivors would get spotted and invited into the bunker, and so the populations grew.

Babies were born and raised underground, educated by the adults that became subject matter experts in various fields. The internet still existed and was a valuable tool in the education of children and, in some cases, adults.

When word spread that people were moving and congregating in old Australia, people packed up their bunkers and their vegetation and moved. For those children born underground, undersea, or in space, it was overwhelming to see so many other people, land, and the sun or moon in the sky.

While establishing the new world order, those forward-thinking leaders created factions and decided amongst themselves that there would be a wealth tax. They picked a cabinet of people to be the rulers of the new world instead of one single person, and they each chose their successor of the faction they'd created.

The leaders decided that instead of money (since no one needed it now), goods decided wealth, and the tax would be their children. The children of the wealthy were promised to one of the factions from age ten to eighteen. They would learn about the faction, and how to improve it and grow it.

Once those children turned eighteen, they could return to the new world and apply their knowledge to advance society or remain in the faction. It was supposed to be a lottery system for picking which child goes where. However, that slid to the wayside in the years since the programs became established.

Because the need for cash was null, the caste system became those who produced goods and those that worked for those people. The faction leaders weren't in either category. No one went without, and the leaders guaranteed equal education for everyone.

With the wealth tax, the parents of the child sent provided goods in exchange for room, education, training, and meals. The children accepted on scholarships paid their way through jobs in each faction. Cleaning, cooking, laundry, and so forth. No one treated anyone differently because of wealth. If anything, those without were a little revered because they didn't have to leave their family for eight years.

Zaralai used plant and soil extracts to create makeup to help alter her appearance. She didn't hold out hope that her scholarship application would get accepted for any of the three factions. There were too many just like her applying. The system that her ancestors created had made the human race rich in ways that pre-nuclear war humans didn't seem to understand.

Zaralai wanted a position in the Habitat. She wanted it more than she'd ever wanted anything before in the history of wanting for all humankind. Space was her forte, or so she thought. She knew she could help and contribute.

The Island or the Fishbowl were good choices too but Zaralai's heart lay in the outer edges of the universe. She wasn't ashamed that her family was considered poor and wasn't looking to move up in station. She wanted to explore, learn, and help. Zaralai might only be ten but she knew enough to understand that she couldn't help if left here to harvest crops.

She packed her homemade makeup in a little bag, slung it over her shoulder and headed outside to let her parents know that she was going to go to Kapua's house to say goodbye to her friend.

"Do they have pictures of us?" Kapua asked Zaralai. "Because that will get us caught if they do. I don't look a thing like Han."

"Didn't you say you wanted to stay here?" Zaralai asked, recalling their conversation earlier in the day. "What if it's just you and me that switch places?"

"Your parents would know I am not you," Kapua pointed out. "How do we make that part work? If we can figure that out, then yeah, let's do it. I don't want to go to space. I don't want to go anywhere. I would have been okay with the Island but the other two scare me."

"Cadets! Line up and hold out your invitations for scanning. You will be issued a uniform with your name, your housing assignment, schedules, and job rotations," the sergeant barked as recruits exited the shuttle.

Zaralai felt a tremor of anxiety race through her body as she held out the summons that Kapua had received. It scanned without issue and the sergeant never looked any of the kids in the eye. Zaralai kept the backpack of limited personal belongings strapped to her back, stood straight, and did her best to keep the paper from shaking in her hand.

Zaralai let out a small sigh of relief when her turn was over and glanced down at her bunk assignment and her list of jobs and classes. She didn't know the people assigned to the room with her. It looked like their jobs were laundry and irrigation for the vegetation in Sector Three.

Classes assigned to her were space engineering, improving the suits for outside the Habitat, and crop variety. None of that seemed like it would be easy to accomplish and Zaralai felt intimidated at the prospect. The crop aspect would probably be the easiest for her to understand, though she never really got into the vegetation part of her family life.

One month on the Habitat under her belt, Zaralai wrote a letter to her family and Kapua but addressed it to herself.

That felt strange for her though it was necessary to remain undiscovered. She would tuck the note for her parents behind the one for Kapua.

Zaralai's parents knew of the deception and were happy to have Kapua there to help with the crops. Zaralai had told her parents about the switch; she had no other choice. They would have seen right through any disguise the girls could have dreamed up. Surprisingly, Zaralai's dad agreed instantly. She figured the most significant resistance would have stemmed from him. Instead, it was her mom who was skeptical of the idea. It took a little convincing for her to agree to the risky plan reluctantly.

Zaralai hadn't gotten to space walk yet, though that was on the schedule for next week for a select few. The instructors wanted to test each cadet on putting on the suit, harnessing and walking down the structure outside, around it and returning without becoming tangled. The instructors drew names at random.

They'd practiced wearing the suit inside and in the anti-gravity chamber. The following week they would start on minor repair work outside the Habitat. Zaralai felt it was too safe and when she suggested the practical training taking place outside, she figured she angered one of the instructors. It was no surprise her name got picked.

Zaralai made it a point to ask many questions, make suggestions, and point out inconsistencies. She didn't do it to make things harder, her goal was to learn and she didn't understand how they taught, so she asked to understand. That made her stand out from the others. A few instructors thought it was good, while others came down harder on her.

Every night she got to look out a window and see the marvel of space. From the vantage point of the Habitat, Earth looked peaceful—a serene place of wonder. There was no obvious sign that there were areas that remained toxic from the bombs dropped. However she chose to look at it, she was getting to live out her dream.

The Island was her second choice of factions to go to because she thought it would be fun to find ways to fix the Earth so that all the land could flourish again. The wars hadn't erased the technological advances; they still existed and had further evolved in the centuries since. Zaralai wasn't a genius though she learned a lot from her study of plants when she learned how to create makeup.

The other thing that struck Zaralai as obvious was that so many changes had taken place after the bombs that it was shortsighted to think that the molecular makeup of everything within those areas hadn't changed. If they changed, then their reactions to other elements had changed. That alone opened the possibility that what once was tested and true could no longer be absolute. She felt it was a logical thought.

Zaralai let out a heavy sigh and told herself to feel grateful that she was there. She moved away from the window and the floating orb that held her family. It was time to sleep and prepare for another day of training.

It had been eighteen months since Zaralai had seen her family or friends. She was almost twelve now and the first thing she wanted to do was hug her parents. She'd written letters and told them of her adventures in space, what it felt like to float free in the universe's abyss. Granted, she had been tethered to the Habitat, not just floating into nothing.

However, Zaralai's fearlessness got her assigned to the team that built a new extension on the east wing. That new pod was for vegetation growth. It would have been more exciting to build a residential pod, yet the crop add-on had nuances that kept it from becoming boring.

Zaralai shifted in her seat while the rest of the crew finished loading. She double-checked her chest straps and tried to curb her anxiousness. She wanted to be underway already. The Earth was in the right spot of the rotation for them to land not far from where she lived and her parents knew that she was arriving today. Kapua would meet her at the Habitat location with Zaralai's parents under the guise that they offered to pick Kapua up because Kapua's parents were busy with a project.

It was tricky and Zaralai wasn't sure they'd be able to pull it off if the girls weren't quick to embrace and switch the bags. Zaralai had let Kapua know what clothes she would be wearing so they could match, and during the hug, they'd change the backpack to Kapua's shoulder. There was always the chance that Kapua's parents would surprise her by showing up.

Finally, the shuttle was in motion and rocketing toward the surface. Zaralai's mind wandered all over and she kept fighting the urge to switch back with Kapua. Zaralai missed her family that much, and the thought persisted that she had learned so many valuable skills and gained infinite knowledge about space. At least to an almost twelve-year-old, it seemed infinite.

The transport shuttle ride didn't take long, somewhere between four to six hours, when they timed it right. During that time, Zaralai mentally built a new residential pod, discussed trading places with Kapua again, and formulated a way to aerate the crops more efficiently. By the time the shuttle docked, Zaralai was exhausted.

The tiredness might have been from gravity's pull on her body after being in space for more than a year. Though the Habitat's atmosphere mimicked earth, medical science dictated that too long in space created issues with the organ tissues in the body. Eighteen months was the maximum allowed for children under twenty without a break to return to Earth, even with the technological advances over the past couple of centuries.

Zaralai waited for the all-clear to unbuckle and depart. The moment the light flickered on, Zaralai was up, her pack slung over her shoulder and out the door. She flew down the stairs, her step only faltering once. Her eyes skimmed the crowd looking for the face of her parents when she spotted Kapua.

Zaralai bolted in that direction only after she saw other kids running toward their parents. She didn't want to attract unwanted attention. Kapua madly waved her arms and Zaralia returned the greeting. Zaralai threw her arms around Kapua and deftly transferred the pack to Kapua.

Kapua spun them around in circles while Zaralai's parents maintained a respectable distance not to give away the girls' dangerous secret. Arm in arm, they headed to the vehicle that would drop Kapua off at her parent's house.

"We have news," Zaralai's mom said over her shoulder when they were safely ensconced in the vehicle. "Your application for the Fishbowl was approved."

"What?" Zaralai's shocked expression froze on her face.

"Yeah," Kapua softly confirmed. "Either you go back to the Habitat as me, or you go to the Fishbowl as yourself."

"What about you?" Zaralai stuttered out. "Don't either of those scare you?"

Kapua nodded with her eyes downcast. Her shoulders slumped forward as a few tears slid down her cheeks. "I have to choose. I don't know which is worse."

The thought of switching to the Fishbowl intrigued Zaralai and she wouldn't have to pretend to be someone else. Exposure to all the factions couldn't be a bad thing. She didn't know how she would get to the Island, but switching to the underwater settlement gave her a burst of unexpected excitement.

"I think you would be fine in space," Zaralai told Kapua honestly. "You don't notice anything different unless you are outside working. Inside, they have simulated day and night for the pods that don't have windows looking out. Plus, you'll never see a more beautiful view of Earth. It's breathtaking and awe-inspiring. Oh, Kapua, you would love it."

Kapua gave Zaralai a teary smile. "That sounds nice. I've always wondered what the view would look like from up there. Does it feel cramped?"

Zaralai gave the question good thought because she didn't want to be dishonest and knew Kapua was claustrophobic. "There are some spaces that are small and feel cramped. But mostly, you don't really notice because there are a lot of windows and the sleeping rooms are spacious, even with four people. The crop pods feel huge and with all the plants in there, I hardly ever noticed I wasn't down here."

"What are the instructors like?" Kapua wondered aloud.

"They are great." Zaralai fudged a bit on that answer. "Some have mean moments, but most are helpful and want you to succeed."

"You sound so grown up," Kapua smiled again. "It doesn't sound so bad. Better than being underwater."

Zaralai's parents didn't offer any opinions and kept quiet the entire ride back to Kapua's house to drop her off with her parents. Whatever the girls decided, they would lose their daughter again to one of the factions.

There were three days left before the departure to return to the Habitat. Zaralai and Kapua sat in Kapua's bedroom and discussed the options of either location. Zaralai leaned toward the Fishbowl but didn't feel tied to it. She thought she owed Kapua the option to choose where she went since Kapua covered for Zaralai during the last year and a half.

"Being underwater in the compressed settlement doesn't bother you?" Kapua asked. "And seeing all those creepy fish outside the windows? What if a shark, or a whale, or a whale shark slammed into it and you drowned?"

"The same could be said for space," Zaralai answered without thinking. "I was up there a year and a half and nothing bad happened once... other than someone stealing food."

Kapua giggled and slapped her hands over her mouth. "Was it something good like chocolate cake?"

"No," Zaralai grinned. "It was green beans."

"Gross!" Kapua laughed. "Who wants that?"

Zaralai shrugged; she never did hear why they stole the produce. The girls fell silent and Kapua watched as Zaralai pulled and picked at a loose thread on her pants. It slowly unraveled and became a small hole that her mother would need to repair.

"Will you be mad at me if I want to go to the Habitat instead of the Fishbowl?" Kapua asked Zaralai with a wavering tone. It sounded better to get sucked into the vacuum of space than crushed under tons of water and scary fish feasting on her remains.

"No, Kapua, why would I be mad at that?" Zaralai asked honestly. "We broke all the rules the first time and now I can go somewhere else and learn something new without hiding who I am. It feels right."

"Will you still write me letters?" Kapua gave her friend a watery smile.

"Of course!" Zaralai promised enthusiastically.

Zaralai stood at the depot waiting for the transport to take her and the other recruits and returning students to the boat. She stashed her invitation to join safely in her pocket and her rucksack was slung over her shoulder, with no makeup this time. It was a relief.

If the experience were anything like the Habitat, the initiation would be the rough spot as she tried to find her place among the others. Zaralai had no plans to rock the boat or make waves for anyone. She was eager to learn.

When the bus arrived, she had a seat to herself and she took the time to blank out and stare at the scenery as they traversed the land on the way to the coastline. The paperwork told her that the bus ride was a minimum of six hours, and then it was a two-day boat ride to the sight of the Fishbowl.

Aside from looking down at Earth from space, Zaralai had never seen the coastline or the ocean before. Her parents were too busy working to take luxurious vacations like that. That was why she did her best to stay awake to get that first look at the water. She wondered if it would be as breathtaking as witnessing the enormity of space for the first time.

Six and a half hours of wandering thoughts and a murmur went through the bus. Zaralai's focus snapped back into place as she popped up in her seat. At first, the blue was so startling she thought she was looking at the sky. Then the sparkles of light off the water peaks that glimmered like millions of little diamonds became evident and she realized she gazed upon the mighty Pacific.

The coastline wasn't in sight yet, though the expanse of ocean spread out before her, blending into the cloudless sky. It was similar to space in the perceived vastness of the blue, yet entirely different. As the bus continued down the road, the first hint of the breaking waves exposed themselves. Then came the sand. It was nothing short of spectacular.

Zaralai felt her face splitting into a grin and she yearned to run barefoot through the sand and splash around in the water like she had no cares in the world. The ocean was life itself. Even the air here smelled different than it did at home. She hoped Kapua didn't regret her choice because Zaralai was as happy as she'd ever remembered.

The bus dropped them off in a location that didn't have a beach, or if there was one, they weren't allowed to access it, to Zaralai's disappointment. The kids were loaded onto the boat and then split into groups of two to share cabins for the ride to the Fishbowl.

It was then that Zaralai learned that they would disembark the ship in two days and enter a submarine that would take them to an airlock entrance where they would go through a decontamination process and then ride an elevator down into the Fishbowl.

A submarine sounded fun in theory, but Zaralai understood the feeling that ran through her was anxiety. She imagined it was what Kapua felt or would feel when she entered the shuttle to depart earth. It was uncomfortable and Zaralai silently praised Kapua for her bravery.

She wondered if she would run into their friend Sunny down there under the sea. She hoped so; it would be nice to have a friend already there to help her through the introduction to life underwater. Zaralai only needed to remember that she had to keep her time on the Habitat to herself so no one got in trouble over their deception.

After stowing her bag in the cabin, Zaralai joined the others in the galley for dinner and then went outside to feel the sea spray on her face. The boat's motion through the water took longer to get used to than she anticipated. When one of the older kids stood near her at the railing and told her to focus on the horizon, she did and immediately felt better.

Zaralai was determined to stand at the railing until the sun went down to experience her first sunset on the ocean. For living on an island, she thought it could be strange that she'd never seen the sea, but to be fair, it was a giant island.

The sun started to sink low and Zaralai marveled at how the water reflected those bright hues back to the sky. If she looked toward the sun, the water sparkled like gold. She let out a squeal of delight when dolphins jumped as if they were chasing the boat, their lithe bodies silhouettes against the brilliant sky. It felt like a dream come true.

Between orientation meetings over the next two days of travel, Zaralai spent every moment she could outside. The ocean was calm, which Zaralai was grateful for. Now the boat slowed down as it approached the bobbing submarine.

They'd learned that it would take two trips on the submarine to get all the kids down. The recruits would be on the last trip as they had to go through more than the returning kids.

Zaralai watched as the anchor dropped, and a small metal walkway stretched out to the seemingly tiny opening of the submarine. It looked precarious at best and she couldn't help but wonder how many people had fallen off on their way to the sub.

As much as she wanted to splash around in the ocean, she didn't want to do it in this deep water with sharks swimming around her. And there were sharks. Someone had pointed out the fins slicing through the water only minutes before the bridge extended.

Zaralai grimaced as the sub rolled again with the currents. The boat was moving, sure, but it looked like the submarine moved a lot more. Too soon, the gangplank got pulled back in, the sub disappeared, and they waited. It seemed like it was only minutes, though she was positive at least an hour had passed before the submarine resurfaced.

Then she was shuffled down the bridge and ushered down the hatch into the metal tube. It was loud inside, and the motion almost made her sick. There was no horizon down here for her to focus on, though her eyes tracked the fish as they darted around the sub in curiosity.

It didn't take long for the world below the surface to capture her attention and divert it away from the sick feeling of rocking around: Jellyfish floated by with countless varieties of fish, including a couple of sharks. They were as terrifying up close as they were from a distance, with only fins showing.

Before long, a thud jolted Zaralai and then the sub began to sink. The rocking motion worsened for about thirty seconds, then you couldn't even tell you were moving. The ride was smooth and you could see clearly through the little windows for a bit. Then all became dark except for what the submarine lights illuminated.

Zaralai watched as a large mass loomed in the distance. It had to be the Fishbowl because sharks weren't that big. The closer the submarine got to the structure, the more she could see. There were lights all around it, and though it had an eerie feel, it was utterly unique and felt like another planet.

From where Zaralai sat, she could watch the docking process and gazed upon the massive structure beneath her and the spooky shadows of large predators that circled outside the bright lights. Add in the creepy hiss of air as the hatch opened and it could be the start of a scary movie. It was a good thing that Zaralai didn't get frightened easily.

They began the deboarding process and Zaralai was almost at the end of the line. It crept along and she finally ascended the ladder into the first lock chamber, where she and her belongings got put through decontamination. Only then was she allowed through to the next, which contained a doctor that screened her for any illnesses. Then she moved through to the next one, where she picked up her uniform and moved to the hallway with the rest of the students.

"Line up, guppies!" yelled an older man blocking the doorway. "I'm Instructor Krebbs. On this clipboard, I have your bunk assignments. You will find your class schedules, training sessions, and chore lists in your rooms. These are non-negotiable. Once I call your name, please step forward. There are two people per room."

Instructor Krebbs went through the names two at a time. Zaralai was near the end again and her roommate was another girl named Amy. Zaralai gave the red-haired girl a shy smile and received a nod in return. It wasn't friendly, nor was it cold. It didn't bother Zaralai; she knew she had a friend here already.

The two girls followed the provided map to their room and Zaralai stepped back and gestured for Amy to choose which side of the room she wanted. Amy shrugged and picked the left side of the room. Zaralai went to the opposite side, quickly unpacked her bag, and stowed it in the small closet before she stripped and donned the uniform.

"I'm going to go look for the shower room and bathroom," Zaralai told her roommate. "Do you want to join me?"

"Don't we have to meet for the tour?" Amy asked after she zipped up her uniform.

"At six," Zaralai reminded her. She guessed that Amy was about a year younger than she was. "I want to get a lay of the land, so I know where I must go if I need to get there fast."

"Okay," Amy shrugged again. "Aren't you nervous?"

"No. I'm looking forward to learning. I try not to think about how far underwater we are." Zaralai had to be careful with what she said and wasn't sure how to comfort the other girl. "I think you'll get used to it. Our schedules are pretty packed, so maybe you'll be too busy to worry."

Zaralai grabbed the map and located the shower room, shared bathroom, and cafeteria. She showed Amy the map, though she didn't look too interested. Zaralai carefully folded the map, put it in her pocket, and led Amy down the hallway.

Amy seemed to keep directly in the middle when they walked through the sections with windows looking out at the dark water around them. Zaralai found the views fascinating even though it was dark. She wondered if it would be that dark during the brightest times of the day; she'd find out soon enough.

Once they'd located the bathroom, which was closer than the shower room, thankfully, they made their way to the shower room. It was large and had individual stalls for privacy, Zaralai was relieved to see. She'd had some awkward encounters on the Habitat, even with scheduled shower times.

It was about a seven-minute walk from the shower room to the cafeteria. It wasn't an easy route, though. The girls had to zigzag their way through several hallways before they accidentally stumbled upon it. Zaralai was happy she'd brought the map with her because finding their way back wouldn't be easy.

The girls grabbed a few snacks and sat there eating them quietly. A few others trickled in and out but didn't speak to them. They got a few smiles of acknowledgment, nothing more. They killed as much time as possible until it was time to return to the room where the tour instructor would pick them up.

Luckily they had an easier time returning to their dorm and made it with time to spare. Zaralai took the time to review her schedule for the following day and made notations on her map of where she needed to be. She colored in her room location as well for reference. She'd just started scanning the rest of the map when there was a knock on their door.

Amy popped up, hurried to answer it, and gestured for Zaralai to join her as if she were afraid to be alone with whoever was on the other side. Zaralai decided that Amy was a nervous individual and got up to stand behind her.

"Hello, ladies. My name is Instructor Ulysses." He was far friendlier than Instructor Krebbs. "I'll be conducting your tour this evening," he said genially.

Zaralai figured he couldn't be all that much older than she was. He had a childlike face and was the nicest person she'd encountered, period. She pushed Amy out the door and closed it behind her, following the instructor. Their group only consisted of four other people.

Instructor Ulysses took them by the bathrooms first, then explained the dorms' layout. The separate hallways with different colored doors signified the occupants' length of time in the Fishbowl. Zaralai learned they wouldn't remain in those rooms as their length of stay progressed.

Instructor Ulysses showed them the cafeteria, the laundry facilities, the housekeeping room where they would find the essentials to keep things clean, and the medical facilities, library, and research labs. The Fishbowl was enormous, much larger than Zaralai expected.

The last place of interest was what Instructor Ulysses called the heart of the Fishbowl. It was the water purification center. He explained that the water supply for the Fishbowl all happened in that wing. The structure pulled in water from the ocean, desalinated it, purified it, and then dumped it into the tanks that provided the Fishbowl with drinking water, shower water, and water for the toilets.

He showed them how the wastewater went through a reverse process. It got purified and then re-salinated to be returned to the ocean so as not to damage the delicate ecosystem that thrived underwater. He described how the pH balances were carefully measured and maintained and that an entire department in the Fishbowl was dedicated to preserving the sea life and water.

Zaralai became hooked with only that tidbit of information. Marine biology as a field choice was something she had never considered before then. Now she wanted to pursue it with gusto.

Zaralai's chores were sanitation and crop irrigation. Both chores aligned with her desire to learn more about marine biology. It had been a month, and though no one had assigned her to any projects, she'd learned a great deal already.

She hadn't made a lot of headway into becoming friends with Amy. However, she had connected with Sunny and they spent time together when they both had free time. Not having to reinvent the friendship wheel was a fantastic help. Sunny also helped Zaralai learn and understand some of the material since Sunny had already gone through those classes.

Halfway through the second month, Zaralai received a summons to the Human Resources department. She hadn't even known there was one of those. The person sent to find her escorted her to the office where she was left sitting outside on a chair; she was relieved that she wasn't alone in figuring out where to go. She wouldn't have found it on her own. She sat there for fifteen minutes before someone stepped out of the office. The lady gestured for her to follow them inside.

The door closed behind Zaralai with a resounding thump that made her feel jittery and jumpy. The large shadow that swam past the window in the office didn't help matters either. The sharks rarely got that close to the facility, though she'd seen them several times in the distance. They seemed to like to swim right on the outskirts of the lights outside. Maybe she'd seen a whale.

"Hello, Zaralai," the woman greeted her as Zaralai sat down, pulling her mind back to the situation. "I'm Director Kim. I head up the Human Resources department. I wanted to have a conversation with you about a communication I received. Would it be okay with you if we talked?"

"Sure," Zaralai shrugged. She didn't see a

problem with it, though she had no idea why they wanted to talk to her. As far as she knew, she was doing everything satisfactorily and hadn't made any mistakes.

"Thank you, Zaralai. I received a letter from Director Sommers from the Habitat. He laid out some issues he has experienced and asked me for input from you. He stated that you were a student of the Habitat for eighteen months. Yet there is no record of you being there, as we looked into that before offering you the scholarship here. Will you tell me more about this accusation? It's a very serious problem that carries heavy consequences and before I make any decisions about your future, I'd like to ascertain the truth as you know it."

Zaralai swallowed the lump in her throat and fought back the sudden wave of tears that flooded her eyes. She couldn't very well lie as the truth had gotten discovered. She hoped that Kapua was okay and that something terrible hadn't happened to have caused her to spill their secrets.

"Well, Zaralai? Is there truth to that accusation?" Director Kim pushed gently.

"Yes," Zaralai nodded and looked down at her lap. "My friend Kapua was assigned to attend the Habitat and she didn't want to go. She is scared of small spaces and had hoped to go to the Island instead. My family are crop workers, so I applied for scholarships to all the factions. I hadn't heard anything when Kapua received her letters and I was sad. We look close enough alike that with some makeup I made with minerals, I could pass for her. I offered to trade places with her."

Director Kim studied Zaralai's face before answering. She took in the child's expression, tone, and disposition. Director Kim had learned of the excellent work Zaralai had done on the Habitat, her scores in class, and the speed at which Zaralai had made friends. It didn't feel right to punish someone who wanted to put in the work to help better society, though there were rules she had to abide by set in place by those above her.

"I'm sorry to hear that." Director Kim frowned before continuing. "I understand why you made the choices you did. However, that doesn't make them right. We still awarded you a scholarship. Sometimes it takes a little longer to process those, though we do our best to accommodate those who want to contribute and can learn the way you do."

"Did something happen to Kapua? Is she okay?" Zaralai let her tears fall.

"She is in the same situation you are in, young lady," Director Kim answered. "She is physically fine and uninjured if that is what you meant. The choices that you two girls made have impacted your families and Kapua's learning in the Habitat."

"What do you mean?" Zaralai wrinkled her brow in confusion.

"Your instructors in the Habitat were expecting a student that has already learned the basics, participated in a substantial project and grown the way they expected. Yet they received a new student who knew nothing about space and how things operate. That jeopardized the classes that Kapua was enrolled in because she didn't hold the same knowledge. Someone could have been seriously injured or killed because of that, Zaralai. How would you feel knowing your friend died because she pretended she knew what to do?" Director Kim explained.

Zaralai's eyes widened and her mouth dropped

open. That was something that neither she nor Kapua had thought about when they switched places back to themselves. She would have never forgiven herself if something had happened to Kapua because of their deception.

"We... I didn't think of that," Zaralai admitted. "I'm so sorry. We just figured it would be easier for her to be herself and me to be me. What happens now?"

"I hate to tell you this, Zaralai," Director Kim replied and bit her lip. "We will have to send you both home, and you will have to face charges for false identities. Since your family was involved, they will also face charges. If you receive a strict judgment, I fear the punishment is banishment to the wastelands."

"W-wa-wastelands?" Zaralai stuttered. "What does that mean?"

"Zaralai," Director Kim steepled her fingers and sighed. "It means that you and your family would be sent away from your home to an area that could still be deemed unsafe. I disagree with decisions like that, but I don't make those rules. I'm going to be completely honest with you about this. Sending someone to the wastelands is how they hand out a death sentence without them saying you are getting a death sentence. As I stated earlier, these deceptions are met with harsh punishments."

"But we didn't mean to hurt anyone," Zaralai protested. "We were helping each other out. We shouldn't have to die because of that."

"I can't say what the outcome will be. I am only informing you of what that verdict means. The crime's punishment will be determined by the judge who hears your case. You are a smart girl; my job is to help you understand the consequences of your actions. I'm sorry that it has come to this, but you'll need to pack up your belongings. A boat arriving later tonight will return you to land," Director Kim explained gently. "For what it's worth, Zaralai, I don't believe a yearning to educate yourself and help others should be a crime."

Zaralai felt hot tears slide down her cheeks. Her selfishness had potentially cost her friend and Zaralai's parents their lives. Zaralai felt her body fold in on itself and slumped forward and sobbed. She was an awful person.

"I've heard the explanations from both students and the instructors as to the possible damage and fatalities that could have resulted. It is my ruling that Kapua Moana, and Zaralai Abara and her family, are banished to a wastelands area no less than three hundred kilometers from an established colony," the judge ruled. "You will have one week to vacate the area."

"I object!" Kapua's father stood up and smacked his hand on the table. "We are one of the established families and I refuse to send my daughter off to some potential area where she could rot and die because she had fears and succumbed to them. She is human."

"I'm afraid the ruling is non-negotiable," the judge droned on as if she'd heard the argument before.

"Then my family and I will be joining her. I will have my crops harvested and take them with us," Mr. Moana declared.

For a brief second, Zaralai thought the judge would change her mind as the Moana crops were extensive and a major supplier. However, she merely sighed and nodded before vacating the room.

"Abara, do not leave without us," Mr. Moana told Zaralai's father. "With my resources, we will start a new community. From the sounds of it, Zaralai is smart enough to help us with building and agriculture. I will need the full week to get everything accomplished and settled. Will you grant me that?"

"Of course, Mr. Moana," Zaralai's father agreed. "I will wait to hear from you. If you need assistance with the crops, you only have to ask and we will all help. We are in this together."

Zaralai's head spun. In less than a week, she had been dismissed from the Fishbowl, sent home, tried, sentenced, and banished. They had a week to pack their stuff and leave the only home she'd ever known. Now her actions had swallowed an entire other family.

"Lift your head, Zaralai," her father admonished her. "We knew what we were getting into when we agreed to allow you girls to switch places. Parents want their children to be happy. We want you to learn and to have better lives than we do. And this may come as a surprise to you, Daughter, but not all parents agree with the factions and sending their kids away. Do not hang your head in shame. I'm proud you followed your heart, and in the end, no one got hurt, regardless of what could have happened."

Zaralai nodded though her guilt did not abate. She felt the tears prick her eyes more than once, yet neither parent mentioned them or did anything to make her feel worse. She dutifully packed up her room when she got home and helped her parents pack the rest of their home.

Two days later, they were all at Kapua's house helping them pack. Half of their workforce chose to follow Mr. Moana, which said much about that family. The crews worked hard digging up the crops to be replanted and loading them on trucks. Considering how much land the Moana family owned, it was an enormous undertaking.

Mr. Moana had talked with Zaralai's dad about their direction, and Zaralai had suggested they travel toward the water. It would take them multiple days to make the trip, but the men located a section of land deemed uninhabitable a couple of decades ago. It was coastline and at least five hundred kilometers from any other known rehabilitated cities.

Zaralai had learned a lot about desalination during her short time in the Fishbowl, and even more, she had books about it. A place near the coast would allow for irrigation for the crops and milder weather in the winter.

It took everyone the entire week, but everything was packed, loaded in a caravan's worth of vehicles and they set out for lands unexplored. It was a bittersweet goodbye for Zaralai but she vowed not to look back and to make do as best as they could. She would utilize the small bits of knowledge she'd gathered and put them to work.

The trip took them a little over two weeks of traveling over rough terrain, to put it lightly, and through areas that were so dry and hot that their vehicles overheated. The landscapes were starkly beautiful in haunting ways.

Zaralai saw more evidence of war than she cared to. Proof of humanity at its worst. Only there were no humans. There were barely any animals or insects either.

Those that survived had mutated genes and were so frightening that she never wanted to exit the vehicle.

But she also saw signs of new life that gave her hope—something to cling to instead of thinking that she was the reason her friends and family would die out in radiated land. Green things were sporadically sprouting up from the cracks in the ground. There were even a few small trees growing in the blackened craters.

When they arrived in their chosen location, they were all pleased to see that some houses still stood, buildings they could use as warehouses and food storage with some alterations. It wasn't a bombed-out shell of a place. Plus, there was vegetation.

Patches of grass, various weeds, and shrubbery grew around some of the houses. That told them that the soil was usable. Plants and water equaled life. Zaralai wondered if fear kept people from branching out and looking at new places to expand. This place appeared utterly livable from what she could see with her partially-trained eye.

They pulled the vehicles over in a neighborhood and used Geiger meters to check radiation levels. When nothing registered, they went through the houses to ensure they were safe—no abnormal readings anywhere.

"Looks like we found ourselves a place to live," Mr. Moana called out. "The houses need a good cleaning and solar panels installed. I'm happy we thought to bring those. That shouldn't be too difficult. After that, we can seek land to clear and till for crops."

So it began. Every able-bodied person got busy cleaning and clearing the houses. That chore, too, took a couple of days, and then the men started the installation of solar panels. Zaralai was able to help them and that went quickly.

Kapua and Zaralai put their heads together and worked out a water purification system for the houses using the books Zaralai brought with her and their combined knowledge from working in the fields. The homes had clean water, solar electricity and heat, and working appliances within a week.

"Look at that, girls," Mr. Moana beamed after seeing that everyone had moved into a house. "What should we call the new settlement?"

"Freedom," Zaralai whispered. "But freedom isn't free." Her thoughts were of the price they all paid for her choices.

"Oh! Yeah!" Kapua agreed. "Freedom."

"You are correct, Zaralai," her father smiled. "It isn't free. However, that is a great name. What do you think, Mr. Moana?"

"Freedom it is. You will do your best to earn it, right?" Mr. Moana glanced at each of the girls.

"Yes, sir," Kapua and Zaralai chirped.

Inside a year, Freedom flourished. Crops grew, children learned, and new people found them. There would be no factions in Freedom, only a sense of community. They taught each other how to thrive and shared their knowledge and skills for the betterment of their society.

Some years later, Zaralai realized she'd received everything she had hoped to obtain from the different factions by simply living within their recreated community. They had turned their punishment into something to be proud of and her guilt was no longer welcome.

Michelle Lee

Now that you know how Freedom was attained, have you decided if history repeated itself? Did society come full circle within two years? Perhaps it was that two young girls from different backgrounds found a way to prove that all you needed to succeed was bravery and ambition. It was possible to start from nothing and have everything.

Reborn

Something tore at the delicately stitched-together seams inside me. It ripped me open, figuratively, of course, but it was almost as if I could feel the tissues separating. A blood-curdling, desperate, angry scream exploded from my throat, much in the way a volcano would erupt. I could hear the metaphorical stitches holding my insides together snap like a guitar string wound too tightly. It was a song of darkness.

Ash billowed out of my open mouth, bleeding into the sky that had only awakened with tendrils of pink reaching across the midnight blue expanse as it receded. If I were a phoenix, I'd rise above it, reborn in magic and start anew. But I wasn't. If I died, I'd stay dead. Something I'd recently learned.

I swallowed the embers of my devastation and let the scream die. Maybe it would carry on the currents to one of my remaining siblings because no one else was left alive... well, that wasn't entirely true. I had two siblings left. Every day the dread of my existence was the sugar in my morning coffee that I shared with no one.

There were only four elementals alive simultaneously, something I had only learned recently. However, I had no idea how a new elemental would be born when there was no one alive to repopulate. I wasn't a fan of incest and the world had died during our family squabble, including my sister.

We'd grown up believing we were immortal. It was true. We were. Only no one had informed us about the loopholes. We would live forever *if no one killed us.* Granted, it wasn't something easy to do, but there it was. Elementals could die.

Even the spirits disappeared. What did that say about the world left when not even ghosts remained? I had yet to find a portal to another realm and my guess was the faerie folk closed them down. No one wanted a part in our drama. I didn't blame them. I didn't even remember how it started.

Hawk, my brother who had the power of the air, was the fight's instigator. I was pretty sure about that. Everest, my other brother who had the power of earth, joined in second in retaliation. My sister, Indigo, felt like she was the victim of Hawk's actions, jumped into the fray, and ultimately died. Now there was no water to balance us out. There is no life without water.

That left me, Alinta. The only elemental not required for life. Guilt ate at me because if one of us had to die, it should have been me. Indigo was necessary. As much as it angered me to admit it, so was Hawk.

Indigo lived to the fullest. Eyes the color of her name, a temperament as unpredictable as the oceans, and hair that flowed the way the water moved. Everyone loved her no matter her mood. Indigo was never alone. We were close; she was my best friend.

Another soul-wrenching sound was about to fall from my chapped lips when I swallowed the boiling lava of my emotions. I needed to find my brothers. I didn't want to. I had the part I played in the apocalypse, and while I owned it, I wanted to be angry at them. Murderously, heartbreakingly furious.

I knew Hawk and Everest were lying low, hiding like snakes waiting to attack. They knew how vital Indigo was to me. I didn't understand which one of them took Indigo's life, only that it wasn't me. I wanted vengeance for Indigo and the world they laid to waste. I was destruction in its purest form. I embodied it, and nothing kept me from razing everything without my sister to dampen my flames. Hiding from me was a wise choice.

There was a double purpose to my traveling by foot, bicycle, or car, aside from the fact that there was no one to fly an airplane and I had no idea where my brothers were. I searched each town I came across for signs of life. I cataloged all the devastation to hold them accountable when I found them.

I wasn't lucky when I found life. My rage was fueled evermore and my heart broke even further. Each decimated city reminded me of Indigo, of lovers that would never happen, of families lost.

Tornadoes, hurricanes, tsunamis, and earthquakes swept through the world like a careless roll of the dice. The fires that broke out weren't even from me. The flames that I had witnessed, I was able to snuff out.

The 'oopsy' I owned was exploding a volcano that resulted in lava flows and decimation of lands and small cities that had lain at the base of the mountain. The only consolation I received was that no one died from my tantrum. I ruined their houses, but their lives ended up taken by the earthquake that swallowed them. It was a hand-in-hand type of thing. One set off the other.

"Where are you, bastards?" I screamed to the sky

with a plume of ash. It wasn't intentional; it was an uncontrolled side effect of my rage.

I caught a glimpse of my reflection in one of the few unbroken windows I walked past in town. My eyes were coal black with the centers appearing as burning cinders; darkened circles framed my eyes and stained my fair skin. My orange hair was a mess of dreadlocks and ratted-out dirty strands that stood out from my head in erratic patterns. Random soot marks smudged any exposed skin.

Given how I looked, it was probably a good thing there were no people left; I'd have scared the life out of them. I looked around for a business or home with a functioning shower and vowed to clean myself up. I knew the odds were slim that I would find anyone alive but there wasn't anything wrong with holding on to a smidgen of hope.

I didn't find a house. However, I found an outdoor swimming pool with a partial locker room that still stood. It wasn't like I had to worry about modesty or perverts. I located some towels, soap, mini shampoo and conditioner bottles, and stripped naked.

I used my fire abilities to warm the water since it was icy. Washing away the dirt, ash, and grime felt spectacular. It was nearly orgasmic washing my hair. It would be pure hell to brush it since it had matted but I'd cross that bridge when I got to it.

I wrapped some towels around me, walked out to the street, and looked both ways. I knew I'd seen a department store somewhere and I hoped they had decent clothes I could wear. The ones I'd discarded needed to be burned.

I found the store five minutes later and dug

through the debris until I found clean clothes that fit. Then I hunted for a brush and possibly some new socks and shoes. I found a toothbrush before I found a hairbrush, but I did find it. I found a backpack, stuffed some extra clothing inside, and then some toiletries.

It took me an hour to brush through my hair using some detangler I found. I was getting up to get back on the road when I heard my name on the air. I thought it was floating on the breeze but maybe it came from the earth. Either way, it was one of my brothers.

I stepped onto the street and sucked in a lungful of air, trying to catch a scent. If you've ever wondered what a bastard smelled like, take a whiff of one of my brothers. The aroma of self-righteousness, condescension, arrogance, and entitlement wafted past my nostrils. It came from the east.

I grabbed snack foods and water from each town I traveled through. I didn't know what would happen when the food ran out. How would we survive? I had yet to find any signs of life indicating animals had survived the melee.

Thoughts plagued me with every step. They flitted through my mind like an angry wraith not ready to show itself as it slithered through the night, looking for its target. My brain was a macabre place to dwell, yet I couldn't help the trajectory of my thoughts. How do we make it past this as a race? As a civilization? I didn't see how it was possible.

Immortal or not, we still bled, felt pain, suffered, and got hungry and thirsty. I understood the nuances of immortality, and after suffering the tragic loss of losing an immortal sister, I knew there were possibilities I'd never thought of before. Dying from starvation was front and center in my head. There was no one left for me to ask if it could happen.

Desolation washed through me at a slow burn. Each mile I walked to the next town felt heavier. I wasn't one prone to depression but the situation warranted it, I felt. No one was left, even if we never had to eat again to survive. It would be the loneliest existence ever, which isn't a life.

Fire would keep me warm at night but it wouldn't love me the way a person would. I didn't have a chance to find a partner now. Honestly, I'd never thought about one anyway. I couldn't imagine loving someone so deeply and knowing you would outlive them. To have to watch them die, or watch your children die? It was the downside of immortality. But with the world populated, I still had that choice until it had been taken away from me.

Fury at my brothers kept me mobilized while grief and anger with my sister immobilized me. I wanted to run and find my brothers, yet stop and wail out my emotions too. I was worse than a train wreck and didn't care because there was no one to witness my countless meltdowns.

I struggled with wrapping my mind around everything. Processing the end of life wasn't an easy task and I figured I'd rather hold on to hope that I would encounter a person than give in to what my eyes told me. Optimism wasn't my usual go-to. I was more of a realist. However, I think optimism was a better choice at the moment, so why not go with it?

I found a bicycle in the next town that was no larger than a block. I rummaged through the food until I found a semi-decent apple and scarfed that down to stop my brain from thinking I was starving to death. I wasn't even hungry. It was nothing more than the toxic wayward thoughts that plagued me. My brain was rotting and I felt like a zombie ready to crack my skull in and sample the goods.

I was now on day four of heading east. I hadn't gotten any sense that I was any closer to either of my brothers. I rode the bike hard and quickly covered the twenty miles between the cities. Eventually, I'd run out of land and face crossing an ocean. I hoped it wouldn't come to that. I could figure out how to drive a boat. However, crossing an ocean on a vessel I was maybe capable of driving was an iffy situation at best.

"Come on," I shouted to the sky. "Where are you?" My scream released another ashy plume that drifted on the currents. "Show yourselves!"

A faint tremor ran under my feet from back to front, and I took that as a sign that I needed to keep heading in the direction I faced. Everest wasn't far from me, it seemed. It was about time I came across one of them. I'd traveled by car, foot, and bicycle and it felt like I'd seen over half of the country.

It was another two days and I don't know how many miles before a sensation of danger crawled over my skin and made my hair stand on end. Fiery heat licked at my skin from the inside in response to the warning.

It had to be Everest, though he'd never used his powers on me before; I didn't like it. It felt like vines were weaving themselves over my skin and holding me in place. I let my skin heat up to burn the sensation away since nothing was physically on me. I kept it going until the feeling receded and I didn't have to focus on making myself move.

"Nicely played, little sister," Everest's voice rang out. "I felt the flames. You've come a long way with your skills."

"This isn't a game, Everest," I barked. I rolled my eyes for added dramatic effect. I was sure he could see me.

"No games. I was merely helping you practice your talents."

There was a rustle of leaves where there shouldn't be since no leaves were there. It had to be Everest up to another of his tricks. He was the oldest of us and I was the youngest. It had taken me longer to manipulate my element than the others and Everest liked to rub it in. He didn't know that while this separation between us had lasted years, I'd mastered fire in that time. I only needed a spark and I could incinerate the world.

"I don't need more practice." I turned and faced the direction I knew he was. "Aside from the fact that there is no need. There are no people to worry about, only you and Hawk. And I don't think either of you are stupid enough to try to fight me with fire. However, you are dumb enough to bring about Armageddon."

"Hardly accurate." Everest let out a peal of laughter. "Do you see angels waiting to pass judgment?"

"Do you see any life at all?" I fired back furiously. "I wasn't trying to be Biblical, but if you want to take it there, then sure, let's do that. What if it were the last battle and only the worthy were taken? What does that say about us?"

Everest's humored chuckles stopped, and I was

staring at him less than two feet in front of me. He needed a shower. I stepped back, waved my hand in front of my nose, and wrinkled my face in disgust. Yes, it was petty, yet I knew it would bother him and his vanity. I wasn't here to make nice with him. I wanted answers and vengeance.

"It's camouflage," Everest argued.

"From what?" I screeched. "There is no one left! I saw not one animal or person the entire trek here. What exactly are you hiding from out here?"

"Old habits die hard," Everest mumbled with a frown.

"What old habits would that be now? Womanizing? Displays of power to woo someone?" I shook my head. Some of my statements might be unfair. I hadn't been around Everest in a while to know if he still did those things. I only remembered him doing them when he was younger.

"I'm not a child." Everest crossed his arms and glared at me. "Why are you here?"

"I want answers." I crossed my arms in a mimicking gesture. "Indigo is dead and it wasn't by my hands. Why is she dead? What started this? Why did the rest of the world have to suffer because of whatever issue arose between you three? And why haven't you bathed?"

I threw the last one in there to jab at my brother again. It was pure irritation for his unwillingness to see the foolishness of his behavior. Also, he honestly smelled awful, like a sasquatch that ate rotten cat food, puked it up, and a stray and starving dog ate it and crapped it out. I told him as much.

I watched in satisfaction as Everest stormed off

and I heard the splash of water. Good. He clearly hadn't experienced people standing up to him or calling him on his childishness and narcissism. I made myself comfortable as he used whatever body of water he'd jumped in to clean himself of the stink.

"Hawk said Indigo threatened and challenged him," Everest told me after he finished his excessively long bath. "Obviously, I didn't believe him and when I joined the madness, it was to stop them both from being destructive."

"Yet you were a destroying force and added to the insanity," I pointed out with a surly tone and expression that matched. The mighty Everest wouldn't win this battle. "You created devastating earthquakes, sinkholes that swallowed cities, landslides that buried roads and towns. Forests came toppling down and took wildlife with them. What exactly were you trying to help with those actions? With Indigo dead, your earthquakes caused tsunamis that couldn't be tempered. Civilizations wiped out in a blink."

"Don't get high and mighty with me, Alinta. You weren't blameless in this." Everest sneered at me. "You act like I single-handedly wiped out the human race."

"Every one of those events I mentioned was solely accomplished by you," I spat. Fire coursed through my veins, begging to be released. "Yes, I caused a volcano to erupt and decimated the village at the mountain's base. Yet I killed no one. I'm not arguing that fact, and I'm not trying to justify it. I was wrong and the guilt is a terrible burden."

"Well, well, well, look who grew up to be an adult," Everest mocked me. He began to pace back and forth and it became apparent that he was uncomfortable. However, you had to really look to see it. Maybe there was hope for him.

"Is the guilt eating at you, Everest?" I did my best to gentle my tone, but that knife's edge was still clinging on tightly.

"I don't know." He paced a few more steps before he came to a complete stop. "I've never felt it before. Is this how guilt manifests?"

"Well, sometimes. It's different for everyone. I want to know how you've never felt guilty about something before now." I huffed out my irritation and vowed to give Everest time to figure it out.

"How do I fix it?" Everest spun to glare at me. "I don't like feeling this way."

"Are you serious?" I growled. "You can't fix it. All you can do is apologize to who you wronged and do something to compensate for it. Only this time, you can't. Everyone is dead."

"Stop harping on that!" Everest yelled at me. The veins on his forehead bulged out and he had a purplish color happening to his skin. I guessed this was Everest's angry look.

"I won't!" I shouted back, getting in his face. "The world is dead. The guilt is yours to carry. We can't reproduce, food will eventually be gone, and we are alone. All because of some trifle spat that probably could have been resolved without Armageddon."

Everest shoved me out of frustration and I flicked the little lighter I carried in my pocket for that spark I needed. The fire that lived inside me roared to the surface and I shot a stream of flames directly at him. He didn't know that, over the years, I'd learned to control and perfect the reach of my flares. My intent was not to burn him but to scare him to see how he would react. That would tell me everything I needed to know.

Everest jumped backward and the ground under my feet began to swallow me. It was as I'd expected. That was why the world went extinct. My brother's responses to fear weren't to evaluate the situation and act accordingly. They leaped to protect themselves instead of what was around them. At least, that was the case with Everest.

I didn't stop him from sinking me into the ground. I patiently waited for him to understand that my reaction wasn't one of aggression; it was a warning. I'm sure my face bore the expression of one with haughty disdain and disappointment.

It took him longer than it should, considering I'm his sister and I sought him out. I would have struck out before if I wanted to harm him. I was tired of his ego. I crossed my arms again and affixed my gaze to his.

"Are you done?" I quirked one eyebrow up.

"We were raised as humans; you know that," Everest deflected. "Our guides wanted us to fit in. That doesn't mean we need food to survive. We eat to fit in."

"That's your defense? We don't need food to survive, so let's kill everyone." I heaved myself out of the hole that Everest sunk me into since he was doing nothing to reverse the action. "I'm done here. You are offering no explanations or anything constructive, so I'm out. I'm going to find Hawk."

I made it to the next town before Everest found me. I'd suspected he'd follow because his pride wouldn't allow anything less than that. His narcissism would force him so he could prove he wasn't the instigator and was nothing more than an innocent victim in all this— arrogant jerk.

I didn't hold out greater expectations for Hawk. He was identical to Everest in his attitude. Their relationship was one of those in that the younger brother idolized the older one. The main difference was that Hawk liked to brag about his exploits, whereas Everest tended to point the finger elsewhere.

I was done talking to my big brother, who filled the silence of his own volition. He followed and talked. He made no notice of the ruins we passed through. The rubble of buildings he made topple over. He ignored the skeletal remains crushed beneath beams and cement. Yet I witnessed the fidgety behavior the more we encountered evidence of his wrongdoing.

A week passed before I caught Hawk's scent on a blustery day. I was on the western side of the country now but I wasn't sure where. I couldn't pinpoint the direction Hawk was in either. Even Everest had fallen silent. That was the advantage of encompassing the power of the wind. You could change directions on a whim and effectively hide.

"He probably doesn't want to be found," Everest whispered. His voice was off, tinged with something close to fear.

I stopped the car we had taken and got out. I walked about ten feet away and stood there staring at the sky. We were almost out of town and climbing a mountain pass. I didn't want to be on foot for that and could only hope the pass wasn't blocked. I was getting tired of walking. It would be just like Hawk to be in the most inaccessible place possible, and that I expected.

"Hawk!" I screamed into the wind. "I need to see you!"

Everest huffed an irritated breath and got out of the car. He searched the sky in the same way I did; only he did not indicate that Hawk was even remotely in this area. I didn't know if Everest was that good of a liar but I wouldn't put it past him.

Without saying anything to him, I got back in the car and started it. I received a small measure of satisfaction watching him bolt back to the car and fling himself inside as I began to move. He deserved it and I didn't apologize. It wouldn't have bothered me to leave him behind.

I headed up the highway to see how far across the pass I could get. I left my window open to see if I caught another whiff of my brother. My instincts told me he was somewhere on the pass in the thick of nature yet comfortably ensconced, probably in a ski cabin.

As I drove, I couldn't help but think I could simply blaze the forest to the ground. Hawk's powers of the wind would only feed my fire; he wouldn't escape. I'm not sure it would kill him, but it would make him easier to find. I itched; I wanted to do it so badly. No. I wouldn't burn the forests. I was one of those that believed in leaving a place better than I found it.

It felt like a ridiculous notion considering no one was left, yet I couldn't help respecting nature simply because of who I was. I think that was something that my siblings forgot. They got too wrapped up in their egos and what people could do for them. Even Indigo did that though she pulled herself back out of it when I called her on the behavior, just as she used to do for me if I stepped out of line.

I missed my sister. I missed people. An immortal lifetime without her seemed impossible. I was jarred out of my miserable thoughts by Everest.

"Stop! He's here!" Everest slammed his palm into my shoulder for added effect. It caused me to veer the car sharply to the left and the front tires slid over an icy patch that hadn't melted yet. The car bumped into the rock wall and spun a little before I corrected it and came to a stop.

"Are you trying to cause an accident?" I glared at my older brother. "The words were sufficient."

"Hawk is around here somewhere. I can feel him," Everest replied caustically. "I thought that's what you wanted. Didn't you just scream for him back there where you stopped?" His tone dripped with condescension like a broken faucet.

I didn't grace him with an answer. I got out of the car and walked in a circle until I felt the fire inside me rise. That was the direction I would go until I found Hawk. If my instincts were warning me about danger, that's where I'd find my brother.

I hiked through the forest over remaining clumps of snow and fallen trees and along a creek with water so cold that even my fire abilities couldn't keep me warm. It was stunning, humbling, and exhausting. Up the mountain, down steep slopes, only to switchback up again. Hawk needed to surface soon.

It felt like I'd hiked half the mountain before we stumbled upon a cabin nestled into a copse of trees. It appeared empty though I knew it wasn't. So did Everest. His entire being changed and his eyes darted around like a skittish cat.

I didn't care about what made Everest so nervous. My skin began to chill with the sudden stopping of movement and I let the fire inside me heat my skin. Steam rose in a vapor cloud around me and Everest took a step away.

That's when I understood we weren't alone. The air was far too still for the setting we were in, on the side of a mountain where the wind always blew. The veil of steam around me didn't shift at all, nor did it dissipate. Hawk was close.

"I want to talk, Hawk," I said evenly. "Everest just invited himself. This gathering isn't to gang up on you."

"Right. Nothing but a good old-fashioned guilt trip lined with some hatred," Everest piped up, his voice rising. "Who doesn't want to listen to that? Come on out and join the fun, brother."

I only noticed the slight alteration to the airflow because the steam hovering over me moved to the left as if disturbed. I lashed out with my right arm and heard the grunt Hawk tried to stifle. Hawk had bent the air around himself to camouflage his presence, as I'd figured.

Hawk didn't expect the aggression from me the same as I didn't expect the retaliation. As my body got blown backward, I didn't miss Everest's smirk and satisfied expression. When my body hit the ground, I rebounded onto my feet and sent the spark as a broad spread of fire to ensure I got Hawk. Any retaliation on his part would only feed the flames.

It appeared that Hawk realized that little fact before it was too late and he materialized, looking a little frazzled. I couldn't decipher the look he shot at Everest but when he finally settled his gaze on me, it was annoyance. He raked his eyes over me and sneered.

"What do you want, Alinta?" Hawk asked me impatiently. It was as if I were keeping him from some important task he had going on out here in the woods where nothing else existed but him.

"Answers." I shifted my stance to a defensive position because Hawk wasn't predictable.

"She's not the same girl we used to know," Everest warned.

"It's the natural process of things to evolve and grow." Hawk smirked at me. "I wouldn't expect her to be the same. She melted a city with lava. Oh, wait, she melted several things when we were kids. I suppose some things don't change."

I ignored Hawk's bait and took in the area surrounding me. There was thick tree cover of pines and a few other trees bare of leaves. Due to the tree cover, there were no snow clumps, yet the small cabin had icicles hanging from the gutters that mainly appeared buried under a layer of moss. The roof was metal under the foliage that piled on top; I guessed it added a layer of insulation to the place.

"What started the fight with Indigo?" I asked Hawk. My tone was stern and Hawk felt the edge. He didn't reply quickly. He stood there and glared at me and I kept repeating to myself that I did not want to burn the forest down.

"Are we facing off against each other or something?" Hawk looked between us and I noticed our distinct triangle pattern. "Why do answers matter now?" For that question, he looked back at me.

"Because it matters to me. We ended the world and I want to know why." I wasn't about to budge or cower under his angry tone.

"Miss High-and-Mighty wants answers." Hawk paced in agitation. "I started a tornado that wiped out a cruise ship."

Yeah, that would push Indigo over the edge into instant rage. It didn't tell me why, only how. Which also begged the question of why he would do that anyway. Yes, part of our role here on earth was to guide the disasters to keep the world balanced. Storms were significant, earthquakes were necessary, floods were critical, and fires expected. Causing a storm on purpose that resulted in death was grounds for disciplinary actions by the fates; if they still existed—or cared.

My silence must have unnerved Hawk because I couldn't shut him up in the next few minutes. His rant was meaningless at first. He called out names I didn't know and cursed their lives, which was moot since they were dead. Then he finally arrived at the meat of the conversation.

"She called me a liar," Hawk blurted out. "It didn't matter how much I showed this woman that I could control the air; she said it was smoke and mirrors. What was I supposed to do? Let that statement hang out there? No way!"

"You started this for some girl you were sleeping with?" I gaped at my brother. "I know Everest used to do that but I figured you learned from his mistakes! How stupid are you? Wait. Don't answer that because your actions already told me." I flung my hands up in the air and pivoted to walk away before I did something dumb.

"Seriously, Hawk?" Everest echoed my feelings in his tone. "Alinta isn't wrong to be furious with you."

"With me? I wasn't alone in that fight. Indigo and

you were there right along with me. Even Alinta took part. You don't get to lay the blame at my feet; I was protecting my reputation and importance in the way of the world. It was a demonstration. How could I know that the hurricane would hit turbulent jet streams and pick up power?" Hawk yelled defensively.

I tuned out Everest's retort after he screamed back that Hawk had the power of the air, who would know better than him that it could happen? Everest was right, and the same thought flew through my head.

Indigo had paid attention to the ebb and flow of the tides to tell her if something were amiss. She'd swim in the water to feel the pollution levels. She'd throw her head back and open her mouth to taste the rain. That's how she'd found out about the hurricane. Indigo had taken her responsibilities seriously.

Just as I did; I monitored volcanoes and magma levels. I watched forest fires and pulled the life out of them at the right moment to maintain the balance of life. I let the sun blast its heat down on the world and then hid it when the time came. Sometimes these events caused a loss of life, but we controlled it. It was ingrained into us from the second we were born and received the powers of the elements.

The start of the apocalypse suddenly made sense. Hawk made his idiotic move and Indigo noticed the change in the water as it got sucked up into the hurricane. She immediately reacted and once she understood how it began and that so many people died, she'd lost control. I'd witnessed that part.

Everest joined in, maybe with the intent to try and dissipate the conflict, but he also couldn't stop himself from his own displays of power and then so it was on.

They all got sucked into this destructive battle with each other for dominance. I didn't help matters any when Indigo died and I erupted that volcano. We weren't watching out for humanity. We weren't helping them; we were the problems.

In a burst of clarity, I understood what needed to happen. I let my power build until it felt like my veins were melting in my body. My power was at a dangerous level; the only time it had been this potent was when Indigo died. I turned back to my brothers and though they still argued, they watched me warily.

The earth preemptively rumbled under my feet and the air currents shifted in a warning. I didn't budge; however, I was ready. I'd trained extensively for battle though I can't say that this scenario was what I expected. Both of my brothers were on high defense.

I wondered if my face gave something away or if my skin changed to give people a warning that hell was about to unleash on them. I can't say I knew the answer to that since I couldn't see myself. I remember that Indigo used to tell me how scary I looked when I was close to this place where the fire inside almost hurt me. Maybe all they were reacting to was my fierce look.

The ground rolled and knocked me off balance. I tumbled neatly into a roll and righted myself right in front of Hawk, who flung shards of frozen fog at my face. I think he forgot that I was fire and they all melted before they hit. I needed the two closer together for my quickly thrown-together plan to work.

I felt a bed of natural gas below and funneled my power into it to cause an explosion next to where Hawk stood. It would take Everest a second to realize that I had intruded on his territory and in that moment, Hawk stumbled into Everest and I burst into action.

"We are the problem!" I yelled at my brothers as I materialized a sword of fire hot enough to cut through diamonds like they were melted butter. I swung my arm in a wide arc while Hawk and Everest were distracted by the explosion. Neither of them looked at me and the sword neatly sliced through the necks of my siblings.

I swallowed the bile that rose in my throat as the two decapitated settled in front of me. My brother's eyes remained open in betrayal and shock as their bodies fell lifeless to the now-still ground. It made me sick that I could do something so horrible but I wasn't wrong in what I said. We *were* the problems with the world.

I think my entire journey has been about coming to that conclusion and this end. I now needed to complete the circle and allow the fates to decide what would happen with the relic of the beautiful world we'd left destroyed and lifeless.

I bent over and set the heads on fire to ensure that part of my plan was complete. My tears fell on the flames though I wasn't worried they would be snuffed out. Once there was nothing left, I went to the cabin to look for any weapons Hawk may have stored.

It didn't take me long to find what I needed, and I walked back outside and sat near my brothers' bodies. I made peace with what I did and looked around me at what I would leave behind.

The forest was breathtaking and I knew there were so many other wonders that the world held that I'd never gotten to experience. My fervent hope was that the universe would intercede and create life here again to explore, care for, and appreciate what we did not.

"Fates, accept my apologies for what my siblings and I decimated without further care beyond our own selfish wants. I offer us up as sacrifices so that life may once more flourish in this majestic place." I took a deep breath, said goodbye, and made a little wish that Indigo awaited me on the other side.

A bird chirped for the first time in months and flew from lush green branch to leafy branch before landing next to the inert, sleeping body of a child amidst the snow drifts that remained. There was no fear from the bird, only innocent curiosity before it retook flight to spread the word through its trilling song that hope remained.

Love Eternal

atty, today, in front of our friends and family, I want to promise you that nothing will stand in the way of my love for you, not even the Reaper himself. I love you and it's eternal. That is my solemn vow to you."

Natasha shut off the video and television it played her saying her vows in return. There wasn't much point in her watching it one more time. She knew how it ended, with Monte breaking his promise by dying. She furiously wiped a stray tear that trailed down her cheek. Sixteen years had not been long enough with the love of her life.

She'd spent the last year watching Monte decline and sitting bedside. The doctors and countless specialists couldn't figure out what was wrong with him. His organs were deteriorating at a rapid pace, and all they could come up with was calling it a fatal degenerative disorder, which could be several things all lumped together. There wasn't a treatment that slowed anything down; it all seemed to progress things further. It was horrific to watch him advance toward the inevitable.

Eight months later and it was still as if he'd passed yesterday. Natasha got up and moved over to the gray plush, overstuffed couch that Monte adored. She settled in the place he'd always sat and stared out the window through the half-closed slats of the blinds.

Her eyes went out of focus and it looked like the stars were twinkling. However, when she blinked, she realized it was nothing more than a reflection of lights on the faux wooden slats; Natasha sighed in disappointment. Nothing but clouds were visible past the street lights.

Since Monte's death, she'd been looking at the stars at night. It was comforting to think that Monte was now one of those stars. He stood watch over her from the heavens. That's what she told herself. She even picked out which star was him and talked to it when things got bad, which was practically every day.

Natasha released a heavy sigh and quietly cursed the clouds. There were times that she wished Monte was a ghost and haunted her. At least that would mean he was still around. She stood up, stretched her arms to the ceiling, bent forward, touched the ground with her hands, and held the pose. She loved the feeling of the slow stretch of her back muscles.

Right before she straightened, Natasha would swear that she felt Monte's hand slide over her butt. She'd know his touch anywhere. She righted herself slowly, with her breath held, and turned around. As expected, there was no one there. She exhaled in a *whoosh* and closed her eyes. Sometimes, her imagination ran to wild extremes.

Natasha rubbed her hand over her backside, shook her head and went to take a shower. It would be an early-to-bed night for her; she'd had a lot of those lately. She hoped tomorrow would be better with fewer emotions flooding her and possibly clear skies.

Natasha woke up with a start, her eyes darting around the bedroom, trying to see shadows in the dark. She was sure she'd heard someone call her name, specifically Monte. It was impossible, she knew, yet it happened. There was no way that it was a figment of her overactive imagination this time. She could feel it resonating in her bones.

"Hello?" Natasha whispered into the bedroom.

She felt ridiculous for even responding and wondered what she would do if she received an answer. Call the cops? Ask more questions? Assume it was Monte reaching out from the beyond? There was no question in my mind whose voice it was; it was his.

She was intimately familiar with Monte's voice. Even now, eight months after his death, she could pick his voice out of a mob of people shouting. Sure, anyone could rationalize the experience by saying she'd imagined it because she wanted to hear him so badly. But she wouldn't have woken up if it were all in her head. It was an audible sound that had pulled her from deep sleep.

Natasha pushed herself onto her elbows and surveyed the room again, looking for anomalies. Not one thing looked different or out of place. The room's ambient temperature was still warm, and the cooler feeling could be attributed to the open window.

A thought clicked in Natasha's mind that maybe someone had said her name from outside her window. She silently climbed out of bed, padded over to the window, and pushed up one of the slats to peek through the blinds.

Natasha's motion sensing flood light hadn't

kicked on and nothing looked strange outside. To be sure, she stayed in place for a couple of minutes and watched the backyard. When nothing stirred, not even a breeze, she crept back to bed and slid under the covers with confusion clouding her mind.

She checked her phone and saw the time was just after two o'clock in the morning. Natasha pulled the covers up to her chin and sighed. Was it an odd coincidence that Monte had died around the same time? *Most likely*, she told herself.

"I feel like I'm losing my mind," she whispered.

Natasha rolled to her side and closed her eyes. It took a while, but she finally fell into a restless sleep, only to wake up a few hours later when her alarm blared out in the silent house.

She let out a weary groan and rolled out of bed. She would feel utterly useless today, and it was a court day, which made it all worse. Her job as a child advocate for the social services department kept her busy and had been a godsend during the past eight months. She needed the distractions to keep her from losing her mind.

Granted, days like today, when she hadn't had as much sleep as necessary, became more challenging. Yet she knew she could focus and get through her reports on the cases being heard by the judge today.

Natasha took an extra long shower and let the heat soak into her bones before she scrubbed herself clean. It would be her last moments of peace for the day until she came home after work.

When she finished and dressed, she looked in the mirror with critical eyes, noted each new line around her eyes and mouth, and bit her bottom lip. She tried not to frown as she carefully applied makeup to mask the dark circles and add some color to her face. She'd let herself go since Monte died.

She dried and styled her hair into a French twist to give her a professional look for the courtroom. Natasha took extra care with her appearance on court days since she was typically in front of many people when she took the stand.

With a final look, she turned and caught a handprint on the bathroom mirror. She stopped and looked again, positive it wasn't there a couple of seconds ago. It must have been the angle of the light and a spot she'd missed cleaning or chose not to clean because the print was much too large to be hers. She reached out to touch it but pulled back at the last second. She didn't want to smudge it. She'd obviously left it there to remind her of Monte.

Natasha shrugged and left the bathroom. She brewed herself a travel mug of coffee, toasted an English muffin and added peanut butter, and ate as she walked out the door into the garage.

She drove as if on autopilot, present but distracted by the earthy smell of pine and the ocean. It was a unique scent, a custom-made cologne that Monte had loved. A bottle of it was still sitting on his dresser at home. She wondered if she subconsciously used some of it after hearing his voice and didn't remember. But even if she had, it would have washed out in the shower.

It was a puzzle that Natasha couldn't figure out and stuck in her mind as she parked, went through security, and made her way to the assigned courtroom. Her preoccupied state of mind continued even as she pulled her case notes out of her briefcase to review before they called her in.

Natasha felt fuzzy in her thoughts and needed a clear head before going in. A few quiet moments of meditation helped. She turned her papers upside down and rested her head against the wall behind her with her eyes closed.

With more of a settled feeling running through her mind, Natasha straightened her neck and slowly stretched it to each side until she felt the pull of the muscles and held the position for five seconds each, then opened her eyes.

Much better, she thought with a tiny smile.

Natasha spared a quick glance around the room to see if the child she was testifying on behalf of had arrived with her temporary foster parents. When she turned her head to the left, the little girl stood beside her.

"Hi, Tasha," Jackie said in her small and timid voice. For a ten-year-old, she was scrawny and fragile-looking.

"Hi, Jackie. How are you feeling?" Natasha asked gently.

"I'm okay. I want to go home. Will I be able to go home today?" Jackie wondered. Her eyes drifted past me and roved over a spot on the wall.

Natasha found that unusual behavior for the child and was curious about what was going through her head. Before she could ask, Jackie's eyes pulled back to her with a frightened look that glimmered behind her big brown eyes.

"Who is that man, Tasha? He looks scary," Jackie whispered with a tremble.

Natasha let her eyes roam over the entire area

that Jackie had stared and went even further on the chance that her peripheral vision caught someone lingering near them. Custody cases could sometimes get heated and Natasha had experienced attempted kidnappings after a hearing before. However, she saw nothing out of the ordinary or any men nearby that could be perceived as scary.

"Where do you see him, Jackie?" Natasha leaned closer to the girl and spoke softly. "What man? Can you describe him for me?" She studied Jackie's facial expressions, watching for any signs of distress.

"Well…" Jackie frowned. "He was right there." The child pointed to the wall. "He had his foot on the wall and he had on a hat. I'm not making it up, Tasha."

"I believe you, sweetie," Natasha whispered to her. "If you see him again, tell me right away." A shiver went down her spine like an ice cube sliding down her back.

Jackie nodded slowly. "What do we do now?" Jackie plopped down on the bench next to Natasha. "Do we have to wait out here? Is my dad here?"

"I haven't seen him yet. What we do now is wait. Someone will come out of those doors and call you; you will go into the room and go on the stand, as we talked about before. They will ask you to tell the truth and ask you some questions. Answer them the best you can and be honest. They'll call my name after, and I'll go in and answer questions, if they have any for me. Do you remember me talking about this with you?"

"Yeah," Jackie responded. "Will I get to go home with my dad?"

"If the judge thinks that's best for you, then yes. We won't know until after it's over." Natasha wanted to hug the little girl but refrained since they were in the open and some might consider it unprofessional.

She had two more cases after this one and settled her mind in for a long day. She needed to be present for the children, not to mention for the sake of her career.

Natasha settled on the couch with a bowl of popcorn and a blanket wrapped around her feet. She grabbed the remote from the antique coffee table that Monte picked from one of the several vintage stores they'd poured through when they bought the house. She turned the TV on and flipped to the channel they used to watch on lazy evenings after work.

Shows where groups investigated haunted locations and sought to prove ghosts existed were a guilty pleasure they'd loved to indulge in together. Something niggled at the back of her mind after all the weirdness and she started to wonder if maybe Monte was trying to tell her something.

She watched and munched her buttery, salty popcorn until the bowl was empty and then sucked down a bottle of water. She chuckled and shook her head as she brought the empty bowl to the kitchen, dumped the kernels in the garbage can, and then put the bowl in the dishwasher.

"Maybe what Monte is trying to tell you, Natty, is that you will have a heart attack from eating too much salt and butter. You should make better choices," Natasha told herself as she returned to the couch to resume her show.

She took mental notes at events that seemed like something she had experienced and began to wonder if Monte or another spirit roamed the house. She fell asleep with that thought, still on the couch with the TV going.

Natasha's sleep was restless and she must have been cold, even in her dreams, because she kept wrapping her arms around herself. It was strange because she could still see the TV on, the blanket wrapped around her feet, and the little clouds of steam each time she puffed out a chilled breath.

After a few minutes, it clicked in her mind that she wasn't sleeping, yet she wasn't quite awake either. That's when she realized she could see herself. Rather than jolting back to reality, Natasha fell still and silent and observed the scene.

The first thing she double-checked was that her physical body was still breathing. The puffs of air from her slightly opened lips confirmed what she had witnessed a few moments ago. Second, she searched the room more thoroughly for signs that there was another spirit present.

Astral projection wasn't one of Natasha's skill sets and she doubted that she arrived in this state alone. She supposed she could be lucid dreaming. However, if that was the case, this was the first time she had managed it and had no clue what to do next.

"Is anyone here with me?" Natasha boldly asked. "Some guidance would be helpful."

A few moments later, it looked as if the air had turned watery. It wasn't real. It was a luminescent film that Natasha couldn't see through. If this experience was lucid dreaming, then that veil was what she wanted.

"Is that the veil between realms?" Natasha asked.

The light the veil threw off was disconcerting. Yet when Natasha moved a few inches to the side, she could see a silhouette, though no identifying marks. It wasn't even apparent whether the figure was male or female. She desperately wanted to believe it was Monte though she was afraid to hope.

Natasha moved closer to the barrier and reached her arm out to touch it. It beckoned to her and repelled her simultaneously. She stopped short of her fingers breaching the mysterious veil. An electric chill crept up her arm and sent warning signals to her brain. The urge to push further was strong; only her self-preservation kept her from doing it.

"Wake up!" Natasha yelled at herself. She didn't know how these things worked. "Natasha! Open your damn eyes!"

It was the oddest feeling she'd ever experienced. A heaviness settled over her chest and it felt like her heart was breaking, yet she yearned for it. Battling for a place with the melancholy was immense fear; she was determined to wake up. Ignoring her instincts never led to anything good. Natasha was at war with herself.

Nothing more than sheer willpower pulled her back to her body. She tried to shake herself awake but her hands went right through herself. With mounting frustration, Natasha screamed and then her mind blanked out to black.

Natasha's eyes blinked open; her mind was foggy and heavy with sleep. She reached for the remote and clicked the power button to turn off the TV. The silence that fell over the living room was absolute. She couldn't even hear the refrigerator's hum and the temperature felt like someone had locked her in the freezer for hours.

As reluctant as she was to remove the blanket

from her feet, she knew it was time to get up and go to bed. She'd had strange dreams while she slept, most likely from falling asleep watching ghost shows. They'd felt so vivid and real that they left her unsettled.

Slowly, Natasha pushed off the blanket and rolled off the couch, her toes instantly cold. She trudged to her bedroom and noticed the temperature difference right away. It felt downright balmy in there compared to the living room. Usually, her room was the coldest in the house, as she slept best that way.

Natasha closed the bathroom door behind her and undressed for a quick shower before climbing into bed. Once she finished, she grabbed her towel and dried off, grateful to the piping hot water that heated her feet back to normal. She dressed in her usual sleep shorts and tank top, pulled her hair into a loose ponytail and brushed her teeth.

In a subconscious move, Natasha glanced at the spot in the mirror where she thought she spotted a handprint earlier that morning. Her knee-jerk reaction to seeing the words *'I'm here'* written in the steam almost had her choking on the toothbrush as she reeled backward.

It was too much for Natasha to handle and her mind shut down. With her eyes closed tight, she finished brushing her teeth and went to bed, thinking that maybe she had a fever and was hallucinating. Things would be back to normal when she woke up in the morning.

It had been a nice thought, but when she woke up, it felt like she hadn't slept but instead had run a marathon. Natasha had tossed and turned all night, and the few moments of actual sleep she'd had, had been riddled with weird dreams that she didn't remember when she woke up. It was enough to drive her mad.

Things continued in this manner for the next two months. The unexplainable events changed and rotated and Natasha ended up beginning therapy. The only thing left for her to do was hire a paranormal investigation crew to examine her house and she wasn't ready to go to that extreme quite yet. Counseling to work through her grief seemed a happy medium.

Natasha's routine was mundane for the most part. She got up, went to work, and came home. The abnormalities were the things that could be considered paranormal. Except for a few instances, they almost always happened at home. There was the courthouse once, but Natasha couldn't prove that it was a ghost there, and once at a grocery store, which she also couldn't prove.

Natasha knew the events were real but it was possible that she read far too much into them and was putting her own spin on reality. As much as she wanted Monte to give her a sign he was still with her, these events felt more sinister than loving and she was tired of them. Aside from the fact that she didn't know if she imagined things because she wanted proof that Monte wasn't gone forever. Grief was a nasty beast.

Three weeks of counseling, three sessions to be exact, still hadn't answered her questions on whether she was sunk too far in or whether ghosts were real. The counselor was frustratingly ambiguous in her comments. Not that she expected a trained mental health professional to tell her she wasn't insane and that something haunted her from the other side.

That is why Natasha found herself outside a ramshackle storefront that boasted tarot readings, séances, and spiritual cleansings. She'd been standing there for more than fifteen minutes staring at the blacked-out window with peeling white letters. Natasha had always heard that places like this were a scam with hooligans only out to steal your money.

Yet, Natasha found herself walking down a street she'd never been on and spotting this clearly old business. Could it be a coincidence? Sure. She could argue for or against it all day, yet in her heart, she didn't believe it had happened by chance. With a defeated sigh, she pulled the door open and walked in.

The smell of patchouli and sage slapped her across the face and she fought back a sneeze, so she didn't appear rude. With a quick glance around the room, she spotted four different incense burners with smoke curling into the air, the wisps fading into nothing. A tad overkill, in her opinion; one burner would have sufficed.

Shelves lined one wall, and across the top shelf were a variety of skulls, some painted, others not. Below that were crystals in several colors and sizes, some stunningly beautiful. The shelf below the crystals had what appeared to be jars of herbs. Then came the shelf loaded with books on spirits, spells, dream interpretation, and many other topics. The bottom shelf held an array of items, including tarot cards, stones, feathers, little bags, jewelry, and things she couldn't identify.

In front of the blacked-out window were stands with leafy plants. True to every stereotypical movie with a fortune teller, palm reader, or someone along those lines, there was a doorway with beaded curtains that blocked you from seeing entirely into whatever room lay beyond.

The wall behind the front counter, which had glass display cases filled with bones, glass sculptures, and random jewelry with crystals or gems, hung various pictures of Jesus, Buddha, and Muhammad. Natasha swore that she would do her best to contain her skepticism and laughter if the establishment's proprietor came out wearing a flowing, gauzy dress and tons of bracelets and necklaces.

Natasha turned full circle looking for someone to speak to and, seeing no one, she approached the counter and tapped her fingers on the glass in nervousness. She fought the urge to whistle and couldn't contain her fidgeting. The rattle of the beads made her looking up.

"Hello," a little old lady greeted her. "How can I help you?"

Natasha's words stuck in her throat and her tongue glued itself to the roof of her mouth. All she could think was that this woman reminded her of the strange old lady from the *Poltergeist* movies. She looked like a grandma that you would talk to and eat the cookies she made while you poured your heart out... only with the understanding that something violent had the potential to erupt from her being at any moment.

"Ah." The lady nodded. "First time talking to a medium. There's nothing to worry about; I won't hurt you. I can't say the same about the spirit attached to you, though. Follow me."

Natasha felt her eyes widen and she robotically followed the woman through the beads into a comfortable little sitting room. There were a couple of comfortable overstuffed chairs with vibrant throw pillows, a soft light lamp, a coffee table with fresh flowers, and a floral print on the wall. There was no sheet-draped table with a crystal ball on it, and the room had an utterly different vibe than the storefront they'd just left.

Natasha sat down on the chair closest to the door and folded her hands in her lap. Her purse was still slung over her shoulder and sandwiched between her back and the chair. She didn't care. She wasn't comfortable no matter what. She might as well keep her purse close on the chance she needed to run away.

"Please, don't be frightened. This room is a safe place. Physical harm won't happen to you here. My guides don't allow it. I'll start with my name. I am Artis."

Artis held her hand out for Natasha to shake. It took several seconds before Natasha extended her hand and shook Artis' outstretched one. Once she did, an odd sensation ran through her body and she pulled back quicker than usual.

"Natasha," she introduced herself. "I'm not sure where to start. What did you mean that I have a spirit attached to me?"

"Well, I can see him, but he isn't speaking or identifying himself in any way. His aura is dark and foreboding. I get the sense that he means harm," Artis explained, looking somewhere over my left shoulder.

"But you have no idea who he is," Natasha mumbled. "That's not exactly helpful."

"No, dear, I suppose it's not," Artis agreed. "Is that why you came here today?"

"No. Yes. Maybe," Natasha blurted out. "I've been having a lot of strange things happening to me lately. My husband died almost a year ago, and I keep thinking he's trying to send me a message. I think maybe I was hoping you'd be able to help me with that."

"Do you think this spirit is your husband?" Artis leaned forward and gave Natasha a concerned look.

"I did until you said it meant me harm," Natasha confirmed. "Monte would not want to hurt me. He promised to love me forever."

"Death changes people, both alive and dead." Artis's tone was grave and her lined face serious. "Monte isn't who he used to be when living."

"I get that," Natasha sighed. "It's just that our love was one of those once-in-a-lifetime types of love. I don't believe death could change how we felt about each other." Natasha heaved out another heavy sigh. "I know I sound like I have a closed mind; I don't."

"I'm not judging you, Natasha. It's not my place to do so. I lost my spouse, too, though not as recently as you have. It's been several years for me. Navigating grief is a difficult thing to do, and it's not something you can do alone. That was a difficult lesson for me to learn. Maybe what brought you here today was learning to let others help you in their own unique ways," Artis shrugged.

"There's merit to that idea," Natasha conceded. "I've never been down this road before and I've lived in the area for years. I don't even remember consciously choosing to go this route. I blinked and was standing in front of your business."

"My opinion is the universe routed you here. It does concern me that you don't remember it and I can't help but think that it has something to do with this spirit that's attached itself to you. Tell me, have you done anything to try and come to terms with the loss of your Monte?"

"Yes." Natasha nodded. "I've been speaking to a counselor. It feels good to talk; however, I don't know how much it's really helping. I've cleaned the house of the things that were distinctly his and didn't hold much sentimental value to me. Other than that, I don't know what else there is for me to do. I work a lot."

"Okay, that's a start," Artis agreed. "Now tell me about the events that led you here or led you to seek help from channels outside the norm."

Natasha began telling her story about the voices, dreams, visions, messages, and everything else that she couldn't find a logical explanation for that had happened. It was a wild tale, yet Artis showed no expression of surprise or disbelief. To top that off, Natasha felt as if Artis had lifted a weight off her shoulders.

"Well, you've certainly had a lot going on, haven't you?" Artis asked rhetorically. "From an outsider's perspective, I see two different interpretations that seem the most likely to me without speaking to my guides. Take it with a grain of salt because I could be wrong. Though, I like to play devil's advocate in situations like this."

"Understood," Natasha replied eagerly. She was desperate for answers or even possibilities.

"Okay. From where I am sitting, if I were you and hoping for a sign my husband was still with me, I could see how some of these events are going to come across as loving and him trying to tell you he hasn't left you completely. However, add in the dreams and the scares, and those events could be seen as sinister. Done by the same person, your husband, because he is unhappy that there is a veil between the two of you. Remember, death changes things."

"I'm following," Natasha said slowly. "I've already considered the sweet side of it and still have that nagging feeling that things aren't as they seem. Talk to me more about the sinister side."

"Consider that death has made Monte bitter," Artis began. She paused to see if Natasha would argue that and when she didn't, she continued. "Look at each event through the eyes of someone who has lost everything and resents it."

Natasha did as requested and sat back to reanalyze each of the anomalies she'd experienced. She couldn't lie; there was a distinct possibility that Artis was onto something. It wasn't easy to see Monte in that light. It contradicted everything she knew about the man she so desperately loved. Natasha wasn't discounting the theory; she merely struggled to reconcile those two images into the same person.

However, if she put herself in Monte's shoes and tried to imagine what it felt like to leave a life so loved behind, along with everything that mattered, Natasha couldn't say that she wouldn't feel cheated and angry. Especially if she could still see Monte and how he was struggling to adapt to life without her, all while not being able to do anything about it.

"I see that side of it now," Natasha finally admitted. "I don't understand how that translates to wanting to cause harm. As hard as I try to imagine Monte wanting to hurt me, I can't see it."

"Naturally." Artis shrugged again. "Consider this: he doesn't actually see that it could harm you. Take the astral projection episode. You saw the veil between our worlds and, in your own words, you wanted to breach that barrier. What if Monte wanted you to be with him so badly that he influenced your thoughts and enticed your emotions to want to be on that side with him so that you would cross over? He's not thinking that you'd have to die; he's only thinking: come to me. His thoughts may have become one dimensional, not seeing the bigger picture."

"How do I find out for certain?" Natasha wondered aloud. "What if that spirit isn't him? What does that mean if it isn't?"

"That's an entirely different matter. The only way we could determine that is if it decided to speak to me or my guides and reveal its intentions or if we try to call Monte and he responds. That would mean a dark spirit broke through close enough to target and attach itself to you. I could try to break the bond and cleanse you of the spirit, though that, too, carries some risks."

"Even if Monte doesn't answer, that doesn't mean the spirit is him. It could still be someone else and Monte could have chosen to move on to whatever is next, right?" Natasha stared at the older woman intently. "What are the risks if we do a cleansing?"

"The obvious risk is that we anger the spirit and he becomes more aggressive. When they are enraged, there's more of a danger that they'll try to physically harm you. If the activity you're experiencing now feels like a lot, it will multiply. It's possible the entity can also attract more spirits of the dark variety that will take an interest in you. I'm not trying to detract you from taking that avenue; I'm merely pointing out the risks involved. The flip side is that cleansing could move the spirit on to where it belongs," Artis explained. "You'd have peace and know that Monte didn't become stuck in limbo, unsettled and unhappy."

"I can't even describe how amazing it would feel to know he's at peace. I want that more than I want peace for myself. I think that reward is worth the risk." Natasha sighed heavily.

"I understand." Artis patted Natasha on the knee. "Let me prepare. I want a few more safeguards to protect us both." Artis stood and began setting up to speak to her guides and possibly Natasha's late husband.

The ambient light from the white taper candles gave the room a gentle glow. The pungent smell of burning white sage filled the room. It didn't stink, but it was a powerful smell. Add in the pings of the little bells that Artis rang before she sat with Natasha on the couch, and it all felt mystical and otherworldly, though oddly calming.

Artis had locked the front door so that no one would come and interrupt and she mentioned that if things went sideways, it would protect someone from walking into a dangerous situation. It alarmed Natasha that Artis kept saying 'unsafe circumstances,' yet Natasha didn't feel she was in harm's way.

"Hello, Spirit," Artis' voice cut through the thoughts in Natasha's head. "Would you be willing to help us today? I have Natasha with me, and she has some questions she would like answered."

Natasha looked around the room as some of the candle flames flickered. She didn't spot anything amiss and went back to watching Artis. Her face was utterly serene; she looked about ten years younger in this state. It was fascinating to watch and nothing like what she had seen on some of the ghost hunting shows she watched.

"I can feel you, Natasha. I'm not a fraud; this is

only my process for diving deeper than merely speaking to the spirits in the room," Artis told her softly. "I don't need to do all this. It just helps me focus."

Natasha's face reddened at being caught. She did her best to clear her mind and waited for instructions on what to do next. Artis didn't take that long to open her eyes, look at her, and speak.

"Ask your questions, Natasha. Spirit is with us," Artis told her.

"I want to know if Monte is with me and trying to get a message to me," Natasha asked immediately.

Artis tilted her head to the left as if she were listening to someone talk to her. Artis' eyes tracked across the room like she watched someone pace as they spoke to her.

"The man you know as Monte is not in the area," Artis responded.

"Is Monte the spirit attached to me but changed from how I knew him?" Natasha bluntly asked, her tone gaining an edge.

"Spirit declared the answer is unclear. He is getting resistance from the entity in regard to his identity. I'm picking up emotions of sorrow, regret, rage, and fear," Artis recited. "This could still go either way on the entity being Monte or not. I'm getting that he's male. He hovers just out of reach and when Spirit gets close, the entity repels him. My guide can't force anything without harming himself. Spirit suggests a spiritual cleansing."

"What does that mean?" Natasha inched forward to stare at Artis' face.

"How are you with modesty?" Artis questioned Natasha.

"I don't understand." Natasha felt taken aback by the question.

"I think that what I would like to start with would be a cleanse for you and your home, including some prayers. The cleanse for you would be a bath with salts, herbs, and crystals. We'd also use crystals and herbs in the house, with some meditative prayers in each room. I'd like you to do a simpler version of the bath each week; I'd bring all the supplies but I need to be in the bathroom with you. I asked about the modesty because you'd have to be naked in front of me," Artis explained. "I'd use Spirit to help purge the energy from the other side of the veil."

Natasha cringed at the thought of being exposed in front of a stranger. She supposed it wasn't any different from going to a doctor's office for a physical, yet she couldn't help but feel vulnerable and nervous at the thought.

"If that's what we need to do, then I'll figure out how to deal with it," Natasha conceded. "I can't keep living like this."

The two women decided on a day and time that worked for them, and Natasha wrote down her address and phone number. She got up and left for home, feeling unsettled yet strangely exhilarated about the process of removing the ghost.

Bath day had arrived. It seemed far longer than three days since Natasha had been in that little storefront. The unusual activity that had felt sporadic had increased over the past few days and reached the point of broken items in her house. One had been the wedding picture of her and Monte.

Natasha had taken the day off work and physically cleaned the entire house to ensure that all areas were free of dirt and ready to accept whatever positive energy this experience would bring.

Natasha had never been overly religious; she believed in God yet followed no particular religion. The entire day she'd been practicing her mantra of inviting only good into her home and her life and asking the universe to remove all negative presence and energy. She followed that up with a generic prayer to suit all deities for the same.

Artis had requested that Natasha be freshly showered and clean by the time she arrived to help with the bath and cleansing of the home. Thirty minutes before Artis was due to arrive, Natasha shed her clothes, started a load of laundry, and then hopped into the shower.

Her clean robe was hanging on the back of the bathroom door and she donned it after getting out of the shower. Two minutes later, the doorbell rang. The timing couldn't have been better and Natasha rushed out of the bathroom to let Artis into her home.

"Welcome to my home," Natasha greeted the woman as she entered.

"Thank you, Natasha." Artis nodded at her. "There certainly is an unhappy presence in this home that I am sure is the same entity attached to you. That is good, as it's only one to remove, not several. Let's not waste any time, dear, lead the way."

Natasha gulped down her fear and led Artis down the hallway to her bedroom and into the bathroom she had just showered in. Artis set her bag down carefully and removed several containers, candles, and bottles.

She moved throughout the bathroom, setting things up in a precise way without explaining.

Natasha had no questions about Artis knowing what she was doing. She just stood there awkwardly while the woman worked around her, setting up black and white candles, empty bowls, water, crystals, bells, salts, sage, other fragrant herbs, and oils. A lot was going on.

"Okay. Once you are in the tub and we pray together, I will set up your bedroom and do one room at a time after we complete the bath ritual. It might seem like overkill or a weird exorcism with the prayers we'll say, but it's effective most of the time and not as traumatic as an exorcism. You aren't possessed and this isn't a demon," Artis said as she completed her placements and preparations.

"Okay," Natasha agreed. "What do we do if this doesn't work?"

"We try to find another way." Artis straightened and looked at Natasha. "Don't go into this with a mindset that it will fail. That's asking for it to."

"Oh." Natasha gave a chagrined smile. "I didn't mean it like that. I was thinking more about the future. I understand what you are saying." Natasha felt flustered. "Even having the thought in my head isn't good. This ritual is going to work."

Artis gave her a gentle smile before turning to pick her bag up and move it to the bed. She returned to the bathroom and gestured for Natasha to fill the tub. "Have the water as hot as you can stand it without burning or turning your skin red."

"How much do I fill it?" Natasha asked, turning the water on to hot.

"As much as you are comfortable having," Artis instructed as she turned to close the bathroom door. "I want you in there no less than thirty minutes."

Natasha nodded to show she understood the directions and adjusted the water to slightly warmer than she usually used. She wanted enough in there to be as relaxed as she possibly could with someone watching her bathe.

In each corner of the bathroom, Artis had lit a small bundle of white sage and two of the dishes had some other herbs sprinkled in. She then lit two of the black candles, then two white ones. There were crystals on the windowsill, one purple and one black. On the ledge around the tub were some white crystals that Natasha assumed were quartz.

The tub filled quickly, and Natasha tested the water with her hand and foot to ensure she wasn't about to boil herself. Satisfied that it was ready, she turned to Artis and let her know.

"Perfect; take off the robe and hand it to me without letting it touch the floor. You'll take these salts, pour them into the water, and stir them around to make sure they dissolve. Then you will take this vial of oil and pour that in as well. Then climb in and say the mantra you've been practicing all day," Artis instructed.

Natasha followed the directions with the salts and the oil, repeating her mantra in her head the whole time. Then she slowly got into the bathtub and sank into the hot water. The sensation of the hot water around her was shocking and soothing simultaneously. The last time she had taken a bath was probably two years ago before things got bad with Monte.

Once Natasha was submerged, Artis placed a few

more crystals in the water and she spoke a prayer in Latin. Then she recited the Lord's Prayer, followed by something in a foreign language Natasha didn't understand.

"Repeat your mantra, and then say a prayer," Artis requested. "Then I want you to submerge your whole body and stay underwater as long as you can. Come up for air, repeat your mantra and prayer, and submerge. Do this three times." Artis left the bathroom then and began to prepare the bedroom.

Natasha did as directed and found that by the third time, her mind and body were relaxed and open to the feeling of being cleansed. The bathroom filled with smoke and steam and Natasha could swear she was no longer on Earth. She was ready to let go of the negativity that surrounded her.

"The entity attached to Natasha is no longer welcome here!" Artis declared suddenly, startling Natasha. She hadn't heard her come back in. "Remove yourself from this woman."

Natasha felt the oppressive weight of gravity resting on her chest. The steam swirled in an unnatural pattern in the room and she forced her prayer out of her mouth and believed it was working or the activity wouldn't happen.

"Thank you, Universe, for all the good in my life," Natasha recited, doing her best to keep her voice level. "I ask your help in removing the negative from my home and filling it with all that is good and light. God, please help me remove the unwelcome entity from my life and my home and fill it with your love and light. Amen."

"Remove yourself, entity!" Artis forcefully declared. "Natasha, rise from the tub and stand on the mat but do not dry yourself."

Thankfully, the air in the bathroom was warm and Natasha climbed out and stood on the mat. She didn't bother to cover herself as Artis stepped up to her with a bottle of oil.

"This is a blend that I make myself. I want you to dab some of this over your heart. Then each pulse point on your wrists, on the back of your knees, on your feet, and then finally on your neck and scalp," Artis explained. "This will help protect you."

Natasha took the small bottle of the oil and held her finger over the opening and she tipped it, followed Artis's directions, appling little dabs of the fragrant oil on her body. She handed it back to Artis.

"I'm going to smudge you," Artis told her. "I'm going to use this feather to cover your body in the smoke that should drive all unwelcome and negative entities from your being. If you could stand with your feet apart so I can cover you that would be helpful."

Natasha felt faintly embarrassed to be standing like this before someone so that they could blow smoke at her genitals, but she did as requested. She kept her mantra and her prayer on repeat in her mind. It no longer mattered to her if it was Monte or not. She didn't want to live knowing he was that bitter or see signs of it every day and wonder if he would convince her to join him.

A squeaking sound pulled Natasha's attention away from the smoke process to the bathroom mirror. A startled gasp escaped her throat as words appeared through the steam. Natasha pushed at Artis and pointed.

"'Love never dies,'" Artis read out loud as the words formed. "'You belong to me.'" Artis glanced up at Natasha and shook her head. "There is a difference between love and obsession. It's no longer love at this point. This entity may very well be Monte, but it's not the husband that you loved and cherished. It's now dark and possessive."

Natasha numbly nodded while Artis finished covering her with smoke. She handed Natasha her robe to put on and told her not to dry herself; she needed to air dry. Natasha slid the robe on but remained standing in place while she stared at the words on the mirror.

"He was always a bit on the possessive side," Natasha whispered. "It never dawned on me that it would warp in his mind to this extreme. I don't want to die, Monte. I still have a life to live; if you loved me, you'd want me to live as long as possible. I want you to move on and be at peace."

"His hold is weakening," Artis said as she ushered Natasha out of the bathroom into the bedroom. "We must keep going; Spirit is keeping track of the tether."

Together, Artis and Natasha went through each room of the house, with Natasha repeating her prayer and mantra and adding in the personal touch of telling Monte it was time for him to move on; he was no longer welcome by Natasha.

The words were hard to say because she loved who Monte had been so much in life this new Monte felt like a betrayal. Artis was right: Monte's spirit now was not who he was. Yes, her life with Monte had showed him to be possessive and jealous at times but it hadn't bothered Natasha because it had showed how much he cared and loved her.

But now, in this situation after his death, it felt oppressive, controlling, and dangerous. This process had shown Natasha how much she needed to let go of Monte and cherish the memories of who he had been, to love and appreciate the time they'd had together.

The words on the mirror haunted her. It made her think of Monte's wedding vows to her, immortalized forever on their wedding video. What once sounded so sweet—like music to her ears—now made her cringe, which felt so wrong. She didn't think it would be possible for her to love someone as much as she had loved Monte—but as he used to be, not this new version of him.

By the time they finished all the rooms of the house, Natasha felt exhausted. She collapsed on the couch and leaned back to stare at the ceiling. She had to admit that she felt different, and not only that, the house felt lighter.

"Spirit says the entity's tether to you is severed. I feel as though I must warn you that it can happen again. Just because the connection has broken doesn't mean he can't remake it. Spirit doesn't feel as though the entity has moved on. The protections we put in place today will help keep it at bay, and I suggest doing the bath at least once a week and smudging the house. It won't have to be as intense as we did today," Artis explained as she sat on the couch near Natasha.

"Will you leave me a list of supplies I would need to get to do that?" Natasha asked wearily.

"I can, or you can stop by the store within the week and I'll have a package put together for you," Artis offered. "I'm not trying to make a sale; I just trust the mixes that I make more than a general store-bought item that doesn't specialize in situations like this."

"That works," Natasha agreed. "Why do I feel so exhausted?"

"Partly because the negative energy is gone and was fueling you for a while. Your energy stores are replenishing with light energy now. A good rest and a healthy meal will help. Aside from that, how do you feel?"

"Sad," Natasha replied after she thought about it for a few moments. "It makes me revisit the episodes where that jealous, possessive side came out of hiding. I don't like questioning my marriage because it was good. I was genuinely happy and in love. We were soul mates; I feel that in the deepest parts of my heart. All this activity here resembled nothing of the boy I fell in love with and the man he came to be as we grew together."

Natasha leaned forward and turned on the TV. Her wedding video loaded and she hit play on it to show Artis. They watched for a few minutes and got through the vows before Natasha turned it off.

"I understand, Natasha. Hold on to those good memories and remember Monte how he was, not who made all this nonsense happen. Move on with your grieving and live again. Not for work, but for you. There's still so much life to experience." Artis stood and stretched. "I'm glad I could help."

"What do I owe you?" Natasha asked, standing. "And I'll come by in a couple of days to get the supplies from you as well."

"Then we can settle up then," Artis suggested. "Right now, I want to go home and rest my old bones."

Natasha leaned forward and gave the woman a gentle hug. "Thank you, Artis."

A year had passed since Natasha's experience with Artis. She'd stopped with the weekly baths after four months of no activity and only did them every month because it helped with the daily stressors that built up.

However, Monte's words that 'love never dies' stuck with her. After everything, she disagreed. The love she had for him when they married remained. However, she did not love the Monte that had haunted her. A distinct end became noted in her mind. There was no love in those actions. After a year, she finally said goodbye to the guilt that plagued her over thinking that way.

Natasha was finally in a place where she could consider the thought of a romantic relationship again, and she had accepted a date with a lawyer she met while working a case. She felt nervous and excited, each emotion battling for dominance inside her.

As she got ready for her first date since her sophomore year (with someone other than Monte), she felt her nerves take control and smeared mascara on her face. She wiped it off, dropped the makeup remover cloth on the counter, and tried again. As she was about to celebrate success, she saw the discarded material take air and soar across the bathroom.

Dread settled in her gut until she saw that the window was open. The logical explanation, she told herself. She picked it up, tossed it into the small trash can, and rechecked her face before walking out to the kitchen.

Natasha kept that unique blend of oils that Artis made in a cabinet with her spices; she felt it was safest there. She pulled it out and dabbed it on several pulse points on her body. She stared outside at the yard while she waited for her date; it dawned on her that there was no wind.

"Monte, if you are here, you are not welcome. Leave, or I will have an exorcist come and remove you permanently," Natasha warned, the awful oppressive feeling returning. Natasha had strategically placed several crystals around the house and she checked to make sure each was still in place.

Crystals had to recharge after use and Natasha performed the tasks every month to ensure her safe place remained that way. When the dark feeling receded, Natasha nodded in satisfaction. To be safe, she quickly smudged the house and hoped like crazy that her date wouldn't mind the scent of sage that clung to her skin. As an added precaution, she wouldn't let him in the house.

Fifteen minutes later, her date pulled into her driveway. Natasha grabbed her purse and keys, put her coat on, and opened the door. Her date was on the walkway and he paused when he saw her coming out the door.

"Hi, sorry I'm late. Court ran a little longer than expected," he greeted her.

"I understand." Natasha smiled. "I was finishing some house chores, so it worked well."

"I hope you're hungry. I made us reservations at this new restaurant that opened. I've heard great things about it. How do you feel about BBQ?" he asked as he gently put his hand on Natasha's back to walk her to the car.

That was when a branch from the tree on the side of Natasha's house cracked and slammed down on his car, the end piercing the windshield where the driver would have sat. Natasha gasped and her date stared dumbfounded at the limb jutting up from his windshield.

"How did that even happen? There is no wind!" he

stammered in shock.

Natasha shook her head, desperate for this not to start again. She had no answers to offer. That could have injured the lawyer if they had been a few seconds quicker. Natasha immediately considered selling the house and moving, though she understood that if the spirit were attached to her again, it wouldn't matter.

"I'm so sorry," Natasha apologized. "I'll pay for the damages, and I certainly understand if you want to cancel the date."

"Nonsense," he shook himself out of the stupor. "I'll call one of those windshield places and have it fixed. Do you mind driving?"

Natasha shook her head, not trusting herself to speak, and handed her date her crystal-filled purse. Hopefully, it would offer him some protection.

She went back inside to get her car out of the garage. As she walked down her hallway she saw them. Words on the hallway mirror. She froze in place and read in a shaking whisper: "'Not everything ends.'"

An Interview with Michelle Lee

When did you start writing and why?

I've written my whole life. I dabbled in short stories when I was in junior high and high school. My main writings were poems, however. To me, writing was an escape. I could say whatever I wanted to say and make the characters into whom I saw them be instead of what they should be like. Writing was also an outlet for emotions that I didn't know what to do with or how to process.

Which authors or books or media influenced you the most as a writer?

I can't say there was one author, book, or genre that influenced me. My reading was broad and encompassed several genres and authors. Someone in my family would hand me a book and I'd read it. I think the most memorable for me was probably A Tree Grows in Brooklyn, Rebecca, and J.R.R. Tolkien.

Which authors or books or media had the biggest impact on you as a person?

Honestly, all of them. I lived several lives through the books I read. The Hobbit opened my young mind to the possibility of other races, magic, and worlds I knew nothing about except in the stories.

Which of your original twelve Prompt stories are you most pleased with?

Out of those stories, the one that pleased me the most was the historical fiction story. That story blossomed into a full-length novel as I wrote it and I was challenged to keep it short. That particular story opened me up to try my hand at a novel based on facts from World War II.

Which of your original twelve Prompt stories did you find the most difficult to write?

November was the most difficult for me. I can't pinpoint why but I struggled with that. It screamed science fiction to me and while I love reading it, I don't see it as a genre easy for me to write. I love researching the fact behind the fiction but weaving it into a story was hard. Perhaps one day, I'll try it again.

What book on writing do you recommend?

The only book on writing I have ever read was one that my mother gave to me as a Christmas gift after my first book was published. I don't remember the name, only that it was satire with little words of wisdom from other published authors.

What advice would you give an unpublished writer?
Don't stop trying. Everyone has a story to tell, whether it's real or fiction. When the time is right, it will come to you. Write down your ideas, and add to them. When things come to me in the middle of the night, I grab my phone and email myself so I don't forget. Do a short story if you get overwhelmed trying to write a novel. Ask someone to read it and offer suggestions if you think it's bad. Whatever you do, don't give up. When you stop trying, that's when you fail. Someone in this world needs to read what you have to say and it may alter their life.

Do you have a "dream project" as a writer? What would it be?
Right now, my dream project is going to be a historical fiction novel my friend asked me to write about her grandfather. I love reading those books and writing one would be amazing, especially one that is based on fact and the life of a person who lived through the subject.

Your stories are published in the seasonal Prompt anthologies but also as a collection of just your own work. Did you have a conscious theme?
No. I went with what came to me. My stories don't stick to one genre. Maybe that itself was my theme. I wanted to stretch my boundaries and try my hand at things I'd never done. My reading patterns vary; sometimes, I'm in the mood for lightheartedness and other times, I want to dive deep. That was my main goal with this project, to keep an open mind and write what came to me. It made

certain months harder than others.

You have a body of work outside your Prompt stories. Share why those works are important to you and how they differ from your Prompt stories.
The Raven's Journey series was important to me because it shows that healing from trauma is possible, especially as an empath. The series is, on the surface, a love story, but for those going through something, they will see the path taken to heal and be the person you want to be, for yourself and for whom you choose to be with romantically and that they accept you for who you are.

The Looking Through the Shadows series was the same but set in real life. It was also a series that challenged me because I went with the not every ending is a happy one. That series focused on PTSD and navigating through it in different ways. I wanted to shine a light on the ways it manifests and how it's perceived. I spoke with several veterans and exposed myself to their personal traumas and how they have adjusted or not and did my best to weave those stories into these characters to give life and light to them. This series also connected me to my significant other, so it had a happy ending for me on a personal note.

The I S.P.I. series was a challenge when the publisher asked me to do a short story, episodic type series. I had a tragic event in my life where I lost a dear friend and her family. Once I was asked to do this series, I decided to make characters out of her and her family to honor them and keep them alive. Since Risa was a funny person and loved to be sarcastic and, well, basically, a smarty pants, the stories in this series flowed easily. It's different from Prompt because I stick mainly to fantasy in this series and I purposely make the stories wild, unrealistic, and funny. I want people to laugh, and while I might touch on some serious subjects, the overall tone will be lighthearted and sarcastic.

The Prompt stories didn't stick with one theme or one genre. It doesn't make them any less important, only different in that the theme varies.

Who do you write for and how does it drive you to create?

That's trickier to answer. I write for myself and for the readers. Myself first. Sometimes an idea strikes me and within minutes, a main character takes shape in my mind and then a story forms. I write the story how the character dictates it to me and try to keep it something that a reader wants, though I stay true to the character and myself. It could be that what sparked an idea was a picture, something that spoke to me on a deep level, something going on in the world, or song lyrics that evoked a powerful emotion in me. Creation comes from everything and it all battles for space in my head. I write to get all those voices out, and if you ask my significant other, he says I write so I don't become the next serial killer.

We're always growing and improving as authors. Talk about how you grew as a writer over the course of the year.

The Prompt project helped me grow the most. It posed several challenges each month, and I tried my best to stretch what I knew. I also talked with other authors and more importantly, with my publisher. I try to always ask for advice on things that should be changed or if an idea merits attention. The other thing that helped me grow was trying my hand at adapting screenplays to stories. I learned that writing that way is not a strong suit for me, which helped me refocus my attention on what I could produce and do well. I think it's important, no matter what field you choose to be in, to stretch your comfort zones. It's when you step out into that uncomfortable place that you grow and you learn. When you do that, you never fail; you learn what you do not like and what does not work for you.

www.ingramcontent.com/pod-product-compliance
Lightning Source LLC
Chambersburg PA
CBHW071545030726
47593CB00001BA/42